Hi Jim,
Thanks again for
being my "Dutch guy."
I enjoy our interactions
on that. Terry Hag

LAST CALL FOR MURDER

A Reverend Rob Vander Laan Mystery

Terry Hager

D1524549

ISBN: 1466407689
ISBN 13: 9781466407688
Library of Congress Control Number: 2011919392
CreateSpace, North Charleston, SC

Printed in the United States of America

» ACKNOWLEDGEMENTS

'd like to thank the following people for their generous help: Cal Dyke for his input on the Grant area and the onion farm setting; Ron Norton, former New Jersey State Police Trooper, for his knowledge of firearms; Rev. Jim Vander Schaaf for helping me with the Dutch words and phrases; Dr. Tom Brink for his medical input; Dick Bewell and Tom Rozema—former Grand Rapids Police Detectives—for their input on police procedure; Ronald Kragt, president of the Michigan Natural Storage Company, for giving me a tour of the section of the gypsum mine used for cold storage; Rev. Tim Limburg for his automotive expertise; Bill Decker for his legal expertise; Rev. Ray Kretzschmer, a colleague who worked with me at the Grand Rapid Youth Ministry, for his input on the phone bugs; Dr. William Stroo and Rev. Al Helder (now deceased) for help on theological questions; Mark Miller, a colleague who worked with me at the Grand Rapids Youth Ministry, for his input on street drugs; Karl Westerhof for his help with denominational data; Daryl Vander Kooi, my brother-in-law, for his help on the Montana section; Julie Hyzy, author/colleague and favorite author of mine, for her feedback on the first few chapters; Paul Haase and Jonas Weisel for their time and expertise in reading the manuscript and giving invaluable feedback.

I owe a special debt of gratitude to Gordon Aalborg, for his editing skills and for teaching me so much about writing a mystery and about how to be a better writer.

Another huge thank-you to Tom Mroczkowski, retired mining engineer, who worked in the Grand Rapids area gypsum mining industry for over thirty years. Under his patient tutelage, the mine gradually came alive for me as I hope it does for you. If there are any mistakes about the mines in the story, they are entirely my own.

Last and most important, thanks to Ruth, my wife and the love of my life, for her readings of the manuscript with an eagle eye and for her constant encouragement.

This Book is dedicated to the staff of the Grand Rapids
Youth Ministry, the hippies, gang members and all
the people in the "Downtown Scene" of Grand Rapids,
Michigan who, from 1968-1973, gave so much to
this small town boy and helped him grow up.
I keep you forever in my heart.

Praise for *Death on the Night Watch*
(Available from amazon.com, Barnes and Noble and Schuler's)

Marcella Gauthier, in the July/August, 2011 issue of
Escapees Magazine:

> *In this fast-paced murder mystery set in 1969 Grand Rapids,
> Michigan, he [Reverend Rob Vander Laan] and his crew of help-
> ers, including his 70-year-old gun-toting secretary, set out to solve
> the murder before someone else gets hurt...*

> *The story's action moves along in gripping... detail as these real
> characters from the gritty, mean streets manage to solve the mystery.
> Readers of this story are easily caught up in this splendid mystery.*

Reverend Don Recker, retired Christian Reformed pastor:

> *Author Terry Hager strips away all the facile stereotypes attached
> to the Dutch Calvinist minister...*

> *[Rev. Rob's] ministry to gang members, street walkers, and night-
> life people... stretches his marriage, family, moral, and faith
> commitments beyond the security of conventional limits.*

> *When members of his "congregation" are found murdered, Rob
> wades into the dangerous whirlpool of amateur criminal investiga-
> tion, only to find himself the murderer's prime target.*

Author Darlene Miller:

> *Terry Hager skillfully weaves a great story that is exciting and
> fast paced with surprising twists and turns.*

Janet Sheeres, book reviewer for d.i.s. magazine, a
publication of the Dutch International Society, in the
December, 2011 issue:

> *If you enjoy a fast paced action story with lots of descriptive street
> language, shoot-outs, car chases, and arson, you will enjoy this story.
> The sentences are short. Dialog, not prose, drives this story forward.*

» CHAPTER 1

The first thing that oozed into my awareness was a stench that made me gag. I opened my eyes, blinking against the rain. I shivered, gagged again. I was soaked, sitting on the ground, my back slumped against a hard surface. Small stones bit into my butt.

I struggled to my feet, wincing at a stab of pain in my shoulder. Once on my feet, I lurched sideways, bracing myself on the thing I'd been leaning against. A garbage bin.

I looked around. Gravel parking lot, lit by a light high on a pole. Smaller light over the open back door of—what?

I stared a moment, till I recognized Gus's Getaway, a bar on the northwest side of town that featured go-go dancers. It was in a mostly residential neighborhood, but on a fairly main drag.

It was mid-August, 1970. I squinted at my watch in the dim light. Almost three on a Friday morning. Unseasonably chilly. I was in Grand Rapids, Michigan. Nixon was president. I could almost hear Jackie, my wife, asking me the questions and pronouncing me oriented as to time and place.

Sound of sirens. Two vehicles turned into the lot, screeching to a stop. Headlights blinded me. I shielded my eyes with my hand.

Car doors opening. A shout: "Police. Hands in the air!" More quietly, "You guys check the bar."

I raised my hands. "I'm a minister," I yelled back. I reached a hand to touch my clerical collar. It wasn't there.

Another shout: "Get those hands in the air, I said! Turn around. Hands on the garbage container. Spread your legs."

A moment later I felt an officer patting me down.

"He's clean."

"Turn around."

I did and faced two uniformed officers. One of them had the curliest black hair I'd ever seen and was, I suspected, a rookie. The other looked to be in his mid-thirties like me, probably six five or six, at least a head taller than me, and lean as a rail. I watched the other two cops entering the open back door of the bar, guns drawn.

"What's your name?" asked the tall, skinny cop.

"Robert Vander Laan from the Street Ministry."

"I doubt it. I hear he wears a collar. Let's see some I. D."

I reached into my pocket for my wallet. Came up empty. "Sorry," I said. "Must have been stolen after I was knocked out."

"What are you doing here at this time of night?"

I had to think for a minute. "I was supposed to meet the bouncer. He wanted to talk. Said his wheels were in the shop. Wanted me to pick him up. We were going to Sandy's Grill."

"Where's your car?"

I looked around the parking lot. My car should have been near the rear entrance. It wasn't. Only the two cop cars were in the lot.

I shrugged and winced at the pain in my shoulder. My head ached, too. "I parked it by the back door over there."

"So you claim you were knocked out."

"Back of my head. Right side."

"Turn around."

I did. The officer shined a flashlight on my head. He put a finger on a growing lump.

I jerked my head away at the pain of his touch.

I was instructed to turn again and face the officers. Tall cop shined a flashlight at my neck. "Could be one a them priest shirts. Look at the collar." Then to me, "Little white plastic thing fits in there?"

I nodded.

"Was the door to the bar open when you pulled in?"

I nodded again. "Figured Hector—he's the bouncer—was inside waiting for me. I was walking toward the door when I got bashed."

"Whoever bashed you dragged you to the garbage bin and took your collar for a souvenir?"

I started to shrug again, thought better of it. "And my wallet. Apparently my car, too."

One of the officers who'd gone into the bar appeared in the doorway. "Clear," he called. "Cash register drawer is open and empty. Looks like a robbery."

"We'd better take you to the hospital to get checked out," said the tall cop.

"I'm fine. I'm not going to the hospital."

After several additional minutes of questioning, two of the officers transported me to the Hall of Justice which housed the police station as well as the District Court and related offices. I was given a cup of bad but hot coffee and began to warm up. I was grilled some more. An officer I'd met before confirmed my identity, and I was asked to sign a statement. When the cops were finished with me, I called Nathan for a ride. Nathan ran Drop-in, a hangout for youth at the Street Ministry where I served as director.

I'd probably wakened Nathan, but he sounded alert. "What kind of trouble you in this time, Reverend?" he asked. Since I'd been ordained a couple of years prior, I tried to get people to address me as Rob instead of using the formal title. Most people had a hard enough time being themselves around a clergyman. The title increased the distance between us, in my opinion. I knew Nathan called me Reverend to jerk my chain a little, but it didn't bother me.

I explained briefly what had happened, and he agreed to pick me up and bring me home.

Waiting for my ride, I felt relieved to be finished with the cops for the moment, but I was still tense. I knew that most members of the Grand Rapids Police Department were highly suspicious of me and my ministry to hippies and gang kids. The fact that I frequented several of the local bars on my night ministry rounds, didn't help either. Despite the goose egg on my head, I wasn't entirely sure I'd been cleared as a suspect in the robbery at the Getaway.

By the time Nathan arrived to pick me up, it was raining hard. I got wet again dashing to his VW van, and he apologized for his heater not working. He dropped me in front of my three-bedroom two story house in a racially mixed neighborhood on the southeast side. With the property values declining as the neighborhood changed, I'd gotten a good deal on the house. I made another dash to my front door. I was chilled again as I fished in my pocket for my keys. Of course they weren't there. They had disappeared along with my car.

I rang the doorbell. After a moment, I watched through the glass as Jackie came down the stairs, putting on her robe and smoothing back her long blond hair. She turned the porch light on and peered out before letting me in.

"What's the deal?" she asked as she closed the door, looking past me and watching Nathan's bus pull away from the curb.

I gave her a nutshell version.

Normally calm in a crisis, she wrapped her arms around me and held me even though I was wet. I shivered again. She looked at the lump on my head. "Any dizziness?"

I shook my head.

"Did the cops take you to get checked at the ER?"

"They wanted to but I said I was fine."

Jackie pursed her lips and shook her head. "Go take a shower. Warm up. I'll put coffee on."

I climbed the stairs quietly so as not to wake Andy, our six-year-old son.

As warmth from the shower seeped back into my bones, I wondered about my attacker. Could it have been the bouncer? Why would Hector ask me to meet him and then assault me at his place of work? It made no sense. Perhaps I'd just been in the wrong place at the wrong time and interrupted a robbery. But then what the heck had happened to Hector?

What really frosted me was the hassle of losing my wallet and my car.

After I dried and pulled a pair of shorts and a T-shirt on, I popped a couple of aspirin for the headache and sore shoulder. I still felt wired when I came back down to the kitchen. I eased into a chair as Jackie poured me a cup of coffee and then took another look at the back of my head.

"What do you think, Nurse Vander Laan?"

"You should have gone to the ER. When your mother finds out, you may not survive her tirade. This is exactly what she's been worried would happen to you in your night ministry. Well, that and a dozen other things too horrible for words. Hungry?"

"Starved."

"I'll fix pancakes. You talk."

I told her what happened in more detail while she prepared breakfast. She placed a plateful of pancakes in front of me and got the syrup from the fridge.

"Why wasn't Lydia with you?" Jackie asked. Lydia was my seventy-one-year-old street ministry partner. She was Roman Catholic but knew my Dutch Calvinist tradition well because her deceased husband had been Christian Reformed, like me.

"Hector wanted to see me alone," I said between bites. "I took Lydia home early."

"So you never saw this Hector when you got to the bar to pick him up?"

"No."

"Could he have attacked you?"

"It's possible, I guess, but that doesn't make any sense to me."

"The Getaway. It's where that young woman works, the one you met at Sandy's Grill a while back?" Sandy's was a twenty-four hour restaurant in the River City Hotel downtown.

"Right. Rochelle's one of the dancers. I told you she invited Lydia and me to stop in at the bar. We've been there a couple of times now. In fact, we were there earlier tonight, and Hector kicked a guy out who was bugging Rochelle. Apparently an old boyfriend of hers."

"Any connection between that guy who got bounced and the break-in?"

"I wonder, too. But why would Rochelle's old boyfriend clobber me?"

Jackie shrugged. "Maybe you just showed up at the wrong time and got mugged by Rochelle's old boyfriends or *whoever* was robbing the place?" Jackie sat down and poured syrup on a pancake for herself. "I wonder what happened to Hector."

"Beats me. Of course, it would hardly be the first time someone made an appointment with me and didn't show." Still, I was worried about him.

"Where's your collar? I noticed when you came in that you weren't wearing it and it wasn't in your shirt pocket."

"The cop who questioned me wondered if the mugger took it for a souvenir. I also lost my wallet, my keys and Night Watch." That was the name given by the downtown people to my uniquely decorated green Plymouth sedan. It had looked like the local vice squad cars—a handicap in my line of work—until a young artist who hung around the Ministry painted it for me according to his own whims: a lighthouse, a cross, a peace sign, flowers and the words "Night Watch."

"Losing our car is a pain," said Jackie.

"Pretty hard to hide. It'll probably show up. Unless it gets re-painted. I'll catch a ride to the airport and rent a car till we see if it's found." I made a mental note to call my insurance company and report the theft.

"Better get to the Secretary of State's Office today to get a temporary driver's license," said Jackie.

I crawled into bed about 5:30, still wide awake. I was a night owl, so working mostly afternoons and nights wasn't a problem for me. For six years, before going to seminary and becoming ordained, I'd taught Reformed Doctrine and English at the city's Christian High School. If only I'd been able to teach night classes, I'd have been much happier. The thing I liked better than teaching was trying to help some of the troubled kids at Christian High. At the Street Ministry I was in my element.

Unable to fall asleep, I rolled out when I heard Andy stir. Jackie's mom arrived a short time later to watch Andy as she normally did on Tuesdays and Fridays since I usually slept till noon after working most of the night. My mother cared for Andy on Wednesdays.

A car horn tooted. Nora, a nurse from the medical office where Jackie worked three days a week had arrived to pick her up. Nora also worked a couple of days a week at St. Mary's Hospital. I'd dated her for a while in college until friends fixed me up with Jackie. I'd not formally broken up with Nora, just didn't call her again.

Jackie gave me a peck on the cheek. "Call your mother," she said as she walked out the door.

"Yeah, yeah." I knew if I didn't call her, she'd hear about my getting mugged anyway.

The phone rang and Jackie's mom answered it. "Just a minute. I'll get him." She covered the mouthpiece with her hand. "It's your mother, Rob. She sounds upset. Are you in trouble again?"

I rolled my eyes as I took the phone. "Hello, Mother."

"You get mugged behind one of those bars you frequent. You're thrown in the trash bin. Your wallet and car are stolen. And you don't think that warrants a call to your mother?"

As usual, she'd gotten *most* of the details right, probably from the Dutch grapevine. "Sorry, Mother. Is Dad on?"

"Are you okay, son? You're not having any dizziness, are you?" That's always the way it went, mother calling, usually to chew me out about something, dad not speaking until I asked. Dad's voice was pinched with the worry I knew they both felt.

After I assured them I was fine and let them know I'd not been tossed into the trash, Mother said something I'd often heard from her. "Why can't you be more like Johnny?" John Vanden Berg was a high school classmate of mine and a minister in Grand Rapids now. He was, like me, the son of a Christian

Reformed minister. Both our dads served churches in Holland while John and I were in high school. My father still served a church there. I'd long suspected Mother would have gladly traded me for John.

I'd had enough of it. I attempted a level tone, almost achieved it. "Mother, you may not be able to help comparing me with John, but I'm tired of hearing it. Please keep it to yourself from now on."

After Mother said a frosty good-bye, my mother-in-law, familiar with this little conflict, raised an eyebrow and said, "You could have told your mother that you'd trade her for John's mom." She immediately put her hand to her mouth and, looking mortified, mumbled an apology.

I laughed and gave her a bear hug. "Why should I tell her that? I've got you."

I made pancakes for Andy and his grandma from the left-over batter and re-hashed my adventure with them.

Andy was excited. "Can I feel your goose egg, Daddy? Are you going to help the cops catch some more bad guys?"

I assured him that was not in my plans as he gently touched my head, but my involvement with the police the previous summer flashed in my mind.

"You can borrow my car for a few days," said Jackie's mother.

"You're the best, Mom."

Since I was too wired to sleep, I spent Friday morning in my study working on a sermon for a preaching date I had in late August at a Methodist church that supported the Street Ministry. One of the things I liked about working in an ecumenical ministry was that I got to preach and to speak about my work in other denominations besides my own. The problem on this particular morning was that I had to keep dragging my mind back from what happened at the Getaway to my sermon.

Shortly before noon, I drove my mother-in-law's car downtown to the Ministry in time for my Friday staff meeting. On the way, I thought about my mother's fears for me in my, to say the least, unconventional ministry. The previous night's assault and the grilling by the cops had left me more shaken than I wanted to admit.

The Ministry was located in a two story house built in the early 1900s. The home had been turned into offices and show-rooms for a furniture store in the forties and then vacated in the mid-sixties until the Ministry had moved in.

Because our group was small, staff meetings were pretty informal affairs. Lydia, my street ministry partner, and I usually reported on our contacts. Nathan kept us posted on the vol-unteer staff and on people frequenting Drop-in, the hang-out for youth we provided. Stacy, Lydia's niece, had taken Lydia's job as our receptionist a year ago when Lydia had joined me on the streets. Since Drop-in was closed during the day, we sat around the low table in that area of the building and ate our sandwiches.

Twenty-two-year-old Nathan pushed his long red hair away from his face, making more visible the sideburns that came down to his chin. "I see you spiffed up your ministry uniform. You almost look cool now."

I was dressed, as usual, in jeans and a clerical shirt.

"What?" said Lydia. "Rob almost always wears ..." Then her eyes dropped to my feet. "Oh, engineer boots. I liked the wingtips better."

I complimented Nathan on his powers of observation and then reported what had happened to me at the Getaway.

"I told you I should have stayed with you," snapped Lydia. With her solid frame, grey hair tucked into a bun and round face, she often conveyed a cozy grandmotherly air that masked her flinty side until those bright blue eyes pierced you.

"You have to watch out for that Lone Ranger streak in the Reverend, Lydia," said Nathan.

"Tell me about it. Next time you need to talk with somebody alone, Rob, I'll just wait in the car or sit at another table in the restaurant."

After staff meeting I got a temporary drivers license. By the time I finished, I could barely keep my eyes open and decided to get some sleep. As I drove home, I realized I was more worried than I'd let on about Night Watch being stolen. While I'd been initially freaked out by the way my car had been painted, I'd since grown very attached to it. And young people all over the city, not just the kids who frequented Drop-in, recognized it.

Of course, the cops recognized it too. That wasn't always an asset.

» CHAPTER 2

"It really frosts me that my wheels were stolen," I fumed to Lydia as I drove to the Getaway.

"Night Watch sticks out like a sore thumb," said Lydia. "I'll bet it turns up soon."

As usual, I'd picked Lydia up about 8:00 for our Friday night ministry rounds. We'd stopped at a few bars on South Division where we mixed with customers and staff. One guy talked with us about his recent job loss and his fears regarding finding a new one, another about his worry for his son serving in Vietnam.

After a short silence, Lydia said, "You know, I'm not so uncomfortable anymore seeing the go-go dancers."

I nodded. "Now that we're getting to know them, they're just part of our congregation."

"I agree. First time we went to the Getaway, I wasn't sure I could handle it. You telling me that you were uncomfortable made it easier."

As we entered the go-go bar, Hector jumped off his stool at the door. He was stocky, with long dark hair and a jagged scar on his right cheek. He welcomed us with a look of chagrin. "Sorry about last night, Rob. Had to take one of the girls home with her car. She was too smashed to drive. Time I got back to meet you, the place was a crime scene. I'm really bummed about what happened to you. I told the cops I was supposed to meet you."

"It's cool, man," I said. "I'm glad you're okay. You want to re-schedule?" If he was involved in the robbery and my mugging, he was certainly covering it well.

"No. I think I got things straightened out. I'll let you know if I change my mind. Ned wants to talk to you." He hooked a thumb toward the bartender, a man in his forties with a fringe of red hair on his mostly bald head. He was polishing glasses and looking our way.

The place was moderately full, mostly guys, a few couples, two of them on the dance floor. A pair of raised tall cages stood at the far end where two dancers clad in bikinis were gyrating energetically. Waitresses, dressed in short dark cocktail uniforms, moved about with trays of drinks or empties. The air was filled with cigarette smoke, laughter and a loud buzz of conversation.

"Rochelle's in the dressing room now," said Hector. "She comes on in a little while for the next set. *She* wants to see you too."

We grabbed a couple of stools at the bar, and I introduced Lydia and myself to the bartender.

"Ned," he said, extending his hand. His sleeves were rolled up showing arms with hair as red as that on his head. "I noticed you guys in here a couple of other times, but I was too busy to meet you. Now I got a new bartender, so I can be a little more sociable. A guy named Blaine used to stop in once in a while. Wore a collar, too. Haven't seen him for a long time. Know him?"

Blaine was my best friend, a Methodist minister and the founder of the Street Ministry. "He's the director of a counseling center in town now," I said. "I've taken his old job."

"So you're hanging out with the hippies and gang kids and hitting the bars like he used to?"

I nodded.

His eyes dropped to my clerical collar. "Should I call you Father or Reverend?"

"Call me Rob," I said.

"Rob it is. Sorry about last night. You all right?"

I assured him I was. "How about you? Did the thieves get much?"

"Nah. Took most of the cash home with me." He looked down the bar, then back at us. "Blaine's a good guy. Some of my dancers and waitresses used to talk about their problems with him. Customers would bend his ear, too. Truth is, I leaned on him a time or two myself. He never preached at anybody. I asked him why he didn't. He said he was doing a ministry of presence, accepting people wherever they're at. He said the clerical collar meant he was representing the church. You two on the same page with him?"

We both nodded.

When Ned brought us our beers, Lydia asked him about the name of the bar.

"I used to have a buddy named Gus." Ned looked into the distance. "Killed in the Korean War. He always talked about his dream of owning a bar and calling it Gus's Getaway. So when I bought this place, that's what I named it."

When Ned moved to wait on other customers, Lydia and I swiveled on our stools and faced the dance floor and cages. A petite brunette danced in the cage on the right. Georgina, a tall young woman with dishwater blond hair and a dazzling smile, was in the cage to the left. We'd talked with Georgina the last time we were in. She was friendly and welcoming. When the music stopped, the two women emerged through gates in their cages. As the applause dwindled, Ned turned down the recorded music and hollered his usual announcement, encouraging patrons to show their appreciation to the dancers with tips. As the music resumed, the dancers wandered among the customers collecting their tips and chatting. Then they disappeared through a door at the rear which led to the dressing room.

A customer sat down on a stool next to mine and asked what brought Lydia and me to the bar. My answer triggered more questions, so Lydia and I didn't notice that two new dancers had entered the cages until we heard the enthusiastic applause. We both turned and saw that Rochelle was now dancing in the cage on the right. The young woman in the other cage wore her long dark hair in a pony tail, just as Rochelle did. Like the previous dancers, both wore bikinis.

I recalled our meeting Rochelle at Sandy's Grill a few weeks prior. Lydia and I'd been waiting for a table to open when Rochelle invited us to join her. Her long blond hair framed her beautiful oval face, and she had innocent blue eyes I wanted to fall into. Lydia told me that Rochelle's innocent, vulnerable face reminded her of her nineteen-year-old goddaughter and grandniece. Before we parted, Rochelle informed us that she was a go-go dancer at Gus's Getaway.

Rochelle's wholesome look and her working as a go-go dancer was something Lydia and I both had trouble wrapping our minds around.

Rochelle was the prettiest and sexiest of the four dancers. Her eyes were half closed, and she moved as if the music were inside her body. Occasionally she opened her eyes wider and smiled seductively at a patron, not looking so innocent any more. I listened to the sound of the Beatles singing "Hey Jude," a favorite of mine, and wondered if I'd ever be able to hear it again without visualizing Rochelle in her cage.

The two young women who had been dancing earlier emerged through the door behind the cages. Wearing miniskirts and tight tops, they headed across the room, each stopping at a different table and accepting invitations to sit down.

When the set ended, Rochelle and the other dancer cruised the audience for tips, then disappeared through the rear door. After a short time, the two original dancers were back in the cages. Rochelle, wearing the between-sets uniform of miniskirt and tight top, stopped at a table near the door to the dressing room where a man sat alone. As she spoke to him, she gently touched his cheek, then walked directly to us. She smiled, but her smile looked forced, like maybe she wasn't so happy to see us.

"I didn't think you'd come after getting mugged here last night," said Rochelle.

I spread my hands. "Hey, wild horses couldn't keep us away."

"Why don't we sit at a table for a few minutes?" She turned and signaled Ned, who filled a glass with water.

"Rochelle, if you're uncomfortable with our being here, tell us." Lydia had apparently picked up on Rochelle's discomfort, too. "You don't have to hang out with us."

Rochelle's eyes misted. "No, no. It's not that. I'm just upset tonight, that's all. Sorry. It's my job to be pleasant with customers between sets, and I feel like I'm blowing it with you guys." She took a drink of water, then set the glass down, clutching it with both hands.

Lydia smiled. "Could Rob and I be two customers you don't have to be pleasant with? What's bothering you?"

I kept my mouth shut and felt grateful that Lydia was my ministry partner. It was a familiar feeling.

Rochelle's eyes glistened. She squeezed them shut, then opened them again and looked at Lydia and me. She took a deep breath. "You know Georgina, right? And Hector? Well, Hector's been going out with Georgina for the past six months. I started working here two months ago, and Hector's been coming on to me lately. Georgina threw me against the wall in the dressing room tonight. She told me I'd better stop messing with him or I'd live to regret it." Rochelle squeezed her eyes shut again. "And that dumb Benny …"

"Former boyfriend?" I asked. "The guy Hector bounced last night?"

"Yeah. He doesn't understand the meaning of 'no.' The guy I just talked to back there is one of Benny's Vietnam buddies. I'm surprised Pookie's coming in without Benny, but I'm glad he is. Pookie is such a sweetie when he's not around that darn Benny."

We sat in silence until Rochelle pulled herself together. "I'm sorry," she said again.

"You don't have to be pleasant with us, remember?" I said.

Brave smile. I wanted to put my arms around her and take her home with me. But I knew I had more than comfort on my mind. I felt a bit like a dirty old man, but I couldn't change my emotional response. I *could*, however, keep it from getting me into trouble.

"I'd like to talk with Pookie," I said. "How about introducing me?" I knew how much the trust building process was accelerated when I was introduced by someone already trusted.

"He's really shy. How about if I talk to him later tonight. Maybe I'll introduce you next time you're here. He comes in quite often."

"That's cool."

"I have to get out there and mix with other customers before my next set. Thanks for coming, guys. Really. Come see me again?" She flashed that brave smile.

We stood, and Rochelle gave us each a hug. She felt very good in my arms.

As Rochelle moved away, I glanced back at Pookie. Short, skinny, in his early twenties, blond brush cut. He quickly looked away when he saw me looking in his direction.

Lydia and I left the bar. As I put the key in the ignition, Lydia reached out and touched my arm. Just a minute, Reverend. Now it's your turn to talk."

Besides calling me "Reverend" when she was irritated with me, she also called me that when she was exercising what she said was her God-given calling to keep me on the straight and narrow. I knew what was on her mind, and I'd have brought it up if she hadn't.

"I was thinking how I'd like to take Rochelle home with me and make it all better."

"I'm sure Jackie would be supportive of you taking in troubled go-go dancers," Lydia said with a deadpan expression.

"Right. So what's your take on Miss Sweet-and-Innocent?"

"She comes across as the genuine article. But, if she knows she has the effect on people that she has on you, it might be tempting for her to take advantage of that. And did you see the looks she gave some of the customers while she was dancing?"

From the Getaway, Lydia and I headed downtown to the Street Ministry offices and Drop-in. A warm front had moved in during the day and, at 11:15 that night, it was still in the eighties and humid. The front door of the Ministry was open to allow the cooler night air in, but it was still stifling inside. Behind the reception desk sat one of my seminary volunteers.

I glanced toward the large space to the left of the reception desk, bursting with youthful energy. The windows were wide open. From a portable radio in the corner came the latest hits. Several gang members, or heavies, wore their colors—denim vests with the gang name, Lost Souls, stenciled on the back. There were also a number of hippies, better known as heads, and several straights or conventional kids. One of the straights was aiming a Polaroid camera at two of the heads who were posing in front of a poster of a peace sign on the wall. Both the heads had long hair and beards and beads around their necks. One of them wore a tie-dyed T-shirt.

The kids that frequented Drop-in got along well most of the time, probably because of their shared disillusionment with the establishment. That disillusionment with conventional society was even evidenced by many of the straights we attracted at Drop-in. Of course, any one of them could turn into a head or heavy in a matter of a few weeks.

Several people were sitting around the low table or on pillows scattered along the walls. Some stood talking in small groups, smoking, drinking coffee. A couple was making out in the far corner, interspersing their intense kissing with intense conversation. A handful of volunteers including a couple more seminary students, a nurse and a nun were scattered among the kids. All of us staff members and volunteers were white, despite the fact that a few of the gang members and a few other Drop-in regulars were black. I'd set up visits with a couple of local black pastors for the following Monday, hoping to entice them to become supporters of the ministry and to provide a couple of volunteers.

"Where's Nathan?" I asked the volunteer at the desk.

"He's been upstairs for over an hour with someone who's having a bad trip." Nathan, besides being our Drop-in coordinator, was also our drug pro—well experienced in using them and counseling kids who were messed up with them.

"What do you bet Caleb's got another runaway there?" said Lydia quietly, nodding toward the door of my office which adjoined Drop-in. Caleb was a member of the Lost Souls Gang. It wouldn't be the first runaway he'd latched on to.

As Lydia spoke, I noticed Nathan descending the last few steps behind us with a young woman whose pupils were dilated. She floated past us into Drop-in and Nathan said to Lydia, "The runaway I just heard you mention is fourteen. Her name's Crystal. That was my next project. Since you and Rob are here, how about if you deal with her instead."

Caleb, in his early twenties, was short and stocky with messy brown hair in need of a wash. He wore his colors, jeans and engineer boots. He'd been busted for harboring a runaway several months earlier. His arm was draped around Crystal, a young girl in cut-offs and a dirty white blouse, who watched the scene in apparent fascination. She wore dangly ear rings and took a drag on a cigarette.

I was about to suggest to Lydia that we invite them into my office when she said, "Why don't we see if they'll take a walk with us. That might be a little less conspicuous."

Now that we knew the situation, we could be charged with harboring a runaway ourselves if we didn't call the police immediately.

Caleb accepted my invitation but didn't look happy about it. We walked toward Veterans Park which was a couple of blocks from Drop-in.

"How long ago did you run away, Crystal?" asked Lydia. We'd already learned that she was not fourteen, but only thirteen. She was from Byron Center, a town just south of the city.

She looked at Caleb, who nodded at her. "Three days." She looked uncertain, but not scared.

"Bad scene at home?" I asked.

"Yeah. My step dad's a real pig! I am not going back there!"

"If you stay on the street the police will find you and take you to Juvenile Hall," I said.

"Juvy's got to be better than home."

"There's another possibility," I said. I told her about the new runaway house I'd helped get started the previous year. So far, the police were warily respecting our referring kids there and the house staff's determination as to where the kids should be placed.

"I don't see why I can't just stay with Caleb," she said.

I turned to Caleb. "Did you tell Crystal about the trouble you can get in if she stays with you?"

Caleb stopped and gave me a hard look. I knew I was on shaky ground here in my relationship with him, but I saw no other choice. I returned his stare.

Finally, he shrugged and said to her, "I could get busted for harboring a runaway."

She looked bug-eyed. "You shoulda told me, Caleb."

A half hour later, Lydia and I dropped Crystal off at the runaway house. Afterwards, we stopped at a couple more bars where we drank pops, having consumed our two-beer limit. When last call was announced, we went to Sandy's Grill.

I looked around, first at the long counter that snaked through the room, stools mostly occupied, then at the tables, finally spotting an empty one.

The waitress served Lydia coffee and set down a lemonade for me. I yawned and checked my watch: 2:45. "I'm bushed, Lydia, I said. "Didn't get any sleep last night. I'd like to skip breakfast and call it a night."

"That's fine by me," she said as I stifled another yawn. "How's the shoulder doing?"

"Better. I barely noticed it tonight."

I took a swallow of my lemonade as a commotion near the lobby door caught my attention. I saw Rochelle entering the restaurant with Hector. When he touched her arm, she jerked it away. The scowls on their faces and the intensity of their discussion suggested they were having a fight. I couldn't hear their words above the din of conversation around us. Rochelle marched to a table with the bouncer at her heels. Neither appeared to notice us.

"Lydia, don't look now, but Rochelle and Hector just came in." They sat down behind Lydia and a few tables to her left. "They look like they're fighting."

Lydia waited a moment, then casually looked over her shoulder. "They're really going at it."

Our waitress came by and refilled Lydia's cup, blocking my view of the Getaway pair. When the waitress moved on, Hector was sitting alone. I watched Rochelle stride out the front door of the restaurant and hop in a cab at the curb. The whole episode took less than a minute. I reported to Lydia what she'd been unable to observe.

"What's Hector doing now?" asked Lydia.

"He's getting up, leaving by the lobby door."

"It's probably just a lovers' quarrel. Are you ready to go?"

We left a moment later. I dropped Lydia off at her place on the West Side and drove home. Lydia didn't think the fight between the Getaway employees was anything to be concerned about, and she was probably right.

So why was my stomach in a knot?

» CHAPTER 3

I woke Saturday morning with what I thought was a fly, buzzing near my ear. I tried to brush it away. The fly buzzed again. This time I rolled over to see Andy lying in bed next to me and grinning from ear to ear.

"So you're the fly buzzing my ear," I said, glancing at the clock. Only 9:30. My gaze returned to Andy. "Do you know what I do to pesky flies who bother me when I need to sleep?"

Andy climbed on top of me. "I'm not pesky, Daddy. I'm a fly with a secret to tell you. Two secrets." He put on a serious face.

"Okay, Mr. Fly, I'm listening."

Andy put his mouth to my ear and whispered, "I love you, Daddy. And Momma says you got a important telephone call."

"I love you, too, Mr. Fly," I gave him a squeeze before he ran off.

The caller was Dr. Elliot Rietsema, a professor at Calvin College, a Christian Reformed institution and my alma mater. Besides teaching Greek at the college, he'd taught a New Testament Greek class at seminary that I'd taken. For the life of me, I couldn't imagine why my former teacher would be calling. I hadn't seen him since my seminary graduation a few years prior.

He cleared his throat and apologized for disturbing me. "I'm, ah, having some problems with my daughter. I mentioned it to someone at church last week and he suggested I call you. I don't know where else to turn. Is this is a bad time?"

Perhaps if I scheduled an appointment with him for the afternoon, it would relieve some of his anxiety. And I could go back to bed.

"Any chance we could talk this morning?" he asked before I could speak. "I know I'm imposing, but I'm so worried about Rochelle."

Same name as the go-go dancer. Now I was wide awake.

I'd been to Dr. Rietsema's home a few times with a handful of seminary classmates, so I knew where he lived. "I'll be there in half an hour," I said.

As I drove to his home after a quick breakfast, my curiosity outweighed my irritation over my beauty sleep being interrupted.

Soon I was sitting on the couch in the living room, remembering the lively discussions we'd had there about New Testament translation issues. After laboring through Introductory, Classical and then New Testament Greek in college, I'd finally had some fun with it in Rietsema's Gospel's class at seminary. Greek would never be my favorite subject, but Dr. Rietsema had a way of bringing out the best in his students, and he'd done that for me.

The professor was in his early fifties, high forehead, bushy eyebrows. He wore glasses and was dressed in slacks and a white dress shirt, no tie. I knew his wife had died, but I couldn't remember when.

"I'd like to get right to the subject of Rochelle," he said. What might be worry lines, creased his face around his eyes.

I nodded.

"Rochelle's twenty-one," he continued. "She's always been a handful. Strong rebellious streak, I guess you could say. Always thought she'd grow out of it. I still hope she will."

I shifted into a more comfortable position. "So, how do you think I can help?"

"I thought you might have run across her in your ministry or could look her up." He gazed at the floor for a moment. Then, in a voice that sounded laced with disgust and embarrassment, he said, "I don't know how to say this except to just come out and say it. She works as a go-go dancer, whatever that is, at a bar."

I could hardly believe it, but I nodded. "At Gus's Getaway."

Elliot's eyes widened. "Do you know her?"

"I do, though I didn't know she's your daughter. The Getaway is a bar I stop at sometimes on my night ministry rounds."

"Well, I'm wondering if you could ... I don't know ... keep an eye on her?"

My stomach did a summersault. The last time parents asked me to watch out for their daughter, she'd turned up dead a few days later.

"Can you be more specific about what you hope I can do for Rochelle?"

"Get her to quit her job, come home, go back to church and join the choir." He smiled a sad smile. "Can't blame a dad for trying."

I waited.

"Okay." He sighed. "Maybe you can be somebody she could talk to. I know you can't work miracles, but working at a bar! Dancing! It's not the way her mother and I raised her.

Dancing was high on the list of forbidden activities among most Christian Reformed folks. I'd finally broken the dance barrier the previous summer and frequently danced with Jackie in our living room. Jackie had learned to dance while she lived with a cousin in Amsterdam, The Netherlands, after high school.

"I talked to Rochelle, uh, yesterday," Elliott continued. Uh, I called her. She said she was, um, too upset to talk."

Elliott was usually fluent. I assumed his hemming and hawing was a reflection of his worry about his daughter.

"Did she say what she was upset about?"

Elliot shook his head.

"Are you and Rochelle close?"

After a pause during which he studied the floor and rubbed his hands together, he said, "We don't see each other as much as I'd like." He glanced at me, then looked away. "She calls once a week or so."

I had the feeling he was being less than frank with me. "Did you talk to her after that phone call you mentioned?"

"I tried to call her today but didn't get an answer. I even went over to her apartment this morning, but she wasn't there."

I thought about Hector. "Maybe she's staying with a friend."

Elliot just nodded, his fist to his mouth, what looked like worry in his eyes.

"All I can promise," I said, "is that I'll continue to be available to her, like I've already been doing."

I imagined Jackie saying, "Not too available!"

"I'll tell her about our conversation," I added.

"It might be better if you didn't."

"That point isn't negotiable. If I'm going to gain her trust, I need to tell her about our visit. And I won't report to you what she's doing or what she says."

A scowl creased his forehead and a dark look clouded his eyes. "I'll have to trust your judgment on that." He let out a deep sigh.

I stood up and extended my hand. "Good to see you again, Dr. Rietsema."

"Since I'm not your professor anymore, how about calling me Elliot."

Back home a short time later, I found a note from Jackie. She and Andy had gone to the park. I lay down on the couch and picked up *The Autobiography of Malcolm X* from the coffee table. I knew that Malcolm X had become a powerful voice in the black community after his conversion to Islam while in prison and that he'd been assassinated by members of the Nation of Islam in 1965. But that was all I knew, and I was eager to learn more. The problem was that my short night of sleep was catching up with me and my eyes were heavy.

When the phone rang, I considered not answering it, then heaved myself off the couch. My irritation quickly turned to surprise when the caller identified himself as Detective Sid Johnson of the Grand Rapids Police Department. Lydia and I'd gotten to know him during the course of a murder investigation the previous summer. Our relationship had grown from one of mutual hostility and suspicion to guarded respect. We'd even gotten on a first name basis with each other.

Johnson got down to business in his usual gruff manner. "Your name's come up in an investigation. Yours and Lydia's. At least I assume it was Lydia with you last night at Gus's Getaway."

"This isn't about the robbery there or my getting mugged?" I asked, surprised.

"It's about another matter."

Dread coursed through my veins. I had a feeling I was not going to like where this was headed.

"Anyways, I'd like you to come to the station to answer a few questions."

"Right now?"

"Sooner the better."

After leaving a note for Jackie, I drove downtown to the Hall of Justice. Johnson met me at the information desk in the lobby and ushered me into the detective bureau. He dropped heavily into the chair behind his desk. He was a beefy man with a comb-over, and I noticed some graying at his temples, not there the last time I'd seen him.

He raised his eyes and gave me a grim look. "Sit." He gestured toward a chair that faced his desk. "You and Lydia talked with one of the dancers at the Getaway last night." He shuffled papers. "Rochelle Rietsema."

I nodded.

"One of the dancers, not Rochelle, hasn't been seen since she left work last night." I let out a breath, not realizing till then I'd been holding it. He ran a thick finger down the page. "Here it is. The girl's name is Georgina Watson. Know her?"

"Tall, darkish blond hair?"

"Right."

"I saw her at the bar last night, but I didn't talk with her. I did meet her last week when Lydia and I stopped in."

"Her car was found abandoned on Veterans Memorial Drive down by the river. What were you talking to Rochelle about?"

"Is Rochelle a suspect in Georgina's disappearance?"

Johnson scowled. "Everyone who was in the bar, including you and Lydia, are suspects till I rule them out. Nothing personal."

"I understand. But I thought you only worked homicide cases."

"Well, I don't. Now are you ready to stop avoiding my question?"

I squirmed in my seat for a moment as Johnson's eyes drilled me. I was about to open my mouth when he spoke again. "It's that blamed confidentiality thing, isn't it?"

I nodded.

He harrumphed. "Just forget your damn clergy scruples and help me out here. What were you talking to Rochelle about?"

"How about I see if Rochelle's okay with me telling you, or better, she tells you herself?"

He glared at me, and hit the desk lightly with a hammy fist. "I could bust you for obstruction of justice."

I held his gaze. "We've each got a job to do, Sid. Do what you have to do."

Would he really bust me? I was pretty sure he was bluffing, but it was hard to tell.

He puffed, then threw up his hands. "Anything you can give me that might help?"

"Lydia and I ended our rounds this morning at Sandy's Grill. We saw Rochelle come in with Hector—he's the bouncer from the Getaway. Looked like they were having a fight. Rochelle went storming out the front door. Hector left by the lobby door a minute later."

"So, what time was this?"

"About 3:00 a.m."

"Know what they were fighting about?"

I shrugged.

"Anything else?"

I shook my head.

"And I don't guess I'll get anything more out of Lydia."

"Not unless she wants to be in trouble with me."

Johnson raised an eyebrow. "Somehow I think she could handle that."

"If Georgina's only been missing since last night, how come you're on it already? I thought you waited longer on missing person cases."

"There were traces of blood in her car. Plus, this Georgina's got lupus, I think it is. She's on two or three medicines, and she's gonna be in a load of trouble if she doesn't have them."

I hardly knew Georgina, but I liked her. I said a silent prayer for her.

When I stood to leave I asked, "Is Kincaid still your partner?"

"Yeah. He stepped out for a few minutes."

"Give him my best," I said.

Later, after lunch with Jackie and Andy, I filled Jackie in on my morning. We sat on lawn chairs in the back yard together under the maple tree, its leaves rustling in the afternoon breeze. We watched as Andy moved truck loads of sand from one end of the sandbox to the other. Jackie pulled her blond hair together in the back and slipped a rubber band around it. Her white short shorts showed off her great legs. I could see she had no bra on under her yellow top. While she still wore a bra in more formal settings, she'd become more comfortable without it. If that was part of women's lib, I was not complaining.

"Mom called today," she said. "Wondered if our car had been found. She said we can keep hers through next week if we need to. Dad can bring her here or she'll use his car to come and take care of Andy."

I nodded.

"Keep the sand in the sandbox, Andy," Jackie called. Then, turning back to me, "Sounds like there wasn't much help you could give Detective Johnson regarding this Georgina's disappearance?"

"None, really. You think what he said about her lupus could be exaggerated?"

Jackie frowned and shook her head. "Probably not. One of the meds she'd be on would probably be Prednisone. I'm surprised she wouldn't be too ballooned up to display her body in a bikini at the bar. She must be on a maintenance dosage."

Jackie's words intensified my worry about Georgina. Suddenly my life seemed to revolve around the Getaway.

"The way you talked about this Rochelle—Little Miss Sweet-and-Innocent. You're attracted to her."

I nodded. Jackie didn't miss a thing.

"Planning to see her only with Lydia?" she asked.

"That's the plan."

She elbowed me in the ribs. "You'd better make sure you stick to it."

CHAPTER 4

"Detective Johnson demanded I tell him what Rochelle said to us at the bar, but I clammed up," said Lydia as I pulled away from her house to begin our Saturday night rounds. "That man can be very pushy. I have to say, though, the detective has a point, especially given Georgina's lupus. I think we should tell him what Rochelle told us."

Georgina's lupus had been worrying me too. "I've never been in such a quandary about confidentiality," I replied. "Let's go to the Getaway right now to check on how Rochelle and the other staff are doing and see if Georgina has turned up. If Rochelle hasn't told Johnson what she told us, I'm hoping I can convince her to do so."

Lydia buckled her seat belt. "I did tell Detective Johnson about what we observed at Sandy's Grill with Rochelle and Hector."

"So did I," I said, then went on to report my conversation with Rochelle's father.

When we entered the Getaway, Hector greeted us with a dark look and a nod.

"Any word on Georgina?" I asked.

He grimaced and shook his head slowly. "It's a bummer, man. I used to go out with her. She's got to have her medicines or she could die."

Lydia slid past me into the bar. I noticed there were only about a dozen customers at this early hour.

"It's got to be tough," I said, turning back to Hector, "not knowing what happened to her."

He said nothing.

"Did Detective Johnson interview you?"

"Yeah, he did. Truth is, I'm sick of answering questions."

"Okay. Let me know if you do want to talk."

When I joined Lydia, she was engaged in conversation with Ned and handing him a Street Ministry business card. An attorney friend had recently showed me his card, and I'd had a small batch printed for Lydia and me with the Street Ministry name and phone number. Two beers stood on the bar next to Lydia. I saluted Ned and took my beer to a table. I watched the two young women in the cages for a moment, and then Rochelle emerged from the dressing room. She stopped at a table where "sweet Pookie" sat with another young man who was tall, well built, with dark hair. She smiled at Pookie and said something to him. The dark haired guy made a comment. She turned to him and scowled, then abruptly headed toward the bar. She spotted me, veered off to my table and sat down, tension lines creasing her forehead.

"Who's that with Pookie?" I asked.

"That's Owen. He's another Nam vet. A friend of Pookie and that darn Benny. Owen's a hard case like Benny. I don't know why Pookie hangs around with them."

"Maybe I could meet them both."

"Forget about Owen. You'll stand a better chance with Pookie when he's here alone. Did you hear about Georgina?" she inquired, changing the subject.

I nodded.

"Can't say I like Georgina, especially after she got on my case so bad, but I'm really worried about her. Did you know she's got lupus? She told me once that, without her medicines, she probably wouldn't last more than a few weeks. The cops said they searched her apartment and her medicines are there."

I felt helpless. I hated that feeling. It made me mad. Rochelle's eyes told me she might be feeling helpless too. She looked like nothing so much as a lost little girl.

She closed her eyes a moment and then opened them. "The other girls and I drew straws to see who would dance alone till Ned hires someone to replace Georgina. Or till Georgina comes back. I got the short straw."

"How soon do you go on?"

"Sadie and Sylvia—the ones in the cages now—just started their set."

We sat in silence for a few minutes. She squeezed her eyes shut again, then took a napkin and blew her nose. "I'm always such a basket case when you're around."

"That's not a problem. You have a right to be upset."

She gave me a soft-eyed look, reached out and touched my hand. "Thanks, Rob. You're an easy guy to talk to."

I was relieved when I heard a chair scrape the floor.

Lydia sat down. "How are you holding up, Rochelle?"

She withdrew her hand from mine. "Hanging in there, Lydia."

"Has Detective Johnson interviewed you?" I asked.

"Yes."

"Did you tell him what you told us about the hassles with Georgina and Hector and you."

"No. It doesn't have anything to do with Georgina disappearing."

"I think you should tell him so *he* can determine whether it's relevant. He's a good detective, Rochelle. He asked me about our conversation with you last time we came in, but I told him he should hear about it from you. How about it? Will you tell him?"

A look of irritation crossed her face. She looked from me to Lydia.

"Rob's right," said Lydia.

Rochelle sighed. "Okay, okay! If he talks to me again, I'll tell him."

"How about calling him now," I suggested.

"I've got a job here, you know!"

"I wouldn't push you if it weren't for Georgina and her lupus."

"Geez! Okay, I'll call him. You're starting to sound like my dad."

I chewed my lip. "Speaking of your dad ..." I figured I might as well get it all out on the table so Rochelle could decide if she wanted to fire the "easy guy to talk to." I told her about my conversation with Elliot.

"Geez!" she said again. "I don't want my dad in my business. The last thing I need is you checking up on me for him. I'm not a child."

"I wouldn't tell him anything you didn't want me to. Just like I didn't tell Detective Johnson when I wasn't sure if it was okay with you. And I've told your dad that I wouldn't report on you to him, that I'd just be available if you need somebody to talk to. I told him I'd be doing that even if he hadn't asked me to. If I have any further contact with him, I'll tell you about it."

Rochelle crossed her arms, shot me a surly look. "I have to think about this."

"He's worried about you. Call him so he knows you're okay."

"I haven't talked to him for six months. I hate to break a good streak."

It sounded like the truth, but I was beginning to wonder if I should take anything from Rochelle at face value. If it was true, why had Elliot told me they talked about once a week? Perhaps he was too embarrassed or too guilty to be honest about it.

"One more thing." I shifted in my seat. I could lose her if I kept this up. "Lydia and I saw you with Hector at Sandy's Grill last night. Looked like you were having an argument."

"Oh, that was nothing. Benny—the old boy friend from high school I mentioned—he's been bugging me. Hector was upset about it, that's all. He gets overly protective sometimes." She shrugged.

When I'd watched them fighting, it didn't look to me like it was no big deal. What was Rochelle hiding?

"I mentioned to Detective Johnson that I'd seen you arguing," I said. "He may ask you about that, too."

A look of fury painted Rochelle's face. "Just get the hell out of here, Rob! And don't come back." She got up so abruptly that her chair fell back onto the floor. Heads turned in our direction. Rochelle marched to the bar, said a word to Ned and disappeared into the room behind the bar.

I gave Lydia a weak smile and raised my eyebrows. "That went great, don't you think?"

"If she puts us in the parent role now, we're dead ducks with her."

After a moment, I said, "I saw you talking with Ned before you joined Rochelle and me. How's he doing?"

"Hard to tell," Lydia answered. "He complained about having to find another dancer to replace Georgina. Seemed kind of cold. I'm surprised he didn't show more concern about Georgina. He knows about her lupus. What did I miss with Rochelle?"

"She was upset about Georgina's disappearance, but didn't open up much."

Lydia picked up her beer. "Let's go see if Ned feels freer to talk with you."

Ned was no more forthcoming with me than he'd been with Lydia. Rochelle reappeared, walked past us, looking away, and sat down at a table with some guys. She was soon laughing with them, and she punched one of the guys lightly on the shoulder.

Ned looked at me quizzically.

"I'm in the doghouse with Rochelle," I said.

"Did you bug her to call Detective Johnson? That's why she wanted to go into my office."

I nodded, relieved that she'd apparently made the call.

When Sadie and Sylvia emerged from the dressing room a little later, Ned signaled them over to the bar. "Rob and Lydia here are good people to talk to," he told the two young women. Then he moved down the bar toward a guy who was holding up an empty beer glass.

We stood for a moment in awkward silence with Sadie and Sylvia until Lydia said, "I've got a niece about the age of you two. I know it would be tough for her to deal with someone she worked with vanishing into thin air."

Another moment of silence while Sadie and Sylvia looked at the floor. Then Sadie said, "I'd better get out there and mix with other customers, but it was nice meeting you."

"Me, too," echoed Sylvia.

Both young women were all smiles and confidence again as they went in separate directions and began mixing with customers. The bar was now nearly full. As we watched Sadie and Sylvia, Lydia said, "That went great, don't you think? We're batting a thousand tonight. At least it sounds like Rochelle called the police."

We spent the rest of the evening visiting other bars and then hit the parking lot downtown about one in the morning, mixing with some of the straight kids who'd been cruising through downtown and gathered here to hang out. It was another warm, humid night. We were about to leave when a battered old Chevy pulled into the lot and squealed to a stop. It was one of the jalopies that belonged to the Souls. Usually it was filled with gang members. Now it was just Caleb who climbed out and sauntered over. He looked like he was doing his best to act casual while bursting with important information.

"Guess what we found at the gravel pit?" He asked. The gravel pit along the Grand River was one of the gang's party spots.

"I give up," I said.

"Night Watch," he said, looking like the proverbial cat who'd swallowed a tasty canary.

"That's fantastic!" I said, feeling immensely relieved. "Did it look okay?"

"It's got a bad scratch along the driver's side," he said. "Keys were in it, too, but I was afraid if I drove it back to town, I'd get busted for stealing it. You guys could come and get it and join us. We got a big bonfire going."

"We're right behind you," I said.

"Thanks, Caleb," said Lydia. "We'll join the party." She turned to me as Caleb jumped back into his car and waved as he squealed out of the lot. "Okay with you, Rob, if we hang out with the gang for a while?"

I grinned. "Is it the skinny dipping you wanted to participate in, or the beer drinking with under-aged kids?"

"Oh, gracious!" said Lydia. "How come I never heard about that? Guess God wants you to keep *me* on the straight and narrow, too."

We followed Caleb out to the gravel pit on the River Road. The bonfire was blazing cheerfully. Gang members and several straights stood around drinking beer, making boisterous conversation interspersed with loud laughter. Even though the temperature had cooled down to the 60's, the sound of water splashing, screams and more laughter suggested that several people were in the water on the other side of the fire. Four or five cars were parked around the clearing.

Just to our left I saw Night Watch. I walked over and glanced inside. The keys were in the ignition. My Bible was on the dash. A toy Jeep, a favorite of Andy's lay I the back seat. I walked around to the driver's side to view a long scratch running across both doors through a peace sign and flowers. Looked like it had been deliberately done with a key or some other sharp object. I was relieved to find my car but really ticked about the scratch. If I found out who did it, maybe I could sic a few of the Lost Souls on the SOB.

Not a very Christian attitude, a voice in my head challenged. The voice sounded a lot like my mother's.

For Pete's sake, it was just a fantasy, I argued back.

After a few minutes of talking with the kids and making our excuses, Lydia drove Night Watch back to my house. I followed in Jackie's mom's car. Lydia went inside with me and waited while I ran upstairs to report the good news to Jackie who was reading in bed. After I called the police station to notify them that I'd found my car and reported the scratch, Lydia and I headed back downtown in Night Watch to Sandy's Grill.

With my wheels back, breakfast felt to me like a celebration. Lydia, however, was stewing about not being hip to what went on at the gang's party spot at the gravel pit. When Lydia served as our receptionist before becoming my night ministry partner, we always said that she knew all the secrets of the kids as well as the staff, that nobody at the Street Ministry was more in-the-know than she was.

I couldn't resist teasing her about it. "We may have to re-evaluate your title as Communication Central," I said.

Lydia scowled at me.

One thing, however, dampened my relief at getting Night Watch back: the clock was ticking on Georgina. That had remained on my mind all night after leaving the Getaway. I wished there was something I could do besides turning my worries into prayers for her safety.

» CHAPTER 5

Sunday: the second day for Georgina without her meds. I forced myself to get up for church since I'd not been there for a while and a friend was the guest preacher. After dinner Andy sat with Jackie in the living room reading to her. Although he didn't start first grade for a couple of weeks yet, he'd been devouring children's books for the past six months, thanks mostly to Jackie's mom teaching him to read on her child care days and when he stayed with his grandparents at their farm.

Mid-afternoon my mother called. "I saw on the news about the missing girl," my mother said. "The one who's car was found by the river. Do you know her?"

After establishing that dad was on the extension, I said, "I know Georgina slightly. Did you only hear about her on the news?" It made no sense that mother would think I knew Georgina unless she'd also heard something via the Dutch grapevine.

"I have my sources," Mother replied. "The news said she was a go-go dancer at a bar. What's a go-go dancer?"

"You don't want to know, Mother."

She let out a short huff. "You're not playing detective again, are you, Robert?"

"No, Mother. Lydia and I stop in sometimes at the bar where Georgina worked, but that's it." Then I added, "I was at the bar the night she disappeared. The cop who's working on Georgina's case says I'm a suspect until he clears me."

She knew I was needling her and ignored me. "I still worry about you being on the streets at all hours of the night," she said, "going to those places you go to. You have a family to consider."

I braced myself, ready for the *take-a-church-and-become-a-real-minister* lecture.

"Don't worry," she said icily. "I'm not going to say anything about your taking a church." Short pause. "Since that subject is now *verbieden*." Then, in a more conciliatory tone, "I hear you got your car back."

I was dumbfounded since I'd just gotten it back late the previous night. Then I remembered that I'd driven it to church, so Mother had probably talked to someone from my church. Still, it was pretty fast, even for the grapevine.

"Dad," I said, changing the subject, "weren't you friends with Elliot Rietsema, my Greek prof, when you were in college? I talked with Elliot the other day."

"Yes, we were friends. We used to visit as couples during seminary years."

"His wife smoked those filthy cigarettes," said mother. "No sense of how to be a minister's wife. Shame that the cancer took her, though."

"How long ago did she die?"

"About six years ago," said dad.

Rochelle must have been about fifteen or sixteen. What had it been like for her to lose her mother at that age?

"You could take some lessons from your professor, Robbie," said Mother. Your dad said that he had clear career goals: to teach Greek at the college, and to be either president of the seminary or stated clerk." The stated clerk was the chief honcho in our denomination. "Your dad says Elliot was being considered for the seminary opening, but his wayward daughter has probably ruined his chances for that."

"Now, dear," said Dad.

"What do you mean about his daughter being 'wayward,' Mother?" I asked.

"I'm not one to spread gossip, but I heard she works in a bar."

I didn't tell her that Rochelle was a go-go dancer at the same bar as Georgina and where I'd been mugged.

"Two more things," said my mother. "We just got off the phone with your sister. She said to tell you hello and she's keeping you in her prayers." My sister, Beth, four years younger, lived in Orange City, Iowa. "Also, we wanted to let you know that we're going to Iowa for a two week vacation the end of August."

* * *

Monday: Day three for Georgina.

After lunch I visited the pastors of two black churches near downtown, acquainting them with the Street Ministry and inviting them to become supporting churches and to provide volunteers for Drop-in. One of the pastors didn't see us fitting with their ministry. The other offered to spend an evening in Drop-in with one of his deacons to evaluate the possibility of their involvement.

When I got to my office, I found Stacy, my secretary, in her usual cheerful mood. She was forty-eight, dark haired and plump. She looked a bit like a younger version of her Aunt Lydia. She'd raised six kids and handled well the sometimes chaotic and disorganized atmosphere of the Street Ministry.

She looked up from her typing. "Detective Johnson called. He said to thank you for getting someone—Rochelle, I think he said—to talk to him. I assume this is related to the disappearance of that dancer Aunt Lydia told me about. Are you helping the detectives on another case?"

I held up both hands. "No, no. Lydia and I are acquainted with Rochelle, one of the other dancers. I just encouraged her to tell the detective some things she told Lydia and me."

"But Aunt Lydia told me that the dancer who disappeared has lupus and could die without her medicine. She said the two of you were going to help the detectives all you could."

"Well," I said dryly, "she hasn't mentioned that to me."

When Stacy answered the phone, I went into my office. I spent the next couple of hours signing checks and preparing a financial report for the board's September meeting. We were slightly under budget for the year. My board president had gotten a laugh at the last meeting when he commented that they'd been wise to put a Dutchman at the helm.

Next I prepared a report on my work for the monthly meeting of the Urban Mission Committee, the arm of my denomination to which I reported. They'd changed their meeting this month to Tuesday to accommodate schedules. I valued the committee's support and active interest in my ministry.

Except for good old John Vanden Berg, the guy my mother often compared me with, who'd been appointed to the committee the previous summer. John managed to ask me at least one loaded question at every meeting. He'd made no secret of the fact that he was, to use his words, "troubled by my theology." When I'd riled him at one meeting, he threatened to bring me up before Synod, the ruling body of the Christian Reformed Church, on heresy charges. If convicted, I could be booted out of the ministry. So far, the chair had been successful in discouraging John from taking such action.

Suddenly a thought struck me. *Could my mother be behind John's appointment to the committee?* I dismissed the idea as pure paranoia.

I pulled my attention back to the report. Under the best of circumstances I didn't like doing paperwork. Now I was particularly restless. Visions of Georgina's empty car with blood on the seat was static on my brain. At 5:00 Stacy and I locked up. Nathan would re-open the building for Drop-in at 7:00.

I was about to get into my car when I heard my name called. Rochelle ran across the street, waving frantically. She wore blue jeans and a red blouse. Her blond ponytail bounced as she ran.

"Have to talk to you," she said breathlessly.

"I thought you didn't want to see me again" I said.

"Oh, that. Sorry I went off on you last night. I have other problems now. Thought you could help me."

"Go ahead," I said, puzzled at the sudden change.

"Could we talk in your office?"

Red flag! Red flag! I thought. I wasn't about to be alone in the building with the volatile and unpredictable Rochelle.

"I just have a minute," I said. "Tell me what's bothering you."

"Okay. First Georgina goes poof, and now everybody at work has it in for me. I don't know what to do."

"What do you mean, everybody has it in for you?"

"Sylvia and Sadie are mean to me. They're jealous because I make better tips than they do. Hector's down on me because I won't move in with him, and Ned ..." She threw her hands up in frustration. "He's on my case for every little thing because I won't put out for him."

"Have you thought about finding another job?" *Maybe moving back in with your dad and joining the church choir?*

"I get such great tips. I can't think of any place I could make as much as I do at the Getaway. What should I do, Rob?" She looked at me with those innocent, helpless blue eyes, a tear running down her cheek.

I wasn't buying it. "You need to think about whether the money's worth the hassle. What do *you* think you can do?"

That dark look flashed in her eyes for a split second. Then she smiled her brave smile. "I don't know. That's why I came to you."

Rochelle was one tough helpless cookie.

"Listen," I said. "I've got to get home now. I'd like you to think about what you might do. Lydia and I will stop in at the bar again tonight to see what you've come up with. If for any reason we can't make it, look for us after work at Sandy's Grill."

"Okay, Rob. Thanks. You're the best." She lit up with a big smile.

I wondered if she was about to hug me, and I quickly crossed my arms.

"See you tonight," she said.

I watched her run back across the street and get into a new green Mustang. She started the car and revved it, the dual exhausts crackling and popping, and then squealed away from the curb.

What was she doing with a hot car like that? A gift from her dad? But she said she hadn't talked with him for six months. Maybe she was borrowing the car. If she'd bought it herself, her tips really were good.

After supper later, I put on a new album by Smokey Robinson, the King of Motown, and sat down on the couch with my Malcolm X book. Before I got through the first sentence,

Jackie came into the living room, moving to the music. She pulled me up from the couch and we danced. Andy must have heard the music, because he came flying downstairs from his bedroom and joined us. Andy would not grow up with the same hang-up about dancing that Jackie and I had had to deal with. Ten minutes later the doorbell rang and one of Andy's friends asked him to come over. After the boys left, I pulled Jackie over to the couch. I told her about my conversation with Rochelle in front of the Ministry. I wanted her take on the young woman, even if it was second hand.

Jackie responded in her usual direct style. "Sounds like she's got innocent and helpless down to a science and uses it to manipulate guys to get what she wants."

"That seems a little harsh." Truth was, it reinforced my own thoughts.

"You asked. By the way, nice job of sticking to the plan of only seeing her with Lydia."

I shrugged. "I definitely don't want to be alone with her. She makes me uneasy. I'll be vigilant and keep you posted."

"You'd better get going," said Jackie. Then she pulled my face toward her and kissed me deeply.

Maybe I'll stay home and skip night ministry, I thought.

Jackie, however, pulled me to my feet. She snatched the white plastic insert out of my shirt pocket and slipped it in the collar. Then she prodded me toward the door.

Normally, Lydia and I didn't work Monday nights, but because of Georgina's disappearance, we'd agreed to make an exception. Maybe we could learn something. Time was running out for the dancer. On the drive to Lydia's, I slipped back into my worry mode.

As she boarded Night Watch, Lydia looked worried too. "Did you know Georgina is Wild Bill's sister?" she asked. Wild Bill was one of the heads in the downtown scene.

My heart dropped. Suddenly, because of my relationship with Wild Bill, I felt much more connected to Georgina. "How'd you find that out?"

Lydia threw me her inscrutable look. "I have my sources."

Shades of my mother, I thought. I wondered if my ministry partner was compensating for her embarrassment at not knowing what went on at the Lost Souls party spot. "You must have just learned that," I said.

"Right. I just called Nathan and Wild Bill isn't at Drop-in, so why don't we stop at his crash pad?" A crash pad was an apartment with a revolving group of roommates. "Maybe Wild Bill can use some support, and maybe we can learn something new about Georgina."

On our way, I told Lydia about my conversation with Rochelle that afternoon in front of the Ministry and about Jackie's take on the young woman.

"I think Jackie's right about Rochelle manipulating men," said Lydia. "And I wonder if she knows more about Georgina's disappearance than she's letting on?"

A recording of Arlo Guthrie singing "Alice's Restaurant" wafted into the hallway accompanied by two or three other voices, one slightly off key, as we knocked on the door to Wild Bill's pad a little later. Someone turned the volume down, and we waited a moment or two before the door opened. The sweetish aroma of marijuana greeted us.

"Oh, it's you two." Wild Bill, wearing jeans, t-shirt and love beads, brushed his shoulder length hair away from his eyes. He spoke with a bit of a drawl, an echo of his Texas roots. It was there, he'd told me that he acquired his nickname during his rambunctious early high school years. His family had moved to Grand Rapids when he was a junior in high school, and it was hard to see any wildness left in his gentle eyes. He smiled at us, then turned and yelled back into the apartment, "Don't flush it down. It's Rob and Lydia."

He led us into a room full of young people sitting around on chairs and big pillows scattered around the floor. Most wore some variation of the dress code: jeans or bell-bottoms, long dresses or skirts, colorful shirts, some embroidered with peace signs, necks draped with beads, sandals or bare feet. Almost all of the faces of the kids were familiar. They waved and smiled in response to our greetings, looking mellow. Wild Bill asked that there be no toking while we were with them. The group fell back into conversation and someone turned the music up.

Bill ushered us into the kitchen and swung the door closed to get away from the noise. "I hear you guys know about my sister disappearing."

"That's why we stopped in," I said. "What can you tell us about Georgina?"

"She and I were never close," he said. "Don't see her much. She ran away a few times when we were growing up, and my folks told me she took off and left town without saying anything to them a couple of times after I moved out. I wouldn't be worried except for her car being found by the river. And she needs her medicines bad."

"Is she into drinking or drugs much?" I asked.

"Yeah, and she's not too careful about it. She told me she's experimented with heroin a time or two. She's been kind of messed up for a long time."

"Do you know when her lupus was diagnosed and how she was coping with it?" I asked.

"Three months ago. We all expected her to really go off the deep end, but a couple of weeks ago, I ran into her as she was about to go into the soup kitchen on South Division. I couldn't believe it, but she was volunteering there three nights a week before her dancing gig."

Was she attempting to turn her life around? I wondered.

"When she took off before," said Lydia, "do you know if it was with a boyfriend or by herself or what the circumstances were?"

"Boyfriend or girlfriend. She goes both ways. Are you two trying to help the police find her? Anything you can do would be really cool." He blinked several times.

"I'm not sure what we can do, bro," I said, "but I'll keep you posted if we learn anything."

I was about to suggest to Lydia that we be on our way, when Wild Bill's girlfriend came into the kitchen, wearing her usual spacey grin. She took a plate of heavenly smelling brownies off the counter. She offered the plate to Lydia who reached to take one. I put my hand out to stop her and shot Bill a questioning look.

He grinned sheepishly. "I think Rob and Lydia are ready to leave, babe."

Wild Bill's girl smiled. "One for the road?"

Lydia started reaching again. I took her arm and steered her out of the apartment.

On our way to the car, Lydia bristled with irritation. "So what's the all-fired hurry? I really like brownies." Then she put a hand to her face. "Oh, wait! I remember Wild Bill talking one time about marijuana brownies. Oh Lordy!" she said, looking at me. Then, shaking a finger at me, "You wipe that grin off your face, Robert Vander Laan!"

As we drove past Veterans Park a couple of blocks from the Ministry, we spotted Caleb sitting on the edge of the shallow pool there, cooling his feet in the water. I parked and we got out. He looked up as we approached and gave a lazy salute.

"You did good work with helping us get the runaway to the shelter," I said.

Caleb shrugged.

"I think you might have a knack for helping people," I went on. "You've got a good head on your shoulders. I see people looking up to you more."

His eyebrows sprang up, then down into a questioning frown. Maybe he didn't know what to do with the positive feedback.

"Another thing, Caleb," said Lydia. "You deserve a girlfriend your own age. I don't want you getting busted for contributing again. If you find another underage kid who's on the run, how about getting her, or him, to somebody on staff as quickly as you can?"

I liked Lydia adding the "or him" even though Caleb had thus far only taken underage girls under his flawed wing.

» CHAPTER 6

"Good grief. Was that Rochelle?" I asked.
After saying good-bye to Caleb, we'd hit a couple of our regular bar stops on South Division where we made little contact. No women working the street either. It was a slow night, as Monday nights usually were, and that's why we didn't normally work them. As we pulled away from Partners, I'd noticed a young woman getting into the passenger side of an older, black Caddie. Lydia and I both rubbernecked as we drove by.

"I wondered if it was Rochelle too," said Lydia, "but I didn't get a good look at her."

"You suppose she could be working the street on her nights off?" How messed up was Elliot's daughter?

When we arrived at the Getaway a short time later, Lydia said, "With all the police around and our being here last Friday and Saturday nights, folks here might feel ganged up on."

"Harassed by the cops and by God, huh? But I really want to know if Rochelle is working tonight. If she's not and if she was in the red light district on South Division, what the heck was she doing there?"

I followed Lydia inside where we found Hector a bit friendlier than he'd been on our previous visit. Before we could ask, he said, "Georgina's still missing."

I frowned and nodded.

Sadie and a young woman we'd not seen before were dancing in the cages while Sylvia sat at a table with three male customers.

Ned waved to us from the bar as we approached.

"Hector says still no word on Georgina." said Lydia.

"Nothing." He drew two draughts for us.

"New dancer?" I asked.

"Yeah. I hired her today. She's a little wooden. Not sure she'll work out."

I looked around. The new dancer was moving stiffly and self-consciously in her cage.

"Rochelle taking a break?" Lydia asked in a just-making-conversation tone.

"Called in sick tonight. As if I don't have enough problems." He moved off to fill an order from one of the waitresses.

I gave Lydia a questioning look, but she just shrugged.

I saw Pookie and Owen sitting at their usual corner table. Owen poured himself a little beer, emptying the pitcher on the table. Like Pookie, he had a brush cut.

I debated about going over to meet them, even though I preferred an intro from Rochelle first. They were friends of Benny. Could they have robbed the bar in retaliation for Benny's getting bounced and then mugged me when I showed up?

I saw Hector signal me. I decided to forget it, and Lydia and I headed for the door.

Hector said, "I'd, um, like to talk to you, Rob. That thing I thought I fixed, it's kind of a problem again."

We stepped aside as three young guys entered, eager looks on their faces. They did a double take when they saw my collar and quickly moved toward the far side of the bar. At the same time Pookie and Owen slid past us and out the door without so much as a glance in our direction.

We waited a few minutes as a couple more guys came in and made small talk with Hector. Then I set a time for coffee with him for the next day.

As we approached Night Watch from the passenger side, I said, "Oh, shit!" The right front tire was flat. By the light from the pole I saw a new long scratch along both passenger side doors. I was furious. I looked around. Saw no one in the lot. Owen and Pookie? No way to prove anything.

I unlocked the trunk and pulled out the spare and the jack. When I pulled off the flat, I could see a puncture in the side of it and showed it to Lydia.

"I'll check with Hector and Ned about this," said Lydia.

I was putting the jack and the flat back in the trunk when Lydia returned.

"Hector talked with a few of the patrons, but no one saw anything."

I was back to my fantasy of recruiting some of the Souls to do some serious damage to whoever was messing with Night Watch. Instead, I used the payphone in the bar to call the police and ask to have the additional damage noted on the report about my car.

* * *

Tuesday: Day four for Georgina.

The Urban Mission Committee was scheduled to meet in one of the meeting rooms at the River City Hotel. On my way to the meeting a little before noon, I remembered an incident a couple of months prior. I'd come early for the meeting and inadvertently eavesdropped on a conversation the chairman was having with another member about John Vanden Berg. I heard the chairman say, "... my wit's end with John. He's never supportive of Rob, and you know how he's interfered with some of our other work." I'd backed off and then hummed a tune so they'd hear me coming.

I didn't envy the chairman's challenge of dealing with John on his committee. I shook off the memory and entered the meeting room. At the end of my report, I told the men about Georgina's disappearance and asked for their prayers for her. The chairman inquired about the welfare of my family, and then there was a moment of silence as he tamped the tobacco down in his pipe. I was just beginning to think I had escaped the veiled judgments of John's questions when he cleared his throat.

"One thing troubled me in your report, Rob. You said that the colored pastor who's considering supporting the Street Ministry is from a Pentecostal Church. Don't you have any theological reservations about that?"

I took a breath and counted to three. "Your question is a reflection of the same song and dance you've been doing since you got on the committee." I should have counted to ten. I'd reported about people I'd had contact with in the past month who were hurting and about Georgina who could be dying. All John could think about was my theology. My neck felt hot.

John crossed his arms and glared.

"To you, John," I said, "association means approval and agreement. It doesn't mean that for me. I would welcome any church that could participate without judgment and with compassion to work with us at the Street Ministry. Which might not include some Christian Reformed Churches."

The room was deadly quiet. Was John counting to ten? After a moment he cleared his throat again and shook his head. "That kind of thinking is an indication your theology is slipping away from the truths of the Reformed Faith. It pains me to say this, but I don't know how long I can sit by and watch it happen."

Crap! I'd definitely gone too far this time. Even the chairman was staring daggers at me.

I thought quickly. "I have an idea," I said in a conciliatory tone. "How about joining me for a night on the streets, John. I don't think we've communicated very well, and maybe that'll give us a better basis for understanding each other."

The chairman brightened. "That's an excellent idea. The rest of us have spent an evening or two with Rob, and it really helped us understand his ministry."

There were murmurs of agreement in the room. John wore a sour look.

At last he spoke. "All right. I'll go with you. It can't be a Saturday night, though. *Some* ministers have to preach on Sunday mornings."

"I'll call you soon to set it up," I said.

I fumed my way out of the meeting. I knew I'd better talk to someone. Jackie was at work, so I decided to see if Lydia was home. I drove to her place and caught her coming out her front door with a few books in her hand. As we walked the two blocks to the Westside Library, I told her about the meeting and my hassle with John.

Lydia frowned. "You've taken other pastors with you on night ministry and it's gone well. So what's the problem?"

"I've thought of inviting John before, but I haven't really wanted to do it. Now I have to follow through."

"Why haven't you wanted to?"

"We have a history and we're not exactly on the same wavelength."

She wiggled her fingers in a tell-me-more gesture.

"John and I were high school classmates. College, too, for that matter. He went to seminary after graduating college while I went on to teach first. At any rate, we were very competitive in high school."

"How did you compete?"

"Basketball, debate team. John did better than me in both." I thought for a moment. "But I beat him in the election for student body president our senior year. I'm not sure he ever got over that."

"Were you competitive in college?"

I shook my head. "I figured we'd outgrown that."

Lydia narrowed her eyes. "I think going out on night ministry together is a good idea. Make sure there's time at the end of the evening to discuss not just the night, but your relationship, too. Talk about what you've told me."

I glared at Lydia. "Sometimes I hate it when you're right. Maybe I can schedule John for sometime in September or October."

"No, no, no!" Lydia wore her exasperated schoolteacher look. "See if he can go with you tomorrow night. I've got a family gathering that I said I couldn't make because of night ministry. But if John can go with you, I'll go to my sister's."

"I thought he'd go with both of us so he can see a typical night."

Lydia closed her eyes and sighed.

"Okay, okay! I'll ask him."

I returned to my office and called John. I didn't know if I was more relieved or anxious when he agreed to go with me the next night. I told him I'd pick him up a little before 8:00. I gave Lydia a buzz to let her know, then went to Sandy's Grill for my meeting with Hector. There were only a handful of customers. I waited a half hour but Hector didn't show. Fortunately,

I was able to immerse myself in the story of Malcolm X while I waited. I didn't think much about Hector's missing the appointment.

At the Ministry later, I cleaned out a back room we wanted to use for an art space and library for the kids. Some of the kids had volunteered to paint it. I was in my office, getting ready to leave when Stacy buzzed me to say that Detectives Johnson and Kincaid were there to see me. When the detectives appeared in my doorway, I greeted them and motioned them to take a seat.

Johnson looked more disheveled than last time I'd seen him—tie askew, rumpled sport coat, comb-over mussed, dark circles under his eyes. He dropped heavily into a chair across from my desk. Kincaid, looking dapper in a dark suit and maroon tie, nodded at me as he sat down in the other chair.

I frowned. "You look tired, Sid."

"Working our butts off on this Georgina thing."

I nodded. "So what's up?"

"We got a dead one," Johnson said. Before I could wonder if he meant Georgina, he added, "The bouncer from the Getaway. His body was found in his house, shot in the head, gun in his hand."

I felt stunned. "So that's why Hector didn't show for the appointment. Last night when I left the Getaway, he said he wanted to talk, so we scheduled a meeting for earlier this afternoon."

"Yeah. We found one of your cards on his coffee table. On the back of the card it said: Sandy's, two o'clock. That's why we're here."

"He committed suicide?" I was having trouble wrapping my mind around it.

"We're still investigating, but it looked to me like he was posed to make it appear like a suicide. If he murdered this

Georgina, he could have killed himself out of remorse or to avoid prosecution. But it doesn't feel right to me."

"Why not?"

"No note. No registration for the gun. No serial number either. It was filed off. We're waiting on more tests."

I glanced at Kincaid to see if he was showing his usual objection to his partner sharing information with me. Kincaid's lips were pursed in what might have been disapproval. If I was reading Kincaid correctly, Johnson, in typical fashion, was ignoring him.

"Neighbors hear the shot?" I asked. "Did they see anyone leaving Hector's house?"

This time Kincaid huffed.

Johnson stared out the window without answering. He seemed distracted. After a moment he turned to me. His unfocused eyes slowly cleared. "Did Hector say what he wanted to talk to you about?"

"No."

"Did he seem down in the dumps or sad?"

I thought a moment. "Worried maybe. But he'd dated Georgina, so I don't know…"

"Did you know he'd signed up for classes this fall at Junior College?"

"No." Trying to better himself? I wondered again what the problem was he wanted to talk with me about. Was it something bad enough for him to take his own life? Or was the problem that someone was after him and his life was in danger? Or something else entirely?

Johnson heaved a sigh. "Got anything else for me?"

"Lydia and I stopped at the Getaway last night. Rochelle wasn't there. Ned said she'd called in sick. Problem is, Lydia and I both thought we saw her hop in an older black Caddy on South Division across from Partners fifteen minutes before that. We didn't get a real good look, though, and we're not absolutely sure it was Rochelle. Of course she could have lied to Ned and gone on a date or something."

"Or turning tricks in her spare time? What else?"

I told him about Lydia's and my conversation with Wild Bill, Georgina's brother.

"Yeah we talked with him. So what else?" He shot me his intimidating glare, but it lacked its usual punch. He always seemed to think I was holding something back. Of course, I often was.

I held my palms up and shrugged. "That's it."

"I'm sorry to hear about the problems with your automobile," said Kincaid. "Do you suppose someone finds it offensive?"

I raised an eyebrow. "Don't know why anyone would."

Kincaid rewarded me with a trace of a smile.

"Anyways," said Johnson, "get a hold of me if you pick up anything that might be important."

After the detectives left, I stared for a long time out the big picture window in my office to the street. The fact that Hector had twice tried to make an appointment with me felt like the beginning of a connection with him. A connection that was short-circuited.

I said another prayer for Georgina.

I felt like I was being pulled by an invisible force into the Getaway trouble. Was this God's leading? He moved in mysterious ways. I only wished I could be as certain as some folks seemed to be about God's leading in their lives.

Suddenly the vandalism done to Night Watch seemed trivial.

CHAPTER 7

"I'll bet you ten to one your phones are bugged." said Wild Bill Tuesday evening as he straddled a chair, his arms resting on the back it. "Feds are bugging everybody these days."

Lydia and I were spending the early part of Tuesday evening at the Ministry because two of the volunteers couldn't make it till later. I was playing greeter at the front desk while Lydia mixed with people in Drop-in. My first thought was to dismiss Bill's suggestion as paranoia.

The other three heads gathered around the desk with Wild Bill nodded in agreement with him.

"Don't look so skeptical, Rob," said Bill. "I'm not high enough to be paranoid."

I grinned. "But you're paranoid about the establishment even when you're not high."

"Just because you're paranoid, it doesn't mean they're not out to get you. Can you dig it? But think about your phones. That's all I'm saying."

Upon reflection, I remembered hearing clicks on my home phone after Jackie had mentioned it to me. Then I'd noticed the clicks on the phones here, too. It seemed unimportant, and I'd forgotten about it. Maybe the clicks were normal, or maybe Wild Bill was on to something. I made a mental note to check further.

"Thanks for everything you're doing to try to find Georgina," said Wild Bill, changing the subject. "It means a lot to me. My mom and dad are really worried. She can't have much time left."

I nodded, feeling like a failure and wondering what more I could be doing.

When the other two volunteers showed up a little before 9:00, I turned over my greeter job to one of them. I asked Caleb and Lydia to join me in my office.

"Oh, oh," said the gang member. "What'd I do now?"

I laughed. "Nothing, man. I have a question that you might have an answer to. Did you hear about the disappearance of Wild Bill's sister?"

"Yeah. Met her a couple times in the lot downtown."

"I didn't know she ever hung out downtown. Did you know that the bouncer from the bar where Georgina worked is dead? Detective Johnson said it's not clear if it was suicide or murder, but he suspects it's murder. He told me the gun that killed the bouncer had the registration filed off. If you wanted a gun that couldn't be traced, where would you go?"

"Van," he said without missing a beat.

"Who's Van?"

"Guy's got a pawn shop on South Division, across from Partners."

"So, you'd get the gun from Van."

"No. I'd go to him because he'd know where I could get one." Caleb peered at me through lowered lids. "Not that I'd want an untraceable gun."

"Okay. Thanks, Caleb."

"No problem. So you're playing detective again."

"No, no! Just trying to get a little information to pass on to Johnson."

When Caleb left, Lydia shot me an amused look. "Not playing detective, huh?"

I shrugged. "I suppose I'm snooping a little, but I'm not chasing any bad guys."

"As you found out last summer, sometimes you're in a better position than the police to get certain information. You know you can count on me to watch your back, partner. Should I start carrying again?" She referred to the Walther her deceased husband had taught her to shoot.

I threw up my hands. "No! Let's stick to ministry."

"Whatever you say, *Reverend* Vander Laan."

Suddenly I remembered that Jackie had asked me to visit her uncle in Saint Mary's Hospital sometime during the evening. He was recovering from gall bladder surgery. I told Lydia I was going to duck out for a half hour or so to make the hospital visit, then come back to pick her up.

Lydia looked at her watch. "It's too late. Visiting hours are over at 9:00."

"You've forgotten about the magic of the clerical collar," I said. Actually it wasn't just the collar. Any clergy, collar or not, had pretty much free rein to visit patients any time.

As I drove to the hospital, I reflected on my protestations that I wasn't playing detective. Again, I felt like I was being sucked into trouble with a capital "T."

* * *

Wednesday: Day five for Georgina.

It was my mother's day to care for Andy. She woke me about 11:30 and told me that Stacy had called. She said that Nathan wanted me to join her and Lydia for lunch with him at the Ministry. I took a quick shower and drove to the office, wondering if Nathan had had a chance to check the phones for bugs.

The four of us were soon seated around the table in Drop-in, opening our bag lunches. I looked expectantly at Nathan.

"I didn't find anything *on* the phones," said Nathan, "but in the basement, at the central box, there's a wire coming out with a device attached. I had a friend who knows about these things look at it this morning. He says it's a pretty crude set-up, but it does the job."

Lydia and Stacy were aghast.

"Did you remove it?" demanded Lydia.

"Uh-uh," said Nathan. "I figure they'll just replace it with something more sophisticated if I do. I propose we tell people when they call here to say hello to the bug," he added with a grin.

"Why on earth would somebody tap our phones?" asked Stacy.

"Probably because of all our contact with heads and heavies," said Lydia.

"That," said Nathan, "but more interesting to the feds and local cops might be Rob's connection with a couple of the local Black Power leaders. Blaine worked with them, you know, during and after the '67 riots here, and Rob has continued working with them in the high schools during the school year. Did you find anything at home, Rob?"

"All I did was unscrew the mouthpiece covers. Couldn't detect anything, but I'm not sure I'd recognize a bug. Can your friend come over to check my phones?"

Nathan promised to have his friend check mine at home as well as those of Lydia and Stacy. His own phone, he said, was clean.

The black pastor I'd talked with called just before we broke up the meeting. "I had a meeting canceled tonight, Rob," Pastor

Washington said. "My deacon and I could come to Drop-in tonight. Otherwise I'm afraid I couldn't do it till sometime late next month."

As if I didn't have enough on my plate with John Vanden Berg joining me for night ministry. But I was eager to get Washington's church involved if I could, and I hated to put him off. I'd manage it somehow. I alerted Nathan and asked him to take care of the pastor and his deacon when they arrived.

"Lydia's taking the night off, Nathan," I added. "A guy on my Urban Mission Committee is going out with me. We'll come by before you close. Can you join us afterwards to go out with Pastor Washington and his deacon to talk about their experience."

"No problem."

After the meeting, I changed into some old clothes I'd brought along and spent the rest of the afternoon with Nathan painting his office.

During supper later, Jackie said that Nathan's friend had stopped in when she got home from work and found a bug on our phones.

"What kind of a bug, Mama?" asked Andy. "Did Nathan's friend squash it?"

"No, he didn't squash it. Remember what you learned in Sunday School about being kind to all of God's creatures?"

"We figure if we remove the one at the office," I said, "they'll just put another one on."

"The thing that frosts me most, " said Jackie, "is some stranger coming into our house to place the bug."

"Me too. But how much energy to we want to put into this?"

Andy looked alarmed. "A stranger came into our house?"

"Yes," said Jackie. "But he didn't do any harm and he won't come back." Then, to me, "You're right. Let's leave it. Maybe we can bore the eavesdroppers to death."

I told Jackie that John was accompanying me on night ministry later.

She arched an eyebrow. "You might bear in mind that John has lived a sheltered Christian Reformed life compared to you. Between your Street Ministry experiences and your seminary internship, you've rubbed elbows with lots of folks John never has." The internship Jackie referred to was the year we spent living in the Chicago area where I worked with a pastor in an almost all black church. "Knowing how John pushes your buttons," she added with a grin, "I'll say a prayer for you."

By 8:15, I was parked in front of John's home. It was a warm, sticky evening. Dressed in my usual uniform of blue jeans and clerical shirt, I walked up to the front door and rang the bell.

John answered, dressed in his usual clerical uniform of dark blue suit, white shirt and dark tie. "Come in, Rob. Say hello to my wife."

I knew her slightly from college and seminary days when our paths had crossed a few times. She greeted me warmly. "Don't let my John get into trouble tonight in any of those worldly places you visit." She flashed a mischievous grin. I'd always liked her, and the two seemed an unlikely pair. Jackie, who also knew her, had once described their marriage as a mismatch made in hell.

As John glared at his wife, I said, "I'll take good care of him."

Outside, John walked all the way around Night Watch. "I read about your car in those *West Michigan Times* articles about your ministry last summer. Those are ugly scratches," he said as he got in. "Vandalism?"

I nodded.

"You had all that stuff painted on the car so people wouldn't think you were a police officer? That wouldn't be all bad. Might restrain some of their illegal activities."

At this rate, it was going to be a long night.

"It would be fine for my car to look like a cop car if I were a cop," I said. "But I'm a minister."

John wrinkled his nose but didn't push it. "So what's our schedule for tonight?"

"I mostly play it by ear. We'll start at Koinonia Coffee House. A guy I know, Wild Bill, is playing his guitar and singing there. It's his sister who went missing. We'll have to swing by Drop-in eventually because the black pastor I mentioned at the committee meeting yesterday and his deacon will be there tonight. We'll go out after Drop-in closes to talk about their experience. For the rest, we'll see."

"Hmm. I'm surprised you don't structure your evening more carefully."

Was everything John said to me loaded, I wondered, *or was it just me?* "It's a ministry in an unstructured setting, so an unstructured approach works best. Now, ground rules: no preaching to people, no criticizing. Your job tonight is to listen and observe. Save the commentary for afterwards when we'll talk about the evening."

"You mean I can't say anything?"

"No, I didn't say that. Just don't preach or criticize." Maybe I was being too harsh. I wasn't so pointed with others who'd gone out with me, but I knew how John could be.

John turned his head and looked out his window.

I was worried about Georgina not having her meds. It would be harder to snoop with John along. I wished it was Lydia instead of John in my passenger seat.

At the coffee house Wild Bill was between sets. Some straight kids—soon to begin their senior year at Christian High—that I'd talked to a few times invited us to join them at their table. I introduced them to John who straightened his perfectly straight tie.

One of the kids, asked John why he was out with me.

"I'm the minister at Woodhaven Christian Reformed Church, and I'm on the committee that supervises Rob's work. I wanted to get a better look at what he does."

"So you're Rob's boss?" The kid shot me a look I couldn't read.

I wondered it he was pulling my leg or being genuinely curious.

"I'm one of his supervisors." John looked happier and more relaxed.

"Well, John," the kid said, "Rob's a really cool night minister. Just thought you should know." He glanced at his friends with a cocky grin. Definitely being a smart aleck, especially calling John by his first name.

John backed up in his chair, but he didn't say anything. After a moment he looked closely at the kid. "Let me ask you something. Do your folks approve of your coming to this place with all these hippies?"

The kid looked down.

John looked at the other two kids. "How about your parents?"

Now there were three kids squirming in their seats. *Nice going, John.*

Wild Bill's voice came from the mike. He'd moved to the small platform in the front that served as a stage. "Peace and love, people." He spotted me and gave a casual wave. "Are you ready for some more music, folks?" There was enthusiastic applause, especially from the three kids at our table. Bill launched into his set with "If I Had a Hammer," making it difficult, fortunately, to continue the conversation. We listened to most of the set, and then I said we needed to leave.

When we got back in my car, I said, "New rule. No loaded questions."

"What do you mean? I was just curious whether their parents approved."

"Did you notice their reaction?"

"I assume their parents don't approve, if they even know where their kids are."

"That may be true, but what was their reaction?"

"You mean the guilty looks on their faces? Maybe it will help them re-think their behavior."

I unclenched my jaw. "Maybe. But probably not. You don't have a relationship with them, John. They don't trust you. You have to do a lot of listening, a lot of trust-building before you can confront. Most of these kids don't trust established authorities. My work is building that trust through accepting without judging and by listening. That way, when there's a crisis, they can talk to me. In a congregation, a lot of the trust is there already."

"Don't you ever confront them?"

"Sometimes I do, but you have to choose your battles. You can't confront everything you disapprove of. Your job tonight," I went on, "is not to minister, but to observe."

I drove to South Division where we stopped first at the Alibi and then at Partners, the gay bar. At least John seemed to be intimidated enough, especially at Partners, where gay couples slow-danced, that he pretty much kept his mouth shut. That gave me a chance to interact with bartenders, waitresses and a few of the customers. I had debated having a beer, then decided not to change my usual routine. I couldn't escape John's judgments no matter what I did, so I'd ordered a draft. John drank water.

As we left the bar, I stopped to observe Van's Pawn Shop across the street. I made a mental note to inform Detective Johnson what Caleb had told me about Van being a connection for unregistered guns.

"Hey, Robbie, you been avoidin' me?"

I turned to see Dolores, a black prostitute I'd gotten to know the previous summer. I hadn't run into her for the past month or so. As usual she wore a short skirt, blue this time, and a low cut yellow top. Her hair was still bleached and straightened.

I grinned. "Good to see you, Dolores. How you doing?"

She gave me a hug. "I be doin' okay. Yourself?"

Before I could introduce her to John, Dolores spotted a car pulling to the curb near us and moved off.

"Sorry, Robbie," she said. "Business. Catch you later."

John looked stunned as he stared after her. "Is that woman a ...?"

"A prostitute? Yes, John, she is."

CHAPTER 8

John was quiet on the drive to River City Lounge. The bar was moderately busy. The gorgeous Samantha, in her low-cut short cocktail dress, greeted me in her usual flirtatious way.

"You've been ignoring me, Rob," she said, eyes flashing. "It's been over a week since you've been here. You haven't found a cocktail waitress you like better, have you?"

I laughed. "No, Sam, you're still my favorite."

I introduced her to John.

They barely exchanged perfunctory greetings before she turned back to me and said, "Where's Lydia tonight?"

"She had a family gathering at her sister's, and I wanted to show John what I do on night ministry."

Sam, her back to John, rolled her eyes at me. Then she said, "Have you heard about the trouble at Gus's Getaway? A dancer missing and the bouncer dead? Do you ever go there?"

"Yes, I know about the trouble, and I've been at the bar."

"Do you know Georgina?"

"Talked to her once. Did you know Hector, too?"

"Yeah, he tried to get into my pants a couple of times."

I kept eye contact with Sam, carefully avoiding looking over the top of her head at John, but I sensed he was bristling. "Detective Johnson is suspicious that Hector's death was murder and not suicide."

She put a hand to her mouth. "Oh, my gosh. I hadn't heard that. Hey, do you know Rochelle?"

I nodded.

"I went to the Getaway a few times on dates and met her there. She came in here, too. She wanted me to cage dance with her. Oh, sorry, gotta wait on some customers before the boss gets on my case."

John and I each ordered a pop at the bar and, while we waited, John said, "What did you say that girl's name was? I thought you said 'Sam.'"

"Yes, Samantha."

John's mouth twisted downward. I was anticipating more judgment from him when I felt a tap on my shoulder and heard a "Hey, Rev." I turned to see two high school classmates I often talked with here. They'd started calling me "Rev" in high school, long before I'd decided to go into the ministry. Of course, they were John's classmates, too, and Christian Reformed.

John turned and the three recognized each other. I wished I had a picture of the shocked looks on all three faces. After shaking hands and a bit of small talk, they recovered. Apparently the two had been arguing about the Reformed doctrine of Providence on the way to the bar and wanted John's input. John looked really comfortable for the first time all night. After fifteen or twenty minutes, I interrupted the discussion and said it was time to go.

"But this is the first important conversation all night," protested John.

As we began to head for the door, someone grabbed my arm from behind and I turned.

It was Sam. "Do you know Rochelle very well?" she asked.

"I've talked with her a few times."

Sam looked at me closely. "You be careful with Rochelle."

I nodded. "I'm planning to be."

Sam grinned. "It's okay. I know you like me better than her." She gave me a quick peck on the cheek and went back to work.

Great. More juice for John's judgments.

Later, at Drop-in, to my surprise, John looked genuinely interested. When we closed at midnight, John and I went with Nathan, Pastor Washington and his deacon to Sonny's, a soul-food restaurant on Franklin Street near South Division.

Washington was enthusiastic about our Ministry. He asked how long black kids had been hanging out at Drop-in. I told him the two who were gang members had been coming for years. The other handful of black teens had been coming in for the past six months. He wasn't sure if his church could contribute financially right away but thought he could come up with one or two volunteers and a representative for the board of directors. He said he'd like me to speak at his church about our ministry and would get back to me about that. We broke up about 1:00.

John yawned as he got into the car and said, "The night has been quite an eye-opener so far. In spite of your reports, actually seeing what you do is an entirely different thing."

I didn't know what to make of that comment, and I didn't ask. I decided to wait till our talk-down when our evening was over.

Next stop was the Getaway. John had survived running into a prostitute, hanging out in a bar with gay couples slow dancing and having a snack in a soul food restaurant. But what about a go-go bar? I wanted to check on how the staff at the bar was doing and whether they'd heard anything about Georgina. But what if, God forbid, John and Rochelle knew each other? Rochelle had grown up in the Christian Reformed Church, after all, and ours was small world. In addition, my relationships with Ned and some of the employees were tentative at best. Coming in with a guy who was wearing a suit, a tie and a very stuffed shirt was unlikely to enhance my standing.

But time was running out for Georgina. I mentally tossed up my hands.

I led the way into the drinking establishment, figuring we'd stay at least till "last call." I headed for the bar. Rochelle and Sadie were dancing in the cages. I was about to greet Ned when John grabbed my shoulder hard. Even in the dim light, he looked red-faced.

"I will not stay in this, this place with you," he sputtered. "Talk about an example of Total Depravity!" he added in a fierce whisper. He referred to John Calvin's teaching that people are prone to all sorts of evil, enslaved to sin, unless they are restrained by the grace of God.

The problem I had with the teaching was the way it was too often used. We frequently failed to acknowledge the depravity in ourselves and in our denomination, seeing it only out there, "in the world," and missing all the grace floating around in surprising places and people—even a go-go bar.

"Go back to the car," I said to John. "I need a word with the bartender, and then I'll be out."

I watched John turn and walk to the door, casting furtive looks over his shoulder at the dancers. I turned to Ned who was watching John and grinning.

"I'm not sure your new night ministry partner is going to work out, Rob."

I mentally rolled my eyes. "Not my new partner. Just out with me for the night."

"Lucky for you."

If he only knew.

"Listen, Ned. I told Rochelle I'd try to stop in and check with her tonight. Can you tell her that I couldn't stay? Lydia and I will try to come back tomorrow night."

"I'll tell her." He grinned again and pointed his thumb toward the door. "Good luck with the stuffed shirt."

I returned to the car and found John sitting stone-faced and silent. I'd put off the hard part of my evening long enough. "Let's call it a night, John," I said as I drove out of the Getaway parking lot. I decided to go back to my office for our talk-down on the evening so we'd have privacy.

When we got to the Ministry, I unlocked the front door, turned the lights on and then relocked the door. We went into my office and sat in the chairs in front of my desk. I suspected this little chat would test to the limit my listening skills. I slipped off my little plastic collar, put it in my shirt pocket and loosened the top button of the shirt. I wondered if John would loosen his tie and collar. It didn't happen.

"It's a lot to absorb, Rob. I'm not sure where to start."

I reminded myself how foreign my night ministry world was to John, how sheltered his whole life had been. Not so unlike my own before I took the job at the Street Ministry. I waited.

"Let me begin," he said after a moment, "with that last dive we stopped at with the naked girls dancing in those cage things." His voice reeked with disdain.

"The dancers were wearing bikinis," I said, then reminded myself to listen.

"Do you even remember," asked John, "that it says in First Timothy 2: 22 to flee youthful lusts?"

I looked at the Bible on my desk. Thought of pointing out that the passage he referred to was in *Second* Timothy. "Go on, John," I said, determined to try to hear what he was saying.

"You shouldn't be in places like that or those bars you took me to on South Division either. It looks like you're condoning a worldly and godless lifestyle."

I breathed deeply.

"I can sort of see the value of your Drop-in here," he went on, "but don't you think it would be better if the Christian Reformed Church were to have its own place? That way we wouldn't have to water down our message to make it acceptable to non-Reformed churches. Don't get me wrong. It's not that I'm anti-ecumenical. Maybe the Christian Reformed and Reformed Churches could run it together. I doubt the Protestant Reformed Churches would go for it."

That pretty well trashes the evening, I thought.

"What was your reaction to our first stop, the Koinonia Coffee House?" I asked.

"I sort of get your thinking about how I might have come on too strong with the kids for a first meeting. I treated them like they were kids in my church. But maybe the Spirit will use my words to get them back on the right path. I'm sure being at the coffee house exposes them to drugs by the looks of all those long-haired hippies. Not to mention that unpatriotic music."

I took another deep breath. "How about our stop at River City, the bar where we got into the discussion on Total Depravity?"

"That was really interesting. Do you get into that kind of thing sometimes on your rounds?"

"I do."

"Huh. I didn't realize that. But don't you have to tell our classmates at some point that they're flirting with worldliness by going to the bar? They should be having these theology discussions in their church's men's society meetings."

With difficulty, I relaxed my jaw.

"Another thing. The way that waitress at River City hung all over you and flirted with you was a disgrace. I mean, you're a man of God. She's a regular Delilah, and you allow her to act that way with you? If Jackie saw that, what would she say?" He shook his head.

The sound of someone banging on the front door washed over our conversation like a blessing. I found Caleb standing at the door with a young girl. It wasn't exactly a re-run of the previous Saturday night because, to my pleasant surprise, Caleb had done the groundwork with this runaway. After talking with Caleb, she'd already decided she wanted to go the shelter.

It was 2:30 when John and I got back in the car after dropping the girl at the runaway house. John yawned. "I'm ready to head home," he said. "Glad I didn't miss your helping the runaway though. That was a good thing you did."

A compliment? I sat in stunned silence.

"Of course, it seems more like the job of a social worker than a minister. Maybe you're missing your calling."

That was a relief. The man was consistent.

"I'd like to get together with you sometime soon, John, after you've had more time to digest the evening."

"Of course, Rob." Ministerial tone now. "How about on Friday, say 2:00?"

I dropped him off at the parsonage and drove home. I spotted a parking spot a couple of doors down. That meant I wouldn't have to park in our garage off the alley. I only kept my car in the garage during the winter and when I couldn't find a parking spot.

Kicking my shoes off a few minutes later in my living room, I sat down on the couch with a cup of tea. On an impulse I grabbed a tablet and pen and recorded the evening in as much detail as I could remember, hoping the exercise would help me sleep.

I said a prayer for Georgina. I experienced again that hated helpless feeling.

* * *

Thursday: Day six for Georgina.

I woke with Jackie snuggling against my backside. "Hey, babe," I said sleepily.

"You seemed pretty restless. How was your night with John?"

I looked at my watch and yawned. "I wrote about it when I got home. My notes are on the desk in the study. Since you're off today, maybe we can talk about it later."

I woke again around noon. Maybe writing those notes *had* enabled me to get some sleep. Normally I slept well, but I didn't usually take John with me on night ministry. Andy's playing in the morning and noises in the neighborhood rarely bothered me. After lunch Jackie and I lingered at the kitchen table.

"How are things going at work?" I asked.

"Mostly okay. I just get so bugged by Nora sometimes She has this thing where she caves in to male authority figures. I've seen her do it with our boss, even when she knows she's right. Yesterday it happened again. I've tried to talk with her about it, but she may be a lost cause."

"Nobody intimidates *you*, Jacks. That makes it hard for you to understand Nora. Some people are just born timid, or things have happened to them that make them afraid of others."

"I get intimidated by others sometimes, but that doesn't keep me from saying what I think is right. Why are you defending her? You don't still have a thing for her, do you?"

I knew Jackie was just needling me and I refused to take the bait. "Did you read about my night with John? What do you think?"

"I thought John was kind of cute in high school."

I scowled.

"Got you." She nudged my leg with her foot. "It's not news that he's a sanctimonious snob with a broomstick up his butt. How did you manage not to jump down his throat when you were talking about the evening with him? Or did you just leave that part out?"

I laughed. "No, I didn't get on his case. Restraining grace, I guess. It helped to remind myself that his whole life has been so sheltered."

"So what would you like to have said to him?"

I whispered so Andy, who was playing in the living room, wouldn't hear. "You're a sanctimonious prick. John. With a broomstick up your butt." I reverted to my normal voice. "I really like the broomstick part."

As Jackie brought the dishes to the sink, I said, "Jacks, maybe this is silly, but do you think John could still resent me because I won the election for student body president in high school?"

"Knowing John, I think it's likely."

I frowned. "By the way, which one of us did you vote for?"

She merely looked down her nose at me and smiled.

"What about you?" she asked. "Are you carrying old resentments toward him?"

I bristled. "Are you suggesting it's *my* problem?"

"Pushed a button, did I? All I'm suggesting is that, even if only a small part of it is your problem, that's the part you can do something about."

I had a flash of punching John in his pious face. That gave me an idea. "Let's go to your folks' place this afternoon." Jackie's family had moved to the farm when her dad had taken the job as principal at Borculo Christian School. "I'll chop some firewood for your dad since he's got that shoulder problem again." It sounded kind of crazy, but maybe the exercise would help me let go of some resentment. Just in case Jackie was right. I had no appointments, so I called Stacy and let her know I wouldn't be coming to the office.

A couple of hours later we were at the farm near Borculo. I left Andy and Jackie drinking lemonade with her folks and eating *olieballen*—balls of raisin-filled dough, deep fried and rolled in sugar. I went out behind the shed, grabbed the axe and started splitting the big chunks of wood into manageable ones for the woodstove in the family room. I hoped Jackie would discourage anyone from joining me because I wanted to focus on John and not be distracted.

With each blow of the axe, I pictured the Reverend John Vanden Berg in his dark suit, white shirt and tie. I thought of all his judgments about my ministry, about his threats to get me before Synod on a heresy trial, his bulldozing the kids at the coffee house. Each blow felt good. Then I thought about his outscoring me in basketball and on the debate team. I chopped some more. Bashing in his smug adolescent face felt good, too. So good, in fact, that I had to admit Jackie was right about my carrying old resentments. And then, gradually, I began to feel finished, drained and energized at the same time.

I split some more wood, but it was, well, just splitting wood.

CHAPTER 9

A s I watched Lydia come down her front steps on Thursday evening and climb aboard Night Watch, I realized I hadn't thought about John since I'd left the farm. But I was back to worrying about Georgina.

"So how did it go with John last night?" Lydia asked.

Instead of starting the car, I told her about the evening.

"I'm beginning to see what you mean about this guy," she said. "I'm surprised you're so upbeat after an ordeal like that."

I told her about my brief foray into being an axe murderer at the farm.

"Wish I could have done something like that after my husband died. I was really mad at God for a while. Of course, that would be taking the axe murder thing to a whole new level!"

I laughed. I felt horrified and fascinated at the thought of using an axe to get out anger at God. I'd have to do some theological pondering on that.

I started the car. "Let's go to the music gathering at Riverside Park first." Maybe we'll catch Wild Bill. See if he knows anything more about his sister."

On the way to the park, I told Lydia about Rochelle and Sam knowing each other and about Caleb's help with the runaway.

"We may have to get Caleb on the volunteer staff," she said.

I liked the idea, but I wanted to take some time to observe him.

Ten minutes later, at Riverside Park, we found a large gathering of kids—heads and straights. There were some "older folks" like me, but no one else as old as Lydia. A dozen police officers observed the activities. We ran into a member of the Drug Help Team who told us they'd already worked with two kids having bad trips.

The concert was getting ready to start. Two guys were arranging speakers and microphones on the stage. A van with its back door open was dropping off a band with its instruments. Nearby we spotted several familiar heads standing around Wild Bill who was tuning his guitar. We went to greet them.

"Great to see you here, Lydia," said Wild Bill.

"Hey," I said, one eyebrow raised. "I've been meaning to check something with you. I thought you couldn't trust anyone over thirty."

"That's true," said Wild Bill. "But Lydia is, well, you know, Lydia." The other heads with him smiled and nodded. "*Your* days may be numbered though, Rob," he added. "We've been letting you squeak by, but you gotta be way over thirty. Don't know how long we'll be able to make an exception for *you*." He grinned as he strummed a chord.

"Now you've got me worried," I said. Then after a moment, "Any news on Georgina?"

"Nada. My parents haven't heard anything either." He had no new ideas about her disappearance.

We listened to Wild Bill open the concert with some of his own stuff, then turn it over to the band from Chicago which was the main feature. They did many of the standard protest numbers and were quite good. After an hour, a light drizzle started falling. The concert was scheduled to end shortly, and we decided to move on.

We stopped at two coffee houses that catered to local high school kids in communities near the city. Both had been started after I spoke in nearby churches and each was sponsored by a handful of area churches. Ministry staff had helped in the planning. After the coffee house visits we went to the Getaway. We met the new bouncer and then parked at a table where Rochelle joined us. She wore a dark green mini-skirt and a light green top that fit like a second skin. She looked as hot as the green Mustang I'd see her driving.

After we exchanged greetings, I asked, "Have you come up with any ideas about how you can deal with your troubles here at the bar?"

Rochelle flashed a smile and waved a dismissive hand. "It's no big deal. Everything's fine." One foot tapped rapidly. Her fingers drummed the table. I wondered if she was on speed.

I tried again. "You're not concerned any more about how you're getting along here."

"Like I said, it's no big deal. I'm handling it."

"I notice Pookie's here again," I said.

"He comes most nights," said Rochelle. "He's such a little puppy dog. I think he's got a crush on me."

"Did you tell him about your hassles with Georgina and Hector?"

"I may have mentioned something. You're thinking he might have told Benny about it?"

"I'm wondering."

Rochelle glanced toward Pookie's table. He was watching us. Rochelle smiled and waved at him. He nodded once, then looked away. "Not a chance he'd say anything to Benny," she said. "He promised me he wouldn't."

I wasn't so sure. After a moment I said, "I wanted to ask you, is that Mustang you were driving your car? That's a really hot set of wheels."

She brightened an already thousand-watt smile. "Yeah, it is hot, isn't it? Got it last month. Told you my tips here are great. Well, better change. One more set."

As she got up, she told us that she had heard nothing new about Georgina.

When Rochelle left the table, Lydia and I went to the bar to talk with Ned. After a moment, the subject turned to the bouncer's death and Georgina's disappearance.

Ned leaned with one hand on the bar as he scanned the crowd. "I'm really sick of that fat slob of a cop and his Madison Avenue sidekick bugging me. I keep going over the same stuff with them. I wish they'd stay away and let me run my business. Don't get me wrong. I feel bad about losing my bouncer and I hope they find Georgina, but I have customers who are going to find another bar if the cops keep hanging around."

Lydia moved down the bar to talk with Sadie and Sylvia. I could tell by the change in music when Rochelle started dancing, but I stayed engaged with Ned.

He pointed a finger at me. "Bad enough I got God's special squad coming in."

I thought he was kidding, but figured I'd better check. "Seriously, Ned, are we making customers uncomfortable?"

"Nah. I was just razzing you. Customers talk about you and Lydia, but you guys are more than welcome. You two add a bit of class here in a weird sort of way."

I wasn't sure how I felt about that. I thought of John's concern about my presence implying approval.

When Ned moved off to fill drink orders, I checked Pookie's table. He was nursing a beer. Lydia appeared to be intensely engaged with Sadie. Sylvia sat with a bunch of guys gathered around two tables pushed together. I was about to get up and go over to talk to Pookie when the customer next to me struck up a conversation. He talked about his strained marriage. I asked if he'd considered marriage counseling. He was interested. I took out one of my cards and wrote Blaine's name and number on the back. He said he'd talk to his wife.

When "last call" was announced about 1:45, Lydia and I left the bar. Pookie was already gone. We headed to the Windmill Cafe, a restaurant on Michigan Hill that displayed pictures on it walls of windmills and other scenes in the Netherlands, honoring the roots of the many Dutch immigrants who'd settled in Western Michigan. The establishment had long ago passed into non-Dutch hands, but the name and decor remained.

Over burgers and coffee, Lydia told me about her conversation with Sadie and Sylvia. "They were a little more open with me tonight. And, boy, have they got it in for Rochelle. They say her sweet-and-innocent thing is as phony as a two-dollar bill. They say she gets vicious when she's crossed."

"Did they say anything about her tips?"

"I brought that up with Sadie after Sylvia went to sit with some customers. But Sadie snorted when I used the word tips. She sort of implied that Rochelle is, um, trading her body for these tips, if you know what I mean."

"She's turning tricks?"

Lydia looked away and then turned back to me. "Sadie said that Rochelle can spot a guy with real money a mile away and latch on to him before anyone else has a chance. And Rochelle's horned in on more than one man that Sadie was being friendly with."

"Could Sadie be making that up because she's jealous of Rochelle?

Lydia shrugged.

I felt sad as I thought about Rochelle.

Lydia brought me out of my reverie. "Have you talked to Johnson lately? I wonder if he's making progress on the case."

"I wonder, too. He's probably way ahead of me, but I want to tell him about Caleb's tip on this Van who owns the pawn shop."

Lydia looked up. "Speak of the devil."

Johnson lumbered to our table, Kincaid a few steps behind. Both sat down.

"We were just talking about you," said Lydia as a waitress served the detectives coffee. "You must have spotted Night Watch out front."

"If you hadn't regained possession of your automobile," said Kincaid, "you'd have made our lives more difficult. We wonder if you have any new information for us?"

"This will probably be old news for you, but I asked somebody where one might get an unregistered gun, or one with the registration filed off. This person said that somebody named Van who owns a pawn shop on South Division is the guy to go to."

Johnson grunted. "The joker's been on our radar for some other things but not for unregistered guns. We'll check him out."

"My source said that Van didn't supply the guns, but could refer to a supplier," I added.

Johnson took a sip of coffee and set the cup down. "So who's your source?"

I looked at him evenly and said nothing.

"Okay, okay," said Johnson. "By the way, how are the Lost Souls doing these days? You keeping them in line?"

The detective was a lot smarter than he looked, but I already knew that.

"By the way," said Johnson," I understand the uniforms were called out to deal with a disturbance in front of the Street Ministry a little while ago. By the time they arrived, no one was around."

I wondered what had happened.

It was almost three when we left the restaurant. I dropped Lydia off, intending to head for home. But, after what Johnson had told me, I decided to swing past the Ministry to check things out, though I didn't expect to find anything. I drove down Jefferson and parked in front of the darkened Ministry. All was quiet. Just to be sure, I hopped out and ran up the steps to make sure the door was locked. It was.

I was walking back to my car, yawning and thinking about how good the bed would feel, when a green Mustang screeched up to the curb, behind my car, one tire rolling up on the sidewalk. I waited and watched as Rochelle emerged from her car. Was she drunk or high? She was dressed in the mini-skirt and top she wore between sets at the bar.

Ambushed again.

"Rochelle, are you okay? What are you doing here?"

She collapsed into my arms. Managing to keep her upright, I opened the passenger door of Night Watch and helped her get in. She did not appear to be hurt, but she smelled of beer and looked thoroughly plastered. I crouched down next to the open car door.

"Sorry, Rob." Her words were slurred. "Jus hafta talk to you."

She was in no shape to drive. The light rain that had ended the concert was still falling.

I closed the passenger door, went around to the driver's side and got in. "So what's up?"

"Iss Ned. We were the las to leave tonight. We had some drinks together. Wanted me to go home with him. Wouldn't take no for an answer." She buried her head in her hands, her long blond hair hiding her face.

"Did he hurt you?"

She nodded and sobbed.

I got a packet of tissues from the glove compartment and handed it to her. She blew her nose.

"Did he rape you?"

"I got away and took off."

"Do you want to report this to the police?"

Rochelle looked horrified. "No. No. I can handle this." Her words were less slurred, as if her fear at the thought of reporting what happened had sobered her some. "I probably should have gone to see Uncle Van and not bothered you." She reached for the door handle and started to get out.

Without thinking, I reached across her, brushing my arm on her breasts, and pulled the door closed. I hoped the darkness hid my embarrassment at touching her. "You're too drunk to drive, Rochelle. Let me take you home."

She looked up with grateful, innocent eyes. "I am a little drunk, aren't I? Could you take me home? I hate to bother you."

"Need anything from your car?"

She shook her head and slouched down, head resting on the back of the seat, skirt riding up to show even more thigh.

"Let me have your keys for a moment. I want to park your car better."

"Bet I went over the curb. Thas what that bump was." She fished in her purse for her keys, then just handed the purse to me. I found a small ring of keys, doing my best to ignore the condoms and the small plastic bag with a couple of joints mixed in with her wallet and girl stuff.

I re-parked her car, then climbed back into Night Watch, putting her keys back in her purse which lay on the seat between us. "Where's home?" I asked, fixing my attention on the job at hand.

She directed me to a house on the near northeast side. It looked like it had been divided into three or four apartments. As I pulled up to the curb, Rochelle said, "I think I'm going to be sick."

I shut off the ignition, jumped out and ran around to the passenger side. I helped her out, careful to stay to the side in case she did as she'd threatened. She leaned against me.

"Better," she said after a moment, "but I'm so dizzy. Can you help me walk." She hiccupped.

I reached into my car and grabbed her purse, then took her by the arm and led her up the sidewalk. She managed with my support.

"Issa back apartment upstairs. Right side of the house."

I followed the sidewalk around till I came to a door with a short roof over it and a light on. I noticed a light go off in a front room of the house.

I found her keys again in her purse and she pointed at one. "Issat one," she said, bracing herself with one hand on my shoulder.

I opened the door and steered her up the covered stairway. She pointed at another key. I opened the apartment door and led her into a small kitchen.

She gave me a tentative smile. "Seems like I'm always bothering you." She stumbled over the word "bothering."

I helped her to a kitchen chair and put her keys and purse on the table. She buried her head in her hands again, crying softly.

"Are you going to be okay, Rochelle?"

"Ned was so angry when I said no." She quickly unbuttoned her blouse, with no drunken fumbling, took it off and dropped it to the floor. "Look where he scratched me." She peeled down her right bra cup—or it might have been the bikini she wore dancing—to where I could just make out a bit of pink areola. An angry scratch marred an otherwise beautiful breast.

For a moment I was too stunned to react.

Then a Scripture text exploded in my head: *Flee youthful lusts.* John was right. I didn't know if Rochelle was trying to seduce me or not. I just knew I'd better get out of there. Pronto!

"Uh, I've got to run, Rochelle. Put some disinfectant on that scratch. I'll see you later." And I was out the door. Not a graceful exit.

When I reached my car, my heart was pounding so hard I almost worried it would wake the neighbors. I felt guilty for leaving Rochelle so abruptly when she was hurting. But I'd probably have felt a lot guiltier if I'd stayed.

I turned on to my street a little later and found all the parking spots near my house filled. Rather than park way down the street, I circled the block, pulled into the alley and parked in my garage. When I got to bed, I couldn't sleep. There was something about my encounter with Rochelle that was nagging at me, something she'd said. Images of her beautiful face, gorgeous legs and the breast with the angry scratch kept playing in my head, preventing me from remembering.

CHAPTER 10

Friday: Day seven for Georgina.

I awoke with a start. Uncle Van.

Rochelle had said that she should have gone to Uncle Van. It was a common enough nickname in Western Michigan where page after page of the phone book contained Dutch names beginning with Van. According to Caleb, Van, a pawn-shop owner, was a source for unregistered guns. Hector was found holding an unregistered gun. And Lydia and I thought we'd seen Rochelle near Van's Pawn Shop.

Even though I'd only had a few hours of shut-eye, I felt too wired to go back to sleep. I slipped quietly out of bed so as not to disturb Jackie who didn't need to get up for work yet. I threw on some clothes and went down to put the coffee pot on. I glanced out the front window and spotted an empty parking spot in front of the house. Jackie had told me the previous evening that Nora was sick and wouldn't be picking her up. Jackie would need the car or I'd have to drop her off at work. If I moved it now, it would be more convenient for Jackie in case I went back to sleep and she took the car. I went out the back door to the garage. It felt like it was going to be another hot and muggy day. I drove my car out the alley and into the spot in front of the house.

When I went back upstairs to the bedroom, Jackie stirred. I pulled my jeans off and climbed back into bed.

"I'm awake," she said.

I reached over her and turned off the alarm which was set to wake her in half an hour.

I filled her in on my encounter with Rochelle, keeping my voice down so as not to wake Andy.

Jackie frowned. "Ambushed again, huh?"

"I'm actually grateful to old John because the text he threw at me about fleeing youthful lusts blazed in my brain in neon lights."

She raised an eyebrow. "Neither you nor John are that youthful. Still, I guess it worked. So you think Uncle Van is the guy who owns the pawn shop?"

"I don't know."

"You should tell Detective Johnson."

"I'd rather talk to Rochelle tonight at the bar first and ask her about Uncle Van. Or maybe I'll try to call her later this morning if I can get her number."

I thought about how wasted Rochelle had been the previous night. And it was late when I'd dropped her off, so she'd probably be sleeping till noon. Which was what I should be doing. Then I remembered she didn't seem so drunk when she was taking off her blouse. The more I thought about it, the more leery I felt about initiating *any* contact with Rochelle, even a phone call, unless Lydia was with me. I decided to wait a little and then call her father to ask about Uncle Van. I sat up and swung my feet off the bed.

Suddenly, Jackie bonked me on the head with her pillow.

"Hey! What was that for?" I whispered.

"That's for playing detective," she whispered back. "I'm not sure if I'm up for another round of that." She referred to my snooping the previous summer because of the murders.

"I'm just going to pass any information on to Sid."

"Right. Just like you won't spend any time alone with Rochelle."

I held up a hand. "That's not fair," I continued in a hushed voice. "You know I was ambushed." I rolled a leg over Jackie and straddled her. "I decided I'm better off calling her dad to find out about Uncle Van." I tried to kiss her, but she turned her head.

"You're cruising for a bruising." She pinched my arm.

"Hey!" I exclaimed again, still whispering to avoid waking Andy.

"Serves you right, pervert, for attacking a defenseless woman."

"Defenseless? Give me a break."

When I tried to kiss her again, she parted her lips and gave me some tongue.

"That's much better," I said.

"Okay, up, big fellow."

"Oh, I'm up, believe me."

There was just time for a quiet quickie before Jackie had to get ready to leave.

When Jackie's mother arrived to take care of Andy, I took Jackie to work, then returned home for breakfast. Afterwards, I went to the phone in the study, hoping I'd catch Elliot. Fortunately his first class wasn't until 10:00. I told him I'd seen Rochelle and talked with her.

"Thanks for that. She, uh, did call me. Said it was your idea. I was relieved to hear from her."

"Question for you," I said. "Rochelle mentioned an Uncle Van to me. Who's Uncle Van?"

A long pause. "Walter Van Oostenberg," he said finally.

I recognized the name from gossip during my seminary days. Something about his being canned from the ministry, but I didn't recall the details.

"Van and I became friends in college," said Elliot, "and our families were close. "Rochelle grew up calling him 'uncle,' because he was like family. We were both pastors of churches in the Seattle area for several years.

"Do you know if Rochelle ever confided in him about things that bothered her?"

Another pause. "When she was a teenager, she told me once that she could talk about things with him that she couldn't talk about with her mom or me."

Elliot was quiet for another moment, then cleared his throat. "Van and I were both candidates for the professorship I was appointed to. It was strange to be competing with one of my best friends for a position. Van never admitted to any hard feelings about my getting the job, but he seemed to start going downhill after that."

"Didn't he move to Grand Rapids shortly after you came here, maybe late 50's or early 60's?"

"Yes. 1960. He served the Northland Church."

Some of the gossip was starting to come back to me. "He got into trouble there as I recall."

"There were rumors of an affair, and Van had to leave Northland. That's when he took the job as director of the Good Samaritan Mission downtown."

"Didn't he get arrested for embezzlement of mission funds there?"

"Charges were dropped. Shortly after that, his affair with the secretary at Northland came out. As I'm sure you know, he was deposed."

"Know what he's doing now?"

"I heard he has a pawnshop somewhere downtown. Haven't seen him for three or four years."

There it was. Uncle Van—former minister, confidante of Rochelle and contact for unregistered guns. It blew my mind.

I knew I wouldn't sleep if I went back to bed, so I spent the morning doing yard work, running errands and playing with Andy, all with little thought of John and our upcoming meeting. My mind was too busy wondering about Van and worrying about Georgina who'd been missing for a whole week.

At 11:15 I knocked off and took a quick shower before heading downtown for my noon staff meeting. After the meeting I drove to Woodhaven Church. Since we'd had the first part of our discussion in my office, it seemed only fair to continue on John's turf.

I introduced myself to the church secretary who gave me the once over. It was probably the first time she'd seen someone in the church office wearing blue jeans and a clerical collar. She asked me to have a seat and buzzed John.

Fortunately, I'd brought along my Malcolm X book to read. I was not surprised that I had to wait for fifteen minutes till the door of John's study opened and he appeared, dressed in his usual dark blue suit, white shirt and tie. He seemed as committed to his uniform as I was to mine.

John's face held a broad smile. "Sorry to keep you waiting, Rob." His voice radiated ministerial authority, a deep sonorous voice that contributed to making him a well-loved preacher in the area. "Why don't you come in?"

Maybe because I'd rather sit out here and read my book? I gave myself a mental shake.

I took in the study walls, lined with bookshelves filled with theological tomes, sermon study aids and devotional reading. I noticed a small table upon which rested a large, ornate open Bible. John stepped around his desk to sit behind it rather than take one of the chairs in front of the desk. I walked to the table. As I had suspected, it was an old Dutch Bible.

"Family heirloom?" I asked.

"It was passed on to me when my wife's mother died. It belonged to her grandfather who was a minister in the *Gereformeerde Kerken* in the old country." John referred to the Church in the Netherlands from which the Christian Reformed Church had sprung.

"It's beautiful. I have one at home that belonged to Grandpa Vander Laan," I said as I took a seat.

After a moment, John leaned back in his chair, elbows on the arms, hands steepled in front of him. "I've thought a lot about my time on the street with you. I couldn't do what you're doing. And I'm still not convinced that you should be doing it or that the Christian Reformed Church should be supporting you. But I concede that your ministry is a witness of sorts. I do believe that witness needs to be more explicit, and I hope you'll come to realize that. At least I came away from the night with some good illustrations for my sermon a week from Sunday on Total Depravity."

I nodded, feeling only a slight irritation. I didn't think, however, that I wanted to hear the sermon.

"There are two things I'm still most concerned about," John went on. "The first is what may happen to your theology in that ministry, what may be happening to it already. The second is your ability to withstand the temptations you face in your work."

Only two points? I thought a good Calvinistic sermon had three points. I mentally shook a finger at myself and tried to be charitable.

John leaned forward. "Now that I think of it, there is a third concern, and I've mentioned it to you before. I think that working in a ministry supported by liberal churches and, now, a Pentecostal church, taints the purity of our *distinctive Reformed witness.*"

In seminary as well as from the pulpit, I'd often heard that phrase. Perhaps folks in every denomination felt they had, if not a corner on the truth, as least the closest approximation to the truth, and a responsibility to "let their light shine," so to speak, among other denominations. Because I never heard even a suggestion about what we could learn from other churches, I felt the phrase suggested a feeling of superiority that seemed all too evident among many in my church.

John continued. "However, I'll not bring my concerns to the Classes. Not at this point. As you well know, there are four Classes that represent the eighty Christian Reformed churches in the Grand Rapids area, not counting chapels, missions, household churches, underground churches, or any other kind of irregularity, aberration or non standard expression of the Reformed faith. The Urban Mission Committee members that you report to are appointed by the Classes. You represent those eighty churches on the streets of our city. I want you to think and pray about my concerns."

So, the threat still hung over my head, but that was no different from before John's accompanying me on the streets.

"Okay, John. I will. And I want to ask you to do the same about the areas in which I've challenged your thinking."

John sat back again. After a moment, he said, "All right. Fair enough. By the way," he added, "I've heard rumors of an *underground church* made up of some confused Christian Reformed folks. Why is it called an underground church? Do they meet in the gypsum mines or basements or something? Know anything about this so-called church?"

I shuddered at the mention of the gypsum mines under the streets of Grand Rapids. I didn't know much about the mines, but dark places like that frankly scared the crap out of me. I laughed, however, at John's taking the word *underground* literally. "The underground church is a group of several couples and individuals that meet in members' homes." I didn't tell him that I'd been invited by the group to preach for them in September. I'd be reporting on that to the committee at its next meeting. I figured John and I had enough to deal with without adding that to the mix now.

John shook his head and pursed his lips. After a moment he said, "Anything else on your mind, Rob?"

I drew a calming breath and nodded. "I want to talk with you about our relationship back in high school, in case there are any leftovers to deal with."

John seemed to flinch. Then he gestured with hands open, arms apart. "What do you mean?"

I plowed on. "We were quite competitive with each other in high school—basketball, debate, school politics. Not to mention the fact that both our dads were ministers in Holland. We got compared a lot." I smiled. "In fact, I'm rather sure my mother would have preferred you for a son."

At the mention of my mother, his eyes darted to his right. Then he looked at me again and smiled. "I don't think she truly feels that way. You know how mothers can be."

"At any rate," I went on, "I know I felt competitive with you. You were better than me in basketball and debate. Then I won the election for student body president."

He blinked, or was it a wince?

"You ever think about all that stuff?" I asked.

His laugh sounded forced. "Honestly? That's all water under the bridge. I never think about it. If you feel competitive with me, I'm sorry. Maybe it's the Spirit calling you to become a real minister." He laughed again, this time sounding pleased with himself. "Anything else?"

I shook my head. I'd tried.

"How about if I offer a word of prayer before you leave," he said. We bowed our heads.

"Our Creator, Redeemer God, Thou Who hast made the heavens and the earth and all that is in them, it behooves us to come humbly before Thy throne of grace in the afternoon hour of this day. We come as Thy covenant children, recipients of thy gracious promises handed down through the prophets and the apostles ..." John droned on in a typical pastoral prayer.

I'm almost positive I didn't doze off. I began thinking of my father's sometimes long-winded pastoral prayers in church. People in the pews referred to the pastoral prayer as the "long prayer." I noticed that my father's long prayer was longest when his sermon was short. I suppose he felt the need for the whole service to take up a certain amount of time.

My mind drifted to Rochelle dancing in her cage. When I was a teenager, my mind had often wondered during my father's long prayers in church, sometimes to sexual fantasies. I suspected this was common enough among Christian Reformed males, though few would admit it. When I began to feel a stirring in my groin, I forced my attention back to John's prayer.

"... that thou wouldst bestow thy blessing of protection upon Thy servant Rob as he ministers to the wayward youth of our city, holding him ever in the hollow of Thy hand. Keep him from falling into temptation as he seeks out the lost in places of depravity and wickedness. Keep his faith strong, ever rooted in the faith of the fathers, strong against the heresies of the liberals and Catholics and Pentecostals among whom it is his calling to serve. May he shine as a witness to the Reformed faith among those who flounder in paths of error and untruth. Forgive us for falling so far short of what Thou hast called us to be. Truly, the best of our works are as filthy rags in Thy sight, oh, holy God. We ask these things only in the name of Jesus Christ, our Lord and Savior. And bless that girl who's missing and who Rob is worried about. Amen."

I looked at John, and said, "Thanks for praying for Georgina." And I meant it.

As John showed me to the door, he said, "I understand your folks are headed to Iowa for a vacation. I've been invited to do pulpit supply at your dad's church on one of the Sundays they'll be gone."

So John would be preaching in my father's church. I wondered if John knew that after I'd last preached there, shortly after graduating from seminary, the elders had banned people with long hair and beards from their pulpit. When I'd heard about it, I considered reminding the elders of the long hair and beards on their first two preachers back in the eighteen hundreds. Their photos still hung in the consistory room. I'd felt hurt and angry.

John placed a hand on my shoulder and smiled. "You know," he said, "if you'd shave that beard off and get a decent haircut, *you* might be invited back to preach there, too."

It was a low blow. I wanted to punch his lights out. Did John intend to hurt me, or was he just that insensitive?

Then it dawned on me that I really had no desire to preach again in my dad's church, and I laughed. "I doubt the haircut would do it," I said. *Not if the real reason I was banned was because I was on such a different wave-length.*

I left John's and drove downtown to my office.

As I stepped through the front door of the Ministry, Stacy greeted me with, "Detective Kincaid wants you at the police station right away." Her grim look matched her tone.

nodded at Stacy, did an about-face and returned to my car. I noticed Rochelle's Mustang was gone. She must have come to pick it up.

As I drove to the station in response to Kincaid's summons, I reflected that, although John was hardly my first choice for someone to spend time with, I'd found it much easier to be with him than before. Could chopping wood at the farm and being more open with him have made that much difference?

My mind quickly returned to Kincaid's summons. I wondered if I was about to learn more regarding Hector's death or Georgina's disappearance. I prayed I'd hear that Georgina had been found. Alive and okay. As an idle after-thought, I wondered why the call to my office had come from Kincaid rather than Johnson.

At the Hall of Justice, I told the uniformed officer at the information desk that I knew the way to the Detective Bureau. He signaled the Communications Lieutenant, however, then ushered me to the hallway behind the information desk, past the other bureaus toward the Detective Bureau. I was surprised when he stopped at one of the interrogation rooms, ushered me in and told me to take a seat at the table. Always before I'd talked with the detectives in the Detective Bureau or the small break room. The uniform stood by the door, arms crossed, saying nothing.

I looked around, but there was really nothing much to see. The room was about eight by eight with enough space for a table with the chair I sat in and two chairs on the other side, no windows, nothing on the walls except for the mirror I took to be an observation window. Perhaps there was something going on in the Detective Bureau and the break room so that the detectives couldn't talk to me in either of those locations.

I began to picture the interrogations I'd seen on TV cop shows in rooms like this. I felt nervous perspiration in my armpits. I wished I had my book with me to distract me from worrying. Several long minutes later, Kincaid arrived. He sat down in one of the chairs opposite me and the uniformed officer left, closing the door. Kincaid greeted me with a curt nod.

"What's up, Detective?" I asked, beginning to feel increasingly uneasy.

"Rochelle is missing. The lady in the downstairs apartment reported that a gentleman brought Rochelle home in the early hours this morning in an automobile that could only be yours. She further stated that the gentleman accompanied Rochelle to her apartment, with Rochelle, quote, hanging all over him, end quote. The lady went back to bed then and didn't see the gentleman leave. This morning, some other gentleman knocked on the lady's door and demanded he tell her where Rochelle was. He forced his way in and roughed her up. She told him which apartment was Rochelle's and then called the police. She stated that this second gentleman left alone after breaking Rochelle's door in. Apparently Rochelle was not at home. That makes *you*, Reverend Vander Laan, the last one to see her."

I sat in stunned silence, my brain feeling like mush. For the life of me, I couldn't find a coherent thought.

"You can see how this appears," he said. "Forget confidentiality."

I tried to force my brain to function. "It's not that."

"Then what were you doing with Rochelle at her apartment?"

I needed a moment to collect my thoughts, but I wasn't going to get it. I told the detective everything I could remember about my encounter with Rochelle the previous night.

Kincaid scribbled in his notebook, then frowned. "What time did Rochelle approach you in front of the Street Ministry?"

"Must have been about 2:45 or 3:00 this morning. Like I said, I'd dropped Lydia off and was on my way home. The reason I stopped at the Ministry was because I wanted to check the door after Sid told me about the disturbance there earlier."

Kincaid looked up from his notebook, pen poised. "And what time did you leave Rochelle's apartment?"

"Five minutes to get her there. I couldn't have been in her apartment five minutes. So, 3:00 or 3:15."

"You went home immediately afterwards?"

"I did."

"Jackie will verify that?"

I nodded. I couldn't remember if she'd awakened when I came to bed. Sometimes she didn't.

"Have you had any contact with Rochelle since then?"

"No. And that was the last time anyone saw her?"

"Didn't I just say that?"

"I talked to her dad," I said. I told the detective about my conversation with Elliot on the phone that morning regarding Uncle Van.

"I just spoke with Doctor Rietsema," said Kincaid.

The detective's questioning went on for a long time, many questions repeated several times. I'd never been grilled like that before. So this was what a real police interrogation was like. I didn't care much for it.

Finally, Kincaid said, "Don't leave town without my permission, Reverend Vander Laan."

I nodded, feeling wired and drained at the same time. "Am I a suspect in Hector's death, or in the disappearances of Georgina and Rochelle?"

"Most certainly." said Kincaid. With that, the detective sent me on my way.

I was so rattled that I didn't even ask where Detective Johnson was.

Back at the Ministry, Stacy asked, "What did the police want? You were gone a long time."

I told her about Rochelle's disappearance and my interrogation. Not too many days ago I'd thought my connection to the Getaway thing was tangential. Now I seemed to be in the middle of the mess. At least until Jackie confirmed the time I got home.

If she confirmed it.

After talking with Stacy, I checked my watch. Too late to hit the jail as I'd planned, and I wasn't sure how well I could focus, anyway. Two of the Lost Souls had been busted on B and E charges, and were awaiting their bail hearing. That visit would have to wait till the next week.

I drove home for supper, worrying about Rochelle now in addition to Georgina. I doubted that it was a coincidence that two dancers from the Getaway had disappeared. Of course, Rochelle might well turn up at work that evening. I still couldn't wrap my mind around *my* being seriously considered a suspect. I thought about that interrogation room and shuddered.

When I got home, Andy was playing with a friend in the back yard. I said good-bye to Jackie's mom and thanked her for taking care of Andy. Then I set the table and put a chicken casserole in the oven. By the time Jackie came home from work and changed out of her nurse's uniform, the meal was ready.

I was quiet during supper, preoccupied with Rochelle's disappearance and my time in that interrogation room. I was glad for Andy's jabbering. When we finished, Andy took us into the back yard and proudly showed us a hideout he'd made out of boxes and boards with two neighbor kids. I doubted it would withstand a mild breeze. I fondly remembered the many hideouts I'd created as a kid. When the two boys who'd helped build it came into the yard, Jackie and I retired inside. While we did dishes, I told her about my afternoon and, particularly, about my ordeal in the interrogation room.

"That must be why Detective Kincaid stopped to talk to me at work," said Jackie. "He asked what time you got home last night."

"What did you say?"

"That I hadn't the foggiest."

"Great."

"What's that over your head?" she asked, peering closely at me as I held a dripping plate. "Could it be a cloud of suspicion?"

If Jackie could joke about it, maybe my being a suspect wasn't that serious. The cops just needed time to rule me out. Still, even though Jackie wouldn't like it, anything I could do to clear myself seemed like a good idea. I washed the next plate, wondering what I could do. I said a silent prayer for Georgina and Rochelle.

When we finished dishes, Jackie said, "Now it's my turn. Let's go in the living room." Jackie sat on the couch, and I took the old leather chair with the ottoman Jackie's folks had given us. My wife sat in silence.

As I looked at her more carefully, I realized she was upset. I'd been too preoccupied to notice. "What's the matter, Jacks?"

"I still haven't had my period. I think I'm pregnant." Jackie had mentioned recently that her period was a couple of weeks late. I had forgotten about it.

My eyes widened. "But how? I mean, you were using the diaphragm, weren't you? I thought you weren't ready to get pregnant."

"Yes, I was using the diaphragm. I told you that it wasn't foolproof and you should use a condom, but sometimes you can be so stubborn."

I bit off telling her that I wasn't the only one who could be stubborn. After a moment I said, "But, Jackie, are you sure? I mean, maybe ..."

"My period is almost three weeks late. I'm starting to experience a little morning sickness."

"But, hey, that's great. It's probably a good idea that we have another kid before Andy gets much older anyway. I mean, it is great, isn't it?"

The look on Jackie's face told me it was a long way from being great.

"You know I want to finish my AB degree before I have another baby, and you're going to start part time on your Masters in Pastoral Counseling next month. I'm not sure I even want another child. If I *am* pregnant, I'm thinking of having an abortion."

"An abortion?" I was stunned. "No, Jacks, we could never do that!"

"What do you mean, 'we?'" Her voice had risen. "I'm the one who's pregnant, who has to deal with the morning sickness and backaches, not to mention the joy of labor pains. It's my body, and *I'm* the one who decides this."

So this was part of women's liberation, too. A small part of me almost admitted that it was basically Jackie's decision, but I wasn't ready to voice that.

My face felt hot. "Jacquelyn, you can't!" My voice sounded muffled to me.

"Don't yell at me. You always call me Jacquelyn when you want to order me to do something. Just like my mother!"

It was only seven o'clock. I didn't need to pick up Lydia for another hour, but I raged out of the house and drove to Lookout Park. As I looked over the city without seeing it, I was furious. And, if I was honest, I was also terrified. My head was a swirling jumble of disconnected thoughts: Hector's death, Georgina's disappearance, Rochelle's disappearance. And I was a suspect in it all. I thought of Jackie's pregnancy, our relationship. I thought of John and his decision to hold off with voicing his "concerns" to the classis.

Where did I go wrong? Maybe I should never have left my teaching job at Christian High. Maybe I shouldn't have taken an internship that challenged so much of my comfortable Christian Reformed life. Maybe I should have been a regular preacher like John. Then maybe Jackie wouldn't have gotten into women's lib. On the other hand, maybe we were both just oddly wired from birth. The truth was that neither of us had ever really felt like we fit in. Until I moved to the Street Ministry. And now everything was a mess.

Lord, help me, I prayed. *I'm pretty lost here.*

No answers, but a calm gradually settled over me. I knew the calm might not last, but I relished it.

By now it was time to go. I drove to Lydia's and found her sitting on her porch swing, dressed in a long denim skirt and white blouse. She got up and slung her purse over her shoulder. If it's possible to step carefully with a bounce, that's what she did as she descended her porch steps and approached my car.

"Your granny skirt is very cool," I said, trying to keep my thoughts light.

"Can't look too square in this line of work. I assume Detectives Johnson and Kincaid have questioned you about Rochelle's disappearance."

So much for keeping my thoughts light. I caught her up on my last encounter with Rochelle, my interrogation and Kincaid's saying I was a suspect.

"Holy smoke, Rob! Looks like you're in the hot seat, like it or not. Have you gotten together with John yet, or is that on the back burner?"

I told her about my conversation with him.

"Doesn't sound like you're any worse off with him than before."

I hoped she was right. I didn't tell her about Jackie's pregnancy. My wife had told me more than once that sometimes I didn't know when to keep my mouth shut.

Lydia smoothed her skirt. "So, what are we going to do to clear your regarding the whole Getaway mess?"

"We need to find Rochelle," I said. "Problem is, there may be amateur detectives who are worse bunglers than you and me, but I sure don't know any."

"Huh!" Lydia snorted. "You think Detectives Johnson and Kincaid don't bungle along on a case? Do I need to remind you that sometimes you can ferret out things the police can't? We might not have known Hector and Georgina all that well, but the Getaway crew is part of our congregation now."

Lydia was right. I had to clear myself and do what I could to find the young women. If I was under suspicion, that meant the Street Ministry's reputation was at stake too. I wasn't a brave guy. But I could be curious and bull-headed when it came to getting at the truth of something.

I threw up my hands. "You're right, Lydia. But there's enough stress in my marriage without my playing detective."

"Want to tell me about it?"

I shook my head.

"Okay," said Lydia. "Oh, I forgot something," She opened the door, hopped out and went back into her house.

I knew my night ministry partner would return with her gun in her purse.

With a mixture of relief and trepidation, I watched Lydia come back to the car and toss her purse on the seat between us. "Now we're both armed," she said.

"What do you mean? I've got nothing."

"Huh. You've got your Bible, which you always keep on the dashboard, although I've got no idea how that could help. And you have your nosiness."

I also had the beginning of an idea. Uncle Van.

As I drove to South Division, I tried to refocus on doing night ministry, thinking we'd hit Partners, the Alibi and Amigos—all in Uncle Van's neighborhood. Passing Van's Pawn Shop, I noticed a light on toward the back of the shop and someone moving around inside.

Lydia noticed, too.

"Let's check for that older, black Caddie that we think Rochelle got into last week," I said. I cruised slowly south on Division. At the end of the block I turned left and then pulled into the alley behind the stores to turn around. Halfway down the alley, a black car was parked. I drove forward slowly until we could see the Cadillac emblem.

As I backed out to the street, Lydia said, "Someone's getting into the Cadillac. I wonder if it's Van."

I drove back to Division and headed toward downtown. As I approached the next corner, the Caddie rounded onto Division heading south. "Don't stare at him," I said. The driver, an older guy with long hair, looked at my car as we passed. A parking spot was open just across the street. There was no other traffic, so I made a U-turn and pulled in. I'd been thinking about trying to follow the Caddie, but it no longer seemed like a good idea.

Lydia said, "Not with your car and, especially, after this guy just checked us out." It was if she'd heard my thoughts. "We'll take my car tomorrow night, just in case."

As we walked toward Amigos, Lydia asked, "Did you recognize the driver? Do you know what this Van guy looks like?"

"Nope and nope." I turned to look across the street at the pawn shop. On an impulse, I said, "Wait a minute." I dashed across the street and looked at the hours posted on the door of the shop. Opened at 11:00 and closed at 8:00. I tried to peer through the window, but I couldn't make out much in the darkened interior. Before my behavior could attract attention, I ran back to Lydia.

After a couple of hours at the bars, we drove downtown and mixed with kids in the lot, the park and Drop-in. I found it hard to focus. My mind kept going back to Jackie and her pregnancy and to the Getaway trouble. When the Ministry closed, we decided to make an early night of it. I dropped Lydia off and drove home.

When I pulled up in front of my house, I was surprised to see a light on in the living room. Blaine Hanson's five-year-old Volvo was parked across the street. Probably Blaine's wife, Sheila, helping Jackie figure out how to handle my freaking out.

Inside, the two women sat in the living room on the couch. Empty wine glasses stood on the coffee table. I kissed Jackie on the cheek. Sheila gave me a hug, and said she needed to leave. Pulling my collar off and tucking it in my shirt pocket, I sat down in the easy chair.

I could see by the tightness around Jackie's eyes that she was still upset. "I'm sorry about getting pissed earlier," I said. "Well, not for getting pissed, I guess, but for storming out of here."

Jackie said nothing.

"I'll try to listen without flying off the handle, if you want to tell me more about how this is for you."

"I don't know what more I can say. Except that we've talked about the zero population growth idea, and you said it made sense."

"But not when it comes to you getting an abortion!" Not flying off this particular handle wasn't going to be easy.

CHAPTER 12

Saturday morning. The start of the second week since Georgina went missing.

Jackie and I got up before Andy. In the kitchen Jackie made coffee. I got out the cereal boxes, bowls and spoons. Jackie got the milk from the fridge. There was a strained silence between us. I finally broke it and told her about probably seeing Van's Caddie the previous evening.

"Do you think Van could have murdered that bouncer?" asked Jackie. "Maybe protecting Rochelle?"

"Maybe. But a Christian Reformed minister? Well, a deposed one, but still ... Seems like a stretch." I was relieved we had something we could talk about.

"And you wonder if Van's involved in the disappearance of Rochelle and Georgina?"

"Yes."

"I don't like the idea of your snooping into this, but maybe you can find out something that'll get you off the hook. You've got me worried about Georgina with her lupus, too. Especially since I know Wild Bill."

I breathed a sigh of relief, although I figured Jackie's support of my playing detective had its limits.

Suddenly, Jackie sat forward, frowning. "Oh, I just remembered something. I was scanning the obituaries last night. There was a Johnson, but I didn't read it, and I didn't think anything of it. Let me see if I can find it." She went into the living room and returned with a section of the paper, found what she was looking for. "Oh, my gosh!"

She handed the paper to me. Johnson's wife had died of cancer. Surviving was her husband, Sidney Johnson, Detective with the Grand Rapids Police Department. The obit mentioned their son, a GR police officer, killed in the line of duty a few years prior.

I closed my eyes, my heart going out to the big guy. "He never said anything about his wife being sick. I guess that explains why Sid wasn't there when Kincaid interrogated me."

"Sounds like Detective Johnson will need all the help he can get. And not just on the case."

"Funeral's Monday," I said. "I'm going."

"I'm glad it's Monday when I don't work. I'll get a sitter and go with you."

"I'll send flowers from the Ministry," I said, feeling a weight of sadness.

Andy joined us a few minutes later, and I fixed him a bowl of cereal. After breakfast I went to my study and worked on a proposal to the Street Ministry board for a twenty-four-hour crisis telephone line. We'd been talking about it in staff meetings for a month. The plan was to install a couple of phones in an office upstairs that wasn't being used and train half a dozen volunteers. Publicity costs would be minimal. If it filled a need, we'd try to spin it off into the community within a year. I thought about the bug on our phones and decided to see if we could set up an office in one of our supporting churches instead.

The phone interrupted me. Lydia had read the obituary notice. I told her that I'd sent flowers and that Jackie and I would pick her up for the funeral on Monday.

I stared out my study window, my mind returning to the Getaway trouble. I had a strong feeling that Van was connected somehow. He was certainly connected to Rochelle.

Georgina had threatened Rochelle. No one knew where the women were. And the lupus was ticking Georgina's life away. Hector and Rochelle had been fighting, and now the bouncer was dead. Could Van be Rochelle's protector? But then why had Rochelle disappeared? Could Van have murdered her? That didn't make sense. Or could he have her imprisoned some-where? Could he be holding both dancers against their will?

On the other hand, Ned had tried to force his attentions on Rochelle and been rebuffed. But why would he kill his bouncer and cause two other employees to disappear. Not exactly the behavior of an astute businessman.

Most of my speculation was predicated upon what Rochelle had reported to me, which might or might not be true. The only thing I could verify was her fight with Hector, and I had no idea what it was about.

I called Elliot Rietsema at home but got no answer. I rang his office at the college.

He picked up before the end of the first ring.

"Wondered if you've heard anything from Rochelle," I said.

"No, nothing." His voice was sharp, strained "Every call I get, I'm hoping it's her. You haven't heard anything either?"

"Sorry, Elliot. I just wanted you to know that she's in my prayers. And you are, too."

"Thanks. I hated her working at that bar, but ... If you could just ... Well, last summer, you did a lot to solve those murders, so I thought ... She's not one of your gang members, but ... Gosh, Rob, I'm so worried that I can't even complete a thought."

"I'm doing everything I can. I consider Rochelle a member of my congregation."

As I hung up the phone, I wondered if I *was* doing all I could? Time to go see Van. Maybe shake something loose.

It was another hot, humid day with rain predicted for the afternoon. On the drive downtown I thought about how I'd approach Van, what I'd say, but nothing felt right. The closer I got to the shop, the more nervous I felt. I thought about going back home. Then I thought about Georgina and Rochelle and I had to follow through. I parked in front of the pawn shop a little after 11:00. A bell sounded as I opened the front door. No one behind the counter, no customers. I looked around at the mess of used items in cases and on shelves: watches, rings and other jewelry, dishes, silverware, TVs and radios, books. Knives and guns in a locked case. People's possessions for sale because their lives had gone downhill. Or maybe had never gone uphill.

"Well, if it isn't little Robbie." Trace of a Dutch accent.

I looked up, startled. I hadn't seen Van come from behind the curtain over the doorway back of the counter. He was a big man, but not fat, over six feet, broad shoulders. Probably, like his classmate Elliot, in his early fifties. Long grey hair fell to his shoulders and a grey beard reached his chest. He looked like the guy I'd gotten a glimpse of in the Caddie. He wore jeans and a white shirt open at the collar, sleeves rolled up. Big nose, the veins prominent. Intelligent eyes, pale blue. His face gave away nothing.

"You must be Van," I said walking to the counter and extending my hand.

He ignored it.

"Apparently, you know who I am," I said.

"I still keep up with the church that fucked me over, Robbie. In fact, I still get the *Banner*." He indicated a magazine on the counter, the official voice of the denomination.

"I'm sorry you've had a bad time with the church."

"Sure you are, Robbie. But then you know about having a hard time with the church, too, don't you? Let's cut the bullshit. Tell me why you're here."

Time to give up any pretense. That made it easier since I had no idea what I'd say when I came in.

"I'm concerned about Rochelle," I said. "Do you know she's disappeared? I thought perhaps you might have an idea what happened to her or where she's gone."

"So you're *concerned* about her. How pastoral of you. You sure you don't just have the hots for her? You been sleeping with her, Reverend Vander Laan? Missing your little lover?"

My face and neck grew warm. "I, I'm concerned, like I said. And so is her father."

"Ah, yes, old Elliot. How is he? We've lost touch. I suppose he feels he has to shun a brother who's fallen from grace. We used to be friends. But then you know that."

"I also know that Rochelle confided in you. Seems like, if anyone would know where she's disappeared to, it would be you."

"Haven't see her for a couple of months, Robbie. I told the cops that." He spoke with an air of lightness, as if he didn't care if I believed him.

I decided to take a chance. "How about last Monday night about midnight? Did you see her then?"

A look flashed in his eyes that I couldn't read.

"Robbie, you are a busy little detective. Now get the hell out of here," he added in a matter-of-fact tone. "Don't make me say it twice."

I took one of my business cards from my shirt pocket, laid it on the counter and left the pawnshop.

I was puzzled by Van's reaction. His bitterness toward the denomination and Rochelle's father seemed understandable, particularly, if he was the kind of man who blamed others for his misfortunes. But why was he so hostile toward *me*? Because I was a Christian Reformed minister? Why accuse me of sleeping with Rochelle? Rochelle had sounded like she still confided in him. If he cared for her and didn't know where she was, why wouldn't he at least be civil toward me in the interest of finding her? Perhaps he was a very private person, especially after what he'd been through, and my prying had just stirred up an irrational reaction.

* * *

"If that man is behind my daughter's disappearance …" Elliot shouted.

Before I left for night ministry Saturday night, I'd called Rochelle's father and told him about my encounter with Van. The only thing I left out was what Van had said about Rochelle and me.

"Don't jump to conclusions, Elliot." I said, holding the phone away from my ear. "I don't know if Van had something to do with Rochelle's disappearance or not. I called because I'd like to learn more about Van and about Rochelle. I'm going to pick up my night ministry partner in a few minutes. May we stop over to talk with you?"

"I guess that would be okay," Elliot said in a quieter voice. After a pause he added, "Who is your partner?"

I heard hesitation in his voice. How open would he be if Lydia was with me? I told him a little about Lydia. "She knows Rochelle, too, and is very concerned about her."

A short time later, I pulled up at Lydia's. As agreed, we took her '57 Chevy coupe in case we saw Van again and wanted to follow him. On the drive over to Elliot's, I filled Lydia in on my encounter with Van. We were soon sitting with Elliot at his kitchen table drinking coffee.

Lydia said, "I hope it's okay that I'm here with Rob, Dr. Rietsema. We feel the more we know about Van and Rochelle, the more chance we can find her or help the police find her."

Elliot nodded, then turned to me. "I'm sorry Van treated you so badly. He never used to be like that. Why did he kick you out when you asked if he'd seen Rochelle last week? What's he hiding?"

Instead of answering, I said, "How about telling me what you can about Van. Don't worry if you're repeating something you told me before because it may be new information to Lydia."

Elliot put a couple of spoons of sugar in his coffee and stirred. "Van grew up on a farm north of Grand Rapids. I don't know much about his childhood. We met at school here when we were pre-sem. We often studied together. He got married in his last year of college, and I was his best man. When I got married after my first year at seminary, he stood up for me, too. We visited back and forth as couples. Then we both got our doctorates in New Testament Studies at the Free." He referred to the Free University of Amsterdam in the Netherlands.

He frowned and blew a breath though his lips. "Shortly after I took the call to the Lynden, Washington church, Van landed at a church in Bellingham, just a few miles away. We sometimes commented on how strangely parallel our lives were, made jokes about dirty pennies and not being able to get away from each other. We frequently visited as families, even took a couple of vacations together. Van and his wife had a daughter, a year older than Rochelle. The two were like peas in a pod. Sadly, Van's girl was killed in an automobile accident when she was ten. It put a real strain on Van's marriage.

"Were you and Van still in Washington when you were being considered for teaching Greek at Calvin?"

"In terms of the strangeness of that whole thing, it gets worse. I'd taken a call to Riverside, and Van had taken one to Northland."

Both were Christian Reformed churches in the Grand Rapids area. It was another example of what a small world my denomination was, but I still shook my head in wonderment.

"We both did some substitute teaching at Calvin," Elliott continued. "The professor I eventually replaced was sick."

"What kind of a father was Van?" asked Lydia.

"Seemed fine as far as I could tell."

"What kind of a pastor was he?" Lydia asked.

"Sometimes he was criticized for being a bit abrasive, but you always have your critics. We often met for coffee to discuss New Testament textual translation questions for our sermons or for the books we were each working on."

It's like they were joined at the hip, I thought. "Of course, I read your book," I said smiling. I'd had to read his book on the Gospels for the class I took with him at seminary. "But what was Van's book about?"

"*Creation Grace* was the title. It wasn't received very well in Christian Reformed circles. It seemed to fly in the face of the doctrine of Limited Atonement. Van argued that God's saving grace embraced all people. We often debated the subject."

I hadn't read it, but it sounded like a book I wanted to read. "Say more about Van's relationship with Rochelle," I said.

"Not much to say, other than what I told you before. The girls would stay overnight with each other back in Washington, sometimes with us, sometimes at Van's. After Van's girl died, Rochelle had little contact with him until she was a teenager here. She ran into him accidentally downtown once. After that, she would sometimes call Van to talk with him."

"When I talked with you at church, you said Van started going downhill when you got the teaching job. Anything else you can say about that?"

"You know about his involvement with the secretary at Northland. I lost contact with him after he left Northland except for seeing him a couple of times at Classis meetings while he was at the Good Samaritan Center." Then came the embezzling business at the mission. *Alleged* embezzling, I should say, since the charges were dropped. Synod deposed him shortly after that. I heard he hit the bottle pretty hard for a while, then pulled himself together enough to get a job as an editor at a publishing company in town. Eventually he bought the pawnshop.

I finished my coffee and set the cup on the table. "As I mentioned earlier, Van said that perhaps you broke contact with him because—let me think what he said—because he'd 'fallen from grace.'"

Elliot looked into the distance, a fierceness in his eyes I'd not seen before. "I couldn't have my friendship with him tarnishing ..." He seemed to catch himself. He glanced at me with a look of embarrassment and said in a calmer voice, "I just didn't know what to say to him. I was uncomfortable around him. Disappointed. Ashamed, maybe. Like his troubles were my fault in some way. If I hadn't gotten the position at the college, if I'd been a better friend, maybe he wouldn't be where he is. He grew a beard and let his hair grow long. Looked like a hippie or like the winos he worked with at the Good Samaritan." He glanced at my beard and longish hair. "No offense, Rob."

"None taken."

"It was almost as if he wanted people to reject him," he went on. "I felt like I didn't know him anymore."

"What about Van's wife?" asked Lydia.

"They divorced just before he got deposed. Last I heard, she was in P.R." Pine Rest was the local Christian psychiatric hospital. "No wonder, given all she's had to endure."

As Lydia drove us downtown a few minutes later, I said to her, "Know what bothers me most about what Elliot said?"

"You mean the comment he almost made: he couldn't have his friendship with Van tarnishing ... What? His reputation?"

"Exactly. I can sort of understand it, but it suggests he may not be the kind of friend you'd expect to stick with you 'through thick and thin,' as the saying goes."

When we got downtown later Saturday night, Lydia cruised past the Ministry looking for a parking spot. Three heads were standing on the sidewalk. Wild Bill spotted us and ran to flag us down, waving both arms over his head.

» CHAPTER 13

When Lydia stopped in the traffic lane, Wild Bill squatted down by the open window. "My mom called me here at Drop-in. She says dad's drunk. He's frantic about Georgina and he's headed for the Getaway. I don't have any wheels to get there, and there's no one here with wheels who can take me now. I'm afraid he's gonna do something stupid."

I looked at Lydia and she nodded. I opened the door, slid forward and pulled the back of my seat up for him.

"It's over a week, man, since Georgie disappeared," said Wild Bill as we crossed the Grand River to the West Side. "Over a week! She can't last a lot longer."

A few minutes later we pulled into the lot at the Getaway, and Bill pointed at a Ford sedan a few years old. "There's his car."

We rushed inside in time to see a bald middle-aged guy stripping down in one of the cages. Customers were laughing, applauding and whistling. All eyes were on him. The new bouncer was making his way to the cage.

"Oh, shit," said Wild Bill, shaking his head.

Ned looked in our direction. I waved at him and headed toward the cage with Wild Bill and Lydia trailing me. I doubted any heads had frequented the bar before. At any rate, as they watched our parade, customers added foot stomping to the general melee, and the noise increased to a roar.

By the time we caught up with the bouncer, he was reaching for the cage door. Wild Bill's dad, in his underpants and socks now, was clutching the door tightly from inside the cage.

I tapped the bouncer's shoulder.

"I think we can help," I yelled in his ear.

His eyebrows shot up as he looked us over. He glanced toward the bar where Ned stood with his arms crossed and a grin on his face. He shrugged and then indicated with a gesture that we had his okay.

The bouncer stepped back.

I faced the rowdy customers and motioned with my palms down for quiet. To my surprise the noise quickly diminished. Someone turned off the music and the low buzz turned to silence.

Bill stepped forward and said, "Dad—"

It was as far as he got. Bill's dad ignored his son and focused on the audience in front of him. He said in a loud voice, "Now I got your attention, I got somethin' I wanna say." His words were slurred and had a Texas drawl.

"Dad," repeated Wild Bill. Again Bill's dad ignored his son. Dad might be drunk, but he clearly had a plan and was sticking to it.

I put a hand on Bill's shoulder. "Give him a minute."

Bill's dad nodded at me. "Some of you guys have been watching my daughter, Georgie, dance here practically naked. I ain't proud of what my baby's been doing. But she's been missing now for over a week. You maybe don't know that she's got lupus, and she ain't got her medicines. She could die in a few days if she don't get 'em. I got a feeling somebody here knows where she is. What if it was your daughter?" His voice broke. "I just want my baby back. I want your help. I want ..."

It was all he could manage. His control broke and he fell to his knees, sobbing.

I opened the door of the cage. Wild Bill helped his dad out. Sadie hopped into the cage and grabbed the discarded pants, shirt and shoes. She jumped back out and motioned for Wild Bill, who was supporting his dad, to follow her into the dressing room.

I looked at the customers, mostly male, all looking serious now. The room was so quiet you could have heard the proverbial pin drop. I noticed Pookie sitting by himself at his usual table, eyes aimed at the floor.

I looked toward the bar. "Ned, may I add a word?"

"Okay, Rob, just so it's not going to be a long-winded sermon." He grinned.

I smiled at my audience as laughter rippled across the room.

When it quieted, I said, "You've heard from Georgina's father. What he says about her lupus is true. Some of you know that Rochelle, another dancer here, has also disappeared and that Hector, the former bouncer, is dead. If anyone knows anything about any of this, even if it seems unimportant, please tell me or Lydia. or Ned. Or you can make an anonymous call to the police if you need to do it that way. Thanks."

A moment later, Wild Bill's dad emerged from the dressing room supported by his son and Sadie who guided him out of the bar.

Lydia and I found ourselves more popular than ever at the nightclub. Several customers talked with us about the Getaway trouble. No one had any information that seemed helpful. One man did tell us that he was suspicious of Pookie. When I pressed him, the only reason he gave was that Pookie was a loner, except for a couple of times when he came in with Owen.

The man said he knew Owen from high school, and that his father had worked with Owen's father in the gypsum mines.

I shuddered at the mention of the mines. I'd often driven past the plaster mill by the Grand River where they processed the gypsum. The mines didn't fit with my notion of Grand Rapids, and the idea of mines under the city always seemed unreal and more than a little spooky to me.

I glanced toward Pookie's table and found it occupied by two men I didn't know. Apparently Pookie had slipped out and we'd missed him again."

* * *

Monday: Day three of week two.

On Sunday I'd spoken about my work at one church and preached in the evening at my own. When I went down for breakfast Monday morning, Andy was sulking on the couch in the living room. "What's the matter, Andy?" I said, plopping down next to him.

"I want to go to the farm, but Mama says I can't. Can I go, Daddy?"

"Not today," I said. "Mama and I are going to a funeral this afternoon. Did Mama tell you your sitter from across the street will be here to take care of you?"

"But I want to go to the farm!" Andy sat with his arms crossed, lower lip protruding.

"Sorry, but you can't do it today."

Andy got off the couch and stomped upstairs to his room.

"No stomping, Andrew," Jackie called from the kitchen.

I went to the kitchen. "Hey," I said. "Stomping is vastly underrated. My mother says I was a stomper."

Jackie shook her head as she flipped the French toast on the griddle. "It's rude. He's got to learn other ways to handle his disappointment."

"He's not just disappointed," I said. "The kid is pissed. If it helps him get it out of his system, what's the problem?"

As I finished setting the table, Andy came down the stairs and into the kitchen, no pouting, no stomping. "Mama, can I go to the park with my sitter?"

"If it's okay with her."

"Okay. Who died?"

"The wife of a policeman Daddy and I know."

"She went to be with Jesus, right? Can I have three pieces of French toast, Mama?"

Standing behind Andy, I smiled at Jackie and stomped lightly. Jackie rolled her eyes.

* * *

From the heat and humidity of the parking lot, we walked into the cool interior of the old Catholic church. With its spacious sanctuary, all the statues, the smell of incense, and the candles, it felt very different from the rather ascetic plainness of most Christian Reformed churches. I soaked up the peacefulness. A half hour after the service Jackie, Lydia and I finally got to express our condolences to Johnson. It was the first time I'd seen him neatly dressed in a white shirt, tie and suit. His face was drawn, and there were dark circles under his eyes. He made a weak attempt to smile that looked more like a grimace as he shook our hands.

When Jackie and I got back home, we found a note from the sitter saying that she and Andy were at the park. We considered taking a walk, but decided it was too hot. Instead we sat in the living room with glasses of iced tea.

"Still no period?" I asked.

Jackie shook her head. "I know we have to talk about this, but are you ready to recognize that the decision is ultimately mine?"

I didn't say anything. I removed my suit coat and tie and unbuttoned the top two buttons on my shirt. I felt *benauwd*, as my father liked to say—like the room was stifling, like the moist summer air was difficult to breathe. But it was more than the weather.

Instead of answering Jackie's question, I said, "I've thought about my storming out on you the other night. If I ever feel the need to do that again, I'll at least try to tell you, um ..."

Jackie shook her head again. "Puleeze! What's the good of storming out if you have to talk about it first?"

I laughed. "You mean it didn't bother you that I did that?"

"Well, sure, it bothered me, but so what? I can handle being upset. It's a difficult thing we're dealing with."

"How'd you get to be so wise and mature? You're younger than I am!"

"Right. Two whole months." Jackie sighed, undoubtedly aware I was still avoiding the issue. Then she changed the subject. "Do you think Detective Johnson is capable of finding Rochelle and the other dancer, given his wife's death?"

"I don't know if he's even on the case. I don't know how he could be."

Jackie held the glass of tea to her forehead. "Working might be his best way of coping, though."

"You may be right."

Although I'd not answered her question about the pregnancy, I kept hearing it in my head, as if a phonograph needle were stuck in a record groove. I drove to the office, put in a couple of hours on desk work, then returned home.

Jackie was fixing a chicken salad for supper. I noticed small beads of sweat on her forehead. Through the screen door I heard sounds of Andy and a friend playing in the back yard.

I gave Jackie a squeeze as she stood at the counter, chopping up celery. She dumped the celery into the salad and stirred it with a big wooden spoon. "Anything exciting happen with Andy while I was gone," I asked.

"He had a bit of trouble with his asthma, but his medicine took care of it. Maybe it was the heat. He also did his stomping number a couple of times again."

"*And?*"

Jackie sighed. "Well, he was pretty happy again shortly afterward."

"*And?*"

Jackie poked the salad with the big spoon.

"*And?*" I repeated.

She shook off the spoon on the side of the bowl and turned to face me. "Okay, okay! You were right. Now you'd better wipe that smirk off your face before I wipe it off with this spoon." She shook it in the air menacingly.

I did as Jackie demanded and turned to go into the living room to read the paper. As I walked out I said, "I can see the headlines: WIFE HATES BEING WRONG, ATTACKS HUSBAND WITH BIG WOODEN SPOON."

I didn't hear her coming, but I sure felt the whack of the spoon on my butt.

CHAPTER 14

A s I drove to Lydia's Monday evening, I felt guilty that I hadn't done anything for almost two days to try to find Georgina and Rochelle. Lydia's car was parked in front of her house and I pulled in behind it. She came down the steps and went to her car. Before joining her, I rolled my windows up in case of rain because the sky looked threatening. The heat was still oppressive.

Lydia drove us downtown. We talked with some of the kids in the lot where they congregated and brought a girl having a bad trip to Nathan at Drop-in before we headed down Division Avenue.

"The light's on at Van's shop," I said as Lydia parked a few places up from the pawn shop and on the other side of the street. "It's been closed for over an hour. Looks like somebody is moving around in the shop." Lydia slid down in her seat, apparently having decided to stake out the pawn shop for a while instead of heading into Partners.

I looked at her as she peered over the dash toward the pawnshop.

"What? It's how they do it on the cop shows and in detective mysteries. If he takes off in his car, we'll tail him."

I slid down in my seat too, feeling a little silly. We listened to the Top 40 with the radio turned low. After about fifteen minutes, I said, "I never realized this part of playing detective could be so boring. How long are we going to sit here?"

We sat for several more long minutes. "Hey!" I said. "The light just blinked off in the pawnshop."

A few minutes later, Van's black Caddie appeared and swung north on Division. Lydia waited a moment, then started her car. A couple of cars went past following the Cadillac. Lydia made a quick u-turn to follow as well.

Van took Leonard Street across the river, swung north when he got to Alpine Avenue. We lost him when he crossed 4-Mile and we got caught behind another car at the light.

Lydia hit the steering wheel in frustration, then looked in her rearview mirror. "Shoot! I'm blocked in here or I'd run the light."

"With that cop there turning on to Alpine?" I asked.

"Oh, Lordy. I never saw him there. Maybe we can catch Van when the light changes."

Ten minutes later, after no further sign of the black Caddie, we headed back into town.

"Suppose, for the sake of argument," I said, "that Rochelle hasn't been abducted. What if she decided to hide out. Why would she do it?"

Lydia frowned. "Rochelle could think whoever shot Hector and made Georgina disappear will come after her next."

"Uh-huh. But if Rochelle is behind Hector's death, she may have left to avoid prosecution."

"Maybe Van hid her or sent her away to protect her. Or maybe, if Van is responsible for Hector and Georgina, then Rochelle is afraid Van will come after her."

"Maybe she thinks Ned is the murderer," I said, "and she's disappeared to get away from her crazy boss. He already attacked her once, if that story is true."

We were spinning our wheels.

Back, once again, on South Division, we visited the Swinging Doors and then spent the rest of the night at Partners before stopping at Sandy's Grill for a bite.

We weren't getting any closer to finding Rochelle or Georgina. I was so frustrated I wanted to stomp like Andy did.

* * *

Tuesday: Day four of week two.

In the afternoon my presence was demanded again at the Hall of Justice. Kincaid brought me to the same interrogation room I'd been in before. No sign of Johnson. When I asked about Johnson, Kincaid ignored me.

"Your wife was unable to verify the time you arrived home after transporting Rochelle to her apartment," the detective said.

"She told me."

"One of your neighbors observed you park your vehicle in front of your house a little before 6:30 that morning. The neighbor speculated that you were just getting back from night ministry. What were you doing between the time you were seen at Rochelle's and the time you got home?"

"I got home when I said I did. I parked my car in my garage because there were no open spaces on the street. I woke early and couldn't sleep, so I put it back on the street about 6:30 so Jackie could drive to work. Turns out I drove her to work instead. That's why my neighbor saw me park it about 6:30." My story sounded awfully convoluted, even to me, as if I'd made it up.

"If you worked late, why were you up so early? Do you always operate on such a minimum of sleep?"

"I woke up early, remembering Rochelle had mentioned that she should have talked to Uncle Van. That made me wide awake, and I wanted to find out about Uncle Van as soon as I could. Which I did a little later when I called Rochelle's father."

"Will Jackie verify that you moved the car from the garage to the front of the house about 6:30?" he asked, giving me a hard look.

It seemed like she'd just woken when I crawled back in bed with her. Shit. I shrugged in answer to Kincaid's question.

Being interrogated for the second time in a cramped little room left me with a gnawing sensation in my gut. In addition to fearing for the safety of Rochelle and Georgina, I had to clear my name and protect the reputation of the Street Ministry. *Ah yes, the spotless reputation of the Street Ministry*, I thought wryly. I was determined to find Rochelle, come hell or high water, unless the police found her first.

That evening, when I picked Lydia up for night ministry, she said her brother-in-law was tuning up her car. It wouldn't be finished till the next day. We started our rounds by visiting Drop-in, the park and the lot. Then we did the slow ride on the circuit—the several block loop through downtown that had, for years, been luring dozens and dozens of teens in cars from the suburbs. The circuit was a cross between a traffic jam and a party. It was only Tuesday, not as busy as it would be on the weekend. It was a cooler night, thank goodness, but windows and convertible tops were down. I had brief interactions, mostly just exchanging greetings, with several kids as they crawled along in their cars in the opposite direction.

As we left the circuit and turned onto South Division, I was surprised to see Elliot Rietsema getting into a car in front of Van's Pawnshop.

"Hey, that's Elliot," I said. "Wonder what he's doing here at midnight."

"He told us he doesn't have contact with Van anymore," said Lydia.

I pulled into an empty parking spot as Elliot made a U-turn and drove past us. He seemed not to notice us. I let him get a block ahead and then followed him till he turned east on Franklin Street.

"Since Elliot lives near the Calvin campus, I assume he's headed home," I said. "I'm not going to follow him any further."

"Plus," said Lydia, "we agreed your car's not so hot for surveillance. Elliot must have gone to see Van. He's got to be desperate about Rochelle and probably thinks Van knows where she is."

Suddenly a black Cadillac cut me off sharply, and I veered into the curb to avoid hitting it. The car pulled to the curb in front of me, cutting off my escape in that direction. Had to be Van. Although, I remembered Dolores telling me her pimp drove a black Caddy. It was Van. As he emerged from his car I heard Lydia's purse click shut. I glanced over to see her gun in her hand, which she covered with her purse.

Then Van was at my window. "Well, well, well. If it isn't little Robbie. I thought I told you to keep your nose out of my business. Yet here you are, following my old friend Elliot after he pays me a social call. Just a coincidence? I think not. Now how do I persuade you to leave it alone?"

As he reached into a pocket Lydia set her purse aside. "I'd be careful if I were you."

Van looked surprised, then amused. He placed both hands on the edge of my open window. "So, Robbie, you have your granny with you for a body guard! Well, I can see how you need all the help you can get."

"How about the three of us go for coffee at Burger Joint up the street," I said. "If you know me so well, you should know that I'm too nosey to leave this thing alone. Maybe we can help each other."

Van ran his fingers through his beard, then eyed Lydia's gun again.

I looked into my rearview mirror as a police cruiser with its flasher on pulled up behind me. "Put it away, Lydia," I said.

Lydia glanced back, then returned the gun to her purse.

As the officer got out of his car, Van stepped back. "Evening, officer. Sorry about blocking the street here. Just ran into a friend, and we were deciding to meet up the street for coffee."

The officer nodded at Van, then aimed his light at Lydia and me. When he saw my collar he said, "You're Reverend Vander Laan from the Street Ministry."

"That's right, officer."

"Everything okay?"

"It's like Van said."

"Okay. Just move your cars out of here and have your chat somewhere else." He returned to his cruiser.

Van saluted me. "Burger Joint," he said and went back to his car.

A few minutes later we were in a booth at the restaurant. After introducing Lydia to Van, I studied him as he sipped his coffee. With his long grey hair and beard, he looked like an old guy who'd tuned in, turned on, and dropped out. All that was missing were beads around his neck and a peace sign on his shirt. I reviewed in my mind the bits and pieces I'd learned about what the man had been through. He'd served a couple of churches, lost his daughter, lost out to his friend on the teaching post at the college, had an affair, lost his congregation, served as director of a skid row mission, was accused of embezzlement, lost his wife through divorce. Plus, he'd been kicked out of the ministry. As I studied him, I realized his pale blue eyes were studying me.

"You called this meeting, Robbie," he said, eyes narrowed.

I had. Now what in the world was I going to say? Asking him questions at his shop had gotten me nowhere. I decided to level with him, just share everything I could think of regarding Rochelle from my first contact with her. The truth never hurt, especially when I couldn't think of anything else.

"Let's talk about Rochelle," I said. "Feel free to jump in anytime, Lydia."

We told Van everything from our first meeting Rochelle at Sandy's Grill to Hector's death, Georgina's disappearance and, finally, Rochelle's disappearance. I told Van about my conversations with Rochelle's father. I even told him about taking Rochelle to her apartment when she was drunk, about her almost baring her breast to show the scratch. I shared my concern about Johnson's ability to work the case and find Rochelle, given the loss of his wife. I told him about my being interrogated by Kincaid.

Van's eyes went back and forth between Lydia and me as we talked. He took a pipe from a pocket, a tobacco pouch from another. He filled the pipe, tamping down the tobacco and lighting it. He blew smoke over our heads.

"We just want to find Rochelle," I concluded. "Make sure she's okay."

Van sat for a few minutes without saying anything, puffing occasionally on his pipe. After tapping the dead ashes into the ashtray, he re-lit it. His face gave away nothing. I wanted to ask him what he was doing earlier in the night with Elliot, whether he had murdered Rochelle's coworkers, whether he'd killed Rochelle or hidden her somewhere. I kept my mouth shut, deciding that waiting was better if I was to engage his trust. Lydia, too, held her peace.

At last Van laid the pipe carefully in the ashtray, folded his hands, elbows on the table, chin propped on his hands. "The cops of our fine city think I murdered that bouncer from Gus's Getaway or had it done." His lips curled into a smile. "They think I'm responsible for the disappearance of Rochelle and that other dancer. Elliot came tonight accusing me of everything from molesting his daughter to kidnapping her to killing her. I've gotten used to people believing the worst of me. You two think I'm responsible, too. Don't you?" He looked from Lydia to me.

I held my hands open and shrugged. Silence still seemed the best course.

His pale blue eyes bored into me. "Don't you, Rob?"

It was the first time he'd called me 'Rob.' He wasn't going to let me off with silence.

"I honestly don't know what to think, Van. I *want* to believe that you really care about Rochelle and have her best interests at heart."

There was a flash of something in those piercing eyes, too quick to identify. If the eyes were the windows to the soul, Van had the shades down.

He cleaned out his pipe again and put it away. The smile was back. "This has been fun, Rob. We'll have to do it again sometime." He nodded at Lydia, slid out of the booth and left the restaurant.

Lydia frowned. "Seems like Van learned a lot, but we didn't learn much."

"He *did* tell us that the police see him as a suspect and about Elliot's visit, and I tend to believe him. Did you notice that he switched to calling me Rob instead of Robbie? It's the first time. I wondered if I glimpsed pain in his eyes when I said that I wanted to believe he had Rochelle's best interests at heart."

"Sometimes you're too gullible. You always want to see the best in people. It can make you blind to the bad stuff. Not to mention, a lousy detective."

There was truth to what Lydia said.

Acutely aware that Rochelle was still missing and the clock was ticking on Georgina, we moved on to the Getaway. After a moment of conversation with the bouncer, we made our way through the busy nightclub to the bar. Not a bad crowd for a Tuesday night. Sylvia and the new dancer whom we hadn't met yet were dancing in the cages. Sadie sat at a table with some guys. When Ned set a couple of beers in front of us, I said, "Looks like all the trouble hasn't hurt business any."

"That's the only bright side to this mess." Ned looked past us at the space full of patrons. "Lots of new customers wanting to check us out."

"No news on Rochelle?" Lydia asked.

Ned shook his head. "Doesn't help that I had an argument with her just before she disappeared. Don't know how the detectives found out about that." He looked sharply at me.

"So she hasn't made any contact with you?" I asked.

He shook his head. "No new information from customers either, though several have talked to me since your little performance here the other night."

When Lydia began talking with the customer next to her, I looked around and spotted Pookie at his table. I picked up my beer and went over. I introduced myself and extended my hand. "Rochelle said your name is Pookie," I said. "My name is Rob. Mind if I join you?"

He reluctantly shook my hand in a weak, moist grip, but kept his eyes aimed at the floor. "I'd just as soon be by myself. Don't really want no company." Pookie's voice had a distinct nasal tone.

I sat down anyway. "May I just ask if you have any idea what might have happened to Rochelle? I know you're a friend of hers. You must be worried about her, too."

He glanced at me and then returned his gaze to the floor. "Yeah, man. I'm worried. I got no idea what happened to her. Now, like I said, I'd just as soon be by myself."

"Okay," I said getting up. "If you hear anything or have any ideas about where she might be, give me a call." I gave him my card and returned to the bar.

Sadie, Sylvia and the new dancer were too busy to talk with us. After chatting with a couple more customers, we left and hit two of the bars in the River City Hotel. When last call was announced, we headed to Sandy's Grill for breakfast.

* * *

Wednesday: Day five of week two.

I rolled over when the alarm went off for Jackie.

"Hope your day goes well, babe," I said groggily.

Jackie said, "I made an appointment at Planned Parenthood for Monday to talk about ending the pregnancy. Will you come with me?"

Suddenly I was wide awake. "Why not your OB-GYN doctor?"

"He's rabidly anti-abortion. If we want to talk to someone who can be objective and help us think about all the options, Planned Parenthood's our best bet."

"You're not saying you're going to get an abortion Monday, are you?"

"When I called, I found out Planned Parenthood doesn't do abortions. It's a counseling appointment."

"Okay." How could I refuse? I suddenly realized how much I longed for another baby, especially if it would be a daughter. I felt a heavy weight of sadness and changed the subject.

I told Jackie about the encounter with Van the night before. Jackie's interest was piqued.

"Van plays his cards close to his chest, doesn't he?" she said.

"That's an understatement."

"If Van is genuine, maybe he'll come to trust you. Suppose he's a good guy who's made some mistakes. Most people are so quick to judge when they don't understand what a person has gone through."

Jackie swung her feet off the bed and sat up. "Rochelle's dad may be losing it. But then, if I were in Elliot's position, I'd probably be losing it, too. Anybody at the Getaway that could be behind all the crazy stuff going on?"

"Ned, Rochelle's boss. One of the other dancers. Benny, Rochelle's ex-boyfriend. Maybe someone who thinks he's God's agent to stop the evil of a go-go bar." I thought of John's reaction the night we'd visited that particular den of iniquity.

"Somebody like John?" Jackie grinned, reading my thoughts.

"Onward, Christian soldiers."

CHAPTER 15

"I haven't been doing anything on the case for a couple of days," said Johnson on Wednesday night as Lydia and I sat in front of his desk in the detective bureau. I was relieved not to be sweating it out in an interrogation room. Johnson's chair squeaked as he leaned forward. He propped his elbows on his desk, hands clasped.

I wondered why he was back to work so soon. Maybe Jackie was right, that working was helping him cope with his loss.

The detective wore a clean white shirt and tie with a neat-looking brown suit, but his eyes and face looked haggard.

"Dealing with my wife's death and everything," Johnson went on. "That's why I wasn't here yesterday when Detective Kincaid questioned you, Rob." He swallowed a couple of times, his Adam's apple bobbing.

"I understand, Sid."

"Anyways, I want to thank you guys again for coming to the funeral." He cleared his throat. "It meant a lot to me." He cleared his throat again, more forcefully this time.

I nodded. "I'm surprised you're not taking more time off?"

He shook his head. "Not working would be the worst thing for me. Chief wanted to assign the case to another detective team. I talked him into letting me and Kincaid keep it. So, back to the case. I know how nosey you two can be." His glance shifted from me to Lydia. "No disrespect intended, Lydia. Why don't you start with why you were talking with Van on South Division last night?"

I wasn't surprised Johnson had learned about our meeting with Van.

Kincaid slid over in his chair from his desk, pen and notebook ready. It looked like they were back in their usual roles.

Lydia and I reported our conversation with Van. Johnson asked a few questions about our visit with Elliot Saturday night and our time at the Getaway dealing with Wild Bill's dad, all things Kincaid had already interrogated me about. Then he said, "Okay, I don't have anything new at this point. You guys got anything else?"

I passed on the Getaway customer's suspicion of Pookie.

"Doesn't sound like much, but maybe we'll try to talk to this Pookie guy. Know his real name?"

I shook my head.

"Anything else?"

"Only that maybe Van is genuinely concerned about Rochelle."

Johnson shook his head. "You're too gullible, Rob."

"That's what I keep telling him," said Lydia.

"Am I still a suspect?" I asked.

"You're still a suspect in Rochelle's disappearance. We have only your word that you were in her apartment for just a few minutes, that she was okay when you left and that you left alone. Only your word on when you got home."

Johnson pushed his chair back. He shuffled papers. "Anyways, I guess we're done."

I wanted to hear Elliot's side of the story of his encounter with Van the previous night, so I called the professor from the pay phone in the lobby of the Hall of Justice. He invited us to stop by. Lydia was driving her car again, just in case.

Elliot met us at his front door, wearing a worn-out white dress shirt with holes in the elbows. His thick brown hair was disheveled. There were dark smudges under his eyes. Walking ahead of us, he sat down in a recliner next to a table piled with magazines, books and a dirty ashtray with two pipes in it. No offer of coffee, no invitation to sit down. Lydia and I parked on the couch.

He looked off into the distance, then brought his focus back to Lydia and me. "You have something new?"

"I wondered how you're holding up." I also wondered if he'd volunteer information about his visit to Van without my asking.

"So this is a pastoral visit?" His voice was tinged with sarcasm. Then He shrugged. "Sorry. That was uncalled for. The longer Rochelle is missing, the more I fear something really bad happened to her." He pushed a fist against his lips. "I feel like I'm letting her mother down. I'm the only parent Rochelle has, and I can't protect her."

I studied him as we sat in silence. A worried father? Or worried about his career? Or both? I considered cutting our visit short. Why ask him about his exchange with Van the previous night when he seemed to be suffering so much? Problem was I'd promised to help, and I didn't know what else to do. And why wasn't he telling us about his encounter with Van?

I decided to confront him. "We saw you leaving Van's pawnshop last night. We talked with Van a few minutes later."

He shot me a dark look, then covered his face with his hands.

After a moment, I told him what Van had said about their visit. I waited. I sensed Lydia was about to say something, and signaled her with my hand to wait.

At last he looked at me, resentment blazing in his eyes. "It was stupid of me to go see Van. I should have known that, even if he knew something about Rochelle's disappearance, he'd never tell me anything. He was always so secretive about his conversations with Rochelle. Never recognized my right as her father to know what was going on. I didn't trust him around her." He rambled on about Rochelle and Van for a few minutes, adding nothing new. Then he said, "Rochelle was always so pretty. I just didn't trust his feelings toward her. You know what I mean."

"You were afraid he had sexual feelings toward your daughter?"

Elliot's shoulders slumped, and he nodded.

"Do you think he molested her?"

"I never actually confronted him with my suspicion till last night. I thought he was going to punch me. He stood there and looked at me. It was like his eyes were shooting sparks. The veins in his neck were throbbing and his face was red."

"What did he say to you?"

"He accused me of being a failure as a father." Elliot bunched up his shoulders and pounded his knees lightly with his fists. "Said I was never there for Rochelle. Too busy worrying about my career. I don't know what he was talking about. I was always there for her. He said maybe I needed to look at my own sexual feelings for Rochelle." He shook his head. "As if I could feel that way toward my own daughter. It made me want to throw up. Shows how far into evil the man has slipped."

"Did you ever ask Rochelle if Van molested her?"

"No! Of course not. Would you, if you were her father?"

"Yes, I think I would," I said. The more I learned about sexual abuse, the more I was beginning to feel that confronting it head on was best.

Elliot showed a tight-lipped smile. "But then you don't have a daughter, so you can't be sure about that."

We sat in silence again. Then I leaned forward, elbows on my knees. "Do you remember anything else about your conversation with Van last night?"

"Van knows where she is. I'm sure of it."

"When we talked about Van before, I got the impression that you felt okay about Rochelle's confiding in him."

"I don't like to speak ill of people and I had no proof of anything." After another moment he said, "I asked Van if he'd inherited the farm he grew up on when his parents died. Thought maybe he could be holding Rochelle there. He said he'd sold it." His shoulders slumped.

"You need to tell all this to Detective Johnson," I said.

"When he asked me questions before, he seemed a little out of it. I hate to say it, but he doesn't seem too smart."

So much for not wanting to speak ill of people, I thought. "He just lost his wife, Elliot. He's a good cop and a lot smarter than he looks."

"That explains it then. I know what he's going through."

The phone rang as Lydia and I stood up to leave. Elliot asked us to wait a moment, then walked into the dining room and picked up the phone. We listened to one side of the conversation. "Okay, Detective. Any word on Rochelle? I see. Can I call you back in a few minutes?" He wrote something on a scratch pad by the phone and hung up the receiver.

The sound of a plate or glass breaking erupted from the kitchen. Lydia and I both jumped, but Elliot just turned toward the closed door to the kitchen and said, "Come on out, Benjamin. Some folks here I want you to meet."

The door swung open and a well-built young man with a dark crew-cut and bushy eyebrows, wearing cutoff jeans and a tee shirt, appeared in the doorway. His narrowed blue eyes were set too close together and his chin seemed to protrude. "Sorry about that, Dr. Rietsema, sir."

"Don't worry about it." Elliot made introductions. "Benjamin got out of the army in the spring and he's starting Calvin next month. I've been tutoring him in English and Greek since he's thinking of going pre-sem. He's still pretty scared of Greek. Tell him it's not that bad, Rob."

I smiled. "It was pretty scary for me, too, Benjamin, until I got to New Testament with Dr. Rietsema. New Testament Greek turned out to be one of my best courses. Were you in Nam?"

Benjamin gave a quick nod, avoiding eye contact."

"If you handled that," I said, "I expect you can handle Greek."

He said nothing and returned to the kitchen.

I turned back to Elliot. "Tell Detective Johnson everything you've told us." I shook his hand.

As soon as we got in the car I said to Lydia, "Benjamin! Rochelle's old boyfriend, you think? The one who was harassing her? She said Benny was a Nam vet. Her dad tutoring him?"

Lydia pulled away from the curb. "That would be weird. Probably a good thing Benjamin doesn't know we're a couple of war protestors. Where to now?"

"Since we've got your car, let's see what Van is up to tonight?"

Lydia headed back downtown. After a moment she said, "Just had a thought. Didn't you tell me that Elliot used to invite you and other students to his home to talk about New Testament Greek?"

"Yes. It was always four or five students whenever I went. I never heard of him having just one student over. I hope Elliot's not messing sexually with Benjamin. No, he wouldn't do that."

"Maybe not, but don't write it off as your obsession with Total Depravity." Between her deceased husband being Christian Reformed and hanging out with me, Lydia had learned quite a bit about Christian Reformed theology.

"Strange that Elliot didn't mention Benjamin earlier this evening," I said. "We probably wouldn't have known he was there if he hadn't dropped something in the kitchen."

"Maybe Elliot was just too preoccupied to tell us about Benjamin."

"What did you think of what Elliot told us about his meeting with Van?"

I braced myself against the dashboard as Lydia braked hard for a light.

"I thought the professor sounded like a genuinely anxious and loving father. But if we're going to keep an open mind, what about the possibility that Van is right, that Elliot wasn't there for Rochelle and that Elliot has, you know, those feelings for his daughter?"

"I'll level with you, Lydia. I don't understand how he couldn't have sexual feelings toward her. I think I would, even if she were my daughter. I'd have to work at being open with Jackie to keep from getting into trouble with those feelings. I can, however, imagine Elliot being so frightened and guilty about the feelings that he'd bury them too deep to recognize."

"What about the possibility that Daddy molested Rochelle?"

"Now who's obsessed with the evil nature of people?"

"An open mind, Rob, an open mind. Can't be a good amateur sleuth without it. Let your obsession with Total Depravity work for you."

Now there was new thought.

There were no parking spots on the street near Van's shop, but lights were on upstairs. Did Van live up there? Lydia drove around the block. At the alley behind the pawn shop, she turned in. Her headlights showed Van's Caddie parked in its usual place. When she got back to Division, a car was pulling out of a space near Van's and she pulled in.

Following Lydia's cue, I slouched down, feeling silly.

To my surprise, Lydia opened her purse and pulled out her knitting. I wished I'd brought my book, though, on second thought, there was probably not enough light from the street lamps for me to read. Maybe I'd have to take up knitting, too.

"This part of detecting is really boring," I said after a while.

Lydia smiled as her hands and the knitting needles moved. Finally I said, "What do you say we give it up?"

"Patience, Rob."

Several minutes later, Lydia said, "Stop squirming. And next time take some knitting with you."

I'd had a hard enough time reconciling myself to snooping as part of my ministry, but this waiting to snoop was killing me. I was ready to get out of the car and walk to Drop-in by myself if Lydia refused to give up our surveillance.

That's when the lights winked off above the shop. We didn't have long to wait before Van's Caddie rounded on to Division and headed north, just as it had two nights previous. Lydia followed Van to the West side of the river. North again on Alpine. This time, however, he turned west on Richmond. Lydia dropped back because there were no cars between us and Van. When she got to the top of the Richmond Park hill, the black Caddie was nowhere to be seen.

We drove a few blocks further, checking the intersecting streets. Then I said, "Maybe he suspected a tail or is just being careful. Let's go back to Thrifty Acres on Alpine and wait in the lot there." Thrifty was the local supermarket chain.

At Thrifty we watched cars go by as they headed north. Ten minutes later, we spotted Van's Caddie.

I smiled.

"Okay, super-sleuth," said Lydia. "Here we go." She pulled out of the lot, and we resumed our tail.

There were three cars between us and Van. He slowed as he approached the green light at 4-Mile. When it changed to yellow, he shot through at the last moment.

"By Jiminy!" said Lydia. "He's going to lose us again!

And he did.

CHAPTER 16

Thursday: Day six of week two.

I woke late in the morning with a growing sense of urgency to find Rochelle and Georgina. If Rochelle had gotten into trouble in high school for breaking rules, as I suspected she had, she would have had to deal with my friend Gordon, associate principal at Christian High. We'd become friends during my teaching days. When I started working at the Street Ministry, Gordon had shown a lot of interest, even coming to Drop-in a couple of times and going out with me a few times on night ministry.

After lunch I gave him a call. He knew about Rochelle's disappearance, and he'd been following the news on the other two Getaway employees.

"I can't imagine what Rochelle's poor father must be going through," said Gordon. "Rochelle was a very bright student. I always had the feeling she didn't have to work to get A's. Her grades started falling off in her junior year though. By 'falling off,' I mean she started getting B's. She probably would have been valedictorian if she'd stayed focused on her studies."

"Do you remember if she had any special friends?"

"In her junior year she started hanging out with a couple of the wilder girls. By her senior year she had a reputation for dating lots of different boys."

"Any discipline problems?"

"That's how she came to my attention. She was pretty wild for Christian High—smoking in school, drinking at a game, skipping classes, helping other kids cheat on tests, dressing immodestly. I came close to expelling her, but she had a talent for talking her way out of trouble. She must have been a real handful for Dr. Rietsema and his wife. Now he has to deal with her disappearance without his wife's support. I'm keeping him in my prayers."

"Do you know which girls Rochelle hung out with?"

"Lois Baxter and Manetta Vander Stern."

"Is Manetta's dad the Vander Stern who owns the furniture company?"

"That's the one."

"And the Baxter girl?"

"I can't remember her folks' names."

"I'd like to talk to Manetta and Lois. Know what they're doing now?"

"Let's see. I heard Manetta is starting Calvin this fall. I have no idea what Lois is doing."

I followed up right away and dialed Manetta's father at his store.

He spoke with a gravelly voice. "Rob Vander Laan. You're with the Street Ministry, right? I knew your dad when we were students together at Calvin. And I think my pastor was a classmate of yours. John Vanden Berg?"

I mentally smacked myself on the forehead. Why did old John keep turning up in my life? Was God sending me a message? If so, what the heck was it? I explained to Manetta's father that I wanted to talk to his daughter about Rochelle.

"Manetta is living in an apartment downtown with some other gals. I don't get these kids today. In my day, girls stayed home till they got married. I don't approve, but what can I do? As my father would say, *'Tis wat hier en Amerika.*" It's really something here in America.

After getting the number from her dad, I called Manetta. She knew about Rochelle's disappearance. I asked if we could meet for coffee.

"Sure, no problem," said Manetta. "I've been really worried about Rochelle. How would it be if one of my roommates comes too. The three of us have hung around together forever."

"Would that be Lois Baxter?" I asked.

"Yup. Did my dad tell you we were friends?"

"No. I talked to the associate principal at Christian High."

"Really? Oh, okay. Let's see. We're gonna be downtown to shop anyway. How about Sandy's Grill in the River City Hotel? How will I recognize you?"

"I'll be wearing a clerical collar."

"No sh ... I mean, really?"

Next I called Lydia. "I've arranged a coffee date with two of Rochelle's high school buddies."

"I suppose I can tear myself away from my knitting," she said. "What time?"

Lydia's tone reminded me of Andy when he jumped up and down with excitement.

An hour later, Lydia and I were seated in a booth at Sandy's. I'd just finished telling her about my conversation with the assistant principal.

"Two girls came in and are looking around," said Lydia.

I slid out of the booth and moved to Lydia's side but remained standing. The young women spotted me and headed over.

I signaled the waitress and, when she came to our table, both young women ordered chocolate malts. They wore jeans and sleeveless tops and had long blond hair, probably helped along by peroxide. A couple of real bombshells. A bit of small talk revealed that Manetta was indeed registered to begin

Calvin in the fall, but I noted little enthusiasm. Lois would be starting Junior College as part of the nursing program at Blodgett Hospital.

When the waitress delivered the malts and warmed Lydia's coffee and mine, the girls began slurping noisily, holding the bottom ends of the straws close to the top of the malts.

"So you're friends with Rochelle?" I asked, steering the conversation toward the purpose of our meeting.

Manetta grinned. "In high school we were inseparable, in fact—"

"—the three musketeers," finished Lois.

"Yeah, that's what some of the other kids—" Manetta, still grinning.

"—called us." It was back to Lois "The three of us had—"

"—quite the reputation." Manetta giggled.

Lois giggled.

"Pardon me," said Lydia. "I know what 'reputation' meant in my generation, but help me understand what you mean."

"Probably the same thing," both girls said together, looking at each other and giggling.

"A lot of—"

"—different boys, know what I mean?"

"Actually, it all seems—"

"—yeah, kind of innocent now. I mean we were—"

"—just kids then. Didn't know what we were doing."

They looked at each other and giggled.

Ah, the wisdom and perspective of age and maturity, I thought.

Lydia bumped my leg with her foot as if she knew what I was thinking. I didn't dare look at her.

"Was there any particular boy who was after Rochelle?" I asked.

The blond bombshells looked at each other. "Benny," they said together.

The girls went on to describe how Benny fell head-over-heels for Rochelle, wouldn't take "no" for an answer, didn't give up on her even after he graduated. Rochelle, they said, sometimes went nuts trying to fend him off.

The girls looked at each other. "El jerko productions!" they said in unison.

Listening to the two young women was a bit disorienting. I blinked, took a breath and continued. "Was Benny still in contact with Rochelle when she disappeared?"

In the same alternating fashion, they informed us that Benny was out of the picture for a couple of years while he was in the army, but that he resumed trying to see Rochelle when he returned.

"Yeah, the jerk came around to our place a few weeks ago," said Lois. "Rochelle made us swear—"

"—yeah, that we'd never tell him where she lived."

Then they told how Benny had grabbed Rochelle on the street a week before he showed up at their apartment. They said that Rochelle had threatened to scream. She'd showed them a bruise on her arm where Benny had grabbed her.

"A real rat fink!" they chorused.

How do they do that? I wondered. *They're worse, or better, depending on your point of view, than an old married couple.*

"So as far as you know," said Lydia, "the last contact Benny had with Rochelle was several weeks ago when he talked to her on the street and bruised her arm?"

"No. The last time was at the bar a couple of weeks ago," Manetta said.

"Yeah. The bouncer kicked him out for hassling her there," said Lois.

"Can you describe Benny."

The two young women drew a word-sketch that sounded like the young man we'd met at Elliot's.

"When did you last see Rochelle?" I asked.

Manetta and Lois looked at each other again. I was betting they'd say the day and time together.

Instead, Lois said, "At the bar."

"Yeah," echoed Manetta, "Last Thursday night when we went to the Getaway. The bartender—"

"—wondered if we wanted to dance in the cages." Lois grinned and elbowed Manetta. "Said he was thinking of starting an amateur night."

"Free drinks for dancing," added Manetta.

"We might do it," said Lois. "We can dance as good as Rochelle."

Manetta and Lois noisily finished their malts. I mean, they finished at exactly the same time.

"Have the police talked with you about Rochelle's disappearance?" I asked.

The girls exchanged sober looks. Lois, on the verge of tears, sniffed and rubbed her nose. Manetta turned to me and said, "The cops haven't talked to us. We're really scared for Rochelle. You think we should go talk to the cops, tell them about Benny?"

"Yes." I produced one of my cards, wrote the detectives' names on the back and handed it to Manetta.

"We'll do it," said Manetta."

When they left the restaurant, I signaled the waitress who returned with the coffee pot.

I looked at Lydia and she was grinning. "Aren't they a fun pair? You sure know how to spice up a dull afternoon."

I shook my head. "I was afraid that if I looked at you, there would be one more giggler in the group."

Lydia held up two fingers. "I don't remember the last time I giggled, but I had all I could do to keep it in."

"So what about our boy, Benny?" I asked.

"He's looking more and more suspicious in the whole Getaway business."

I rubbed my forehead, thinking about meeting Benjamin at Elliot's house. "If Benny and Benjamin are one and the same—and it sounds like they are—why would Elliot be tutoring a guy who's been harassing his daughter?"

"I think it's time to talk to the detectives again," said Lydia.

At the police station we learned that neither Johnson nor Kincaid were in. I wrote a message for Johnson, briefly stating what we'd learned from Manetta and Lois, where they worked and where they lived. I added a P.S. to the note: "If you have the opportunity, interview them together."

I dropped Lydia at home and headed to the office.

I felt like I was on a countdown till the Planned Parenthood meeting with Jackie. I doubted that the Apollo astronauts could feel any more tense than I did as they awaited their blast-off. Between Jackie's pregnancy and the Getaway trouble, I was feeling like a basket case inside. The plan was for Jackie to walk to Planned Parenthood where I would meet her at 3:30.

I was in my office, glancing over the rough draft I'd made on the crisis line proposal, not really seeing it, when Stacy came in and dropped into one of the chairs.

"I need to talk to you about my daughter."

"Go ahead, Stacy," I said.

"She's engaged to Aaron Boertje, a really nice guy."

"That's great," I said, then noticed the look of concern in her eyes.

"Well, I think so, too." She frowned. "Except that, as you know, we're Catholic."

I had a hunch I knew where this was going since her daughter's fiancé's name was Dutch. "Let me guess," I said, "Aaron is Christian Reformed or Reformed."

Stacy nodded miserably. "Christian Reformed. Aaron tried to explain the problem to me. He said his parents and pastor told him he couldn't marry someone from another religion. I told him we weren't from another religion, that because we are Catholics doesn't mean we're not Christians. I told him Islam and Judaism were other religions."

"In the Dutch-American community in this area," I said, "even the Methodist Church is referred to by some as another religion."

Stacy shook her head. "He also said what he called 'intermarriage' is always frowned upon. The marriage would be that much more difficult, depending on how different the churches were in which each partner grew up. And the worst thing, according to his pastor, was the Catholic Church required their children had to be raised Catholic. I knew most Christian Reformed folks were down on the idea of marrying Catholics, but I never heard all this stuff before." She held her palms up, a look of confusion on her face.

It was possible that Aaron was trying to get out of the engagement, but I knew of other situations that were exactly as Stacy had described. "I'll try to explain," I said. "The closer another denomination is to the Christian Reformed Church in its beliefs, the less it's frowned on to marry someone from that church. Say, if a Christian Reformed person marries a member of the Reformed Church or the Protestant Reformed Church, it will barely raise an eyebrow. Churches like the Methodist or Presbyterian will upset a greater number of folks because those denominations are more liberal, as will the Baptist Church because of its fundamentalism."

"So where does the Catholic Church fit?"

"That goes back about five hundred years. Because of the split during the Reformation and the continuing reaction by protestant churches to the Catholic Church, marrying a Catholic is the worst. You have to realize that your daughter's boyfriend was probably taught that Catholics worship idols because of all the statues in your churches, that they pray to the saints instead of praying only to God and that the mass is 'an accursed idolatry.'"

Stacy's mouth dropped open. "I know that a lot of Christian Reformed people are really down on us, but I never heard that before. I guess I just thought a lot of CRC people were as open-minded as Aunt Lydia's husband. What about you? Did you get all this anti-Catholic stuff growing up, too?"

"I guess it just didn't take with me."

Stacy shook her head. "I don't know what those kids are going to do."

"I don't suppose they can talk to his pastor from what you've said."

"The pastor said he'll only talk to them if my daughter agrees to become Christian Reformed."

"What about your priest?"

"They talked to Father O'Conner once, and they have another appointment set up with him. Aaron says he really likes Father."

"Then they may have all the help they need, but if they want to talk to me, just have them call. By the way, do you know which church Aaron goes to?"

"He said he goes to Woodhaven. The minister is Vanden Berg or something like that."

Why does this keep happening to me? I wondered. With eighty Christian Reformed churches in the Grand Rapids area, what were the odds of Aaron belonging to John's church?

I glanced at my watch: 3:40. *Oh, shit,* I thought. *The meeting at Planned Parenthood and I'm already ten minutes late.*

Fortunately, the agency was less than three blocks away. When I was ushered into the counselor's office, Jackie looked at me without saying anything, but her eyes told me she was really ticked at me for my tardiness. After introductions and a minimum of small talk, the counselor presented the options of keeping the baby, giving the baby up for adoption and, finally, abortion.

"Jackie already indicated to me," said the counselor, "that she's thinking of having the pregnancy terminated, Rob. I'm wondering how you feel about that?"

"I'm not comfortable with abortion." I said. "I can see, however, that in some situations it's the best option." I went on to elaborate what I thought was a pretty noble and open-minded position.

"That's not what I asked though, Rob," said the counselor, cutting through my bullshit. "What I'm wondering is how *you* feel about the possibility of Jackie having the fetus that *she's* carrying aborted."

I studied the counselor's diploma and license on the wall, the photos on her desk of two small children. Since that wasn't working, I began studying my hands, which to my surprise were shaking. I blinked back tears, which surprised me even more.

I swallowed and cleared my throat. "I think the idea of Jackie having an abortion is the pits. I mean it's *our* baby." I choked down the flood of emotion that threatened to overwhelm me. Why couldn't I just be pissed like before? "If it's just for Jackie's convenience … But I also want to support her getting her degree, and I've decided to go back to school myself, so the timing of the pregnancy is rotten. It's probably my fault anyway for not using condoms."

Time to shut up. I took a shaky breath and risked a look at Jackie. To my surprise her eyes were soft and glistening.

"This has been a good start," said the counselor. "Let's schedule another appointment for next week."

» CHAPTER 17

Van's Pawn Shop was dark. It was a little after 9:00. Van had left a phone message at the Ministry for me earlier in the evening, saying that he'd like me to stop by, to come around to the back of the shop and ring the bell. I was driving Night Watch since we didn't want to take a chance on Van seeing Lydia's car in case we tried tailing him again.

We made our way around the building through the shadows to the back alley where a bulb over a door provided a bit of illumination. I rang the bell and heard rapid footsteps. Van opened the door. He was dressed in worn slacks and a sweatshirt with paint stains on it. He turned around without a word and headed back up the stairs, taking them two at a time. Lydia and I followed.

Van led us through a small kitchen with a tiny table and two mismatched chairs, stove, fridge, cabinets, and sink, dishes neatly stacked on the drying rack. A coffee pot, toaster and radio stood on the counter. In the living room was an old TV set with rabbit ears on it next to an easy chair upholstered in bright red flowers with matching footstool. The easy chair clashed with a black and white striped chair and a worn green French provincial couch. End tables were piled with magazines and books, in contrast to the neatness of the kitchen. A coffee table in front of the couch was strewn with magazines and newspapers. Most of the wall space was lined with bookcases filled to overflowing. Van plopped down in the easy chair, propped his feet on the footstool. Lydia and I sat down on the couch. So far not a word had been spoken.

"Check the envelope on the coffee table," said Van, pointing. It was addressed to Van. No return address. I opened it and pulled out a neatly penned letter.

"Why don't you read it aloud, Robbie?"

So, I thought with a bit of irritation, *it's back to "Robbie."*

"Dear Uncle Van," I read. "I wanted you to know I'm okay. I can't tell you where I am. Please show this to anyone who's worried about me. Sorry to be so secretive." It was signed, *Het beste,* Rochelle. Dutch for "the best."

I looked at Lydia, then back at the envelope. I checked the postage cancellation and noted that it had been mailed a couple of days earlier in the city.

"Yeah," said Van. "Mailed in town."

"Rochelle knows a bit of Dutch," I said.

"She made me teach her when she was a little girl. She said it always ticked her off when adults around her would talk Dutch because they didn't want her to understand what they were saying. She figured the topic was usually sex, and she didn't want to miss it."

"Adults shifting gears into Dutch irritated me, too, when I was a kid." I said. "And for the same reason."

Van went on. "My parents immigrated here with me from the old country when I was ten. We spoke mostly Dutch at home, so I remained fluent in it. Rochelle liked to have conversations with me in Dutch. She got pretty good at it."

"Why are you showing this to us?" I asked.

"Rochelle says to share it with anyone who's worried about her."

I could read nothing in Van's face. "Did you show it to Rochelle's dad?"

"I was thinking maybe you could do that. I'm not too eager to go another round with good old Elliot."

"I can do that. What about the cops?"

"Same thing applies there."

"They'll come to question you about it anyway."

"I'd still rather you show it to them first. If you're not comfortable with that ..."

"I'll be glad to do it."

Van stood up and showed us to the door. Not a man to stand on formalities.

"On to Elliot's," I said as we walked to my car. "We could phone him, but I like the idea of surprising him with the letter so we can observe his reaction."

I drove in silence, pondering what had happened at Van's. I assumed Lydia was doing the same. As we turned on to Elliot's street, I said, "Do we take what happened at Van's at face value?"

Lydia shrugged. "I guess." Her voice lacked conviction, reinforcing my own uncertainty.

Elliot's lights were on. He met us at the door, his face tight with worry. "You have news?"

"I have a letter from Rochelle," I said.

After he ushered us in, I took the letter from my pocket and handed it to him. He read it quickly, then looked at the envelope. "I don't know what to feel. I'm relieved, I guess."

"You recognize the handwriting as Rochelle's?" I asked.

"It's from Rochelle. I'm not happy that she sent this to Van instead of to me."

A flash of something in his eyes. "Sometimes that girl ...! I guess this means Van doesn't know where she is either."

"We'll have to show this to the police," I said.

He nodded.

"Mind if I call Detective Johnson?"

"Go ahead." He pointed to the phone.

While I dialed the police station, Lydia asked Elliot how Benny was doing. I didn't hear his response as I told Johnson about the letter and that we were at Elliot's.

"Stay put. I'll be right over. Don't touch the letter any more." The detective did not sound happy.

When the detectives arrived, Kincaid put on gloves to hold and read the envelope and its contents, Johnson reading over his shoulder. Kincaid looked up. "Can you verify that it's your daughter's handwriting, Dr. Rietsema?"

"It's Rochelle's writing, Detective."

Kincaid asked Elliot if he had a larger envelope. Elliot retrieved one from a small desk in the corner and handed it to Kincaid who slipped the smaller envelope and Rochelle's letter into it.

Johnson looked at me, scowling. "You've most likely ruined any chance we had of getting finger prints from this. You should have called me right away from Van's. Van should have called me before he contacted you."

Johnson huffed, then turned to Elliot. "Have you gotten any ideas about where Rochelle might be, Dr. Rietsema?"

"She had a couple of close girlfriends in high school that she may still keep in touch with."

"Manetta and Lois," said Johnson. "Yeah, we visited their apartment and talked to them." He tossed me a glance, stone faced, and winked. "They told me about a guy named Benny that Rochelle dated for a while in high school. Know him?"

Elliot started to shake his head, then shot a quick look at Lydia and me before returning his attention to Johnson. "I've been tutoring him, helping him get ready to start his freshman year at Calvin. Why are you asking about him?"

Johnson scratched his chin. "Manetta and Lois said Benny has harassed Rochelle. Did Rochelle ever complain to you about him?"

"That was back a few years ago, before Benjamin went into the army. Now he's thinking of going into the ministry. Rochelle has never mentioned him to me since she was in high school. Could it be a misunderstanding? I believe the boy still cares about her."

I remembered Rochelle saying that she hadn't talked to her dad for six months before I pushed her to do so. I doubted Elliot knew much about what was going on currently in his daughter's life.

"Manetta and Lois said Benny was still giving her a bad time," said Johnson.

"That's news to me," said Elliot.

I turned to Johnson. "May I ask something?"

"Fire away," said the detective.

"The first time we talked about your daughter, Elliot, you knew she was working at a bar as a go-go dancer. Did Rochelle tell you that, or how did you find out?"

Elliot shot me a look I couldn't read. "Sorry," he said. "I'm just embarrassed about it. I got an anonymous phone call."

The look I'd seen in his eyes wasn't embarrassment. But what was it? Irritation at what I was asking?

Sid nodded. "Anyways, call me if you hear from Rochelle or if you get any ideas where she might be, Dr. Rietsema."

Lydia, the detectives and I walked out together. We stood for a moment by my car.

"Sorry about messing up the evidence," I said. "It's hard to get good help these days."

I was rewarded with a smile from Kincaid and a raised eyebrow from Johnson. The burly detective rolled his head and stretched his shoulders back. "Anyways, Manetta and Lois sure are a pair!"

"I'm pleased you suggested we interview them together," added Kincaid. "It wouldn't have been nearly as amusing interviewing them separately."

After leaving Elliot's, we swung by the Ministry. A couple dozen kids were in Drop-in with three volunteers. Lydia sat down at the table with them while I stayed in the reception area talking with one of the seminary volunteers.

"Nathan counseling someone in his office?" I asked.

"He's up there with Caleb and a runaway," said the volunteer.

"Let me guess," I said. "The runaway is female and in her early teens."

"She's fourteen. I don't know how Caleb does it."

"It's his gift," I said. "Let's just hope he keeps bringing them to us."

"Actually, I heard a couple of the other Souls talking about her. Sounds like she's been hanging close to Caleb for a couple of days."

"His gift may need a little fine tuning," I said.

I looked up, then, to see Nathan preceding Caleb and a young girl down the steps.

Nathan introduced the runaway to me, Aretha Vander Stern.

I clamped down to keep my jaw from dropping open. "Any relation to Manetta," I asked.

Aretha brightened. "My sister. Know her?"

"Yes, I do." That meant, of course, that Aretha's pastor was John Vanden Berg. The man's shadow was dogging me.

Since Nathan had to get Aretha to the shelter, Lydia and I stuck around till Drop-in closed, then went to the Getaway. Sadie and Sylvia danced in the cages while Ned filled drink orders. "Any word on Rochelle or Georgina?" he asked a few minutes later as he placed two foaming glasses of beer in front of us.

We told him about the letter from Rochelle.

He frowned. "Guess I'm happy she's okay, but I can't go on holding her job for her. If she's not back by Thursday, I'll have to hire somebody else. A couple of friends of Rochelle's said they might be interested."

"Manetta and Lois?" I asked.

"Hey," said Ned, grinning, "you know them? They're quite the pair. Can you guys vouch for them?"

"We can vouch for the fact that they're 'quite the pair,'" Lydia said, "but we only met them once."

If Ned hired them, that would make three Christian Reformed dancers at the go-go bar, counting Rochelle. Rochelle had told me that Sadie and Sylvia were both Catholics. I didn't know about the new dancer. And Manetta was a member of John's church. My stomach did a flip-flop. If John blamed me for this, there could be hell to pay.

Changing the subject, I asked, "How are you and your staff managing with the trouble here?"

"We've all been feeling uptight. But, like I said the other night, it's been good for business. That'll probably wear off soon enough, though. The thing is, without Rochelle, it's just not the same. She was the best." He looked down, nervously swabbing the bar with a towel.

Was Ned just reacting as a businessman or was it more personal?

Before I could ask what he meant, he moved off to wait on a customer at the far end of the bar. Sadie and Sylvia had finished their set and approached us. We told them about the note from Rochelle.

"Did you meet Rochelle's former boyfriend when he came in a while back?" asked Lydia. "The guy that got bounced out of here?"

"I didn't meet him," said Sadie, "but Rochelle sure bitched about him."

"What did she say?" I asked.

"What a pain he was, didn't understand the meaning of 'no,' that sort of thing."

"She made sure to leave work with one of us for a while after that," added Sylvia.

Since Pookie was in his usual spot, I left Lydia at the bar and approached his table.

"Hey, Pookie," I said. "How's it going?"

He avoided eye contact with me and mumbled, "I don't want no company."

So, no friendlier than when I'd introduced myself to him. I sat down anyway and told him about the letter from Rochelle. "Since you're a friend, I thought you'd like to know."

"Thanks," he mumbled. "But I still don't want no company." He drank the last of his beer.

"Okay, man," I said pushing my chair back but leaning forward. "One other thing. Apparently your friend Benny was giving Rochelle a hard time. Did she tell you about it?"

He pushed his chair back and stood up. "Sorry, man, but I gotta go." He headed for the door.

As I watched Pookie go, I remembered that Nathan had a friend who was a Nam Vet. He'd come to Drop-in a few times, and expressed an interest in volunteering but was too busy at the time. Maybe I could get him to come to the Getaway and see if Pookie would open up more with him about Rochelle and about Benny.

Conversations with other customers at the bar kept us occupied till last call.

In the parking lot, I sat tapping my key against the steering wheel. "If Benny's responsible for Hector's death and Georgina's disappearance, what would his motive be?"

Lydia frowned. "If he knew about Rochelle's hassles with other Getaway staff, maybe he thinks he's solving her problems for her."

"But how could Benny know about her fights with them? Doesn't seem like Rochelle would tell him. Seems like someone else, Pookie, maybe, would have to be informing him, even though Rochelle says he wouldn't do that."

I thought for a moment. "We haven't eliminated Ned as a suspect either. But if he was Rochelle's problem fixer, seems like he'd just fire Hector and Georgina?"

"Good point," said Lydia. "Hard to see Ned behind all this unless he has a very different motive that we don't have a handle on yet."

Lydia squinted. "And there's still Van. Rochelle could easily have confided in Van about her troubles at the bar. If he's overly protective of her, he might want to get Hector and Georgina out of her hair."

The more we dug into the Getaway trouble, the more I liked the idea that whoever was behind it all was motivated by a desire to solve Rochelle's problems. And, given the volatile woman Rochelle was, I hadn't ruled out that she could be her own problem solver.

» CHAPTER 18

Friday marked two weeks for Georgina without her meds. I woke late morning, light streaming in my bedroom window, thinking about Georgina and about Jackie's pregnancy. A pleasant breeze from the fan blew across my bare chest. But my stomach was in a knot. I was still avoiding the abortion issue. I heard Andy's laughter from downstairs, followed by my mother-in-law's, "Shhh. Don't wake your daddy."

The knot in my stomach let go, and I felt a rush of pure joy. "It's okay," I called. "I'm awake."

I smiled as I listened to the sound of Andy pumping full tilt up the stairs. He came flying into the bedroom, climbed on the bed and threw his arms around me. "Daddy, I love you so much it makes me cuckoo!"

Andy's laughter made me almost giddy. "I love you, too, Cuckoo Kid." I held him tight and never wanted to let him go.

The hug lasted two seconds till he pulled away and bounced off the bed, calling over his shoulder, "I built a hideout in the living room, Daddy. Gotta go back down."

* * *

At 10:00 that Friday night it was eighty degrees and humid—the dog days of August. Lydia and I cruised slowly down South Division with the windows open.

As we rolled past the pawnshop, Lydia craned her neck. "The light's on in the shop. I thought Van closed at 8:00. Wait!

Slow down. There's a guy facing the counter. Van's *behind* the counter. Stop a minute."

There weren't any cars behind me, so I stopped, watching my mirror for traffic. "Tell me what's happening."

"Van's looking our way. Now the guy at the counter is looking too. It looks like Benny."

I eased the car forward, looking for a parking spot. "Let's find out what's up."

I continued half a block and, seeing no empty spaces, made a U-turn, then watched as Benny got in a green Chevy sedan and squealed away from the curb. He stared straight ahead as he drove past us. I made another U-turn and pulled into the spot he'd vacated.

By the time we got to the front door of the pawn shop, Van stood in the open doorway.

"Can't resist checking up on me, huh?" he said, his eyes and face their usual mask.

"Just driving by and noticed the light on," I said. "Was that Benny with you?"

"Actually, I'm glad you two came along when you did."

"How so?" I asked.

"Benny was pushing me hard about Rochelle. Said if I didn't tell him where she was, I'd regret it. Everybody seems to think I know where she is." He produced his pipe from one jacket pocket, tobacco from another. He went through his pipe lighting ritual. An aromatic blend.

"I had my hand on the shotgun I keep under the counter," he continued. "I got the feeling Benny was about to pull a weapon on me. He ducked out when he saw you two."

"It sounds like Benny doesn't know where Rochelle is either then," said Lydia. "We wondered if he might be responsible for her disappearance, even though her letter made it sound like her disappearance was voluntary."

"Was tonight the first time you met Benny?" I asked.

Van puffed away for a moment. "I ran into him once before when I took Rochelle out for dinner. Benny showed up and wanted to join us. Rochelle was having none of it, so I sent him on his way."

"You want us to hang around with you and make sure Benny doesn't come back?" I asked.

"Got a Bible with you so you can beat Benny up with it if he tries anything?" Van's eyes carried a hint of laughter.

"As a matter of fact, I do," I said. "I've never had to use it for that before, but you never know. I've heard more than one sermon, though, in which I felt I'd been beat up with the Bible."

"No doubt," Van said, then turned to Lydia. "What about you, Lydia? You packing?"

"Let's just say I believe in being prepared," she said, raising her chin a notch.

Van shook his head. "You guys hit the road. I doubt that Benny will come back, but I think I can handle him if he does."

Lydia waved to Van as we pulled away from the curb. "I'm definitely warming up to the guy," she said.

"I'm still suspicious he knows where Rochelle is though."

"He sounded like he doesn't know, but I suppose it could be an act."

"I think Van is beginning to trust us," I said, "but maybe not enough to let us know where Rochelle is. If he knows. He might have mailed Rochelle's letter himself. I wish we could tail him if he heads north on Alpine Avenue again. Of course, if he spotted us we'd probably lose what little trust we've gained."

At the Getaway, a short time later, we were surprised to see Manetta and Lois, moving pretty well in the cages, looking great in their bikinis. *What is the deal with Christian Reformed young women these days?* I wondered, feeling really old. They had to be the exception, though. The dandy duo spotted us and waved. Ned was behind the bar, and Sadie and Sylvia sat at separate tables with groups of guys.

I noticed Nathan's friend sitting at the table with Pookie. I'd talked to him earlier that evening, and he'd readily agreed to check Pookie out. At least Pookie was letting him sit with him. Maybe we'd learn something helpful.

Ned raised two beer glasses in the air. Lydia and I nodded. He filled them and set them in front of us. "Any news?"

I shook my head. "Did you let the other young woman go?"

"Yeah, her dancing sucked, and she wasn't that good with customers. Manetta and Lois showed up, so I'm giving them a try. If Rochelle ever comes out of hiding or whatever she's doing, she may have to find another job. Unless her attitude is radically improved."

That doesn't jive, I thought, *with Ned's saying Rochelle was the best.* "What was wrong with her attitude?" I asked.

"Oh, it's just that she was, uh, well ... Oh, better fill that order." Ned moved to the waitress station.

Lydia and I exchanged looks.

Manetta and Lois left their cages, cruised for tips and then ducked out the door to the dressing room. Sadie and Sylvia soon entered the cages for their set. When Manetta and Lois emerged from the back, they made straight for the bar and greeted us.

"We're still worried about Rochelle," said Manetta, with a frown, but we really dig the dancing and—"

"Yah," said Lois, "and hanging with the customers is a hoot. They really—"

"—dig us. Well, some of them, you know—"

"Yah, a few are a big pain in the butsky, but most are okay."

"Think you can handle school and your jobs here when the semester starts?" I asked, knowing I was sounding like a parent. It wasn't like me. Maybe all the stress in my life was getting to me more than I realized. If the college got word Manetta was working here, she'd be out faster than you could say "John Calvin." Same was probably true for Lois and nurses training.

Manetta waved a hand dismissively. "Maybe school will have to wait. We'll see how it goes."

"Yah, we're having way too much fun. We're—"

"—getting older, you know. Gotta—"

"Yah. Gotta sow some oats yet while we're young."

"The clock is running."

"Tick tock," they said in unison.

"Speaking of the clock," said Ned, tapping his watch.

The girls headed off to mingle with customers.

"You were telling us about Rochelle's attitude." I said, turning my attention to Ned.

"Oh, no big deal. All the girls I get in here have attitude problems."

What was Ned hiding? If one of his female employees wouldn't put out for him, did she have "attitude problems?"

* * *

Saturday: Week three, day one. Georgina couldn't have much time left.

At noon I was running at the Y with my friend Blaine Hanson, the man I'd replaced at the Street Ministry. We'd vowed to work out regularly together but, in reality, only managed to do it semi-occasionally. Afterwards we showered and then went out for burgers and fries, undoing whatever we'd gained by our workout.

Blaine was forty-five, medium height and build, balding, with a full dark beard. He might have passed for ordinary were it not for his intense green eyes. If Blaine wanted to convince you of something, he'd look at you with those penetrating eyes and you were halfway there. If you had reservations, his ready wit soon had you laughing at your foolish resistance. Finally, if you weren't persuaded, he left you feeling respected. No wonder he could talk people into most anything. I considered him a mentor as well as a friend.

I'd been battling in the back of my mind for days whether to talk to Blaine about Jackie's pregnancy, her considering an abortion and about how I was handling the whole thing. With great misgivings, I told him all about it.

Blaine said, "Why didn't you tell me sooner?"

"This is the first chance I've had."

His eyes sparkled. "What, the phone company cut off your service at work and at home?"

I winced. "I was embarrassed about feeling so out of control and confused."

"Sounds like the best time to talk to a friend. You've got to stop acting like the Lone Ranger when things bother you."

"You're right. It really bugs me that I stormed out of the house when Jackie first told me she was thinking of an abortion. Seems kind of juvenile now."

"Heaven forbid that Reverend Vander Laan would ever act like a juvenile!"

"Screw you," I said. "You think I could still be working on one of my basic hang-ups here?"

"I'd say at least three hang-ups: taking yourself too seriously, the Lone Ranger thing and your Messiah complex. Good thing God has a special place in his heart for slow learners. You Calvinists keep Him pretty busy." Then he sobered. "Just hang in there with Jackie on this. You'll sort it out."

I wished I could be so sure. I mentally set that aside and told him about the trouble at the Getaway. Some of it he'd caught on the news.

"I got to know Ned pretty well when I used to stop in there," he said. "Did you know he has a record?"

"Huh. He didn't mention it and Sid didn't tell me."

"Don't think Johnson tells you everything. Just what he wants you to know to get more from you. The Chief says Johnson's the best detective he's got, but he doesn't always do things by the book. Is he still partnered with Kincaid?"

I nodded, appreciating the inside information that came from Blaine's friendship with the Chief.

"So what was Ned busted for?" I asked.

"He did time for assaulting his wife about ten years ago. She pressed charges and divorced him."

That made Rochelle's story about Ned's assaulting her more believable.

After Blaine left for work, I finished my coffee while reflecting on my reluctance to talk about my problems. I didn't have to wonder where that reluctance came from. The occasional dream still kept that early memory vivid. My real mom sat on my bed. I was too terrified to do anything but lay there with my eyes closed and pretend to be asleep. I could still hear her quiet crying as she said, "I'm sorry I can't take care of you. You'll have to take care of yourself and your little sister for me. I'm so sorry, my baby."

The next day, when dad returned from a church meeting, he found mom lying on the bed, empty bottle of pills on the bedside table.

I'd learned early that I couldn't depend on someone else to take care of me. Leaning on Blaine or Jackie or Lydia didn't come naturally.

After leaving the restaurant I went home and picked up Jackie and Andy. We spent the rest of the afternoon playing and swimming in the pool at Franklin Park, several blocks from our house, before returning home for supper. Jackie made her delicious garlic chicken pasta.

At quarter to eight that evening, I left to pick up Lydia for night ministry. On the way, I stopped at a drugstore near my house to grab some breath mints to compensate for the garlic chicken. I returned to my car and was reaching to put the key in the ignition when I was startled by the passenger door opening. A young man slid in.

"Benny!" I said. "What's up?" I observed his closely bitten fingernails and dark circles under his eyes, as if he hadn't slept for a while. He'd looked better a few days ago at Elliot's.

"You've got to tell me where Rochelle is."

"No idea. I know you demanded the same thing of Van. She wrote a letter to him saying she's okay. Why are you so anxious to find her?"

"I'm worried about her." His jaw moved from side to side.

"If she doesn't want to be found, there's nothing we can do."

"You know where she is." His eyes bored a hole into me.

I looked back steadily. "No, Benny, I don't. You've got to quit worrying about Rochelle and get on with your life."

"If you're messing with me ..." He didn't finish the threat. He got out of the car, slammed the door and stalked off.

» CHAPTER 19

As I drove to Lydia's after my encounter with Benny, I was aware of how unsettled the incident had left me. Once again, Lydia drove her car. She pulled away from the curb and I told her what had happened.

"That young man sounds dangerous," she said. "It would make sense for Rochelle to be hiding from him. Did Nathan's friend learn anything from Pookie?"

I reported what I'd been told earlier in the day by Nathan's friend. "Pookie saw some pretty bad stuff in Nam," I said. "Still has nightmares. He also said he never met anyone who could sniff his way around at night in the jungle like Owen, that Owen killed over two dozen North Vietnamese by sneaking up and throttling them or cutting their throats. Owen's nickname over there was Ghost. Once Owen slipped up though, and Benny saved his butt. Owen is completely loyal to Benny."

"They sound like the deadly Three Musketeers," said Lydia.

"Except that Pookie says he doesn't like to hang out with Benny anymore. He didn't say why. Apparently Pookie is really freaked out about Rochelle disappearing. He's hanging around the bar in hopes of learning something about where she is. Pookie says Rochelle talks about her problems with him, that she needs him. Nathan's friend thinks Pookie has a huge crush on Rochelle."

"Does Pookie have a job?" asked Lydia.

"Pookie didn't want to talk about that. Said it was a dirty job, he hated it and didn't want to even think about it when he's not at work."

"Garbage collector, maybe?"

"He said something about not seeing any daylight in his job, so maybe he works in a room or building with no windows."

"Anything else?"

"Owen came in and joined them after they'd talked awhile. He was civil but real closed-mouthed. Nathan's friend said he might have misread Owen, but he thinks Owen was furious at Pookie for talking to him."

"Interesting, but I don't know how it helps us," said Lydia.

"I agree. What say we drop in unannounced to see Elliot? Maybe we're going in circles, but I don't know what else to do."

A short time later we were standing at Elliot's front door. He was dressed in slacks and a sport shirt, looking better than he had for a while. "Do you have news? Oh, come on in." He ushered us into the living room.

"I don't have news about Rochelle," I said. "You haven't heard anything more either?"

He shook his head, then pointed to the couch as he sat down in an easy chair.

I eased back on the couch and propped my ankle on my knee. "Is Benjamin here tonight?"

"No. Why?"

I told him about my encounter with Benjamin at the drugstore.

Elliot shook his head and rubbed his hands together. "I'm not so worried about Rochelle since I saw the letter from her. But Benjamin's another story. I'm beginning to think it wasn't such a good idea for me to offer to tutor him."

"Why do you say that?" asked Lydia.

Elliot looked at her. "I wonder if Benjamin has just connected with me as a way to try to get closer to Rochelle. I'm not even sure he'll start school next month. He seems distracted lately, and it's getting worse. At first I thought it was nice that he was so supportive of me and worried about Rochelle, too. I felt less alone. But lately he seems overly-concerned about my daughter."

"How do you mean?" I asked.

"He starts talking about her when I'm quizzing him on Greek vocabulary and grammar. The other day I found him looking through photo albums with pictures of Rochelle. He'd gotten the albums from the shelf in the closet over there. How he found them I don't know. He must have been snooping. He demanded I tell him where she is."

"Do you think he'd do anything to hurt Rochelle?" I asked.

Elliot hesitated, then said, "No, I don't think he'd hurt her. He really cares about her."

I wasn't so sure.

As we were saying good-bye, I suddenly thought of something. "Elliot, where did you say Van grew up?"

"On a farm off 7-Mile Road, west of Alpine. I don't remember exactly where. I went up there a couple of times when we were in college. Like I told you, Van sold it after his parents died."

"Oh that's right. You did tell me."

Lydia tossed me a questioning look.

I heard thunder rumbling in the distance as we climbed into Lydia's car. Maybe we'd get some relief from the heat and humidity.

"You were thinking maybe Van lied about selling the farm and has Rochelle stashed there." said Lydia.

"You know," I said, an eyebrow raised, "it's a little scary when you read my mind like that." After a moment, I added, "Both times we tailed Van, we lost him heading north on Alpine. Let's check a phonebook at Drop-in and see if there's a Van Oostenberg listed in that area.

Ten minutes later we darted inside the Ministry, dodging raindrops. I went into Drop-in while Lydia searched the telephone directory at the front desk.

A few minutes later, Lydia poked her head in and motioned to me. At the front desk she took my elbow and ushered me out the front door. We had to make way for a few kids who were running into the building to get out of the rain.

Back in her car, Lydia said, "There's a Van Oostenberg on Jenkins. I think that's off 7-Mile. My sister lives out that way. It's starting to get dark, so let's hustle."

As Lydia drove up Alpine, the windshield wipers beat out a steady cadence. We found Jenkins without difficulty in the growing dusk and drove north checking addresses on mailboxes.

"Bingo," I said as I read the name we were looking for on the fifth mailbox.

The farmhouse was set back off the road, a few large old oak trees in the front yard. The lights were on in the house. I pulled into the driveway. I felt a surge of excitement when I saw Van's Cadillac parked near the back door. As I pulled up next to the Caddie, the back door of the house opened.

Van stepped out. He stood under the overhanging roof, with his arms crossed. He closed his eyes briefly as we stepped out of the car into the rain.

I screwed up my face and shrugged. "I thought maybe we could have coffee with you and Rochelle."

Van turned around and walked back into the house.

I looked at Lydia, shrugged again. We followed him inside and into the kitchen.

"We've got company, Rochelle," Van called.

Rochelle emerged from another room looking a little bug-eyed. "What are you two doing here?" She scowled at Van. "Uncle Van, I thought you said you didn't tell anyone."

"I did not tell them. I did not invite them. I'm as surprised as you are. I have no idea how they found us." He motioned us to sit in the chairs around the kitchen table.

Rochelle wore jeans and a purple short-sleeved top. She still wore a look of irritation, but otherwise seemed fine.

When we were all seated, I explained how we figured out where they were.

"But why couldn't you leave it alone?" asked Rochelle, looking at me. "You read my letter."

"I can answer that, Rochelle," said Lydia, smiling. "Rob's really nosey. It's kind of a problem."

I shook my head at Lydia, who wore her grandmotherly smile, then turned to Rochelle. "I was suspicious that Van had mailed the letter from you to himself, and I wanted to make certain you were okay."

Rochelle's eyes softened. "Well, you can see for yourself." She leaned back in the chair and stretched, arms over her head, back arched, probably not even aware of the seductiveness of her pose. Then, again, maybe she was.

"Who are you so afraid of?" I asked. "Is it Benjamin?"

Rochelle dropped her arms abruptly. "If you knew him, you wouldn't ask."

"I do know him. At least I've met him a couple of times." I explained, then told Rochelle what her father and Ned, as well as Manetta and Lois had said about Benjamin.

"You met Manetta and Lois?" Rochelle leaned forward. "You really have been a busybody. It's kind of sweet, in a way."

The letter from Rochelle had told me and anyone else who was worried about her to butt out. Now she was telling me it was sweet of Lydia and me to check up on her. I wondered if she typically sent out such mixed messages.

"Manetta and Lois are dancing at the bar now," I said.

She pulled back in her chair. "At the Getaway?"

I nodded.

That dark look flitted across her face. I was getting better at recognizing it, even if I wasn't sure what it meant.

"Well, Ned had to do something when you disappeared." Why was I defending Ned and the dynamic duo.

Rochelle looked away. "I suppose."

"Let's get back to Benny," I said, "He demanded your dad and I tell him where you were. And, as I'm sure Van told you, he also demanded that *Van* tell him where you were hiding."

Rochelle shot Van a hard look and clenched her fists on the table. "Why didn't you tell me, Uncle Van?"

Van shrugged. "Didn't want to worry you, pumpkin."

Was the fleeting look in her eyes one of fear this time?

Rochelle passed a hand over her face. "The time he caught me on the street, he said that if he couldn't have me, no one else could either."

"Is Benjamin the only one you're afraid of?" I asked.

"Ned was being a jerk again, getting real possessive. You saw what he did to me when I wouldn't go home with him." She paused, looking at me. Trying to read my reaction to the memory? "I told Ned," she went on, "I just wanted an employer/ employee relationship, but he wouldn't let it go. I don't know why men get so possessive with me."

She wore the vulnerable little girl look I'd seen before. Was it real? I glanced at Van, but his expression was inscrutable, as usual. I returned my attention to Rochelle. "You have to call Detective Johnson. Benny could be involved in the disappearance of Georgina and in Hector's death. Maybe it's his way of taking care of you, misguided as that would be."

"But I thought Hector committed suicide," she said.

"Maybe. Or maybe not."

"Oh my gosh. Okay, I'll call him."

"You should also call your dad."

"I don't trust him not to tell Benny. They're so palsy-walsy. I found that out last time you made me call my father."

"Then write your dad a note, and I'll bring it to him."

Rochelle huffed. "Did anybody ever tell you that you can be really demanding?"

"I've told him," offered Lydia, flashing her grandma smile again.

Rochelle frowned and abruptly got up from her chair. "Excuse me while I carry out Rob's orders." She marched into the other room where I heard her dialing the phone and asking for Detective Johnson.

"It's probably a good thing, you guys coming here," said Van. "Rochelle made me promise to tell no one where she was. But if you two figured it out, it's just a matter of time before Benny or Ned does too."

"Or Elliot, for that matter," I added. "He sounded like he believed your tale that you had sold the farm, but he might have second thoughts about it."

"Where's Rochelle's car, by the way?" asked Lydia.

"Hid it in the barn," answered Van.

When Rochelle finally came back into the kitchen, she handed me a folded piece of paper. "Give this to my father, but promise you won't tell him where I am. I don't want him meddling in my life. He's caused me enough grief. He's always tried to control me through my friends and even through my bosses at other jobs I've had. Nothing I do is ever good enough for him."

On our way back into town, Lydia said, "Rochelle really unloaded about her dad. Just normal rebellion against parental authority, or do you think there's more to it?"

"No idea. I take everything Rochelle says with a grain of salt."

"To change the subject, it seems like our primary suspects in Hector's death and Georgina's disappearance are Benny and Ned. Of course, that's assuming the bouncer's death was a murder."

"Let's not rule out Van just yet, though. And what about Elliot?"

"Seems like he's one of the men who want to protect and control Rochelle. But you'd expect some of that from a father."

I blew out a puff of air in frustration. "I don't think we're getting any closer to finding Georgina. She doesn't have much time left."

"If you had to pick one suspect now, from your gut, who would it be?" asked Lydia.

"I'm torn between Benny and Ned. I guess I'd pick Benny, but maybe that's just because of the confrontation I had with him earlier tonight. He could be just having a hard time adjusting after returning from Nam, but I've got a bad feeling about him."

Back in the city, we headed to Elliot's. It was a little after 11:00, but lights were still on. This time Elliot greeted us dressed in a bathrobe and slippers.

He turned the porch light on. "More news?" he asked. "Come on in." He opened the screen door.

"We won't stay," I said, remaining on the porch. "We saw Rochelle." I handed him her note.

Elliott read quickly, then looked back at me frowning. "She says she's hiding from Benjamin."

"Is Benny here now?"

"No. He wouldn't be here this late. Where is Rochelle?"

"I promised her I wouldn't tell you. It's the only way she would agree to write you the note."

I resisted his efforts to make me tell him, despite his increasing frustration about it.

Back downtown, we spent an hour at Partners, then hit one of the bars in the River City and stayed till last call.

I got to bed shortly after three. I tossed and turned, in and out of sleep, in and out of dreams that didn't make sense. I was in a bar. "Last Call" was being announced endlessly and it terrified me.

CHAPTER 20

Day two of week three for Georgina.

Sunday morning just after 9:00 Jackie roused me from a fitful sleep. I'd gone to bed relieved that Rochelle was okay but still worried about Georgina. I wondered if the cops had given up hope. I needed more sleep.

"Rob," said Jackie again, shaking my shoulder this time. "It's Van. He says it's urgent."

Now I was wide awake. I took the call in the study.

"Rochelle's gone," said Van.

"You mean she's disappeared again," I asked, "but this time you don't know where she is?"

"Right. After you and Lydia left last night, we talked about finding another place for her to stay. The detectives came out and questioned us both. Then I came back to town. When I called her about an hour ago, there was no answer. I waited a bit, then tried a couple more times. So I drove out here and found the back door forced open. Rochelle was gone."

"Okay," I said skeptically.

"I know, I know," Van said. "Why should you believe me since I deceived you before? But it's true, I swear."

"What about her car?"

"It's not here."

"Any idea what might have happened?" I asked.

"I don't know. I worry it was Benny or Ned who took her."

"Any possibility Rochelle would just force the lock herself to make it look like she'd been abducted and then drive away?"

"I don't think so, though she can be unpredictable, to say the least. Seems like whoever took her had an accomplice since the car's gone too."

"Have you reported this to Detective Johnson?"

Silence.

I sighed. "I'll call him. If you're going to stay at the farm, give me your number there so Johnson can reach you."

I disconnected and called the cop shop. Johnson and Kincaid were off for the day. I declined to speak to another detective. With some misgivings, I called Johnson's home number. He'd once told me to call him anytime, day or night, if I had something important on the case. But that was the previous summer.

"I hope it's okay I called you at home," I said. "Rochelle's disappeared again."

"You mean, from Van's farm? Since last night?"

"Yes. Van just called me from the farm. He says the back door was forced open and Rochelle's car is gone too."

"And where did *you* go after you left the farm last night?"

I reported on our ministry stops the rest of the evening. I told him when I'd gotten home. "I know Jackie woke up when I came to bed. You want to talk to her?"

"I'll follow up later with Jackie if I need to."

"Have you found anything else on Hector's death that you can tell me?"

"Got a witness who says she saw a man leaving Hector's place the night he died, but her description of the guy was very general."

When Johnson had first told me that Hector was dead, I'd asked if any neighbors heard a shot. He hadn't answered. "What if the killer used a silencer on the gun," I said, "and then removed it and placed the gun in Hector's hand?"

"You might be missing your calling."

"I get that a lot."

Johnson grunted. "Thanks for the call. You got Van's number at the farm?"

I gave it to him, then called Elliot and got no answer. He'd probably gone to church. I was too wired to go back to sleep, so Jackie, Andy and I made the morning service at Alexander Church.

Afterwards we were talking in the parking lot with Howard Minema, a grey-haired elder with a jowly face that made me think of a bulldog. He spoke with a pronounced Dutch accent—w's sounding like v's, th's like d's, r's rolling like waves on Lake Michigan. Howard said, "I was going to call you to see if we could set up a time for *huis bezoek.*" He used the Dutch phrase for the official visits that the elders made to all parishioners' homes.

We agreed on a time. Jackie sounded matter-of-fact, but I knew she disliked the whole idea of *huis bezoek.*

On the way home, I could tell by the way she sat rigidly and stared straight ahead that she was fuming silently. Finally she said, "Do they think they can take your spiritual pulse in a half-hour visit?"

"Well, if they're good at it, they might get some idea," I said. "Depends on the elder."

"It's a game. Everybody puts on their most saintly face, mumbles pious platitudes and can't wait for the elder to hit the road."

"I don't think everybody feels that way, Jacks. Some people are lonely and like the company. Sometimes there's a sick family member or a recent death, and the prayers of the elder can be very comforting."

I watched Andy in my rearview mirror, looking from me to Jackie to me, not missing a thing.

"They're just going to put *me* on the spot about why I don't come to church more often. And you'll be able to weasel out of it because of night ministry and occasionally preaching in other churches on Sunday nights."

I suspected Jackie was right.

From the back seat Andy asked with keen interest, "Can I stay up for huiszook, Mama?"

"Oh, yes," said Jackie, "I wouldn't want you to miss it."

You'll want him there as a distraction, I thought.

"Why are you defending the whole business?" asked Jackie. "You don't like it either."

It was true. I'd put off the elders last year successfully. It was time to get it over with.

I gave a noncommittal shrug.

I dropped Jackie and Andy at home, then swung by Elliot's. I could have called, but, again, I wanted to see his reaction to the news about his daughter. He was walking up the front sidewalk as I parked. He looked better than he had recently, and now I would have to break the bad news to him. He spotted me and walked to my car. I opened the passenger door, and he hopped in.

"Thanks for bringing me the note from Rochelle," he said. "I slept better last night. It would be nice to see her, but I guess I can live with her secretiveness as long as I know she's okay. Maybe now she'll have sense enough to quit that dancing job. I'm sorry I got so upset with you last night."

"That's okay, but I'm afraid I've got bad news, Elliot."

He stiffened.

I repeated what Van had told me.

"Rochelle was staying at Van's farm, wasn't she?" said Elliot. "I should have known Van was lying about selling the farm." He shook his head. "To think of my daughter staying out there with that reprobate—"

"I don't think Van was staying there with her," I interrupted. "I think he was just providing her with a safe haven."

I didn't know that. Why was I sticking my neck out to defend Van now?

Elliot pounded the dash. "That girl is more trouble! Maybe Van just found another place for her to stay since you two figured out where she was."

"Maybe. Or maybe she force the lock on the door herself and drove away."

He was silent as he wiped a hand across his face. A distraught father or a good actor?

"Or maybe Benny took her," I said.

Elliot shook his head, then looked at me uncertainly. "He called me before I left for church. Wouldn't he have said something? He's decided he's not ready to start school. I think he's right."

"Did you notify the police."

Elliot looked into the distance, then shook his head.

"The police are looking for him," I said with a note of exasperation. "They need to question him. You have to report your contact with him." I wondered if he'd freak out again at my pushing him about Benny.

Elliot looked at me and sighed. "I'll call the police."

"Good. Why isn't Benny ready to start school?"

"He can't seem to focus. He's not the same boy as he was before Vietnam."

"You knew him when he was growing up?"

"Not well. I preached at the Grant Church for a summer and got to know the De Groot family a little."

Elliot sat up straighter, squared his shoulders. Pulling himself together? "Benjamin really cares about Rochelle. He just needs a little more time to recover from his military experience."

"Can you be more specific about what he went through in Nam?"

"I'm sorry. I can't. I counseled him some and I consider that information confidential. I'm sure you understand."

"I've been in your shoes on the confidentiality thing," I said. "But it may be your daughter's safety we're talking about here."

Elliot looked into the distance again, then turned back to me. "I won't violate Benny's confidence. I still don't think he'd hurt Rochelle."

On my way back home, I had a new thought. I wondered if Benny was like a son to Elliot, the son he'd never had. Elliot might have a blind spot with Benny.

Back home I called Johnson again, but got no answer. I called the police station and left a message for him about my conversation with Elliot.

* * *

Blaine and Shelia came for supper that evening with their two children. After we ate, the kids played Bloody Mary in the basement. The adults sat in the living room and talked about the vacations we'd taken earlier in the summer. I wondered if Jackie would bring up the pregnancy issue since she'd already talked about it with Sheila and I'd told her that I'd talked with Blaine. She may have been wondering the same of me. The phone interrupted our conversation about Blaine and Shelia's trip to Maine.

The call was from the director of the runaway shelter. "We had some trouble here today with the Street Ministry's latest referral. I believe Nathan brought her in.

"Aretha Vander Stern." Manetta's sister. "I met her just before Nathan brought her to your place."

"Her father and his pastor showed up here this afternoon and demanded we release her to them. Aretha heard us talking and climbed out her bedroom window, so she's on the run again. I think the pastor accompanied you when you came with a referral a couple of weeks ago."

The location of the runaway shelter was unknown to most of the community, and we tried to keep it that way. Emotions surfaced in me in rapid-fire order: embarrassment, shame, anger, guilt. "I'm really sorry for taking the pastor there. He was out with me on night ministry to get a better idea of my work."

"I don't blame you for what happened, Rob. I just thought you should know about it."

When I hung up the phone Jackie said, "Let me guess: The Reverend John Vanden Berg strikes again."

Blaine and Sheila gathered their kids soon after and we said our good-byes. After our visitors left, I called Lydia and brought her up to date. "I'm just too antsy to sit still here," I said. Want to go with me to check with Manetta and Lois, if we can, and with Van. Doubt if it will do any good, but—"

"Georgina can't have much time left," Lydia interrupted, "and I'm really worried about Rochelle. My only plan tonight was to meet Sam for coffee at Sandy's Grill at 10:30. I can call and cancel."

"Hold off with calling her. We may just be checking out two dead-ends."

A short time later, Manetta and Lois met us at Sandy's. They greeted us with a worried, "Hey, guys." They reported that Detective Johnson had talked to them earlier in the evening.

"He said you found Rochelle," said Manetta, "and she disappeared again." "Anything new?"

"Afraid not," I said. "If Benny took her, any idea where he'd go with her?"

The girls shook their heads. "Nada."

After twenty more fruitless minutes of speculation, we said good-bye to Manetta and Lois. I called Van from a phone in the hotel lobby to see if we could stop over. He said he wouldn't mind the company. That was new.

As we stepped out of the lobby to the street, we ran into Wild Bill who begged a ride to his apartment. He thanked us for helping with his dad. We sat in front of his apartment for several minutes trying to reassure him about Georgina and promising that we would not give up on finding her.

Then we drove to the pawnshop, parked on the street and cut through between the shop and the dry cleaners. Suddenly, the sound of a car starting in the alley caught our attention. I heard it peel rubber as I raced to the alley. I caught a glimpse of it, not enough to tell the make or color. Van's Caddy was parked in its usual spot.

"Look!" said Lydia, pointing.

The rear door that led into the pawn shop and the stairs to Van's apartment was wide open.

"We've got to check on Van," I whispered.

Lydia's purse clicked as I moved toward the door. I hesitated. Lydia put a hand on my arm, gently pushing me to the side, as she pointed her gun at the doorway. She poked her head inside and quickly withdrew it. She poked her head in again and looked up the stairs.

More tactics from her favorite cop shows, I thought.

We both stepped inside. The door that led into the shop was closed. The door at the top of the stairs leading into the apartment was open, light spilling out. No one was in sight.

"Van," I yelled. "Are you okay?"

In answer, a muffled groan.

» CHAPTER 21

I pushed past Lydia and charged up the stairs. I hesitated at the top and Lydia bumped into me hard enough so that we both stumbled into the kitchen.

Van lay on the floor.

Lydia said, "I'll check the rest of the apartment. You see to Van." She closed the door quietly, then slipped past me and into the living room.

I moved toward Van, past kitchen chairs that were tipped over and the table that had been shoved against the counter. Blood oozed from a cut on Van's lip and one on his forehead. Blood stained the front of his torn shirt. The sight of a tooth lying next to his head, gleaming in the overhead light, momentarily mesmerized me.

I knelt beside Van and felt for a pulse. I found one. I could see his chest moving, so I knew he was breathing. I stood up and reached for the phone on the kitchen wall to call for help.

The jangle of the phone startled me so badly that I jumped backwards, almost falling over a chair lying on the floor. I recovered and picked up the phone in the middle of the second ring.

Before I could ask the caller to get off the line, I heard an urgent whisper. "Just listen, Uncle Van. Don't say anything." Then, what sounded like a door closing on the other end of the line. A man's voice said something, too far from the phone for me to hear. Then a female voice, speaking loudly: "You've got to let me go. You'll just get into serious trouble. It's not worth it." It had to be Rochelle.

The man's voice again, still too faint to make out.

The female voice, "You don't do this to someone you love."

A man's voice again, louder this time: "What the hell are you doing?"

The female voice, screaming something in Dutch. The explosion of the phone being smashed onto the cradle made my head hurt, and then I was listening to the dial tone.

I hung up, grabbed a pen and a piece of scratch paper near the phone and wrote the Dutch words I thought I'd heard. I put the piece of paper in my shirt pocket and picked up the phone again to call the cops as Lydia returned to the kitchen.

Lydia gave me a questioning look, but I put a finger up for her to wait. I called the operator and she connected me to the police. I was told someone would be out as soon as possible and that they'd call for an ambulance. I turned around to see Lydia looking at Van, holding her gun at her side, a look of stunned disbelief on her face.

My own thoughts moved through thick sludge.

A sudden pounding on the door interrupted the silence. A shout: "Police. Open up."

That was fast. I hadn't even heard them coming up the stairs. In a fog, I opened the door. Two officers entered with guns drawn as I stood to the side. They looked past me and the already charged air exploded with even greater urgency.

"Drop the gun, lady. Now!" One of the officers had his gun aimed at Lydia, the other officer had his aimed at me.

"Oh, but I just ..." Lydia's gun clattered to the floor.

"Both of you, turn around and put your hands behind your backs."

Two clicks and we were handcuffed.

"I have a permit," offered Lydia weakly.

It took a minute for the officer to locate the permit in Lydia's purse as the other checked Van. Then there was the sound of feet climbing the stairs and the ambulance driver and his assistant entered. One of the cops escorted Lydia and me down the steps. I heard the other cop in the apartment saying to the ambulance guys, "Yeah, Vander Laan from that ministry to the downtown punks. He's the character who meddled in those murders last summer."

Lydia and I were ushered to a cruiser parked in the alley and made to sit in the back seat where we were questioned. We watched as the emergency guys carried Van on a stretcher, put him in the ambulance and took off. I urged the officer who was questioning us to contact Johnson. I told him Van's assault was probably connected to a case the detective was working on. The cop flashed me a look that said he didn't appreciate my helpfulness, but he radioed his report and asked that Johnson be informed.

A short time later Johnson and Kincaid arrived. I was surprised since they were both supposed to be off duty that day. After the cop who sat in the cruiser with Lydia and me made his report to the detectives, Johnson and Kincaid went up to Van's apartment. A few minutes later, the detectives returned to the driver's door of the cruiser. Johnson glanced at us as we sat awkwardly with our hands cuffed behind our backs, then said to the uniformed officer, "Let 'em go."

The officer shrugged. "Whatever you say, Detective. I was going to bring them in and sort it out at the station."

"Not necessary," said Johnson. When we were released, he glared at us. "You jokers took a risk charging into Van's apartment before the uniforms came. You're both so damn headstrong. Sorry, Lydia."

As we got out of the cruiser, Lydia snapped, "When do I get my gun back, Detectives?" She had obviously regained her composure.

Kincaid answered. "As soon as we eliminate it as a weapon used in the assault on Mister Van Oostenberg. You're cognizant of the protocol, Lydia."

I knew Kincaid's literate vocabulary was his natural way of expressing himself. He must have known how he was viewed by many of his fellow officers because of this, but he apparently made no effort to change.

That's when I remembered the phone call. I removed the piece of paper from my pocket. "There was a phone call while we were in the apartment, Sid. It sounded like Rochelle." I reported what she'd said. "I didn't recognize all the Dutch words," I went on, "so some of this is just spelled the way it sounded to me." I read aloud what I'd written: "*I schur generaal noord van de groote stormsversneling.* I'd say it's all Greek to me, but my Greek is fresher than my Dutch. All I can make out— maybe—are the words in the middle. Something like, 'general north of the great.' Sorry."

Johnson looked at the note, rolled his eyes and handed it to Kincaid, who studied it, then returned it to me.

"Let me see it," said Lydia.

"Don't tell me a Polish Catholic like you knows Dutch, too?" I said.

"Just a little bit." She'd undoubtedly learned some from her deceased husband. Lydia had no better luck than I did on the translation.

"I'd better keep that," said Johnson.

I removed a little notebook from my jeans pocket. "Let me make a copy first." Afterwards I handed the original back to Johnson.

When the detectives let us go, we returned to Sandy's Grill to wind down over a cup of coffee. I studied the note I'd made of the phone call, shaking my head. "The caller said, 'Uncle Van,' so it must have been Rochelle, and it sounded like her. It makes sense she'd call Van. But what are the chances she'd call while we were in the apartment? And that someone other than Van who also knows some Dutch would answer the phone?"

"That's freaky alright," said Lydia. "Let's suppose that Rochelle had a brief moment to make a call behind her abductor's back. Maybe she figured whoever's holding her doesn't know Dutch and she could make something up about what she yelled."

"Let's run with that theory." I put down my coffee cup. "Obviously Van couldn't be holding her. I'm pretty sure Elliot knows Dutch, so it's not likely that he's holding his daughter. I doubt that Ned knows Dutch, but we'd have to check that out. Benny went to the Christian Reformed Church in Grant, but most kids don't learn the language, even if they hear it spoken once in a while by adults. The fact that Rochelle said, 'You don't do this to someone you love,' fits with Benny's obsessive pursuing of Rochelle, so maybe he's her abductor."

Lydia and I were debating the best way to get help figuring out the Dutch words on my note when Lydia checked her watch. "It's almost 10:20," she said, getting up. "I'd better try to call Sam from the lobby phone and see if I can catch her before she leaves."

"Too late," I said pointing to Sam as she entered the restaurant from the lobby and spotted us.

She walked to our table and slid in next to me. "Didn't know you were coming, Rob. Any progress on the Getaway mystery?"

We told her about the latest developments.

Sam's eyes sparkled with excitement as she examined the note. "It's gibberish to me. But what kind of a Dutchman are *you*, Rob? You should know what this means. Do you really think it was Rochelle? How can we figure the note out? Know anybody who's good at Dutch that would help us at this time of night?"

"We could go to my place," said Lydia. "I've got a Dutch dictionary. I'm sure you have one, too, Rob, but my place is closer."

I considered telling Sam that Lydia and I needed to do this alone, but then I remembered how much she'd done to help us solve the murders the previous summer. And she knew Rochelle. I put money on the table for our coffee and we left the restaurant. Sam followed us in her car.

A short time later, Lydia led us into a room next to her bedroom that I'd never been in before. She turned on the light, and I checked the books on the shelves. This had been her husband's den and reflected his theological and philosophical interests. Looked like my list of required reading at seminary.

"You read all this stuff, Lydia?" I asked.

"Quite a lot of it. Had to keep up with my husband. Sometimes I sit in here at night and imagine I'm having a theological bull session with him like we used to do."

"Where's the dictionary?" I asked.

She pointed. I pulled it from the shelf, sat at the desk, grabbed a pen and a scratch pad next to it.

"Let's see." I began writing. "The first word sounded like 'I.' But there's no 'I' in Dutch. Closest sound would be 'ui.' That's onion. I scowled and shook my head. "*Ui schur*. Onion something."

"*Schuur*, with two u's is 'barn,'" said Lydia before I could look up the word.

I shook my head again, irritated that I'd forgotten that one. "Okay, what's next? *Generaal noord.* General North? This is making no sense."

Lydia put a hand on my shoulder. "How about just 'General.' Keep the north with what follows."

"Okay. *Nord van de groote stormsversnelling* North of the great. That much I know." I paged rapidly in the dictionary, ran my finger down a page. "Here it is. Rapids. Great Rapids? Big Rapids? Yes!" I could feel the adrenalin surging. Big Rapids was a city about sixty miles north. "Or, wait. Can *groote* mean grand? I looked it up. "Yes!" I could hardly sit still. Onion barn, general, north of Grand Rapids. "General. General." I pounded the desk with my fist in frustration.

Sam leaned on the desk with both hands. "How about General Grant? The town of Grant? That's just a little ways north."

I jumped up and hugged Sam. "That's it. Onion barn in Grant! I know there are muck farms in that area." Muck was the rich, dark soil in which farmers often grew onions and celery. "That must be where Rochelle is being held. That reminds me that Elliot said Benny's folks had a farm in the Grant area."

Sam said, "I grew up in Newaygo, just north of Grant. In fact, my uncle Clarence has a small muck farm near Grant. Onions and celery. He might be able to help."

When I called the police station, Johnson wasn't there. I called his home number.

I counted eight rings, before a gravelly voice answered.

"Sorry to bother you at home, Sid. But we think we've figured out the Dutch clue."

"What the hell are you talking about? What frigging Dutch clue? Who the hell is this?" The words sounded slurred with more than sleep.

"It's Rob Vander Laan. We think we've figured out what that voice yelled over the phone at Van's apartment. Are you with me, Sid?"

"Rob? Rob Vander Laan? Why the hell are you calling me now. Call me in the morning."

"I don't think this—" I heard the sound of the receiver being fumbled onto the cradle.

I looked at Lydia and Sam. "I think he was drunk."

We've got to find Rochelle," said Sam. "Maybe Georgina's there, too. Let's go to my uncle's. Maybe he can help."

I needed no convincing. I glanced at my watch: 10:50. "One minute." I picked up the phone again and dialed while Lydia went into her bedroom. I quickly summed up for Jackie what we'd surmised and what we were about to do."

She didn't sound happy. "Make sure Lydia takes her gun."

"Don't worry." I didn't want to explain that Lydia's gun had been confiscated.

"You should come home and get my gun." She referred to the 9mm her father had brought back home with him after his time in France and Germany during the war, a gun that was now officially Jackie's.

"We'll be fine, babe," I said as Lydia returned, purse in hand.

We jumped in my car, and I drove like a bat out of purgatory, clutching the steering wheel tightly and keeping an eye out for cops. We raced north on M-37, slowing down in Grant where Sam had us turn east. She directed me to turn north after a few miles. In the moonlight, I saw muck fields on both sides of the road. After a couple of miles we turned into the driveway of a darkened farmhouse. A sign on the front lawn, briefly illuminated by the headlights, heralded the news: "The Wages Of Sin Is Death." Hello, Uncle Clarence.

We parked in the driveway and followed Sam to the back door. An old brown and white shepherd barked perfunctorily, then came up to Sam, wagging his tail as Sam pounded on the door.

While we waited I looked again at my watch. It was 11: 40. In a couple of minutes, a light went on over the door. A curtain was pulled aside. A man opened the door with a look of concern.

"Samantha? What's going on?" He was tall, lean and weathered. He wore a brown robe over his pajamas. His full head of dark hair was disheveled, but his eyes were alert.

Sam gave him a quick hug. "Sorry to wake you like this, Uncle Clarence, but we need help."

The light went on in the kitchen and a short, stocky woman with grey hair appeared, clutching her flowered robe at her neck and her waist. "Father, what's going on? Is that you, Samantha? Well, gracious. Come on in, all of you. Don't stand outside."

When we'd gathered in the kitchen, I explained the gist of our situation.

"So," said Sam, "we hoped you could help us figure out where someone might be holding Rochelle."

Clarence's gaze met his wife's. His look of concern was mirrored on her face. "The old De Groot place, you think, Mother?"

She nodded.

"De Groot!" I exclaimed, looking at Lydia. "I think that's Benny's last name."

"Benny De Groot?" Sam's aunt said. "What's the boy got to do with this?"

We told them our suspicions about Benny.

"Oh dear, Benny was such a nice boy," she said. "A little strange, though. I can't believe he'd do anything like that. But I haven't seen him since he got back from the army."

"Are his parents still living on the farm then?" I asked.

"His dad passed away, let's see, a year and a half ago. Right Father? And she passed last February."

"What's happened to the farm since Benny's parents died?"

Uncle Clarence frowned. "I haven't heard it's for sale or anything." He looked at his wife for confirmation and she shook her head. "Benny was an only child and I suppose he inherited it."

I assume the farm has a barn on it?" I said.

"The De Groot farm is a small one like ours," said Clarence. "They did onion sorting in the barn like I do. Their farm is northeast of here a few miles It's on a small pocket of muck, separated from the rest of the muck land around here."

Clarence gave the directions, and we started for the door.

"But, Samantha, honey, don't you think you should call the police?" asked her aunt.

"Can you call the Grant police and tell them where we went?" said Sam. "We can't wait."

"Have them notify Detective Johnson of the Grand Rapids Police Department," I added.

With that, we were off. Probably barging into trouble.

» CHAPTER 22

idnight. Lydia, Sam and I headed back toward Grant. We turned east through the rich muck land, then north and were soon out of the muck farms. We passed one darkened house. Half a mile further, I slowed as we passed another farm on the right. This one, like the others, was dark, but there was light coming from a window in a building behind the house.

My heart pounded, a mix of excitement and fear. I kept going. "We'll find a good place to park and then walk back," I said. I drove slowly, then turned off on a dirt track into a muck field, hopefully part of the isolated pocket Clarence had mentioned. I shut off the engine.

We ran from the car back toward the farm. Halfway to the driveway I stopped, my hand on Sam's arm, to give Lydia a chance to catch up. We paused and listened. I did not want to be surprised by a vehicle coming down the road or emerging from the drive. I wasn't a hundred percent certain this was even the farm we were looking for, but I thought it fit with Uncle Clarence's directions.

My pulse raced and my chest was tight. I listened to the sounds of crickets, the breeze blowing through bushes and trees along the road, our labored breathing. We resumed jogging to the driveway.

A mailbox stood near the drive, its little door hanging open, an old newspaper shoved inside. I had to look closely in the darkness to make out the name: De Groot. So far, so good.

We walked cautiously up the drive, trying to make as little noise as possible.

We made our way past the farmhouse, past the old windmill, to the weathered white barn. An old outhouse stood to the right. A small patch of light came from one window in the barn. We waited a moment, listening. I looked back at the darkened house. Apparently we'd set off no alarms for anyone who might be in the house. There were no cars in the yard.

I heard the click of Lydia's purse.

Evidently, my ministry partner had more than one gun. She must have picked it up when we were at her house. I shot her a questioning look.

"My sister's," she whispered. "Since we're working on a case again, I thought I'd better have a back-up."

The Boy Scout motto flitted through my mind: Be prepared. I returned my attention to the barn. An outline of light could be seen around the edges of some kind of blackout material on the windows. A piece of the material on the window to the right of the door appeared to be torn off, allowing a bit of light to come through.

I made my way cautiously to the window and peered through the small part of the pane through which light showed. A green Chevy sedan a few years old was parked inside. Crates were stacked in one corner. A short conveyer belt for sorting onions stood near the crates. Next to the conveyer was a large garage door. In the northeast corner of the barn was a door to a separate room. A window on the south side of the barn was bare, the blackout material having come loose and hanging below it. That explained the light I'd seen from the road.

I whispered my findings to Lydia and Sam. Willing myself not to freeze with indecision, I told them I wanted to circle the barn, at least far enough to see if I could look into that separate room. I proceeded along the north side toward that room, Lydia and Sam following closely. We came to another window blocked by bushes, but I could make out a dim light.

I edged as quietly as I could through the bushes and peeked in. At first, I saw nothing through the grimy pane. But after a moment, I saw that a woman was tied spread-eagle to the four corner posts of a bed. It looked like Rochelle, but I wasn't sure. A blanket lay over her. Clothes were draped on a chair.

I ducked back out of the bushes and whispered what I'd seen.

"We've got to get her out of there," hissed Sam.

We quickly returned to the front of the barn, and I made my way to the window with the ripped blackout material to peer inside again. All looked the same. I went back to the door where Lydia and Sam waited impatiently. In a whisper I asked Sam to hide behind some bushes near the outhouse. I handed her my car keys. "If Lydia and I get caught," I said, "you go for help."

I grabbed the door handle and then looked back at Sam as she disappeared behind the bushes.

The door opened with only a slight squeak. Lydia and I stepped through. I left the door open, not wanting to hear that squeak again.

Over a table to the left were three nails with onion shears hanging from them, like the ones I'd used one summer when I worked topping onions with a cousin in the muck fields of Hudsonville, between Holland and Grand Rapids. I grabbed one and we crossed the cement floor toward the corner room. When we reached the door we waited, listened. A latch was unfastened, open padlock hanging from it. I opened the door and stepped inside.

Rochelle lay on the bed looking at us, eyes wide in surprise.

I put a finger to my lips, then stepped quickly to the bed and, with the onion shears, cut the twine that bound Rochelle to the bed. She swept the blanket aside and sat up. She was naked.

I turned away as she reached for her clothes on a chair by the bed, knowing the image of her body would reappear for me at inconvenient times, like during the long prayer at church.

As Lydia squeezed into the small room, I closed the door, but not tightly. "Where's Benny?" I whispered.

"He's in the house," said Rochelle, not bothering to whisper. She didn't sound frightened. Almost matter-of-fact. "He said he was expecting a call from Owen at 12:15. Okay. I'm dressed. How the heck did you find me?"

"Tell you later." Once again I checked my watch: 12:20. Benny could be back any minute.

"Let's go." I said softly, reaching for the door knob.

Suddenly the knob was yanked out of my hand.

I saw Sam standing to the side of the door, Benny right behind her with a gun to her head. Sam looked more sheepish than scared. "Sorry, Rob," she said.

"Drop the gun, lady," ordered Benny.

I heard the familiar click. "It's in my purse," she snapped. "Is that good enough?"

"Back up, Rob," said Benny. When I did so, he shoved Sam into the room. His eyes darted around the space. "All of you, line up by the bed. Toss the onion shears on the floor, Rob." His voice sounded calm, but his eyes continued to move rapidly, perhaps betraying fear.

We did as he demanded.

Rochelle took a step toward Benny. "Benny, please don't—"

"Shut up! Grab the shears. Get over here. Now."

When Rochelle reached his side, he yanked her through the door and slammed it shut. There was a click, and I knew the padlock had been snapped shut. We heard the sound of the garage door rolling up, a car starting and moving. Lydia, Sam and I stood transfixed.

I came out of the trance and tried futilely to open the door. I kicked it once, succeeding only in hurting my foot.

I moved to the window, which wasn't made to open. Six-inch-square panes encased in a metal frame. Even if we broke out some of the panes, we'd still be unable to get out that way. I looked around the room for anything to help us. There was nothing. I looked under the bed. Nothing. Sam and I sat down on the bed.

"At least he let me keep the gun," said Lydia. She went around to the other side of the bed and stretched out. In a few moments, she was snoring softly.

* * *

It was after 1:00 when we heard noises in the barn. Sam had joined Lydia on the bed for a nap, and both sat up. I'd been sitting in a corner of the room, head propped against the wall, dozing. I stood up and banged on the door. "Help. We're locked in here." I doubted it was Benny returning.

"This is the Grant police. Who's in there?"

I answered and we waited. A few minutes later, I heard the sound of the lock being broken. A burly, pleasant looking man in his forties opened the door. For the next several minutes, the Grant cop quizzed us on what had happened. We were all standing in the farmyard later when a car pulled in behind the Grant police car. Johnson stepped out wearing jeans and an old sweatshirt and sporting a stubble of beard. His eyes were bloodshot.

Johnson flashed his badge for the Grant cop. Then he gave Sam, Lydia and me the once-over. "So what's the story this time, Rob?"

We told him what had happened.

Johnson turned his attention to the other officer. "Discover anything that might help us figure out where he's taken her?"

"House is locked. I'll need to get a search warrant. I'll keep you posted on that. Nothing obvious in the barn. Want to take a look?"

I felt exhausted. I looked at Lydia's drooping shoulders and knew she was feeling the same way. Sam looked like she was still bursting with energy. As the two officers headed toward the barn, I called, "Want us to stick around, Sid?"

"Nah. Take off. I know where to find you."

After dropping Lydia and Sam off at Lydia's, I headed home. The light was on in the living room. It was almost 3:00. Jackie was probably waiting up, worried. At least she didn't work Mondays. I yawned as I climbed the steps to the porch, yawned again as I unlocked and opened the door.

Jackie was just coming out of a curled up position on the couch and sitting up. She was wearing a shorty nightie. That woke me up a bit. I plopped down next to her and gave her a kiss. "Were you asleep?" I asked.

"I was too worried to go to bed, but I must have fallen asleep waiting for you to come home. What's the story?"

Between yawns, I told her about the night.

"No idea where Benny took Rochelle after they left the farm?" she asked.

I shrugged.

"So what's next? If I know you, you'll keep snooping." I heard irritation in her voice as well as worry.

"Lydia and I agreed that, after we get some sleep, we'll go see Elliot and Van tomorrow. Rather, this afternoon. That's all we can think of."

Jackie nodded. "If you're spending the afternoon with Lydia, you might as well invite her for supper." Jackie started to get up and sat back down. "So you think Benny is obsessed with Rochelle and that's what's driving this whole business?"

I gave a mighty yawn. "That's the only thing that makes any sense to me."

Jackie stood up, put her hands on her hips and gave me a penetrating look. "From what you've said, Benny's not the only one obsessed with Rochelle." She turned abruptly and headed for the stairs. I followed. If it was possible to stomp quietly, that's what Jackie was doing.

Was I obsessed with Rochelle? Why would I be? I thought about Jackie's pregnancy, a subject always lurking in the back of my mind these days. I had to admit that focusing on the disappearance of the dancers was partly a convenient way to avoid dealing with Jackie's wanting an abortion.

As she climbed into bed, I asked, "How have you been feeling the past few days, babe?"

"Besides the morning nausea, you mean? Just more tired than usual." She sat down on the bed and studied me. "Anything new on your end?"

She was probably hoping I was ready to agree to the abortion. "Sorry. No."

I crawled into bed and dreamed about Rochelle.

CHAPTER 23

Day three of week three.

I woke a little before noon Monday, thinking about John and his visit with Manetta's father to the runaway shelter. I had to deal with that soon, and I didn't look forward to it. I showered and ate lunch with Jackie and Andy. Then I went to the study, took several calming breaths and called John. I conveyed my take on the inappropriateness of his trip to the shelter. I expressed as much understanding as I could honestly manage for his argument that he was doing his pastoral duty. I explained to him how vital it was for the location of the center not to be generally known.

He didn't apologize but he had the grace to at least sound embarrassed, if not sorry.

Next on my agenda was to check on Van. I wasn't sure where the ambulance crew had taken him, but I called Saint Mary's, the hospital closest to his apartment, and got lucky. I picked up Lydia, and a half hour later, we were walking down the hall in the hospital.

"Here's the room," said Lydia.

Van was sitting up in bed. He had bruises on his face and stitches on his right cheek. His lower lip was puffy and split, his left eye black and swollen almost shut, his left arm in a cast. His right eye looked alert. I glanced at the empty bed next to his.

"My roommate went down for x-rays," Van said. Then, "I guess I owe you two clowns." He grimaced as he shifted to a more comfortable position. "I'll try to remember to send you each a thank-you note." He winced as he took a deeper breath.

"How are you doing?" asked Lydia.

"Broken arm, some stitches in my face, a concussion, bruised ribs. The bad news is I'll need dental work. I hate dentists."

"Maybe that's the good news," I said, raising an eyebrow.

"I take your point, Robbie."

I wondered if he could tell that I hated to be called Robbie. He nodded toward two chairs and Lydia and I sat down.

"Has Detective Johnson been here to talk to you yet?" I asked.

"He and Detective Kincaid left a little before you got here."

"Did he tell you we found Rochelle and lost her again?"

"What?" He looked surprised, then angry, then worried. "Johnson didn't tell me anything."

Lydia and I told him about our trip to Benny's farm.

He shook his head. "You two are persistent. I'll grant you that."

"Do you know who beat you up?" I asked.

"I figured it was Benny, but it sounds like he was probably at his farm with Rochelle." He shrugged. "My attacker had a ski mask on. Son of a bitch crashed through the door and took me by surprise in the kitchen. Must have picked the lock on the door downstairs and sneaked up the steps. He hit me with his gun before I knew what was going on. He went to work on me with his fists, then his boots. I don't know how he broke my arm."

"He never said anything?"

"After he hit me with the gun, he said to leave Rochelle alone."

"Did you recognize the voice," asked Lydia?

Van shook his head.

"You sounded surprisingly open to our stopping over when I called you last night," I said. "Was anything special on your mind?"

Van looked out the window for a moment before speaking. "Just thought if we put our heads together again, maybe we'd come up with some idea where Rochelle might be." He paused, and then in a quieter voice, "Sometimes, rattling around in that apartment by myself ...

Lydia said, "I think he's starting to like our company, Rob."

Van scowled at Lydia, then turned back to me. "You said you got a phone call from Rochelle at my place. Tell me about it."

I did.

"Must be Benny doesn't know Dutch. Rochelle probably figured she could make up some cock-and-bull story for Benny about the Dutch words and why she was yelling them. I didn't know Benny's parents had a farm in that area. It's not all that far from mine."

"Any guess where Benny might have taken her?" I asked.

Van shook his head, wincing. "You?" His good eye went from me to Lydia.

We both shrugged.

"Do you know when you'll be discharged?" I said, getting to my feet.

"Maybe tomorrow."

I nodded "Anything you want us to do for you?"

"Find her."

I shook his hand.

He gave me a piercing look with his good eye. "You and Lydia be careful. I mean that."

A short time later, Lydia and I sat in Elliot Rietsema's living room. Books and papers were scattered on the coffee table and couch, and I'd had to move some of it to make room to sit.

"Excuse the mess." Elliot looked around the room. "I can't seem to stay organized, and I can't concentrate worth a nickel."

"Has Detective Johnson talked to you today?" I asked.

"He stopped over this morning. He told me about you two finding Rochelle at Benny's farm and then the two of them disappearing. I just can't believe Benny—"

"You have to stop protecting him!" I said more sharply than I'd intended.

Elliot looked at the floor.

I said, "Um, I'm—"

Lydia cut off my apology with a touch of her hand on my arm. We waited.

It seemed a long time before Elliot spoke, and I was starting to think we should leave.

Finally, he raised his eyes to mine. "He had Rochelle tied to the bed?"

I nodded.

"But she seemed okay?"

I looked at Lydia. "What did you think?"

Lydia shook her head, brow furrowed. "It happened so fast. She looked okay. You asked her where Benny was. She said he was in the house, expecting a call from Owen. But Benny came in almost right away and demanded that Rochelle come with him. Then they were gone. The last thing she said was, 'Benny, please don't—'"

Please don't what? I wondered. I hadn't thought about it before. *What was Rochelle going to say? Don't hurt anyone? Don't what?* My eyes focused on Lydia again. "What emotion did you sense in Rochelle in that room?"

Lydia frowned. "Fear? Concern?"

"Did you get that from the sound of her words," I asked, "or your own imagination?"

"Hmmm. Now that I think of it, I didn't get any emotional tone at all from her words. In fact when you asked where Benny was, you whispered the question. She answered you in a normal tone of voice."

I turned my attention back to Elliot. "I want you to stop trying to maintain your ideal picture of Benny and let yourself imagine the worst. I want you to think of every possible place Benny might take your daughter, no matter how far-fetched."

Elliot shook his head. "You've got the wrong idea about Benny," he said with irritation. "Detective Johnson does too."

I looked at him levelly. "Benny threatened us with a gun. He tied your daughter naked to a bed. He locked us up. You have to stop protecting him. Rochelle's life may depend on it."

Elliot stood up abruptly. "I think you'd better go now. I'm sorry I brought you into this. You're on the wrong track and I think you'd better leave it alone."

In my car a moment later, as I tapped my keys on the steering wheel, puzzling over Elliot's behavior, Lydia said, "What did you make of that?"

"It was strange that he kicked us out. But he's got to be really freaked out about Rochelle's probable abduction. He could be blaming himself. He could be lashing out at us because he feels guilty. I've been wondering if Benny is like the son Elliot never had and so he has blinders on."

As I pulled away from the curb I said, "How about joining us for supper tonight."

"Don't you think you'd better check with Jackie first?"

"She suggested it."

"Oh, okay. I've been missing Andy and I'd like to see Jackie. I get enough of *you* almost every day."

When I parked in front of my house, Jackie and Andy were sitting on the front steps. Jackie looked tired. Andy saw Lydia get out of the car and ran to give her a hug.

"What did you bring me, Lydia?"

Lydia laughed. "May I at least give your mama a hug before I show you? Go give your daddy a hug. I think he needs one."

As Lydia greeted Jackie, I scooped Andy up. He quickly wiggled to get down, ran to Lydia and tugged her hand.

"I didn't forget you, Andy." Lydia opened her purse and began scrounging. Andy was doing his best to look into her purse, so I was glad Lydia was holding it high enough to make that impossible. He didn't need to see the gun. At last, with Andy jumping up and down, Lydia handed something to him.

Andy held up a small plastic magnifying glass. "What is it, Lydia?"

"Why, it's a magnifying glass, like detectives use to look for clues. If you hold it close to small things, it makes them look bigger."

"I'm a detective! I'm a detective!" Andy shouted as he raced around the house toward the backyard, eager to look for clues.

"Andy," I yelled after him, "you forgot to say thank you." I turned to Lydia. "Thanks, Lydia. He treasures all the little things you give him."

"He does treasure them," agreed Jackie, "but a magnifying glass? I'm not sure it's a good idea to encourage him to walk in *those* particular footsteps of his father."

After a supper of grilled chicken, potato salad and Jackie's fresh baked apple crisp ala-mode, Lydia and I sat with Jackie in the living room while Andy played with a friend down the block.

"So, what did you learn this afternoon?" asked Jackie.

I wondered if her interest in the case was in part a way for her to avoid thinking about her pregnancy and her unsupportive husband. I pushed down my guilt and confusion as Lydia re-capped our visits with Van and Elliot. I was eager for Jackie's take on things.

Jackie listened quietly till Lydia was finished, asked a couple of questions, then said, "It sounds like you aren't a hundred per cent sure that Benny is holding Rochelle against her will. There's a chance they're in this thing together. It seems like your guts say Benny or Benny and Rochelle together are behind all the trouble at the Getaway. Not Ned, not Van, not Rochelle's father."

"I'd say that's about right," said Lydia, "but I'm not completely ready to rule out Ned or Elliot."

"Same here," I added.

"I'm thinking about Rochelle's father," said Jackie. "It's in the nature of being a parent to sometimes get over-involved in your kids lives. I guess that's true of all love relationships. The question is: when does that become pathological?" She was silent for moment, then looked into the distance. "But we're not much further ahead than when we started. We haven't really eliminated any suspects except Van."

"Don't forget," said Lydia, "according to Johnson, Rob is a suspect. Do you think we can eliminate him too?" She looked at Jackie with a straight face."

"Nah," they said together.

I rolled my eyes, then said, "There's something odd about the relationship between Elliot and Benny, given Elliot's extreme reaction today when I pushed him to stop protecting Benny. And who beat up Van if it wasn't Benny?"

I was tired and Lydia looked like she was too. But with the clock ticking on Georgina and with Rochelle missing again,

Lydia and I decided to hit the streets for the second Monday night in a row. I had no idea what we could do, but that was nothing new. We'd muddle along as before, with a hope and a prayer.

CHAPTER 24

At Drop-in Monday night, Lydia and I talked with Wild Bill. Nothing new from him. We gave him what support we could.

We'd just decided to move on when Nathan came in from the front desk. "Phone message for you and Lydia, Rob: Detectives Johnson and Kincaid request the honor of your presence at the Detective Bureau."

As I drove to the Hall of Justice, I said, "You think the words of that message were Kincaid's or Nathan's?"

Lydia laughed. "We should have asked. Could have been either one."

When we got there about 8:45, the detectives were both at their desks doing paperwork. Johnson looked disheveled, tie askew, shirt more wrinkled than normally. Even Kincaid didn't look as crisp and neat as usual. Johnson glanced up and motioned to the chairs in front of his desk. Kincaid nodded at us and resumed typing. He was a proficient typist, while Johnson labored over his typewriter using two thick fingers, punching keys as if they were bugs that had no business being on his desk.

When he stopped typing, he pulled the report out of the typewriter and dumped it in a basket. Kincaid noticed and pushed his chair back.

Johnson looked up. "Turns out I was right about the bouncer."

I frowned. "So Hector was murdered. How do you know?"

"Angle of the bullet's trajectory and lack of powder residue on the victim's hand."

"So where is the evidence pointing in the Getaway mess?" I asked.

Sid puffed and squirmed. "If evidence can point in circles, that's what's it's doing. Not unusual. If we just stay at it long enough, things generally start falling into place."

I glanced at Kincaid who said, "That is frequently the nature of the investigative process."

Hmmm, I thought. *That's my method, too.* Of course, the detectives knew a whole lot more about what to look for. They couldn't bumble along as badly as Lydia and I did, could they?

"We searched Benny's farmhouse and didn't turn up anything," Johnson went on. "The place has been on the market for a couple of months. We haven't gotten a warrant yet for Benny's apartment in town. Hopefully, we'll get it tomorrow. His neighbors haven't seen him for a few days. The Grant police are trying to find out about any family or friends Benny may have in the area."

"What about Pookie and Owen?" I asked.

"We're trying to track them down. Don't have a last name on Owen. We talked with Pookie once at the bar early in the case. I'll probably lean on Doctor Rietsema again and see if he knows anything about Benny's friends. I can't figure out why he's so protective of Benny."

"Speaking of Elliot," said Lydia, looking from Johnson to Kincaid, "he acted strange when we talked with him this afternoon."

Kincaid raised his eyebrows. "Can you articulate your observations?"

Lydia reported on our visit, adding, "Something's off about Elliot's relationship with Benny."

I nodded. "Maybe Elliot sees Benny as the son he never had and can't see Benny's faults."

Kincaid nodded. "It's a speculation that warrants careful appraisal."

I was surprised that Kincaid put some credence in my theory and that he was letting us know what he thought.

Fancy theories aside," said Johnson, "I'd rather you had some new ideas where Benny and Rochelle might be holed up. That's why we asked you to come in."

When we told him we had nothing, he pushed away from his desk and stood. "Anyways, this case isn't going to keep us up all night. We're going home now."

* * *

Tuesday, week three, day four.

In the afternoon, I visited a couple of kids at Juvy and had two counseling appointments at my office. Georgina and Rochelle were static on my brain the whole time. Was Rochelle okay? Was Georgina still alive? At least during supper that evening, Andy's lively jabbering about his day distracted me.

At 7:30 the doorbell rang for *huisbezoek*. A few minutes later Jackie, Andy and I were seated with Elder Howard Minema in our living room. For several minutes we made small talk and then I answered his questions about my work.

"What do you think of your daddy's job, Andy?" asked Howard in his heavy Dutch accent.

Andy looked puzzled, then shrugged.

"Do you worry about him spending time with the people he works with?" Howard had never been known for being subtle or sensitive.

"Uh-uh. The people Daddy works with are really nice. Caleb even let me wear his colors. That's a gang jacket. And Mad Dog gave me some candy."

I imagined Andy adding, "Wild Bill gave me a hit off his joint and asked me if I wanted to score some acid." I studied the floor.

Howard shifted in his seat. "How about you, Jackie? You worry about Rob in his work?"

"No."

Silence.

Jackie wasn't giving him much.

"Okay, then." Howard opened his Bible and read a brief passage from the tenth chapter of Hebrews with the favorite text to prove the importance of regular church attendance. Jackie had been right.

Howard cleared his throat. "I want to tell you that the question of your infrequent church attendance has come up in elders' meetings. I said I would talk it over with you—*unofficially*. Now I realize, Rob, that your ministry requires you to be on the street on Saturday nights till the wee hours, so I can understand your missing morning services as much as you do. I know, too, that you preach sometimes in various churches that support the Street Ministry. But, Jackie, it seems like I don't see you and Andy there very often when Rob isn't there."

Andy pulled on my arm. "Mama was right, Daddy. She's on the spot and you weaseled out of it."

Sometimes I was amazed at how much Andy understood from what Jackie and I said to each other. I reminded myself, as I had countless times, not sell him short.

Howard shot Andy a questioning frown, and then brought his attention back to me when I cleared my throat.

"Jackie and I thought that might be part of the reason for the visit," I said. "You're right, and we'll try to rectify the problem." It was obvious to me that since this discussion was *unofficial*, the implied next step would be *official*, that is, the first step in church discipline that could ultimately lead to excommunication, though that seemed unlikely. Even though I was sometimes at odds with my church, it was the church that had formed my faith. There was much in the denomination that I valued, and I wanted to remain a Christian Reformed minister. I hoped Jackie would continue to hold her peace. I noticed Howard's shoulders drop. This hadn't been easy for him.

"Okay then," he said. "May I ask you, Jackie, how is it with your spiritual life?"

"Yah, well," said Jackie, "there are the hills and there are the valleys." She'd have carried off the platitude, but she made the mistake of glancing at me and our eyes met.

She giggled.

The silence that followed was palpable. I knew Jackie had a strong silly streak that was sometimes at odds with her normal serious demeanor, but her little number surprised even me.

Then, apparently deciding to ignore this faux pas or not knowing what the heck to do with it, Howard wrapped up the visit with a brief prayer. "Father in heaven, we thank thee for thy gracious presence in our lives." When he prayed, the Dutch accent became more pronounced and he prayed in a deep monotone. "Bless Rob in his ministry and Jackie in her nursing. Bless them as a family. May thy Kingdom come more fully in our lives. In Christ's name, Amen."

When Howard left, Andy asked, "How come you giggled, Mama?"

"I was making a joke, Andy, but Mr. Minema didn't get it."

"Did you get it, Daddy?"

I looked at Jackie. "Oh, I got it. Don't ask me to explain, Andy. It's a big-person joke."

Relieved that the meeting with our elder was over, I gave hugs to Jackie and Andy and headed to Lydia's.

After a stop at Partners where one of the waitresses made an appointment to see Lydia later in the week, Lydia and I moved on to the Alibi where we nursed our beers at the bar.

"I got my gun back from Detective Johnson," said Lydia.

I looked at her purse hanging from her shoulder. "You don't have two in your purse, do you?"

"No, no. I left my sister's at home."

I glanced up and noticed Dolores, the prostitute I'd run into when I was out with John, parading into the bar. She wore a red miniskirt, a tight, low-cut blue top and red spiked heels. She spotted us and moved toward us with every eye in the place following her. She looked upset.

"Hey, Robbie. Hey, Lydia." For some reason it didn't bother me when Dolores called me Robbie. "You guys still givin' out hugs? I could sure use a couple." She looked vulnerable, a side of her I'd not seen before.

After the hugs she said, "Let's sit at a table."

"What's up," I said as we all sat down. "Rough night?"

"You could say that."

"Want to talk about it?" I asked.

She paused a moment, then said, "Nah. The hugs were good, though. So how you guys doin'?"

"Fine," said Lydia, and the two began chatting about the stretch of hot, humid weather we'd been experiencing. I listened to the sound of Engelbert Humperdink singing "Release Me." I flashed on an image of Rochelle tied to the bed. What happened in that room in the barn occurred so fast, that maybe it was just my imagination that something seemed off.

Joe South came on next, singing "Games People Play." If it hadn't been for those two songs, coming one after the other, I'm not sure my uneasiness would have jelled.

"Dolores," I said when there was a break in her conversation with Lydia, "any of your johns ever want to, um, tie you to the bed?"

Dolores smiled and lowered her eyelids to half-mast. "Why, Robbie. I never dreamt you be into kinky. I done it, but not with no minister. Shall we tell Lydia to take a hike?" She turned to Lydia. "'Less you wanna watch."

I sat with my mouth open. Lydia squirmed and looked down.

Dolores hooted. "The looks on your faces. Wish I had me a camera."

I recovered and smiled. "You got us Dolores. But I was thinking about ..." What? A case Lydia and I were working on? We weren't cops. I started again. "Have you heard about the go-go dancers who disappeared?"

Dolores nodded. "Yeah. You guys doin' more detective work? Need my help?"

"Just need you to tell us about tying someone to a bed for sex."

"Well, I rather tie the john. It's a lot safer. But, yeah, I let myself be tied a couple a times."

I couldn't imagine how being tied or tying someone could be a turn-on. "I guess I don't get it."

"Well, if you be tied, you can prob'ly shove away some guilt, pretend you bein' forced. For the one who ain't tied, it can be a power trip."

Lydia looked at me sharply. "You think Rochelle and Bennie were *playing*?"

"Rochelle didn't seem scared for herself. She had *some* concern about Bennie, maybe that he would shoot somebody? She said, 'Benny, please don't ...' That's as far as she got. Why didn't she look terrified?"

CHAPTER 25

"Spare change, Father?"

I was about to board Night Watch with Lydia after leaving the Alibi when a guy dressed in an old baggy pants and stained sweatshirt with holes in the elbows shuffled up to me. I'd seen him on the street before and greeted him, but this was the first time he'd approached me. He might have been as young as fifty or as old as seventy. He smelled of cheap booze. With effort, I avoided wrinkling my nose. I extended my hand. "Rob Vander Laan," I said.

"Thomas W. Arnsted." He made it sound like one word.

As we shook hands I said, "And what would you like me to call you?"

"You can call me Thomas W. Arnsted."

"Okay, Thomas W. Arnsted, I'm glad to meet you. I don't have spare change for you, but are you hungry?"

Thomas W. Arnsted nodded enthusiastically. "That's what I was going to use the change for, sir. I didn't eat nothin', um, anything, today."

I wondered if he felt the need to clean up his grammar in hopes of making a better impression on me.

Lydia and I spent the next half hour with Thomas W. Arnsted, hearing the hard luck story of his journey from a life of privilege to his present status as he munched on his hamburger and fries and drank his coffee. His father had been a wealthy business owner in the city, but Thomas W. Arnsted had managed to lose the fortune he'd inherited. It was unclear whether the drinking had preceded the loss or was the result of it. When he finished, I paid the waitress and handed her the tip, not wanting to leave it on the table for the man to pocket.

"Lydia and I have to go," I said, "but do you want more coffee?"

Thomas W. Arnsted nodded vigorously. "Yessir. And thank you for the meal, sir."

I looked up at the waitress who gave me a look of long-suffering, but poured the gentleman more coffee.

As Lydia and I were getting up he said, "I seen, um, saw that guy who beat up Mr. Van from the Pawn Shop. That was a bad thing. Mr. Van is always nice to me."

Lydia and I dropped back into our chairs. "What did you see?" asked Lydia.

"I saw that guy get out of the car in the alley, put on a ski mask and go up to Mr. Van's place. I hid behind a car, and I heard a racket up in Mr. Van's apartment. Then the guy came running down the stairs and took off in his car. I saw the two of you go up to his apartment. I left after that because I didn't want to be there when the cops, er, officers of the law, came."

"Did you see what the guy in the ski mask looked like?" I asked.

"No, sir, I did not see him very clearly."

"Do you have a place you call home," I asked.

"Mostly I stay at the Grand when I can afford it, sir." The Grand was a seedy, old hotel down the street.

I nodded. "Detectives Johnson and Kincaid will want to talk to you about this. They're good cops. Will you talk to them?"

Thomas W. Arnsted studied his coffee cup. "I'm not fond of officers of the law, sir." After a moment he looked up at me, apparently having reached a decision. "Since you say they're okay, I'll talk to them."

I got to my feet and was about to extend my hand again, when I said, "Did you see anything else that night?"

He shook his head. As I pushed the chair back to the table, he looked toward the street. "Just the other man in the car, the driver. But I never saw what he looked like either. He didn't get out of the car."

"There was another guy in the car?"

"Yessir."

"Did you notice what kind of car it was?"

"No sir. Except that it was a late model and dark in color."

"Did you see if it was a two-door or a four-door?"

"It was a four-door vehicle, sir."

I was no longer taking anything for granted. "Anything else?"

He scratched his head. "No sir."

I extended my hand. "Thank you. It's been a pleasure."

As we made our exit, Thomas W. Arnsted was repeating for the fourth time, "God bless you," making it sound like one word.

"I wonder who it was that beat Van up," said Lydia. "And who the driver was."

"Owen? Pookie driving maybe? Or maybe some other friends of Benny?"

From my office a little later, I called the police station and left a message for Johnson about Thomas W. Arnsted.

After hanging with kids at Drop-in, the park and the lot, Lydia and I headed for the Getaway.

"I'm baffled about this Getaway business," said Lydia. I just can't make the pieces fit together."

"Try this. Benny finds out Georgina has a thing for Rochelle. He murders Georgina or abducts her or scares her out of town because he sees her as competition or an aggravation to Rochelle. Rochelle is angry with Hector so Benny kills him—intentionally or accidentally—and tries to make it look like a suicide. Since Rochelle is becoming increasingly afraid of Benny, she goes to Van's farm to hide out for a while. Benny finds her, snatches her and takes her to his parents' farm. When we find Rochelle there, he takes her someplace else. He wants her all to himself."

Lydia shook her head and scowled. "That's what I thought too till you threw a monkey wrench in things with the idea of Rochelle's being tied to the bed as part of a game they were playing."

I shrugged. "Maybe I'm wrong about the sex game."

"Maybe. But suppose you're right."

"Okay," I said. "But why, then, would Rochelle call Van's and throw out that Dutch clue?"

"Because she loves high drama?"

I pulled into a parking space in the lot behind the Getaway. "Then we've got Rochelle and Benny as a team in this whole business," I continued. "Or Rochelle, controlling Benny who does what she wants him to. That would fit with the way Rochelle seems to use her sexiness to manipulate and control other people. Of course, if Benny is mentally messed up after Nam, that could be a dangerous game. But then Rochelle being tied to the bed doesn't fit with her being the one in charge, does it?"

Inside the Getaway, the crowd was light. Sadie and Sylvia danced in the cages while Manetta and Lois sat at a table with half a dozen guys who looked to be in their early twenties. A handful of men stood at the bar, far enough apart to avoid conversation with each other. No sign of Pookie or Owen.

Ned drew us each a draft. "The big cop's been in here again. Said you found Rochelle and then lost her again. She hasn't resurfaced?"

I shook my head. "Did Johnson tell you that she was at Benny's parents' farm?"

"No, he didn't say where. So now this guy's stashed her someplace else."

"You think Benny's holding her captive then?" I asked.

"What else? I don't think she'd go anywhere willingly with him. If he's the guy we bounced out of here."

I set my beer glass on the bar. "Maybe they made up."

"Nah. Rochelle wanted nothing to do with that guy."

"Stranger things have happened," I said.

I felt a tap on each shoulder, turned to face Manetta and Lois.

"Heard you found Rochelle and lost her again," said Manetta.

"That's about the size of it," I said.

The girls exchanged a worried look. "Don't give up on her," said Lois.

"And don't leave before our show," said Manetta.

"Yah, our first dance will be for you guys."

"But we wondered if you could meet us at Sandy's after close, say about 2:30 or 2:45," said Manetta.

I looked at Lydia who nodded. "If nothing comes up to keep us, we'll be there," I said.

A short time later, the girls began dancing their first dance of the set. I was happy there was no announcement that this one was dedicated to Lydia and me as they moved sensuously to Frankie Valli's "Can't Take My Eyes Off You."

While we watched the dance, I noticed someone enter the bar and look around furtively. The bouncer appeared to be talking to the man, but the man seemed to ignore him. The man appeared to be middle-aged, short haircut, slacks and short-sleeved shirt. Something about him was familiar, but in the dim light I couldn't identify him. He started to move forward and I realized it was Rochelle's father. I was about to wave to get his attention when his eyes met mine. He quickly stepped back, and then he was gone.

Why would Elliot come to the Getaway? Concerned father desperate to find his daughter? So why duck out after seeing me?

Lydia and I left the bar a few minutes later, Manetta and Lois blowing us kisses from their cages.

When we got into my car, I told Lydia about Elliot's brief appearance.

"Maybe he came to try to see if he could get information about where Rochelle might be."

I nodded. "Makes sense. Then why duck out after spotting me?"

"Maybe he was embarrassed about being seen by you at a go-go bar."

After a bar stop in the River City, where we stayed till last call, we went to Sandy's Grill. We were finishing our breakfasts when Manetta and Lois arrived. They slid into the booth and ordered coffee and breakfast.

"So did you like the dance?" asked Manetta.

"I did," I answered honestly. "How about you Lydia?"

Lydia cleared her throat.

It was kind of fun to be the one putting her on the spot for a change.

"I have to say that you girls are very good at what you do," said Lydia carefully. "And that dance certainly demonstrated your talents."

Both girls beamed.

"Lois thought—"

"Yah, I thought, with you being—"

Manetta picked it up. "—yah, you know, a little older and everything—"

Lydia squirmed.

"—and being a woman—" added Lois.

"—you might not really dig our dancing," finished Manetta.

"Lydia's just a cool granny," I said.

"We figured you'd groove on it, Rob," said Manetta

Lois giggled.

"Yah, I mean, you may be a Christian Reformed minister—"

"—yah, but you're still a normal, horny guy, right?"

Now Lydia was looking smug, saying nothing.

I put on a serious face. "Don't you think you should have more respect for a minister?"

Manetta and Lois instantly sobered.

I tried to keep from grinning, but I could feel the corners of my mouth gradually turning up at the sober looks on their faces, and, more than anything, their silence.

Tentative smiles replaced the sober looks until Lydia said, "He got you, girls."

They giggled.

"Lois wanted to have Ned announce that the dance was dedicated to you."

"Yah, but Manetta talked me out of it."

"Thank you, Manetta," I said, in a level tone. I hoped she realized I was serious about that.

"And, thank you, Rob," Manetta said, "for getting my sister into the runaway shelter. Sorry my father messed that up. He's always coming on like gangbusters."

"Have you seen her since she ran from the shelter?" I said.

Manetta hesitated a moment, then said, "Don't ask."

I wondered if the runaway was staying with her older sister. I decided not to push it.

* * *

Wednesday: day five of week three.

I spent the afternoon at the office with counseling appointments and letter writing. As I was leaving, Stacy reminded me of the birthday party for one of the gang girls at Drop-in that night.

After supper at home later, I got a call from Howard Minema, my elder. Another small-world surprise, two, actually. It turned out he was a good friend of Manetta's father and had received a call from him. Howard said he hoped I'd find Aretha, Manetta's sister, and return her to her father. He also *strongly suggested* that I convince Manetta to quit her job as go-go dancer. As a Christian Reformed pastor I had to protect the reputation of the denomination. He suggested it would go a long way to demonstrate that I was a sincere CRC minister.

I made no promises and thanked him for his call.

I'd no sooner hung up the phone when it rang again. John Vanden Berg.

He blustered on about the need for me to return the runaway to her father. I suspected he felt badly about the mess he'd created, but maybe that was just my trying to see the best in him.

"Even if I could," I said, "I wouldn't make Aretha go back home. You should understand how I deal with runaways after being with me when I referred that other girl to the shelter. If I can get Aretha back to the shelter, I will. But you have to promise not to interfere again. Advise her father not to interfere as well. I understand your concern as the family's pastor, but you have to trust the process on this, no matter what her father says."

John reluctantly agreed. Then he moved on to Manetta and her go-go dancing. He knew about Lois, too, and he knew that Rochelle had been dancing at the Getaway before she disappeared. Apparently, he'd been doing his own snooping. "You have to get them to quit their jobs there, Rob. I'm pleading with you. If you go into that evil place and watch them dance ..."

"Don't give me your speech about my presence conferring approval again, John," I said, trying to remain calm. "I'll continue to try to be a pastor to the dancers and Aretha if I have the opportunity, but on my terms. That's all I can promise."

John sputtered and fumed for another moment. I remained quiet as I tried to imagine how hard this must be for him.

Then he dropped the bomb.

CHAPTER 26

"One more thing, Rob," said John as I shifted the phone to the other ear. "I know Jackie is pregnant and that she is considering having that precious gift of God murdered. I don't even know if Jackie has told you. Don't ask me how I found out because it's confidential. She may have her reasons to be thinking about this, but you are the spiritual head of your family. I won't make the abortion business public since I have that information in confidence, but I felt like I owed it to you as a brother in Christ to confront you with this. I may be violating confidentiality by even saying this much. Now I'm going to hang up and pray that you'll do the right thing."

I'm not sure how long I stood there listening to the dial tone in stupefied silence. Finally I slammed the receiver down and stared at Jackie who was knitting an afghan in the living room.

She looked at me with concern. "What?" she asked.

I walked into the living room but couldn't sit down. I paced the floor as I reported the two conversations. Jackie listened quietly as she continued her knitting until I got to the part about John being aware of her pregnancy and that she was considering an abortion.

At that point, she threw her knitting on the floor and stood up. "You told him!" she yelled. "That's the only way he could know!"

Jackie had never yelled at me before. "I did not!" I yelled back.

"Then how did he find out?" she demanded.

"Someone at Planned Parenthood who's in John's church?" But I didn't really believe someone there would inform John.

Jackie shook her head, and we stood looking at each other in silence for a moment. Then she dropped back on to the couch and pounded the cushion next to her.

"Look at me, Jacks," I said. When her eyes met mine, I said, "The only person I told was Blaine."

Finally, Jackie said in a quieter voice, "Just go. Do your night ministry thing. I'll see if I can figure this out."

On the way to Lydia's, my mind raced with the events of the past half hour. I was angry at John for his meddling. I was surprised at how much he'd learned about the Getaway and its dancers. Most of all I was baffled how he'd learned about Jackie's considering an abortion. I was certain, however, that it was connected to the small ethnic world we lived in. Jackie and I had confided in Blaine and Sheila Hanson, but they were not part of our Dutch culture. I was pretty sure the counselor at Planned Parenthood would not betray our confidence. Somebody else knew what Jackie and I were going through and had told John. I thought about the bug on our phone. Had Jackie said something on the phone about getting an abortion? Had she called Planned Parenthood to make the appointment from our home phone?

I parked at Lydia's, my jumbled thoughts still swirling in my head.

"Van's back home," Lydia said as she got into the car. "I called the hospital and he left this morning. Seems like his being discharged after only a couple of days is a good sign."

I was glad for a chance to focus on something other than John's meddling and Jackie's rage. I drove to the pawnshop and parked. The store was closed. We walked around to the rear of the building. I pressed the doorbell.

Silence.

I banged on the door. "It's Rob and Lydia," I called. When I got no answer, I banged on the door again.

Finally, a window opened over our heads. A gruff yell, "Cut out the damn racket."

We heard Van slowly coming down the stairs. The door opened. He looked at us for a moment, then stepped aside, apparently inviting us in.

We went up the steps and waited in the kitchen for Van to negotiate the stairs. He entered and stood for a moment catching his breath. The swelling on his lower lip and his left eye were down some, but the bruising was even more obvious and turning green and yellow. We followed him into the living room.

When we were seated on the couch and he was comfortably ensconced on his recliner, he reached for a pipe, then put it back. "Hurts to inhale," he said. "It's also a little challenging to manage the pipe with this stupid cast on."

"Are you in much pain?" asked Lydia.

"Pills pretty well take care of it, but they keep me groggy. I'll try going without them tomorrow. Any word on Rochelle?"

I shook my head and told him what we'd learned from the gentleman drunk the night before.

"Thomas W. Arnsted," mused Van. "I find him sleeping it off behind the shop occasionally. Sometimes he sweeps out the shop or shovels snow for me. Other little odd jobs. Any idea who might have been waiting in the car while I was attacked?"

"We were hoping you might have an idea," said Lydia.

He reached for his pipe, drew his hand back. "Elliot? He's pretty angry with me, but that's probably because he's worried about Rochelle. Hard to imagine him conspiring with Benny or friends of Benny to beat me. Maybe one of Benny's friends drove the car."

"Any possibility Rochelle might have been the driver?" asked Lydia.

Van stared at her for a long time. Lydia didn't look away.

"Why would you think it might be Rochelle, Lydia?" As usual, his eyes gave away nothing.

"When Benny came into the barn at his farm after we freed Rochelle from being tied to the bed, something seemed off. Rochelle didn't seem to be afraid for herself and she should have been."

Van picked a pipe from a rack on the table next to his chair. He was quiet as he fiddled with it. "Rochelle can be unpredictable. She's a great manipulator. I was always thankful she wasn't *my* daughter. I felt she respected me, though, even when she was angry with me. I'd hate to think I was wrong about her feelings toward me. If she's in on this thing with Benny, I don't know what to think."

"Let's suppose," I said, "that Benny killed Hector, engineered Georgina's disappearance and had someone beat you up. Now he's abducted Rochelle or they've disappeared together. Why would Benny do all that?"

"Maybe he saw the bouncer and Georgina as threats to his relationship with Rochelle."

"Then are you a threat, too?" I asked. "And how about Elliot? Or me, for that matter?"

Van set the pipe down. "Benny could see me as a threat, even though I'm not a romantic threat. He knows Rochelle confides in me, and maybe he wants to be her only confidante."

"But then why not have you killed? Why just beat you up?"

"*Just* beat me up? *You* obviously didn't get the beating."

"I didn't mean ..."

"Relax, Robbie, I'm giving you a hard time. I've done plenty of thinking about why I wasn't killed. Perhaps it's because Benny knows how important I am to Rochelle. He couldn't take the chance of hurting her that deeply by killing me. But he wanted to send a message for me to keep my nose out of things. Of course, it's all speculation."

We sat in silence for a moment.

"I'd watch my back if I were you," said Van. "You could be next."

But I wasn't nearly as important to Rochelle as Uncle Van, so maybe I'd be in more danger than he was.

As if I'd spoken aloud, Van said, "Don't overestimate your importance to Rochelle, though. Benny might see you as expendable if he catches you nosing around."

I stifled a shiver. I remembered the fear I'd felt when Benny confronted me in my car, demanding to know where Rochelle was. I was familiar with these battles with myself about taking risks to get information. It wasn't that I was brave. It was more a stubbornness that kept me moving into trouble. I remembered hearing my father say to a friend of his once, "Rob toddled into trouble from his first baby steps."

"Let's get back to where Rochelle might be," I said. "Maybe she and Benny are staying with some friend or relative of either of them who lives in the area."

"I can't think of any relatives or friends of Rochelle's around here, besides those two girlfriends from high school. I wouldn't know about relatives or friends of Benny." Van shifted in the chair and grimaced. "I'd offer you coffee, but I'm tired, so you'd better go. If you learn anything about Rochelle, call me." He wrote his number down on a piece of paper and handed it to me. "It's unlisted," he said.

From Van's we headed to Drop-in. The birthday party was in full swing, with the usual mix of heads, heavies and straights. The volunteer staff were mixing with the kids and no one was at the desk, but Nathan was posted close enough to it to spot anyone who walked in the door. All the faces were familiar. The rock and roll music from the portable radio was loud, and people appeared to be finishing up on the refreshments. The cake had been consumed, and Pamela, the birthday girl was apologetic about that. She wore a bright red scarf draped over her colors. She brought us each a dish of ice cream. Lydia gave her a hug and I congratulated her.

A few minutes later, Nathan nudged me and nodded toward the desk. I turned to see Johnson, Kincaid at his side. They'd never been in Drop-in before, other than to walk through it to my office. "Detectives," I said, raising my voice to be heard above the noise. "Want to join the party?" I motioned them to come in and they moved closer to the group.

All conversation died. Someone turned the radio way down. Everyone stared warily toward the cops.

Johnson surveyed the group. "We seem to be putting a damper on things, Rob. Can we talk in your office?"

"The kids just need to get to know you. Hey, everybody, this is Detective Johnson and Detective Kincaid. Remember the cops who worked on the Downtown Murders last summer."

Johnson's face reddened. A grimace shaped his lips, or it might have been an attempt to smile. Kincaid's face was blank as he nodded to the kids. Johnson made an awkward wave with his hand. He turned to me, a kind of desperation in his eyes. "Rob, could we—"

"Detective Johnson?" It was Pamela, two bowls of ice cream in hand. "Welcome to my birthday party. It's the first one I ever had. Thanks for all you did last summer to catch the murderers." She extended the bowls of ice cream to the detectives.

Johnson stood there with his ice cream, looking a little disoriented.

I led the detectives and Lydia to my office and closed the door. I took a seat behind my desk and the others sat in chairs in front of it. "You can set the ice cream bowl on my desk if you don't want it, Sid," I offered.

"Huh?" He looked down as though surprised to find himself holding it. He set in on the desk as Kincaid quietly ate his.

"So what's on your mind?" I asked.

"What? Oh." Johnson frowned. "We were trying to find that drunk you left a message about, but we haven't had any luck yet. Tell us what he said."

Lydia and I reported our conversation with Thomas W. Arnsted and answered the detectives' questions.

"Anyways," said Johnson," we got the search warrant for Benny's apartment on the northeast side. Found a bunch of his letters to Rochelle. Written on the envelopes was 'return to sender.' Pictures of her, too. Some from high school, some more recent. The recent ones look like they were taken with a telephoto lens. Found the camera and the big lens, too. Apparently he hasn't been seen at his apartment since last Friday night. We're keeping an eye on it."

"Any sign of Rochelle's car?" I asked.

"Nope." He pushed his chair back, and we all stood up. "Think we'll get back out to South Division," he said, "and see if we can rustle up this Arnsted guy. Otherwise, I'll get Vice to keep a lookout for him."

I smiled. "You should stop in more often, detectives. Think of it as cultivating your sources. Do the kids good to get to know you, too."

"Yeah, that would be great for my reputation on the job," said Johnson.

Kincaid looked thoughtful. "There might be some merit in the suggestion, Sid. Let's not dismiss it out of hand."

When the detectives left, Nathan appeared at my office door. "Just got a call from a guy named Ned at the Getaway. He'd like you and Lydia to stop in."

We went directly to the nightclub, arriving a little after 10:00. It was a good crowd for a Wednesday night with only a couple of tables open and a little standing room left at the bar. Manetta and Lois blew kisses toward us from the cages as they danced to B.J. Thomas, *Hooked on a Feeling*. Sadie and Sylvia each sat at a table with a different bunch of guys. It looked like Ned was breaking in a new assistant bartender. When Ned spotted us, he motioned us to follow him into his office behind the bar. He closed the door to shut out some of the noise and then sat on the edge of a small desk. Lydia and I remained standing.

"Benny was here tonight," he said.

"Did you call the cops?" I asked.

"As you've no doubt gathered, I'm not too fond of them. Probably should have, but I called you instead."

"They're looking for Benny. You have to report what happened."

Ned picked up the receiver from the phone on his desk and handed it to me. "Be my guest."

Figuring Johnson and Kincaid were still out, I called dispatch and left a message for the detectives.

When I hung up, Lydia said, "How long ago was Benny here?"

"He came in about 9:30."

"What did he want?" I asked.

"He said I owed Rochelle a week's wages, which is true. Said I should hand it over to him so he could give it to her."

I frowned. "What did you do?"

"Told him to go to hell. Said I'd give it to Rochelle and for him to tell her that."

"What happened then?"

"He looked like he was about to take something out of his pocket. Might have been a gun. The bar was already pretty busy. I'd signaled my bouncer earlier and he was standing at Benny's elbow. Benny looked at him, then turned and walked out."

"How did Benny look to you?" asked Lydia.

"He looked like he needed a shave, maybe a shower and a change of clothes. His voice sounded calm, but his eyes were jumping all over the place. In other words, he looked nuttier than a fruitcake."

CHAPTER 27

Johnson and Kincaid arrived at the Getaway a short time later. Lydia and I left the table we'd been sitting at and met the detectives at the bar. The noise of conversation died down, and customers focused their attention on the detectives instead of the dancers. Ned motioned the detectives, Lydia and me into his office and closed the door.

Johnson turned to me. "You and Lydia were here when Benny showed up?"

I shook my head. "Ned told us Benny had been in."

Sid rounded on Ned and glared at him. "Why didn't you call the station right away? You know we're looking for Benny."

Ned raised his gaze to Sid's chest and shrugged.

"I ought to charge you with 'aiding and abetting.'" He added something under his breath that I didn't catch.

"So what time did Benny make an appearance?" asked Kincaid.

"About 9:30." Ned reported what he'd already told us.

Johnson poked a finger under his collar and scratched his neck. "Anybody see what he was driving?"

"You might ask my bouncer, but I doubt it," said Ned.

Lydia and I went back to the bar and ordered beers. I was hoping to get a word with the new bartender. We watched the detectives interview the rest of the staff.

When Johnson was finished, he approached us. "What do you make of Ned not calling us right away himself?"

I shrugged.

His gaze lingered a moment on my beer glass, then refocused on me. I wondered if he was wishing for one. When he didn't say anything, I asked, "Benny's car?"

"Bouncer saw him get into a green 1967 Chevy. We already knew that's what he's driving."

"Learn anything from the rest of the staff?"

"Nothing. But don't let that stop you being your normal nosey self. Just be careful. And get a hold of me if you learn anything."

We watched the detectives walk toward the door. When the new bartender had a moment's breathing space, I asked if he'd observed anything special about Benny.

"What do you mean?" he asked.

"Nothing in particular. Just wondering if anything stood out for you?"

"Just his eyes going all over the place. Looked like a wacko to me." He glanced toward the cages, then said, "Manetta and Lois were between sets, and they sure seemed riled up. They kept watching him when he was talking to Ned and they looked pretty shook."

"Hey, Rob." Two voices.

I turned to face Manetta and Lois. "I hear you two were pretty nervous when Benny was here," I said.

"Well, yah!" Again in unison. They exchanged a worried look.

"Were you afraid for yourselves or Ned or what?" I asked.

They looked at each other, as if telepathically checking signals before responding. Then they shrugged and said, "You never know."

"With Benny?" I said, "You never know with Benny?"

"He's dangerous," said Manetta.

Lois touched Manetta's arm. "Come on. Gotta change for our set."

As we walked to my car, Lydia said, "Do you believe Ned about not calling the police because he's not 'fond' of them?"

"Wouldn't be the first time we've run into that."

"But what if Ned didn't call the police in order to give Benny time to get away. Maybe they're in cahoots."

"But the two really *did* have an altercation about the money owed to Rochelle. If Benny and Ned are in this together, why hasn't Ned already gotten the money to Rochelle?"

"Maybe Ned doesn't want to risk going to the place Rochelle is hiding out."

"Or where she's being held captive." I started the car. "Ned being in on the whole thing doesn't makes sense to me though."

At the River City a little later, the music sounded like something from the Grateful Dead. I wasn't focused enough to be sure because my thoughts were still back at the Getaway. The bartender passed two beers to a guy standing in front of us and pointed at Lydia and me.

The patron turned, smiling, and almost dropped the beers when he saw my collar. He looked to be about fifty-years-old, give or take a few. The smile left his face, replaced by a look of uncertainty.

"What? You think just because he's a man of the cloth, he doesn't drink beer?" Sam was at my elbow, smiling broadly. "Pass them over before they get warm."

The gentleman handed the glasses to Lydia and me as Sam gave me a sideways squeeze and touched Lydia's arm. "Catch you guys later if I can," she said and brought a tray of empties to the server station.

I extended my hand and introduced myself to the man who'd handed us our drinks. He had a pleasant face with a prominent mole on his left cheek, penetrating blue eyes, dark curly hair, with a hint of grey at the temples.

"Quincy De Weerd," he said with a firm handshake.

I introduced Lydia.

He took Lydia's hand in both of his. "You remind me of my dear mother, Lydia. And I couldn't pay you a higher compliment."

Lydia smiled warmly.

Why was I feeling a twinge of discomfort?

"I thought I'd seen everything," said Quincy. "May I be so bold as to ask what brings the two of you here?"

Before I could open my mouth, Lydia explained what we were doing at the bar.

There was a tug at my elbow. "Table's open in the back, and it's not quite so noisy there," said Sam.

"I should probably stick with Lydia," I said, the vague sense of discomfort lingering.

Sam leaned close to my ear. "Lydia is quite capable of handling herself, and she looks like she's making a nice connection to the guy. Let her do her ministry thing, and you talk to me."

I let Sam usher me to the back table. She gently shoved me into the booth and slid in next to me.

"So what's happening on our case," she asked, leaning close, eyes intense.

I briefly caught her up on the latest developments.

She slid out of the booth. "Don't go away. I'll be back after I get this order."

When she returned, she said, "Don't worry about Lydia. They're sitting at a table together, thick as thieves." Her eyes quickly roamed toward her customers. Then she said, "I talked to Uncle Clarence this afternoon. He says the Grant cop told him Benny's been getting into fights since he got back from

Vietnam. He's been arrested twice for assault in Detroit where he goes sometimes to visit an army buddy."

When Sam spotted two customers at a table looking around, she squeezed my arm and headed toward them.

I walked to the bar where the crowd had thinned a bit, took a last sip of beer and set my empty glass down. I looked toward the table where Lydia and Quincy sat, engrossed in conversation. At that moment Quincy reached out and put a hand on Lydia's wrist.

After I talked with a couple of guys at the bar for a while, I went to get Lydia. She looked up at me. "Sit, sit," she said, waving her hand in a downward motion.

"Let me buy you and Lydia a beer," Quincy offered, smiling.

"We've had our two-beer limit tonight," I said, "and we should probably get going."

"Why, we just got here." Lydia looked at her watch. "Oh, for goodness sakes!"

Quincy looked at his watch and laughed, then gave Lydia a soft-eyed look. "It *does* seem like we just started talking. I can't believe it's been almost an hour. I wish you could meet my mother. I know you two would hit it off. Maybe we could have dinner sometime."

"Why, yes. I'd like that." Lydia took a Ministry business card from her purse, wrote her phone number on the back and handed it to Quincy.

As I drove to the Windmill Cafe, Lydia talked non-stop about Quincy. "He grew up in Iowa and New Jersey and Wisconsin. His father was a minister. He's Christian Reformed."

"What does he do?"

"He's a carpenter. Does odd jobs for people."

"Sounds like you two really hit it off."

"Yes. He's such a nice boy."

"Is he married or has he been married?"

"No, never, which surprises me. He's had a couple of girlfriends, but the first went to South America as a missionary and was killed in an automobile accident there. The other woman died of breast cancer. Poor man."

I should have been happy that Lydia was excited about meeting an interesting man who seemed to be bringing out her maternal instincts. So why my uneasiness?

* * *

Thursday: week three, day six.

Jackie was off on Thursdays. After lunch we lingered at the table. She listened as I assured her again I hadn't told anyone other than Blaine about her pregnancy and her considering an abortion.

She agreed that neither Blaine nor Sheila would say anything to anyone.

"Could the counselor have let something slip to someone?" I asked.

"I called her this morning. She swears she didn't and I believe her. I also checked with my boss yesterday, since he gave me the referral to Planned Parenthood. He, too, swears he didn't let it slip. Then I called John and gave him a piece of my mind. I asked him who told him. He insisted it was confidential, like he said to you."

"What about the bug on the phone? Did you call Planned Parenthood from here or say anything to anyone else on the phone?"

"I called to make the appointment from my office. I didn't say anything on our home phone to anyone."

With Andy at the sitter's a short time later, Jackie and I went to Planned Parenthood for our second counseling session. Jackie came out clearly in the session for the first time: she wanted to get the abortion. She'd wrestled with her demons in the previous weeks and was prepared to deal with whatever emotions she experienced after the abortion. I was still not okay with it. We were stuck.

"Abortions are still illegal in most States, including Michigan," the counselor said. "So the vast majority of women get dangerous illegal abortions at the hands of amateurs. Some States now make an exception for rape or incest, and some if the mother's life is in danger. The best option for you, Jackie, would be to get a legal abortion in New York State. I can give you a referral. It would be best to get it done within the next five or six weeks and the sooner, the better."

"There is one thing I'm clear about, Jacks," I said, turning to her. "John's threat to me in his phone call is irrelevant."

"Thanks. That means a lot. I'm willing to give you a little more time, but you have to work it out soon."

"I appreciate your holding off while I try to wrap my mind around this," I said.

* * *

When I picked up Lydia that night, an older Ford pick-up truck was parked in front of her house. I pulled in behind it and peeped the horn. I waited a few minutes, then went to the door. I rang the bell and walked in. Quincy got up from a chair, setting aside the newspaper he'd been reading.

"Hi, Rob. Good to see you again. Come on in."

Frankly, I was shocked. Lydia had just met him the night before. "I'm surprised to see you here," I said carefully. "Where's Lydia?"

"She's almost ready to go out with you. I came for dinner, and time got away from us. Have a seat. She'll be out in a few minutes."

I sat on the edge of the couch.

"There's some coffee left in the pot."

"No, I'm fine."

Quincy settled back into the easy chair he'd been sitting in and put his feet up on the footstool. "So, Rob, Lydia tells me you're a Christian Reformed minister. What led you to work at the Street Ministry after seminary? I mean, obviously, you felt called to work there, but tell me more."

I told him briefly of my inner city internship in Chicago between my middle and last year of seminary and about going out on night ministry with Blaine several times in my last year. I was impatient for Lydia to come. I heard her puttering around in her bedroom. Quincy seemed perfectly at home, a host entertaining his guest. He had no business acting that way in Lydia's house.

Get a grip on yourself, I thought.

"Lydia says your dad was a CRC minister," I said. "What was his first name?"

"Klaas. But he went by Case."

"Case De Weerd," I said. "Doesn't ring a bell."

"He died when I was fourteen."

"And your mother?"

"She's living in Racine, Wisconsin. She has some heart issues. She's eighty-nine."

At that moment, Lydia came into the living room. "I see you and Quincy have had a chance to get acquainted. I'm ready to go unless you want to chat with him some more."

I stood and moved to the door. "Let's hit the streets."

Lydia turned to Quincy who took his time getting to his feet. "Guess I'd better get going then." He gave Lydia a hug. "Thanks for the wonderful dinner. Tomorrow night will be my turn. But I'll spare you my limited cooking talents, and we'll go to a restaurant."

"See you about 6:00," Lydia said and ushered us out.

I sat behind the steering wheel as Quincy pulled his truck away from the curb. I looked at Lydia. "Did you have a nice dinner with the guy?"

Lydia bristled. "The guy? What's with you? Quincy is a perfect gentleman. I'd think you'd be happy that I have a new friend. He deserves a little mothering."

"Sorry. Guess I'm just in a bad mood." Maybe the conflict with Jackie about her pregnancy was clouding my perspective.

Lydia was prickly with me all night as we made our ministry rounds. I couldn't say I blamed her. I had no basis for my negative feelings about Quincy. We were both preoccupied as well. All we could talk about between our stops was the Getaway trouble, even though we didn't visit the bar.

When I pulled Night Watch to the curb to drop Lydia off at the end of our evening, she said, "Even though we're not following Van anymore and have no new leads on the case, how about if I drive my car tomorrow night. That way we're prepared."

"Sounds good," I said. I couldn't bring myself to apologize again about my attitude toward Quincy.

Lydia got out of the car and shut the door without saying good-bye.

CHAPTER 28

Friday: the end of the third week.

I woke late morning remembering a wonderful dream of camping in the mountains. I lay in bed and thought about our trip to Yellowstone and the Tetons earlier in the summer. I recalled the smell of the pines and the breath-taking vista of the majestic Teton peaks.

After staff meeting later, at which Lydia said almost nothing, I asked her if she wanted to talk.

"I just have some things on my mind," she said and left the building.

I worried it was something about Quincy. I worried about Rochelle and Georgina. I breathed a prayer that the dancers would be found soon, that Georgina, against all odds, would still be alive. With my mind's eye I gazed at the Tetons and breathed deeply. It wasn't enough to loosen the knot in my stomach.

* * *

That evening I pulled up behind Quincy's pickup in front of Lydia's house a little before 8:00. He was mowing the front lawn with a push mower. That was really nice, wasn't it? So why did I want to tell him to get lost?

As I got out of the car, Quincy wiped his forehead with the back of his hand and waved.

"Lydia's inside," he said. "Go on in."

I don't need your permission, I thought. I nodded at Quincy, ran up the steps, rang the doorbell and walked in. "Hi, Lydia. It's me."

"I'm in the kitchen."

I found her washing dishes. I grabbed a towel and started drying. "I thought Quincy was taking you out for dinner. Did you eat here instead?"

"Yes. We wanted more privacy to talk, and things are a little tight for Quincy right now."

"You haven't adopted him, have you?" I asked, grinning. "Given him the spare bedroom?"

Lydia drained the sink and dried her hands before giving me a look I couldn't read. "Like I said, he's going through a hard patch. I want to help him a little if I can."

I scrambled for something to say as I dried the last plate. "Well, at least you don't have to mow the lawn." Lame. Maybe he really was like a son to her. Still, it was awfully fast.

Lydia said nothing.

"You don't know him very well," I said. "Are you sure this is wise?"

She glared at me. "Don't lecture me. Quincy has had a rough life. He deserves my help."

"Okay. I'll say no more. Ready to hit the streets?"

"Quincy is pretty upset about some things. He hasn't had a friend to really talk with for a long time. Do you mind awfully if I skip it tonight?"

"We were going to take your car, just in case."

Lydia said nothing.

I forced myself to smile. "Okay. Quincy's lucky to have such a good listener."

"I *am* lucky, aren't I?" I hadn't heard him come in.

I made as graceful an exit as I could and headed downtown. Lydia was a mature woman with way more life experience than I. The problem was I did not trust Quincy. True, he seemed the perfect gentleman, charming, polite, and considerate.

But he sure moved in on Lydia fast. I prayed that God would protect my ministry partner.

There was nothing I could do about Lydia and Quincy, so I might as well get on with my job. But I hadn't worked alone in ages, almost since Lydia had become my partner a year before.

I drove without conscious decision until I found myself pulling into the police station lot. At the front desk, I told the communications officer I needed to speak with Detective Johnson.

A few minutes later, I found the detective seated at his desk talking on the phone. He wore a ragged look, like his grief was wearing him down more than he might want to admit. He looked up, motioned to one of the chairs and finished his conversation. Kincaid was not at his desk.

"What's on your mind?" Johnson asked.

"I'm worried about Lydia."

Johnson shrugged. "Why come to me?"

I told him about Quincy.

"What do you expect me to do? Lydia's a pretty good judge of character, don't you think?"

"Maybe she's got a blind spot when it comes to this guy. Maybe I'm just being paranoid, but I wonder if you could check him out? I've got a real uneasy feeling about him."

"What's his name?"

"Quincy De Weerd."

"How could you be suspicious of a guy with a good Dutch name like that?" he asked, one eyebrow raised. Then, "If it'll make you feel better, I'll do a little checking."

I left the cop shop with a sense of relief.

I swung by Drop-in so I could see how Nathan was doing since he had been feeling a little under the weather at staff meeting.

"Hey, it's his Eminence himself," Nathan said in his usual bantering tone as he sat on a corner of the front desk. "To what do we owe the honor, Reverend?"

I smiled. "Sounds like you're feeling better," I said.

"Just a cold. I'm fine. Did Lydia prefer Quincy's company to yours tonight?"

"Guess so."

He motioned me to lean closer and said quietly, "Wild Bill told me that they identified a narc. It's Reefer." Reefer was a young man who'd been in the downtown scene for about a month.

"I haven't been able to connect with him," I said. "Thought maybe it was my collar."

"Everybody on staff is having the same experience with Reefer. Wild Bill says Reefer never does drugs with the heads except for smoking a joint a couple of times. He talks like he's so experienced with drugs, but Wild Bill doesn't believe him. He's offered to set up buys, but the heads are putting him off."

"I suppose the heads could be wrong, but I'm inclined to trust Wild Bill's instincts."

"That's not all. Wild Bill followed him. Watched him talk to a Vice cop a couple of times."

"Are the heads going to expose him?"

"Not unless things get too uncomfortable. They'd rather have a narc around they're on to."

The phone rang. Nathan reached back, answered and passed it to me. It was Elliot. "Sorry I was so hard on you last week, Rob. I wonder if we could talk?"

"Sure." I said. "Let me get the phone in my office."

"I'd rather we talked face to face. I'd be glad to come downtown."

We arranged to meet in fifteen minutes at Sadie's Café, a restaurant near the Ministry.

I moved into Drop-in and chatted with the kids for a few minutes. Then I walked to the restaurant where I joined Elliot. He slid his coffee cup closer, wrapped his hands around it as if to warm them, then looked up. "Again, I want to apologize, Rob. I had no business being so rude with you when you pushed me about Benjamin."

"Apology accepted."

"My nerves have been shot with what's going on with Rochelle."

"I understand."

Elliot stirred cream and sugar into his coffee in silence. At last he looked up. "Benny's been around."

"When?"

"Earlier tonight."

"Did you call Detective Johnson and let him know?"

He shook his head.

I took a deep breath. Most of the folks I worked with went out of their way to avoid contact with cops, but why would a caring father whose daughter is missing act this way? I wanted to shake him.

Instead I asked, "What did Benny want?"

"He brought a message from Rochelle." He took an envelope from the inside pocket of his sport coat, removed a folded piece of paper and handed it to me.

"Open it and lay it on the table," I said. At least this one wouldn't have my fingerprints on it.

The message read: "Dad, I'm okay. Don't worry about me. I'm not in any danger. It's like when I went into downtown Seattle by myself because I needed to be alone. Don't try to find me."

When he reached out to take the note back, I put up a hand to stop him. "Leave it. Let's not get any more prints on it. The police will need to see it."

"I was hoping we could keep the police out of it."

"And be charged for interfering with a police investigation? I don't think so." I blew out a breath of air. "Is it Rochelle's writing?"

Elliott nodded.

"I wonder why Rochelle or Benny didn't just call you."

"Benjamin said she's in a safe place, but there's no phone."

"What do you make of the note?" I asked.

He swiped a hand across his eyes. "The thing is that when Rochelle went downtown by herself in Seattle, she was twelve years old. She got lost and some guy tried to pick her up, but two women nearby intervened and the guy took off. The point is that she was in danger."

"You think that's what she's trying to tell you? That she's in danger now?"

Elliot nodded, face grim.

"Okay. Stay put and don't touch the note. I'll call Detective Johnson."

When I returned to the table, I studied the note, then the envelope, which lay next to it. I noticed that a bit of course gray powder had spilled from the envelope onto the table.

"What's that powdery stuff?" I asked. "Looks like it spilled from the envelope."

Elliot grabbed a napkin from the holder on the table and made as if to wipe it up.

"Leave it!" I said sharply. "It might be important."

Elliot hesitated, then set the napkin aside and peered at the powder closely. "I hadn't noticed it. I have no idea what it is."

The waitress came by to refill our cups. A few minutes later, the detective duo arrived. The note had been folded twice and didn't lay quite flat. Kincaid carefully turned the note, his finger tips touching only the edges, so he and Johnson could read it. Johnson asked Elliot what he thought it meant, and Elliot repeated what he'd said to me about Rochelle getting lost in Seattle.

Johnson grunted. "What's that gray powder?"

"I don't know," said Elliot. "Rob asked me about it, too. We just noticed it."

Johnson gave me a searching look. He returned his gaze to Elliot. "Could the material have gotten into the envelope after Benny gave it to you?"

Elliott seemed to squirm uncomfortably for a second, then tossed up his hands. "Maybe. I just don't know. After Benjamin left, I sat at my kitchen table with it to study it. Sugar? Salt? But it doesn't look white enough."

Kincaid picked the note up carefully and put it in a plastic bag Johnson had taken from his pocket. The detectives put the envelope in a separate bag which Johnson produced. He patted his pockets until Kincaid produced a third bag. Then Johnson used a napkin to brush the powder into that bag. "I assume the envelope and note have your prints on it, Dr. Rietsema," he said.

Elliot nodded.

"And yours, Rob."

I shook my head. "I may be a slow learner, Sid, but eventually I get it."

Johnson rubbed a hand over his chin. "What time did Benjamin give you this?"

"What time did I call you, Rob? About 9:45? Benjamin must have come about 9:00."

"Did he stay for forty five minutes?" asked Johnson.

"No, no. He just stayed a few minutes."

"But you didn't call Rob for another forty minutes or so."

"Um, I wasn't sure what I should do, if anything."

Johnson grunted. "How did Benny seem?"

"Really nervous. Kept pacing and looking out the window," said Elliot.

"Was he driving his car? The 1967 dark green Chevy?" asked Kincaid.

"Yes." Elliot looked toward the windows and the parking lot.

"Why didn't you call us about this immediately, Dr. Rietsema?" asked Kincaid.

"I feel so protective of Benjamin. He's had a rough time the past few years. I didn't want to get him into trouble with the law."

Johnson huffed. "If he abducted Rochelle he *is* in trouble with the law. You have to stop protecting him, Dr. Rietsema."

Elliot fidgeted and nodded. "I know, I know. Rob told me the same thing. I'm telling you everything I can think of. I apologize for not calling you right away."

"Anything else?" Johnson looked from Elliot to me, and we both shook our heads.

"Anyways," he said, "we've got an A.P.B. out on Benny along with a description of his car. Next time, call us right away, Doctor Rietsema."

When Johnson and Kincaid left, Elliot said, "I should get going, too." He put money on the table. When I reached for my wallet he said, "No, no. I've got it. Keep her in your prayers. And Benjamin, too."

I walked out of the restaurant with him. In the lot I said, "By the way, aside from Benny, do you still do some private tutoring with students?"

His head jerked a fraction. "Why? What's that got to do with anything?"

"Nothing. I just remember the reputation you had among us seminary students."

He took a small step back. "Reputation?"

"For always being there for your students, especially the ones having a hard time."

"Oh. Yes, I still do the occasional one-on-one. Mostly I have a small group of students over at the house like I did with you."

We shook hands, and I walked to my car. I didn't get in right away. I was brooding about the gray powder. Maybe it didn't mean anything. But Rochelle was a smart cookie. Could it be another message? Elliot's reluctance to involve the police in finding Rochelle baffled me. Was he more protective of Benny than his own daughter? I stood at my car, lost in thought.

My asking about the tutoring had popped out unplanned, but I wondered if Elliot might have had inappropriate relationships with any of his students. I didn't know what to make of his reaction, but he certainly seemed uneasy. I remembered a few of my classmates who'd said they were getting private tutoring with Elliot. At the time, it had just increased the professor's esteem in my eyes. Was it my preoccupation with Total Depravity that made me wonder about Elliott's relationships with his students? I remembered Lydia encouraging me to use that preoccupation as I tried to figure out the Getaway trouble.

I hit the Alibi, and then Partners where I talked with a gay couple for half an hour about their fear of being found out, especially in their respective churches. One was Reformed and the other Baptist.

The couple had left and I was about to move on when I saw Van come in the front door. The bar was across the street from his shop. The bouncer, the bar tender and a few customers greeted him in a familiar fashion. The bartender poured him a ginger ale and Van put a bill on the bar. Then, with a look of concern, the bar tender motioned toward Van's face. It looked as if Van was explaining about his beating. After a few minutes the bar tender pointed in my direction, and Van turned to look. He picked up his glass, walked to my table. He lowered himself into a chair with a wince. The arm with the cast was in a sling, and he rested the cast on the table. His face was a Halloween mask of black, purple and yellow.

"I'm surprised you're here," I said.

"You mean here at Partners? I'm friends with the guy who runs the place. How about you? This one of your regular haunts?"

I nodded. "Actually, I meant I'm surprised you're up and about after your beating."

"I was going stir-crazy, but I'm not sure coming over here was too smart. I'm still pretty sore. Anything new regarding Rochelle?"

I told him about the note Benny had delivered to Elliot. I didn't mention the powder.

Van frowned. "The time Rochelle got lost in Seattle, she was in serious danger. She was too young to run off like that, but she was always precocious."

"Elliot told me about the time in Seattle," I said.

Van grimaced as he shifted in his chair. "It's driving me nuts. I just wish we could find her." He swallowed the last of his ginger ale, then stood and left the bar.

I followed him out the front door, then drove to the Getaway. There were lots of cars parked on the street in front of the night club. Looked like a busy night. I didn't see any open spaces. Then I noticed a green Chevy a few cars ahead of me. It slowed as it passed the bar but did not pull in. Benny? If he was still driving his car and the cops had a description, why hadn't he been picked up yet?

One of the cars between the Chevy and my car turned at the corner. Instead of following it toward the lot behind the bar, I kept going. Now there was only one car between the Chevy and me. I dropped back a little.

When the Chevy turned left toward the river I slowed again. I wished my car didn't stick out like a sore thumb. I was irritated that Lydia and I were not following in her car. I made the left turn and spotted taillights about a block ahead. I continued following, maintaining the interval between us. When the car turned right I kept going straight. The danger of being spotted, if it was Benny, was too great for me to stay on his tail.

When I reached Butterworth, I turned right. I saw the taillights of a car a few blocks ahead. I speeded up till half a block separated us. To my surprise, it was the green Chevy again. I slowed down. The Chevy turned right and I kept going, my heart beating rapidly.

I turned left, circled the block and headed back toward the Getaway. I was nosy, but not suicidal. As I turned right to reach the lot behind the bar, I glanced into my rearview mirror and watched what looked like the car I'd been following move slowly through the intersection, not following me toward the lot. Was Benny now checking on me?

I felt sweat trickling down my sides. Instead of pulling into the Getaway lot, I kept going, intending to circle the block. I wanted to report the suspicious vehicle to Johnson. Now that

I thought about it, the quickest way to do that would be by phoning from the bar rather than going to the police station. I debated. Suddenly the headlights of the car moving toward me in the other lane jerked into my lane. I braked and swerved to the curb. A green Chevy. Another car screeched to a stop behind me, close enough to prevent my backing up.

Benny was at my door before I could collect my thoughts. As I punched the horn, he pulled my door open, reached in and released the seat belt as the sound of the horn continued to pierce the night air. He grabbed my shirt and yanked me out of the car. Then he slammed me back against it so hard that I expelled the air in my lungs with a grunt.

He leaned close to my ear, his voice a whisper. "Leave it alone, Reverend Vander Laan. This does not concern you. You get one warning." Then he pulled my little plastic collar out of my shirt and tapped it against my nose. "Next time I will shove this down your throat. That's not a metaphor." He put the collar in my shirt pocket.

Then, confirming my suspicion that he was questionable pre-seminary material, he slammed me against the car again. This time I yelped as my head snapped back against the roof and my shoulders banged against the window.

looked across the desk in the Detective Bureau at my favorite G.R.P.D. detective. The front of my neck was sore, and I had a lump on the back of my head the size of a walnut. I felt slightly dizzy and nauseated. My head was beginning to ache. I'd made my report about following Benny and about his less-than-subtle warning that I back off.

Johnson closed his eyes and rubbed his hand across his face. "You followed him with your *inconspicuous* wheels? That was really using your head!"

I could justify myself by blaming Lydia's preoccupation with Quincy which had prevented us from using her car. I thought better of it and said nothing.

Johnson scowled. "Will you file an assault charge on Benny?"

"Seems kind of minor compared with possible kidnapping and murder charges," I said.

"Thing is, it would be easy to pick Benny up and hold him for assault while we continue to make our case. We already got a warrant on him for his assault on Van, and Van is willing to testify. But it would make a better case if you filed a complaint too."

Kincaid came around to sit on the front corner of his desk. With a deadpan expression, he said, "What my partner is suggesting has to do with witness credibility, and *you*, as an upstanding member of the community and highly respected member of the clergy with no hint of scandal and a reputation beyond reproach—"

I held up both hands to stop Kincaid and gave a short bark of a laugh. I winced as the pain shot through my shoulders and neck. Kincaid had never teased me before. "If you think it might help, I'll press charges."

It was after 1:00 when I made my way through the lobby of the Hall of Justice and bumped into a *West Michigan Times* reporter I knew. He'd been gathering information for a piece on a robbery of a liquor store earlier that night. He wondered why I was there, and I told him.

When I got home, I woke Jackie so she could do her nurse thing with me. She examined me carefully as I sat on the toilet seat in the bathroom and told her what happened.

"Describe the pain," she said, looking at me with what might have been a mix of worry and irritation in her eyes.

"My neck is really sore, front and back. The back of my shoulders and upper back hurt. Even my upper arms are sore. And I have a corker of a headache."

She felt the bump on the back of my head. "This is a rotten time for you to be playing detective," she said. "As if I don't have enough on my mind with the pregnancy."

"I know," I said. Then, trying to lighten the mood, "First time I've received treatment from a beautiful nurse in a nightie. I like it. What's your medical opinion?"

She looked at me severely. "You have a bump on your head and a sore neck and back brought on by your extreme nosiness and delusions of being a detective. Take two aspirin and go to bed. Don't call me in the morning."

At least her diagnosis and advice were free—unless she made me pay later. And she might.

* * *

Saturday: The beginning of week four for Georgina.

I awoke late morning, turning over with a groan. Jackie was quietly putting clean laundry in her chest of drawers. "Take two more aspirin," she said.

I got up and took the aspirin. I thought about returning to bed, but the idea of a hot shower was too inviting to resist. I took a long one that felt as good as I'd anticipated.

When I got down to the kitchen, Jackie and Andy were already at the table.

"Mama made goulash for lunch," said Andy through a mouthful.

I gave him a hug, getting goulash on my cheek. I wiped it off with a napkin, kissed Jackie and sat down. I tried to keep from turning my head too much.

Jackie looked me over, then said to Andy, "Your daddy needs a little T.L.C. He got hurt last night."

Andy jumped off his chair to come around and give me another hug. "Where did you get hurt, Daddy?" he asked.

I took his hand and placed it lightly over the bump on the back of my head.

"That's a big goose egg, Daddy. I had one like that once when Ronnie hit me with his bat. Were you being nosey again, like that time you got stitches? Want to borrow my magnifying glass?"

"Don't think I'll need it, but thanks for the hug. Better get back on your chair, Mr. Man, and finish your lunch."

Andy jumped back on his chair, nearly knocking it over.

Jackie got up and served me goulash and a glass of milk. Normally, I'd do it myself, so it was clearly Jackie's T.L.C.

I was taking care of my dishes when the phone rang. Jackie got it. "Your mother."

Here we go again, I thought. Mother had no doubt heard of my assault through the Dutch grapevine since the Saturday paper wasn't out yet.

I went into the dining room and took the phone from Jackie.

"Robbie, you were beat up? Are you okay? Are you playing detective again? It's got something to do with those people at the awful go bar or whatever you call it, doesn't it?"

Instead of answering all Mother's questions or picking one, I followed our usual script and asked my own. "How did you hear?"

At least her answer was rather straightforward and simple. "A gal who works at the West Michigan Times called her mother in our church. You don't need to know who it was." Sometimes the word traveled through several people before getting to my parents. Truth was, I was always a bit spooked by the Dutch grapevine.

Might as well go to my next line. "Dad on the other phone?"

"How are you doing, son?"

"I'm okay, Dad. The guy just roughed me up a bit. I've got a bump on my head. My neck and back are sore."

Mother said, "I'm sorry to say it again, but that ministry is too dangerous for you, Robbie. I'm not saying you have to take a church, but maybe you could think about becoming a hospital chaplain."

"How about a prison chaplain?" I asked.

"Well, at least the criminals you'd work with there would be behind bars."

Suddenly I envied Dad with his Christian Reformed world of rules and certainties and low physical risk. But I'd seen too much, changed too much, to picture myself in a typical Christian Reformed Church. I felt a weight of sadness.

Andy was standing at my elbow, pulling on my arm.

"Andy wants to talk to you," I said. "Here he is."

Andy took the phone. "Hi Gramma. Hi Grampa. Daddy got hurt because he was being nosey again. He got a bump on his head like I did." Andy went on with his story about his own bump on the head.

Later, my sister called from Iowa. The grapevine to her had been quite circuitous. Plus she'd gotten a call from Mother. Jackie's folks called to make sure I was okay. Elliot called, apologizing again for not calling the police right after Benny had given him the note from Rochelle, blaming himself for my assault. Finally and surprisingly, a call from Van. He couldn't still be tuned in to the grapevine, could he? Perhaps the Saturday paper was out already, though we usually got ours the middle of the afternoon.

After lunch and a nap, I was sitting in the living room thinking about Lydia and Quincy and worrying about Rochelle and Georgina when Jackie opened the front door to pick up the newspaper. She returned to the living room and set the paper in front of me as the phone rang.

I checked the local section. There was a short article: STREET MINISTER ASSAULTED NEAR GO-GO BAR.

The great clergy witness with the impeccable credentials, as Kincaid had pointed out.

When Jackie picked up the phone, I mouthed to her, "I'm gone."

She shook her head at me. "Here he is," she said, and held the phone toward me.

It was Johnson. "I got some information on this Quincy. Want me to give it to you over the phone?"

That reminded me about the bug on the phone. It might be better if I ran downtown to see him, but, with my sore neck, I didn't want to drive more than I had to. I gave a mental shrug. "Shoot."

"The guy's got a record here for burglary and petty theft. Likes to prey on older single ladies—becomes friends with them, gets them to give him money. Locked up for three months at Kent County a couple of years ago. Arrested a couple of other times, but his lady friends decided not to press charges. Lives back and forth between here and Madison, Wisconsin, where he grew up. Well, actually a little town outside of Madison."

I scribbled furiously on the pad by the phone. "Any record on the other side of the Lake?"

"Same kinds of stuff. Seems he likes to leave restaurants and gas stations without paying. Sometimes he sneaks into a motel room in the morning after the guest leaves and sleeps there. He gets out by check-out time, unless he politely requests late check out by phone from the room. His busts have been small-time. Cop I talked to in Madison knows him well. Says he's really slick. You better warn Lydia."

"I intend to."

Johnson grunted. "If he pulls any of this crap with Lydia, I want to know about it. You hear me?"

I holed up for a while in my study on the easy chair and pondered how to approach the matter with Lydia. Finally, I went downstairs and talked it over with Jackie.

"I'm sure Lydia will be angry with me for checking up on Quincy," I said. "Think it will be an unforgivable sin?"

Jackie looked thoughtful. "Probably not. She'd be more likely never to forgive you if you don't tell her and she gets ripped off by this jerk and badly hurt emotionally."

I decided the best way to approach it was directly. *Give me wisdom*, I prayed, *or, short of that, help me not say anything really stupid.* I dialed her number.

As I listened to the phone ringing, I wondered why I hadn't gotten a call from her about Benny roughing me up the previous night. In fact, I resented it. If she'd been with me and we were in her car, it might not have happened. Was she too busy with Quincy to read her newspaper?

Finally she picked up. "Hey, a good afternoon to you, Rob. Bet you're wondering if I'll be going out with you tonight. Well, I'm planning on it. Quincy got a lot off his chest last night. Good thing I stayed home with him."

"Is he there now?" I asked.

"No. He borrowed my car after taking his truck to the shop. Had to see a couple of people about possible jobs."

"You let him drive your car?" Lydia's 1957 Chevy coupe was grey and white. Or, as she had corrected me once, Inca Silver and Imperial Ivory. Her husband had kept it in pristine condition while he was alive. With the help of her brother-in-law, Lydia did the same. As far as I knew, no one else besides her brother-in-law was allowed to drive it. When I'd asked to get behind the wheel once, she'd refused. I considered pointing that out, thought better of it.

Lydia let out an exasperated sound. "What is it with you? Can't you give Quincy a break?"

"Sorry, Lydia. Did you happen to see the paper this morning?"

"No. The paper boy must have forgotten to leave one. I even checked the porch roof and the bushes. Maybe someone walked off with it. That reminds me that I have to call him about it. Something about the Getaway in the paper?"

"Not exactly. Can you have coffee with me this afternoon? I need to discuss something with you."

"Can't it wait till tonight?"

"I'd rather not wait."

"Come over now. I'll put coffee on."

"Um, what time do you expect Quincy to get back?"

"He should be back in a little while." Then in her cranky voice, "Why?"

I took a breath. "Could we go out for coffee? I'd like to talk with you in private."

"Oh, for Pete's sake. If Quincy's in the living room and we're in the kitchen, that's not private enough?"

"No. Sorry, Lydia."

Finally, she said, "Be here at three. But I want to be back by 4:00. Quincy and I have plans."

On the drive to Lydia's, I winced each time I had to turn my head, and I couldn't turn it very far. I rang Lydia's bell, half expecting Quincy to have returned early and to usher me in. Instead, Lydia came to the door.

"We can stay here," she said. "Quincy's got another call to make and probably won't be back till suppertime."

I stayed on the porch. "I'd rather go to Burger Joint in case he comes back early." The chain had a restaurant a few blocks away.

Lydia shook her head in irritation.

Five minutes later, we were seated at Burger Joint. We'd said nothing to each other on the way over. I had the local section of the newspaper folded under my arm. I opened it and placed it on the table for Lydia to see. I pointed to the article on my assault by Benny. I was shamelessly trying to soften her up before broaching the subject of Quincy.

She read for a moment, then looked at me, her jaw dropping. "I had no idea. Are you okay?"

I assured her I was, then added, for a little more softening. "Well, I'm pretty sore yet. He slammed me around really hard."

Her brow furrowed in concern. "What a day not to get the paper. Oh, I called the paper boy, and he said he'd seen it land on the porch but he'd bring another."

I wondered if Quincy had anything to do with the missing newspaper, not wanting her to see the article about me. *Hey*, I reminded myself, *not everything is about you.* I'd scanned the rest of the paper at my house earlier and couldn't think of anything else in it Quincy wouldn't want Lydia to see. Maybe her idea of someone coming by and snatching it was right.

"Guess you need your sidekick with you for night ministry." She grinned. "You have a way of getting into serious trouble by yourself." Then she sobered. "Oh. We were supposed to take my car last night. Benny probably wouldn't have recognized us, and I'd have had my gun. I am really sorry."

Exactly what I'd thought earlier and knew was wrong. "I made my own decision to follow Benny. It's not your fault," I said, and I meant it.

I sipped my coffee, putting off as long as possible delivering my news about Quincy.

Finally Lydia spoke. "Is this why you wanted to talk to me? Why would you care if Quincy heard us talk about this?"

I studied my coffee cup.

"It's not about you getting banged up." Her cranky voice again. "It's about Quincy, isn't it?"

Finally I dropped my shoulders, looked at her and reported all I'd learned from Johnson.

Lydia sat in silence. As her eyes narrowed and her jaw set, I imagined smoke rising from the top of her head. Her eyes seemed to shoot sparks.

That went well, I congratulated myself. *Won't Quincy be in for a nasty surprise when he finds he's on Lydia's shit list.*

Her explosion took me by surprise. "You went to Detective Johnson behind my back." she yelled.

I tried to look around furtively and winced with the pain. Fortunately there were only a few other customers in the restaurant. All were looking in our direction, as were the three employees behind the counter. I waited for the rest of the outburst. I didn't have to wait long.

"And I thought we were friends. Not just co-workers." Her voice was a notch quieter, but, if anything, more intense. "You're the one who likes to preach about accepting people and not judging them. You hypocrite!" Her voice was rising again.

I forced myself to keep looking Lydia in the eye.

"It will undoubtedly surprise you that Quincy's trouble with the law is exactly what he talked about with me last night. He's seeing a counselor and turning his life around. If you think I'm going to abandon him now, you're nuts."

She got up abruptly and stalked out of the restaurant.

I didn't follow her, knowing she would only insist on walking the few blocks to her house. I wondered when she'd be ready to talk to me again. If she ever would. I felt like the lowest life form on the planet. Maybe Quincy really *was* turning his life around. Who was I to judge him so harshly?

After supper later, I was reading to Andy from *Treasure Island* when Jackie came into his bedroom to say that Lydia was on the phone.

Lydia's voice sounded tense. "Quincy isn't back yet with my car. He phoned from Holland just now. Said he'd called on a potential customer there and then stopped at a pay phone to call his mother in Racine. He found out his mom had a serious heart attack. He really sounded scared. Well, I told him to drive on to Wisconsin and call me when he knew the situation there. But after what you told me, I'm starting to worry."

The son-of-a-bitch, I thought. I was livid. Then I reigned myself in. *What if his mom really did have a heart attack? Well, why not find out?*

"Give me fifteen minutes," I said, "to see what I can learn, and I'll get back to you." I hung up without explaining and dialed directory assistance. I asked for Racine, Wisconsin, then for a listing for Mrs. Klaas or Case De Weerd. I was guessing that if she had a listing, she would use her deceased husband's name. Bingo. I took down the number. If I didn't reach Quincy's mom, I'd call area hospitals.

The phone was answered after the third ring.

"Is this Mrs. De Weerd?"

"Yes, it is. Who's calling, please?"

I introduced myself and could hear her voice shift to a more open and trusting tone when she learned I was a Christian Reformed minister. I told her I was acquainted with her son, Quincy.

"Oh, dear. Is he in trouble again?"

I suspected trouble was a way of life for him. "I'm calling because Quincy heard that you had a heart attack. If you're okay, I'd like to reassure him when I see him."

"Why, yes. I'm fine. I have an irregular heartbeat that bothers me occasionally. To tell you the truth, that's not as much of a problem as my bowels. I can get tied up for days. And my arthritis! Why sometimes I can hardly walk. It can get so damp here. Although it would be worse in Michigan. You have so many grey rainy days there. At times I hurt so much I can't sleep. I just sit up in my easy chair and read the Bible. Say, did you know my husband, Reverend Case De Weerd?"

I pounced on my chance to end the conversation and get back to Lydia. "No, I didn't. I just graduated from seminary a couple years ago. Well, thanks Mrs. De Weerd. I have to run. It was good talking to you, and when I see Quincy I'll tell him you're fine."

"Thanks, Reverend Vander Laan. Tell that boy to call me."

I phoned Lydia back and reported. There was a moment of silence on the line. When I couldn't stand it any longer, I asked, "Are you okay?"

"Yes. No. I don't know what to do."

"Let's tell Sid."

"No! I'm too humiliated."

"It's not your fault. Quincy is an expert manipulator. He's got it down to a science."

"I feel so stupid."

"He's. Got. Your. Car."

That got through to her. "Tell Detective Johnson I want my car back!"

I called Johnson. He suspected Quincy kept his leeching confined to the familiar territory of the eastern and western shore areas of Lake Michigan. Johnson told me he would notify appropriate law enforcement agencies.

When I called Lydia again, she sounded more like her old self. "Sorry I unloaded on you this afternoon. You still want me for a night ministry partner?"

Thank you, God.

» CHAPTER 30

"My money's on Reefer." said Lydia.

We were back at Burger Joint near Lydia's before beginning night ministry. I'd told her that the heads had identified the police drug informant in the downtown scene. I smiled. "Sounds like you were on to him, too," I said.

"He had 'narc' written all over him." She looked up and waved. "Here come the detectives. They obviously spotted your car again."

I turned to see Johnson lumbering toward us with Kincaid following. I slid over in the booth, and he sat down next to me. Lydia moved over, too, but Kincaid remained standing.

"We stopped to see if Quincy contacted you again, Lydia," said Johnson.

"No. I'm afraid he really had me buffaloed."

"Refrain from being too harsh with yourself," said Kincaid. "Mister De Weerd has great expertise in deceiving people. We'll find him."

Lydia's face reflected gratitude before darkening several degrees. "He's got my car. I'm so mad I could spit nickels!"

"We'll get your car back," said Johnson. "Law enforcement all along the Lake are looking for it. Did he take anything else from you?"

"Nothing aside from a little of my dignity and time."

"You've checked your valuables?"

"I don't have much of anything worth stealing, except for my car. I told that man how much it means to me."

As Johnson stood to leave, I asked, "By the way, Sid, find out about that powdery stuff yet."

"We've got a pretty good idea on it."

I waited a moment, then said, "We'll give our word not to tell anyone, right, Lydia."

"It might help us help you," she said.

Johnson looked from one of us to the other, brow furrowed.

Kincaid shot his partner a look, probably cautioning him not to say anything further.

"Nope," said Johnson. "You're liable to go barging into another dangerous situation, not to mention doing something to blow the case."

Lydia pulled back in her seat. "Give us a little credit for common sense here, Detective."

"I don't mean to offend, Lydia," said Johnson, "but sometimes common sense takes a back seat to your nosiness."

Lydia huffed.

"What about an exchange of information?" I asked. Johnson sat back down. "I could give you a tidbit, unofficially. In confidence, shall we say? It's something your vice cops will be interested in."

He gave me a long hard look, long enough for me to have severe reservations about my proposal. Finally, he said. "You go first. I decide if it's good enough."

I plunged on. "Everybody in the downtown scene knows who your narc is."

He frowned and pursed his lips. "Who is this supposed narc?"

"He goes by Reefer." I didn't dare look at Lydia.

"Cute nickname," she said.

I breathed a little sigh of relief, knowing she and I were on the same page.

The detective squinted for a moment and pulled on his nose, then spoke quietly. "You didn't hear this from me. The powder is gypsum."

Kincaid sighed.

"From the plaster mines," I said. The mill, where they turned the gypsum into powder for plaster and wallboard, was on Butterworth Drive, a short distance beyond where I'd followed Benny.

"Was it pure gypsum," asked Lydia, "or were there additives in the sample."

Johnson's brows shot up as did mine. "The sample was pure," he said.

"Oh, Lordy!" exclaimed Lydia quietly. "Benny could be holding Rochelle and Georgina in the gypsum mines!"

This time Johnson's jaw dropped a bit. Kincaid closed his eyes and rubbed a hand across his face.

"Even if Benny is holding them in the mines," said Johnson, "there are miles of tunnels underneath the city. Then there's the old gypsum plant to search. We *are* working on it. And don't you two even think about going into the mines," he growled.

When Johnson and Kincaid left, I leaned forward, winced with the pain in my neck and sat back again carefully. "You obviously know something about the gypsum mines?"

"Oh, yes." Lydia rubbed her hands together and her eyes shone. "A good friend of my late husband worked in the mines. When we visited as couples, Titus would tell stories about people disappearing in the tunnels and awful things happening down there. He was just teasing me but my husband would listen intently, as if he believed every word, and then laugh his head off and clap when Titus got to the end of a story. Titus claimed the mines were haunted."

"Did you learn any *facts* about the mines from Titus?"

"Well, if I can sort out fact from fiction, he said the Indians knew about the gypsum beds on Plaster Creek when whites first settled here. The first mill for grinding gypsum was built in the 1840s."

"Do you know how deep the mines run?"

Lydia frowned. "Titus said it varies from fifty to over a hundred feet, depending on the surface features. There are huge rooms down there, carved out of solid rock. The miners left lots of rock columns to support the roof. In the area by the plaster mill, there were three or four seams thick enough to mine. When number two seam played out, the slope was extended down to number four seam which was under and parallel to the old workings."

I hated mines. I took a deep breath, tried to relax and plunged on. "How do they get the gypsum to the surface?"

"In the old workings, mules used to haul the rock out in mine cars on tracks. The mules rarely came out of the mines and went blind over time. The mules were eventually replaced with electric locomotives like the old street cars. In the newer workings, they use shuttle cars and belt conveyors to get the rock to the surface. They've got electric lights along the main haulage ways and power for the mining equipment. There's a shop, an office and a lunch room for the workers down there."

I was amazed at how much Lydia knew about the mines, but my stomach was in a knot and I felt sweat dripping down my side.

"So the rock is grey?" I asked.

"Pure gypsum is white. The rock in this area is marbled with impurities which makes it grey after it's ground. The closer to the surface it is, the more colorful it is. Titus showed me a piece with shades of red, pink, yellow and brown that he'd polished. It was crystalline and translucent. It was so beautiful you wouldn't have believed it was gypsum."

"Must be cold down there," I said with a shiver.

"According to Titus, temperatures are in the mid-fifties year around."

"And they make plaster from the gypsum. That's why they're also called plaster mines, right?"

"Right. Gypsum wallboard and lath are also made at the plant," said Lydia. "but there are many other uses for gypsum. It's even used in toothpaste."

Finally I asked the question I'd been avoiding and wasn't sure I wanted the answer to. "How do you get into the mines?"

"Took you long enough to get the real question. The original entry road at the processing plant goes under Butterworth Drive and slopes down to the mine opening. There's also an air shaft which can be used to enter or you can use the newer portal. Titus said the entrance locations are highly classified, and my husband and I weren't cleared for that information. He said that if he told us, he'd have to kill us."

I forced a smile, gazed off into the distance, shivered again, before returning my attention to Lydia.

She was giving me a squinty-eyed look. "You've been playing with your beard ever since we started talking about the gypsum mines. You look like you've seen a ghost and you're sweating. I've never seen you look so nervous. What's up?"

I squirmed in my seat, looked away from Lydia's scrutiny. I wanted to run. Forget about the missing dancers. If the girls were in the mines, the cops could find them. I didn't want to think about the time I was trapped in the mine, but I couldn't think of anything to say to deflect Lydia's question.

Lydia reached across the table and grasped my hand. "You always tell people they'll feel better if they talk about what's bothering them. Heaven knows you tell me often enough."

I heaved a sigh, thinking I might as well tell Lydia, get it over with. Then leave the Getaway trouble to the cops.

"I've never told anyone, even Jackie," I began. "I was trapped in a mine once when I was a kid."

Lydia's look turned to one of puzzlement. "In a gypsum mine?"

"No, no. It was a gold mine in Montana. I went out to stay for a couple of weeks with my cousin Hank in Churchill just before my seventeenth birthday."

When I didn't say anything more, Lydia nodded, probably sensing my need for encouragement. I realized that if I was going to tell anyone, I couldn't have a better ear than Lydia's.

I took a shaky breath. "It was a hot Friday afternoon. Hank and I and two of his buddies went on a camping trip up in the Gravelly Range near a couple of old mining towns. I remember how beautiful that last stretch of road was—all switchbacks— up to the head of Wigwam Canyon."

I shifted in my seat as the fear in the pit of my stomach intensified. Maybe I'd just tell Lydia I couldn't go any further.

She squeezed my hand, saying nothing. I hadn't realized she was still holding it. My own grip tightened. If I held on hard enough ...

"Dennis and Mooch, Hank's buddies, had taken a couple of cases of beer along. After supper we sat around the camp-fire drinking and telling stories. I'd never had alcohol before. We all got pretty plastered. Then they said they were going to show me a mine they knew about. It wasn't a big deal for them, but it might be fun for me. By the time we set off, it was dusk.

I didn't realize how fast it got dark in the mountains, but I was glad for the two flashlights we had with us."

"Were you scared?" asked Lydia.

"A little. But I was excited, too. I thought it would be fun."

"But it wasn't."

"It only took about ten minutes to reach the mine. We scrambled up the tailings pile. The mine was barricaded with a heavy wooden door secured by a hasp with a wedge-shaped piece of wood through it. Dennis yanked the wedge out, gave me a flashlight and told me to take the lead. When I hesitated Mooch asked if I was chicken. He said they were doing this for me. I took the flashlight, stepped around an old ore cart that lay tipped on its side and moved into the mine."

I tightened my grip on Lydia's hand even more. It was as if I were back in that mine. My hand felt sweaty in Lydia's. She gave me another squeeze.

I forced myself to go on. "As soon as we were all inside, Mooch told me to give him the flashlight so he could show me something. Cousin Hank was quiet. I don't know if he knew what was coming or not. Suddenly I felt a hard shove on my back and went flying forward. I stumbled and fell. I heard the guys running back out of the mine and the door slam shut, the stick jammed into the hasp. When I got to my feet, I couldn't see anything at first. Then I made out faint patches of light coming through the cracks in the door.

"I was more angry than scared. It was totally quiet. Until I stepped toward the entrance. That's when I heard the rattle. There was a rattle snake between me and the door. Why it hadn't struck when I came flying past it, I don't know. I did the most fervent praying of my life. I was petrified. I suspected later that the rattlesnake had slipped into the mine to get out of the heat and probably slithered back out shortly after announcing its presence.

"Anyway, after what seemed like a lifetime, suddenly there was an explosion of sound as the door slammed open, then laughter as the guys returned to let me out."

I loosened my vise-like grip on Lydia's hand. "That's it," I said. I felt bathed in Lydia's look of concern and understanding.

But that wasn't it. There was the piece that really shamed me. I looked at Lydia, silently pleading for her to say something so we could move past this. She must have sensed I wasn't finished. She silently squeezed my hand again.

I looked down at the table, unable to meet her gaze as I said, "When the door banged open, I was so terrified I wet my pants. Dennis noticed it, and they made jokes about it till I went back home."

At last Lydia spoke. "Well, it's no wonder you wet your pants."

I looked up again. I felt the shame retreat to a manageable sensation. We sat in companionable silence.

Finally, I noticed my thoughts moving back to Georgina and Rochelle. "Can you get us to one of the mine entrances?" I asked, suppressing a shiver at the thought of going underground.

She gave me a smug look. "Well, I know where one of the entrances is, but, if I tell you—"

I laughed, winced with the pain in my shoulders and put up a hand.

She leaned forward and lowered her voice to a whisper. "If you swear you won't tell." She didn't wait for me to swear. "The entrance for the public tours is off Judd Street, north of Chicago Drive."

I'd been had. "They give public tours of the mines?"

Lydia smiled. "They stopped mining that area in the mid-forties, and the Michigan Natural Storage Company began using it for cold storage over ten years ago. Lydia shrugged and grinned. "That doesn't seem a likely place to hold the girls, though, because it's too public."

"Clearly, Titus's flair for high drama regarding the mines has rubbed off on you," I said.

Lydia smiled. "Thanks for helping me take my mind off my car and that no good so-and-so."

"And thank *you* for listening to me."

I checked my watch. Almost 9:00. I thought about Rochelle. Was she being held against her will at the plaster mill or somewhere in the mines? Maybe she was hiding out there and sending Benny off on his violent forays. Perhaps we should talk to Titus, if he was still alive. Of course, all I had to do was mention Titus to Johnson, and he could handle it. But he probably had his own sources, and maybe Titus would be more receptive to Lydia, since they were friends.

Lydia stood. "Let's go talk to Titus."

"Hold on a sec." I popped some more of the aspirin I'd taken along and drained my water glass.

Lydia called Titus from the pay phone in the restaurant, let it ring for a while. "No answer," she said, shaking her head and finally replacing the receiver. When she offered to drive my car, I gratefully accepted.

After hitting a number of our usual haunts, she drove to Gus's Getaway. We entered the bar. The cages were empty.

"I don't see any dancers," said Lydia. "They must all be in the dressing room."

The bouncer, sitting at a table near the door with two customers, nodded to us. Ned was arranging some bottles on the counter behind the bar and had his back to us as we approached. When he turned and spotted us, he came over, threw a towel under the bar forcefully and braced his hands on top of the bar.

"What's up, Ned?" I asked.

He closed his eyes for a couple of seconds, then stared at his hands. "Manetta and Lois never showed for work. The detectives just left. Apparently, they suspect foul play. I can't figure out why they got on it so fast, and they wouldn't tell me a thing." When the music changed, we noticed Sadie and Sylvia were in the cages starting their set.

I wondered, too, why the cops would be investigating so soon. "Maybe Manetta and Lois just took off on a lark," I said. "Maybe they're not so dependable." I hoped that was it. I *prayed* that was it.

"Beats me," said Ned. "Can't you two do something about my disappearing dancers? Go find 'em or at least say a prayer. You must have some clout up there," he said, thumb aimed toward the ceiling.

"We'll do what we can," I said.

He moved down the bar to refill an empty glass.

"What say we stop at the police station," I said to Lydia, "and see if we can find out anything about Manetta and Lois."

A few minutes later, as we walked across the lobby, we saw Johnson standing at the counter talking with the officer at the information desk. The detective spotted us and waved for us to follow.

Back in the Detective Bureau, he said, "You heard about Manetta and Lois disappearing. That's why you're here?" Kincaid, sitting at his desk immersed in paper-work, glanced up and nodded at us.

"We just came from the Getaway," I said. "What can you tell us?"

"Not a lot. Manetta's dad called this evening. Said his wife had gone to pick up the girls from their apartment to do some shopping this noon. Their roommate was frantic because Manetta and Lois never came home from work last night."

"That never happened before?" asked Lydia.

"It has, but one of the girls always calls by noon or so. Manetta's father figured they were up to their usual shenanigans and waited to raise a stink till this evening. Manetta's dad's got some leverage with the mayor, so the mayor's leaning on the chief to find the girls. We got on it right after we saw you earlier tonight."

"Learn anything yet?" I asked.

"Just that Manetta and Lois were the last to leave the bar. The bartender locked up, but the dandy duo were having an argument in the parking lot. Manetta told the bartender to go ahead, that they would only be another minute or so. That's the last anybody saw of the young ladies."

"Anything more on the gypsum angle?" asked Lydia.

"We're looking into that. You guys got anything for me?"

I looked at Lydia and shrugged. Carefully.

"Afraid not," she said.

Johnson peered closely, first at me and then at Lydia. "Hard to believe you two haven't done anything since our little information exchange earlier this evening."

"We have a job to do, Detective Johnson," said Lydia. "We're not paid to fight crime."

Johnson grunted. "Anyways, the Vice guys appreciated the heads-up." He raised an eyebrow. "They were pretty surprised."

"That we gave up the info," I asked, "or that everybody is on to Reefer?"

"Both."

» CHAPTER 31

Day two of week four.
I woke late Sunday morning to a quiet house. A note on the bedside table confirmed my hunch that Jackie had gone to church with Andy.

I took a long shower, willing my sore muscles to heal. My headache had lessened, but was still hanging around. I dressed and put on a pot of coffee, then began preparations for dinner. Jackie had already put a pot roast with potatoes, carrots and onions in the oven and it smelled heavenly. I was drinking my second cup of coffee and reading the paper when the phone rang.

It was Lydia. "Detective Johnson called and said that Quincy's been caught. I'm planning to go down and pick up my car this afternoon."

"Where was he caught?"

"Saugatuck. Apparently he was enjoying a little vacation weekend, eating in restaurants and leaving without paying, sleeping in a motel room after the guests left."

"Your car is okay?"

"Yes."

"Are *you* okay?'

"Aside from a wounded ego? I'm so hopping mad I'd like to get a couple of the Lost Souls to teach that guy a lesson. A couple of them were complaining the other night that they haven't busted any heads for a while."

"Your own personal goon squad, huh?"

"You're right. It's probably not a good idea. Still …"

"You haven't had a chance to call Titus again, have you?" I said.

"I did. Still no answer. I'll try later today."

I heard Jackie and Andy come in the front door. Andy raced into the dining room. "Who you talking to, Daddy?"

Andy took the phone and chatted with Lydia. At dinner I told Jackie about the gypsum connection and the disappearance of two more dancers. I also told her Quincy had been busted.

At my mention of the word "busted," Andy looked up. "Who got busted, Daddy? Is Quincy one of the Lost Souls?"

"No. He's a man Lydia knows. Do you know what busted means?"

Andy rolled his eyes. "It means the cops took him to jail. What did he get busted for? B and C?" He casually took a bite of potato.

"You mean B and E?"

"Yah. That's what I meant."

"Something like that. He was eating in restaurants and staying in a motel without paying."

"That's like stealing."

"Right, son. It *is* stealing."

Andy looked thoughtful. "I guess that's not as bad as busting heads or dealing bad dope."

Jackie looked at me, and this time she rolled her eyes. Our son was getting quite an education during his occasional visits to Drop-in.

While Andy played catch in the street with a neighbor boy, Jackie and I sat on the porch after doing the dishes. "Well, one mystery is solved," said Jackie. "I got a call from Nora. Guess who's church she goes to."

"Has to be John's."

"Afraid so. She overheard my boss supporting my thinking about going to Planned Parenthood and assumed I was going there to get an abortion. Nora didn't know they only give information and counseling. She was so troubled that she went to see John. When John pushed her, she did her caving-to-the-male-authority number again. She feels terrible that she talked with him instead of with me. I'm sorry I accused you."

I took her hand. "It's okay. I'm still pretty confused. I realize we have to get it resolved soon, or you'll have to go ahead, even if I'm not on board. Like you said, it's ultimately your decision. Although," I added, raising an eyebrow, "as head of the household ..."

She made as if to punch me on the shoulder, then apparently took pity on my aching body. "If you think you can be the boss of me ..." It was a phrase Andy had tried using with his sitter.

I smiled. Then I suddenly had an idea. "How about if we take a ride to Johnson Park for a change of scenery?" The park was on the Grand River in Grandville.

Jackie wasn't fooled for a minute. "You want to cruise by the plaster mill on Butterworth." I thought she'd veto my idea, but instead she said, "Let's go, Sherlock. I'll get Andy."

As we rode out Butterworth, past the edge of the city, the homes became more spread out and the trees more plentiful. There wasn't a car behind me, so when we reached the gypsum-processing facility, I slowed to a crawl, then stopped on the shoulder across from the entrance. Jackie and I studied the buildings and grounds, deserted now. There was a long, rather dilapidated-looking one-story building and another large building with tall stacks on the roof. I assumed the latter was the main mill building where they turned the gypsum into plaster. I saw four silos near the road that resembled grain silos. A few other smaller buildings completed the complex. Most of the grounds were covered with a whitish gypsum dust. It almost looked like a dusting of snow. I knew the area only appeared this way when it hadn't rained for a few days and there'd been a good breeze. I saw no signs of activity and assumed the complex was closed on Sundays.

Andy jumped up in the back seat, dropping the book he'd been reading. "Are we there yet?" He looked out the window. "That's not Johnson Park. What is that place? It looks spooky."

"It's where they make stuff from the gypsum rock they bring up from the mines, Andy," said Jackie.

"What kind of stuff do they make?"

"Stuff like plaster. It's used to make walls in houses," I said.

I checked my rear view mirror to make sure no one was behind me, then pulled across the road to the entrance gate. Andy went back to his book. I peered at the gate, then got out to check the padlock on it more closely. I kicked the gate lightly with my foot. It was securely locked. I gazed past the gate at the plant, wondering if Johnson had gotten a search warrant and if the cops had searched it. I looked around, trying to picture the mine entrances Lydia had described, but saw no indication of them.

"Let's go," Jackie called from the car. "Unless you plan to get busted for illegal entry and trespassing."

As I got back into the car Jackie was assuring an alarmed Andy that, no, Daddy was not going to get busted since he hadn't gone inside the gate.

We spent an enjoyable hour romping around Johnson Park, climbing the hill used for sledding in winter, throwing rocks into the river and slowly driving the curvy road through the hills in the park with Andy on my lap, steering with my help.

* * *

"That's two services for you today," I said to Jackie as I drove home from evening worship. "You're becoming a typical Christian Reformed housewife."

"As long as I'm married to you," she responded, "I don't think there's much of a chance of that."

I grinned at her. "Or as long as you're you."

When I came downstairs later after putting Andy to bed, Jackie sat at her sewing machine in the dining room. We'd planned to go to an outdoor rock concert at John Ball Park but decided we'd rather hang out at home.

"Try this on," she said, holding up a new blue and red dashiki she'd just finished making for me. I'd mentioned how much I liked the one I'd seen on the guy at Amigo's Bar, but this came as a complete surprise.

"It's beautiful, babe. I love it." I took my shirt off and pulled on the dashiki. It fit perfectly as did everything that Jackie made for me.

She looked it over critically, made a circling motion with her hand. I turned, coming all the way around to face her. She nodded, apparently satisfied. "Want a doo rag to go with it?" she asked with a deadpan expression.

I was about to give her a hug when the phone rang.

"Rob, it's Lydia. How would you like to visit Titus with me?"

"Now?"

"Yes."

"Hold on," I said. I relayed Lydia's invitation to Jackie.

On the short drive to the West Side, I felt the tension in my stomach that was there whenever I imagined the possibility of the dancers being held in the mines. It was more like a hard knot now, as I pictured them, perhaps starving and in total darkness. I pushed the thoughts away. I saw Lydia's car parked in front of her house and eased Night Watch in behind it. I was relieved her car was back.

Before I could ring the bell, Lydia opened the door. "What took you so long?"

I'd come right away and it hadn't taken any longer than usual.

"Wow! That's a beautiful shirt," she said. "It looks like the kind that black guy we talked to at Amigo's was wearing."

"It's a dashiki. Jackie just finished making it for me."

"Cool. Let's move it. We haven't got all night. Let's take my car."

On the drive to Grandville, Lydia said. "Detective Johnson called today. He had a few questions about Quincy. He also told me that their search of the gypsum plant didn't turn up anything. They couldn't get a warrant for the mines."

That's a bummer." After a moment, I said, "Tell me more about Titus."

"He and my husband were friends all their lives. They both grew up in Grandville, attended the same Christian schools and the same church. Titus worked maintenance in the mine for twenty years till he retired. He loved the mine almost as much as he loved telling his stories about it."

I shuddered. *How could anyone love working in a mine?* I wondered.

» CHAPTER 32

Titus's home was a modest white bungalow that looked freshly painted and smelled like it too. An extension ladder lying in the driveway and a neat pile of paint-spattered drop cloths suggested the job was not yet finished. Titus greeted us at the door dressed in khakis, polo shirt and slippers. He ushered us into the living room where a gray-haired, comfortably plump woman sat darning socks. He introduced his wife who then went to the kitchen and returned with four China cups and saucers on a tray. While she busied herself with serving Lydia and me and adding cream and sugar to her own and Titus's coffee, Lydia and Titus chatted away, catching up on each other's lives.

When Titus's wife was back in her chair, he said. "To what do we owe this surprise, Lydia? Did you and Rob decide to do a little night ministry in Grandville? We're not exactly street people. In fact our mortgage is paid off." He turned to me and grinned. "The missus and I actually know quite a bit about you and your ministry, between the newspaper, TV news and Lydia. We missed you when you spoke about your work at our church last winter because we were in Florida. I have to say that most folks didn't know quite what to make of you."

I lifted an eyebrow. "I suspect that's an understatement. As I recall there were almost no questions and no one talked to me afterwards except your pastor."

"I wish we'd been there," said Titus. "I'm sorry you got such a cold reception."

"It was a bit frosty, but I can appreciate how foreign I must sound to lots of Christian Reformed folks."

Titus laughed. "They sure talked about those chains and knives you took along from some of your gang kids. I think you gave a whole new meaning to 'show and tell.'" He laughed again.

"Say," Titus went on, "I think your mother is a cousin to my sister-in-law."

As he went on, I nodded appropriately at the Dutch bingo, the game played in our circles, where connections were established and trust was built.

Titus's wife joined in with enthusiasm. "Yes, and your grandfather's brother Walter's son Gerald married my aunt Anna's cousin Margarite. The connections became increasingly convoluted.

After a brief discussion of my dashiki, Lydia took advantage of a tiny break in the conversation. "Titus, do you mind if I change the subject? We came to talk about the gypsum mines."

Titus leaned forward, elbows on his knees, chin propped on his folded hands. He frowned at Lydia. "Of course you know I've been retired for a few years, but I still have coffee with some of the guys about once a month. I hear the ghosts down there have been really active lately. The guys have been hearing screams and moans and all sorts of weird stuff."

"Stop that!" said his wife, sharply. "Rob and Lydia didn't come over to hear your silly stories."

"I just thought Lydia might be missing my tales from the dark and haunting depths. And Rob hasn't had the opportunity to hear my vast knowledge of the bowels of the earth and their ghostly denizens." Titus shot his wife an unrepentant grin.

She shook her head in exasperation.

"That is sort of why we came," I said, carefully changing my position in the chair. "Let me give you a little background. Some of it you may have caught on the news." I told him about the disappearance of the go-go dancers, Hector's murder, the assault on Van, the message from Rochelle. I didn't mention the gypsum powder in the envelope.

Titus appeared to listen intently, his eyes sparkling. "I think I see where you're going with this. Do you think this Benny may be holding Rochelle and the other dancers in the mines? Any evidence for that?"

"I'm not free to say," I said. "But let's suppose Benny wanted to hide out in the mines or the processing plant or hold the young women captive there. Where might they be? How could they have access? Is this scenario even feasible?"

Titus chewed his lower lip in silence for a moment. "I understand you can't talk about it, but should I *assume* that somebody found a trace of *pure* gypsum, and that's what's driving your curiosity about the mines?" The grin again.

I smiled. "Go ahead and assume that."

Titus nodded "Okay. Let's think about the mill first. The only place you'd find pure gypsum is in the department where the rock is ground up. They couldn't hide there without being detected, though. There's always the possibility of some maintenance or supervisory personal being around, even when the shift is ended."

"What about the mines themselves?" I asked.

"There are a few mining companies and entrances to the mines in the Grand Rapids area. The mines extend roughly over ten-square-miles. I'm most familiar with the Grand Rapids Gypsum operation on Butterworth where I worked."

Because I'd seen Benny heading out Butterworth, I was most interested in the entrances near that facility. "So tell me about the mine near Butterworth."

"Wouldn't be real easy for an unauthorized person to get in." Titus scratched his chin. "Possible, though. I think we can rule out the original mine entrance because it's between the mill and Butterworth right by the plant. No place to park a car or enter the mine without being noticed. Another option would be the air shaft which has a ladder down to the mine, but climbing down it with the girls seems like it would be a hassle. Walking down the incline in the portal off Butterworth Road seems like the best option.

"But if they were holding captives there," I asked, "wouldn't they be seen by the workers?"

"Not if they held them in the old workings on level two. That area's been abandoned for years."

"Can you describe this portal you mentioned?"

"It's a paved slope or ramp with concrete walls that descends into the mine. It's maybe fifteen feet wide, eight feet high. There's a four-inch pipe on the floor of the ramp for water that's pumped out of the mine. Empties into the Grand River. A conveyor comes up the ramp from the mine for bringing out the gypsum. The conveyor is high enough so you can walk under it. Large equipment can be driven down the ramp, too."

Now I had a picture of the portal. "So anybody could walk in or out anytime after the miners finished their shift."

"If they had keys. There's a chain link fence around the site with a padlock on the gate. Another padlock for the gate at the portal is inside a steel cover so bolt cutters can't get at the lock. The cover has an open bottom to get the key into the padlock."

"So, if they had keys, they could go through the portal. Then what?"

"They walk down the slope to where the floor flattens out. That's number two seam. There are two pumps there and a couple of crosscuts—tunnels—that go off to either side. There's a steel door in a steel wall to isolate the old workings from the slope that goes on down to level four. You can enter level two— the old workings—by that steel door. The door is very hard to open due to negative pressure created by the vent fan when it's running."

I squeezed my eyes shut trying to visualize the entrance to the old workings.

Suddenly Titus jumped up, went to an old desk in the corner of the room and returned with a tablet and a pen. He drew a diagram and handed it to me. Lydia and I huddled over it, finally able to make sense out of what he'd described.

"Could any of this have changed since you worked in the mines?" I asked.

"Nope. Not according to the guys I talk with. The only changes are in the area they're actively mining."

The further down into the mine I went in my imagination, the more tense I felt and the more my stomach churned.

"What's it like in the old workings on level two?" asked Lydia.

"The ceiling height varies quite a bit as you move away from the entrance. The rooms and crosscuts are pretty haphazard in that section. Later the mining became more planned and regular. Some hazardous roof areas in the old workings as well and some areas where the roof has collapsed. Lots of water in there. The new workings are much dryer. Pumps on the surface pull the water out, and there's a pump at Scranton Lake I used to maintain."

"There's a *lake* down there?" I said.

"It's just a low area north of the portal. There's a twelve-foot aluminum boat by the lake we'd take to get to the pumps we maintained there."

I thought of the River Styx over which Charon would ferry the dead into Hades. I repressed a shiver.

"They installed a pump outside the mine too," Titus went on, "to keep level two from flooding. There's lots of old abandoned equipment lying around. Footprints in the mud all over the place that could be a few days or even decades old."

"Sounds like it's too dangerous a place to hold the dancers," said Lydia.

"It's dangerous, but you can walk through most of it okay if you stay away from the flooded areas and on dry ground. When we were in level two, we always kept an eye on the roof for potential collapses. We used a roof bar to pry down the loose roof areas."

"It just seems too complicated to hold captives there," I said.

"Not for someone who knows that area of the mines. If you stay near the path where you feel the air flowing, you can stay fairly dry. There's an abandoned maintenance shop and lunch area that might work for holding the dancers. The room has a pit in the middle that was used for working under machinery. At night, after the workers finish their shift in level four, this Benny guy could take the dancers down the slope from level two to level four to use the bathroom. He could make phone calls in the new office on level four as well. He would have to bring in warm clothes, cots, sleeping bags, food, drinks and lanterns. Or miners' lamps. Those suckers will last for eight hours before they need to be recharged."

"Who would know the mines well enough to pull something like this off," I asked.

"Besides me?" The grin was back. "My old partner still works maintenance. Of course he has a new partner now. Any mine worker might be able get access to the keys and have duplicates made. A supervisor would have his own keys."

"Any other areas besides the shop and lunch room on level two that would work for holding the dancers," I asked.

Titus scratched his chin again, looking into the distance. "I can't remember just where the magazine for storing the explosives was on level two, but it had to be a ways from the old shop. Come to think of it, that was dismantled when they abandoned level two. Nope. I think the old shop is the only likely place in the mine for holding those girls."

I shifted in my seat, trying to relax. I gave up. I couldn't talk about a mine and relax. "Would it be hard to find the abandoned shop area?" I asked. "I have the impression from what you said that it's a maze down there."

"Once you're through the steel door into the old workings, there's a guide wire strung up all the way to the old shop and lunchroom area and beyond. You have to pay really close attention to follow it though. Otherwise you'll be lost forever down there and join the rest of the ghosts." Titus flashed his grin.

"I'd like to get this information to Detective Johnson. Would you be willing to talk to him if he wants to speak with you, Titus?"

"Of course." He pointed to the phone on a small table in the dining room.

As I went to the phone, Lydia said she would get the coffee pot from the kitchen.

The officer who answered the phone at the information desk sounded young. He also sounded distracted. "May I ..." After a pause he came back on. "I'm sorry. May I help you?"

There was a lot of background noise, voices yelling, arguing. Sounded like a riot going on in the lobby of the Hall of Justice. I asked to speak to Detective Johnson or Kincaid.

He put me on hold. I listened to silence for few minutes as my stomach tightened and my foot tapped impatiently. When the officer came back on, he informed me that Johnson and Kincaid were both off duty. I heard more yelling in the background.

I told him as quickly and succinctly as I could what Titus had suggested about where the dancers might be held in the mine. I had to repeat some of the information more than once.

Twice more he told me to wait while he said something to someone else and while I listened to the background din. Finally he said he would try to pass the information on to another detective team. I gave him Titus's name and phone number. Titus handed me a note he'd just written with the name, address and phone number of the mine supervisor who lived in Grand Rapids. Although I knew the police might already have this information, I relayed it to the officer.

At last I said, irritation in my voice, "What the heck is going on there?"

"Um, we're having a little disturbance."

Had there been trouble at the concert? I wondered. *Or was there a repeat of the race riot that the city had experienced a few years prior?*

I had no confidence that the police would soon be headed for the mine. *If* they ever got the message. "Is there a supervisor there I can speak with?" I asked.

"The Communications Lieutenant is too busy to speak with you. I have to go now." He hung up.

I quickly dialed Johnson's home phone. I bit my lip as I listened to it ring several times, then hung up and reported to Lydia and the others the chaos at the police station.

We thanked our hosts for their hospitality. Titus put an arm around his wife, squeezing her shoulder. "That was fun, wasn't it, honey?"

She ignored her husband and leveled a severe gaze at Lydia. "You aren't thinking of going into the mines to try to find those girls, are you Lydia?"

"My goodness," said Lydia, with an indignant look I couldn't quite buy. "We have no way of getting in and we're not police officers."

» CHAPTER 33

Lydia abruptly pulled over to the curb a few minutes after leaving Titus's.

"What's up?" I asked.

I watched as she reached into a pocket of her slacks. "Guess what I've got?" She produced several keys on a ring, held them up with a look of triumph on her face.

"Well, let me see," I said. "Could it be keys?"

"Very perceptive, Reverend Vander Laan. But keys to what?"

"Lydia, stop playing games."

"They're keys to the mine!" Lydia responded to my look of incredulity with a satisfied smile.

"How the heck did you get them?" I asked.

"I got them when I said I'd get the coffee pot. I knew Titus kept them on a hook by the back door."

"Why would he still have the keys after retiring?"

Lydia shrugged. "Maybe they were waiting for us to use them."

I shot her a dubious look. "What if they changed the locks?" I imagined Jackie telling Andy that his dad and Lydia had been busted for illegal entry and trespassing. But if the cops didn't get the message I'd left ...

Lydia huffed. "There are four girls missing now. Members of our congregation. And it sounds like it might be a while before the cops can get there."

Were any of the girls alive? I wondered. *What if they were being abused or had been abandoned down there?*

"I thought Titus wouldn't tell you where the entrances are," I said.

"I don't know exactly where they are. But when my husband and I were out for a Sunday drive one time with Titus near the plant, he pointed to where the airshaft was, and the portal is near it. I think I can find it. My husband and Titus used to hunt deer in that area, and we went there for walks a few times. You ready?"

"Can we just drive to the portal?" I asked.

"Should be able to, or at least close to it."

I thought about the confusion at the police station. My terror of the mine paled in comparison to the plight of the dancers. I wanted to get to the portal as fast as we could, but I didn't want to be stupid about it. "Let's do it," I said. "But first we have to think about what we need for our foray into the mine."

Lydia dropped the mine keys into her purse, then turned off the car and pulled the car key from the ignition. "Come and look," she said. She got out of the car, walked around to the back and opened the trunk. I met her at the rear of the car.

Inside lay two jackets, a larger one which had probably belonged to Lydia's late husband, and a smaller one. On top of them lay a large silver flashlight.

I gave her a determined nod. "Lydia, you never fail to surprise me. You had this in mind the whole time. Spare batteries for the flashlight?"

"In my purse." Lydia stood tapping her foot impatiently.

"I'll call Jackie. She won't like it, but somebody needs to know where we're going."

We found a pay phone, and I filled Jackie in as quickly and as fully as I could. She must have heard the resolve in my voice because she didn't argue. She hung up the phone without saying good-bye. I knew she wasn't happy with me, but I couldn't let that stop me.

Lydia crossed the Grand River at Johnson Park a little before 10:00 p.m. and headed back toward Grand Rapids on Butterworth Drive. Before we reached the gypsum plant, she made a left turn on a gravel road. There was no street sign.

"I'm pretty sure this is it." Lydia turned her lights off and drove by the light of the moon.

After a couple of moments, she stopped and pointed straight ahead. "There it is. The portal's got to be beyond that gate."

I saw some structures I couldn't identify enclosed by a fence, too nervous to look carefully. I didn't like how exposed we were. "Drive that way." I pointed to the right. "Let's see if we can find a place to hide your car."

Lydia turned right on to a dirt road, then took a left up a slight hill through the trees on a two-track. In less than a minute of bouncing along, I spotted something and pointed. "That must be the air shaft." In the moonlight I saw a structure surrounded by a chain link fence. The structure was about ten feet high with a Chinese hat type roof about four feet above it, leaving a few feet of open space, probably for the fan to do its thing without getting wet when it rained or snowed.

Lydia drove a little further on the two-track and then parked behind some trees.

After grabbing the jackets and flashlight from the trunk, we hurried back along the way we'd come. When we reached the air shaft, Lydia said, "Now we can approach from the north. We'll stay on top of this hill. With all the trees here bordering the two-track, we won't be so easy to spot."

A big part of me wished we'd be spotted and arrested for trespassing. Where were the cops when you needed them?

We walked carefully, but quickly down the two-track. Tree branches formed a canopy over the road and it was darker here. An owl hooted nearby. Two deer, startled by our approach, darted off. Lydia grabbed my arm, and we both took a few deep breaths. My heart hammered in my chest.

Down the slope ahead and to the right was a bank of transformers outside a cyclone fence enclosure. We scrambled down from the two-track to the gate and peered through the fence. The area within looked much as Titus had described it: a shed with a fuel oil tank behind it, a storage silo for the rocks, miscellaneous pieces of equipment and a truck. Further in and a little to the left was a second gate to the cement portal that opened into the darkness of the earth like the gaping jaws of a monster. A conveyor rose from the blackness like a giant tongue, reaching up to the top of the rock tank where the monster would spit out the indigestible portions of its lifeless victims.

Lydia fished around in her purse till she came up with the keys. She tried a couple of them on the padlock on the gate till she found the right one. I slid the gate open.

When we were both inside, I shoved the gate closed and snapped the padlock shut.

We walked toward the monster's mouth. Lydia reached under the steel cover at the second gate, tried different keys, dropped them once and had to start over.

I felt exposed in the moonlight as I waited, goose bumps rising on my skin.

Finally, she found the correct key. She opened the padlock. The fence moved on horizontal rollers. When I pushed on the gate, it slid open easily with little sound. Inside, I pushed it closed again. I reached awkwardly through the six-inch mesh fence and tried to snap the padlock shut.

"Come on!" said Lydia impatiently. "Leave it unlocked."

"If Benny comes, I don't want him to know someone is inside," I said, almost dropping the padlock and swearing under my breath. I finally managed to snap the lock shut. Opening the padlock from the inside would be more of a challenge, but we'd deal with that later.

We put on the jackets and I turned on the flashlight. I aimed it up at the three foot wide conveyor over our heads, then pointed the light through the portal, moving the beam from one side to the other. There was a four-inch pipe running along the cement floor at the wall, just as Titus had said.

Lydia and I looked at each other. Showtime.

My feet wouldn't move.

Lydia shoved me forward. That was enough to get my feet remembering what they needed to do.

I led the way down into the tunnel. It was approximately fifteen feet wide. The conveyor was on our right. On our left, the floor had a metal grating, probably to help vehicles coming up get better traction on the wet floor. I felt a breeze blowing on my face as we descended. The concrete floor under our feet was relatively smooth, and there were no obstacles to impede our progress. There was only the soft sound of our shoes on the pavement. I noticed the sound of a pump in the distance.

I wished I were home watching TV or reading. I wished I were anywhere but here. I continued downward, walking with a confident step that was a total sham. I shivered as the cooler air moved over my sweaty face. I stopped to zip up the jacket. The sudden sound of the zipper made me want to bolt back the way we'd come.

I took a breath, resumed my descent, Lydia at my side. After a few minutes the concrete floor leveled out for a couple of crosscuts. I saw two pumps and a small pond. One of the pumps was running quietly. It shut off as we watched. A slow, steady stream of water was running into the sump to repeat the cycle. Water hoses lay on the floor. Electrical panels were on the wall. I stopped, pointed the light at the ceiling and noticed electrical wires. The ceiling was a few feet higher here. I swung the light down and to our right. A steel door. Another electrical panel with several breaker boxes on the wall to the right of the door. We had to be at level two, the entrance to the old workings.

I wiped sweat from my forehead with the back of my hand. I turned right, passing under the conveyor and into the crosscut, leaving the main tunnel which continued downward to level four. I stopped in front of the steel door. I heard air being sucked around it into the old workings, warning me that opening that door would be tricky.

Maybe the girls weren't in the mine at all. Maybe this was a complete waste of time. I should leave this to the cops. I tried to tell myself I couldn't even be certain this was the entrance to level two. But it fit Titus's description perfectly.

Lydia must have sensed my indecision. "Think about the girls, especially Georgina."

I passed the flashlight to Lydia, then gazed at the door, listening to the sound of air being sucked around it. The handle appeared to be a homemade strip of flat steel welded to the door. I gritted my teeth and put all my effort into pulling the door open. It opened inch by inch. I hung on for dear life to keep it from being yanked from my hands. I was sweating profusely and my arms shook with the effort. When I'd opened it far enough, I jerked my head at Lydia to enter. She entered and then leaned into the door from the inside.

"Now you," she hissed.

I slithered around the door, hanging on as best I could and joined Lydia in exerting pressure on the inside of the door, stepping backward carefully and attempting to let it close slowly. Despite our best efforts, the pressure on the door thrust us into the old workings. We almost lost our balance, stumbling backwards as the door slammed closed.

I stood for a moment, looking at Lydia and catching my breath as she did the same.

We were greeted in the old workings by a distinct odor of mildew. It smelled like a damp, musty and long-neglected basement. I stood for a few minutes catching my breath as Lydia played the flashlight around the immediate area. I couldn't see very far because of all the columns left in place to support the roof. The surface of the walls and columns was rougher than in the tunnel we'd emerged from, and the walls were darker than they'd been along the incline. The columns appeared to be about thirty feet square. The opening for the air shaft was on the right. As my eyes took in our new surroundings, I could easily see how someone could get lost here and never be heard from again.

Don't think that way! I admonished myself.

"Shine it over here," I whispered, pointing up and a bit to the left.

The light revealed the guide wire Titus had mentioned hanging from the ceiling, a single strand of brown wire that led forward, past a column. The wire was thin, maybe ten gauge. Too thin. Easy to lose track of.

I took the flashlight from Lydia and, with a deep foreboding, whispered, "Let's go."

I proceeded slowly, with Lydia following, moving the light between the wire and the floor. I wished we had two flashlights, one always aimed at the guide wire, the other always aimed at the floor to see where we were walking. I saw and heard water gushing from a hose or pipe, and running downward, perhaps toward Scranton Lake. After a few minutes the sound of the water diminished as it ran beside and sometimes underneath where we walked. We passed a few columns. There were piles of tailings along the sides and in some of the crosscuts. Sometimes we encountered heaps of debris on the floor and had to move around them or step carefully over them. I noticed fungus growing on some of the damp pieces of wood on the floor. I saw some old mine cars for carrying the rock to the surface. They were about four feet wide, three feet high and six feet long. They appeared to be empty. *With a guide*, I thought, *and if I didn't hate mines so much, this might be an interesting tour.*

Suddenly we were startled by a muffled slam. Lydia grabbed my arm. Had to be the door we'd just entered to level two. Someone else had entered the old workings.

switched off the light, grabbed Lydia's hand. We moved cautiously away from the wire, feeling our way down a cross-cut and behind a column. We heard at least two voices but couldn't make out the words. We waited.

The voices moved closer, gradually becoming less muffled.

"Yeah, the sooner, the better." A male voice. Unfamiliar. It didn't sound like Benny.

I did a quick peek around the pillar and saw two lights bobbing toward us. Looked like the lights were attached to helmets. I pulled my head back behind the column.

"I don't see why we have to fill all their stupid requests," another male voice whined. A distinct nasal quality. It sounded like Pookie from the Getaway. "It took us forever to find the raisins. You'd think the grocery store would arrange things where you could find them."

"Don't you ever get tired of complaining?" *Owen?* I wondered.

The sound of their footsteps and conversation and the lights moved past us. I peered from behind the column to see the backs of the two men, mere shadows moving deeper into the mine. It looked like their lights were bobbing between the wire and the floor. Then the men disappeared around a column. The sounds of their voices and footsteps diminished. The lights quickly faded to nothing.

We came cautiously back around the column we'd been hiding behind. I whispered into Lydia's ear, "Let's wait a few minutes so they won't hear us. Then we'll follow them."

Lydia clutched my arm in the total darkness.

After a bit I turned on the flashlight, pointing it at the floor. A confusion of muddy footprints was evident as we inched quietly forward. I pointed the light ahead and saw an old set of rail tracks disappearing into the darkness the way the voices had gone. We followed the tracks as quietly as we could, keeping a close eye on the wire. Occasionally we passed dilapidated machinery and equipment. I stopped at a Y in the tracks where another set of tracks veered off to the right. As I moved on I noticed a drainage ditch at one side of the tunnel. The sound of running water accompanied our footsteps. The passage was damp and the mildew smell was stronger here. Some places the floor was dry and dusty. Wires, in addition to the guide wire, hung from the ceiling, and I saw an old trolley cable above the tracks. I noticed a whiskey bottle along our path and a dynamite box. There was some graffiti on the walls—drawings I couldn't identify and dates. At one place the water crossed our path. A bridge made from an old section of conveyor enabled us to cross it and keep our feet dry.

A few minutes later Lydia hissed, "Where's the guide wire?"

I swung the flashlight around. I didn't see it and felt on the verge of panic. We retraced our steps. At least that's what I hoped we were doing. Lydia clutched my arm tightly.

After several slow steps, swinging the flashlight around and not seeing the guide wire, I stopped. I wanted to run screaming in any direction. I wanted to yell for Pookie and his partner, make a racket until they found us.

I looked at Lydia and saw my own terror mirrored in her eyes.

Instead of surrendering to the panic, I used the light to look more carefully at the floor of the mine, at the chaos of partial footprints and occasional complete ones. That was of no use except that it was helping me to focus, to reign in my terror.

I got an idea.

I put a hand on Lydia's shoulder and felt her trembling. Tears streamed down her cheeks. I'd never seen her look so helpless and afraid. Somehow, that helped my own fear recede a bit.

I leaned close and whispered in her ear. "It's going to be okay, Lydia. We *will* find that guide wire. Here's how we'll do it. You are going to stay right here. I'm going to—"

"You can't leave me," she whimpered, tightening her already viselike grip on my arm.

"I won't go far. You'll be able to watch me and see the light. You'll be my anchor. If I don't see anything, I'll come right back to you and try another direction. I'll keep doing that until we find the wire. If I come to a pillar, I'll walk around it to check all sides and then come back Are you ready?"

Lydia stared into my eyes. I looked back at her with a confidence I desperately hoped would convince her.

"I need you to be my anchor, Lydia."

She gulped a breath of air, released her grip on my arm and nodded.

I looked around again, the flashlight illuminating the floor, walls, pillars and ceiling. I picked a direction at random and walked slowly forward, sweeping the flashlight as I went. Nothing. When I reached a pillar, I turned back and shined the light toward Lydia, keeping it low so as not to blind her. I made a circle with the light. I turned and walked slowly around the pillar, sweeping the light as I went. I prayed I'd see the wire on the other side.

I didn't.

I returned to the side where I'd started, then came back to Lydia.

Once again I gave her a steady look. She nodded. I set off again. I repeated this procedure several times, always returning to Lydia before trying a new direction. I was beginning to lose hope in my plan.

Then I spotted the wire. A couple of the wire fasteners must have come loose from the ceiling or wall and the wire looped down to the floor, then back up to the wall where it turned around a column to go in a different direction. *Thank you, God,* I breathed.

I shined the light in Lydia's direction and motioned her over, lighting the way for her feet. When she reached me, I pointed the light at the guide wire, played the light along it down to the floor and back up to the wall.

"I see it," she whispered.

I told myself not to get distracted by the eerie scenery of the mine.

We proceeded even more slowly than before, making sure not to lose the wire again. Sometimes the wire was attached to the ceiling, sometimes it dropped to the floor, sometimes it hung somewhere between. The floor had cracks in it. I saw wooden pillars shoring up the ceiling in places. Some of the wood looked rotten. I cast furtive glances at the ceiling, praying it wouldn't fall on us. There were places where rock had fallen from above. Some of the rock pillars had cracks and splits in them. Water ran beneath one pillar. Occasionally we had to step over running water. Once we scrambled over old cribbing that had probably been used to prop the roof till it rotted and fell, and a couple of times we carefully made our way over rock heaps that appeared to have come down from the ceiling.

We lost the wire—our life-line—once more.

We quickly found it again.

Our journey seemed like a long one, but was probably only twenty minutes or a half hour. I'd long ago lost track of the turns we made.

I heard a sound up ahead, moved quickly to the stone pillar at our left and switched off the light. Again, the darkness was total. I reached for Lydia's hand as she made a muffled squeak. She squeezed my hand in her iron grip. I waited for my eyes to adjust. It made no difference.

"Breathe," I whispered in her ear, as much to remind myself as her.

"Turn on the doggone flashlight," she hissed. More of the old feistiness than earlier, less of the helpless panic.

"Wait. Listen." I heard muffled voices, a squeak like a door opening. Faint, unsteady light spilled around the stone column next to which we were huddled.

Then, "Don't forget to bring the empty bucket in when you set that one out there."

A clink as if a bucket was set down. The sound of water sloshing. "Got it, Owen." Now both voices were identified. The two Nam vets must have been Benny's eyes and ears at the Getaway.

The sound of the door closing. The light disappeared. No sound of footsteps so Pookie must have returned to the room.

We waited a moment. When we heard nothing more except the indistinct murmur of voices, I moved cautiously around the column, keeping the light off and feeling my way. Lydia followed too closely, clutching my arm. I stopped. A sliver of light lay just ahead along the floor. I gingerly made my way to the wall, one hand in front of me, inching my feet forward. My hand touched a flat perpendicular surface. The wall was smooth compared with the uneven surface of the columns and the mine walls.

I heard low voices. At least one was female. We moved closer to the sliver of light at the floor, listening.

"How long are you keeping us here? It's cold." Manetta's voice.

"Yah, and a real pain in the butsky not to be able to shower." Lois.

After warning Lydia with a whisper, I risked a quick flick of the flashlight. We were next to a plywood wall. The light we saw escaped from beneath the door to a room on the other side of that wall. The old shop and lunchroom?

The muted conversation continued so I turned the light on again, longer this time, and looked around. Another broad column loomed a few paces to our right.

I made my way over to the column and moved behind it, Lydia fastened to my shoulder. I shut off the flashlight. If one of the guys came out now, we'd be hidden behind the pillar. It seemed like a good spot from which to figure out our next move. We were close enough to the room so we could still make out most of the conversation coming from behind the door.

"So when do we get our reward for the raisins?" Pookie.

Silence.

"We could just take 'em, Pookie," said Owen. "Nobody to stop us."

"That's enough!" Rochelle. "Nobody's *taking* ..." The last part not clear.

Rochelle sounded okay. But was she in charge or just asserting herself?

A mumbled "Fuck you. We could take you, too."

Then, a groan.

"Maybe Georgina," I whispered in Lydia's ear. If so, all the dancers were alive. But what condition was Georgina in?

"Give Georgina some water," said Rochelle. "She needs a doctor."

So it was Georgina.

"Give her some water, Pookie."

After a moment, "Untie the others so they can eat something." Owen. "I'll watch them. Better give me your gun so one of them doesn't try something."

Lydia leaned closer, speaking into my ear. "We have to do something."

"We've still got no idea what's going on, Lydia. Let's just keep listening for a bit."

"But Georgina—"

I hushed her with a finger to her lips. We listened as the women apparently settled into their meal.

After a while, Rochelle spoke again. "Georgina is going to die if she doesn't get help. You guys want to go to jail for murder?"

"Maybe we should just finish her off, Pookie," said Owen. "We're in deep shit already."

"Are you crazy, man? I didn't sign up for that. I saw enough of that shit in Nam."

"Give me your gun again and tie them up."

Silence. Then Owen's voice. "Want a hit, Pookie?"

"Yeah. Let's mellow out. No more talk of killing anyone."

The sweetish smell of marijuana seeped out of the room.

More groaning.

"I can't stand to listen to her," said Pookie.

"I'm going to throttle her," said Owen. "Benny told us to kill her if she got to be too much of a problem. It'll help these other bitches know we're serious."

"No!" yelled Pookie. "She ain't no gook."

"Shut the fuck up. Get out of my way."

"No!" Rochelle.

Then silence, except for a quiet trickling of water somewhere nearby.

I felt Lydia's movement and knew that she was going for her gun. I was bending toward her ear to warn her not to snap her purse closed when I heard the click. A small sound that shattered the stillness.

CHAPTER 35

"What the hell was that?" Pookie.

Flickering lights in the space went out. Again the darkness was absolute as we crouched in our hiding place, hardly daring to breathe.

A squeak. The door opening? Owen knew how to hunt out the enemy in the dark. His nickname in Vietnam was Ghost. I sensed him moving toward us. Or was it my imagination? In Nam he choked the enemy to death or slit their throats. I covered my throat with my hand. A feeble defense.

Suddenly, Rochelle's voice pierced the darkness. "Help! We're in here!"

Manetta and Lois added their screams. "Help! Help!"

A thud followed by a groan. Then a hiss: "Shut up or I'll blow your brains out."

It was quiet for what seemed like several minutes. Maybe Owen and Pookie were both hiding in the room, listening. The only sounds I could make out were my shallow breathing, the pounding of my heart and a trickling of water. We would wait them out. Then, when they resumed their activity, thinking they were safe, we would return to the surface and get help from the cops.

All at once I sensed a presence—very close. Or maybe it was my fear messing with my head. We waited.

I remembered the chaos at the police station and wondered if any cops would be available. I prayed for Johnson and

Kincaid to come. Maybe they had gotten my message despite the turmoil.

Suddenly, from behind us, we were bathed in light.

"Drop the gun, lady," said Owen.

Lydia hesitated. Then, rather than dropping it, she set it carefully on the floor.

"Now slowly turn around, both of you. Hands in the air."

I closed my eyes in the glare of the flashlight.

"Turn the light back on, Pookie. We've got company. Won't Benny be surprised!"

The sound of a match being struck, the hiss of a lantern as light came through the doorway from the space where the women were being held.

"Who is it?" yelled Pookie.

"Turn around again," ordered Owen. "You'd better join the others. Get a fucking move on."

I followed Lydia through what must have been the shop area. Steel columns instead of rock here. Workbench and shelving along one wall, a table and some old chairs. Wires dangled from the ceiling. In the middle of the room was the pit Titus had mentioned, maybe five feet deep. In the doorway to a room at the far end stood Pookie with his gun pointed at the floor, his mouth open. He stepped aside as Lydia and I proceeded through, followed by Owen.

"Lydia! Rob!" shouted Manetta and Lois.

Rochelle lay on her side, blood oozing from a wound on her forehead. Next to her was Georgina, lying on a cot and covered with blankets. Lydia went to Rochelle, knelt down to cradle her head and to check her wound.

Rochelle's eyes fluttered open, closed, opened again. "Lydia?" She turned to see me. "Rob? Boy, you guys don't give up."

We were in a large room, walls with drywall over them, wooden floor. It was long and narrow, maybe twenty five feet wide by fifty or sixty feet long. The odor of mold was strong.

Pookie moved to stand beside Owen. "It's the minister and the old lady that hang out at the Getaway. What the heck do we do with them, man?"

Owen rubbed a hand over his mouth. The butt of Lydia's gun protruded from his jacket pocket. "Beats the hell out of me. I don't like this."

I looked more carefully at Owen. Like Pookie, he appeared to be in his early twenties. But, unlike Pookie, Owen was well over six feet, slender, with brown hair and bushy eyebrows. He reminded me of a cat. I thought of how he'd come up behind us without a sound.

"My name is Rob," I said, back to my faked confident tone. "This is Lydia." Maybe the fact that I was a minister and Lydia an old lady lent us a measure of safety, but I wasn't banking on that. "You're in some deep shit here, Owen. The police aren't far behind us." Wishful thinking, no doubt. "Let me help you make it easier on yourself."

"Shut the fuck up, man. I'm trying to think."

"Hey," said Pookie. "Watch your language in front of a minister."

Owen scowled at Pookie. "You shut the fuck up too. Light those other lanterns."

Pookie did as he was told, while Owen watched us.

"We got no more fucking rope," Owen said when the lanterns were re-lit. "Get the fuck over to the new shop and call Benny. Let him know what the fuck we've got here. Tell him to bring some more fucking rope with him when he comes in the morning. It's getting to be a regular goddamn circus down here. The sooner Benny gets back, the sooner we get out of this hole and blow Grand Rapids."

"But, Owen," protested Pookie, "He's a minister. She's an old lady. Your language, man."

"Shut the fuck up and get moving," snarled Owen. "And get back here as quick as you can."

"Okay, man, but you have to watch ..."

Owen silenced Pookie with a look.

Pookie slid his gun into his belt and grabbed a large battery attached to a belt which he strapped around his waist. The battery had a cord running to a helmet which he slapped on his head. He switched on the helmet light and disappeared out the door.

I wished I at least had my clerical shirt on instead of the dashiki Jackie had made me. Maybe a dark suit to go with it, like John wore. Nevertheless, I mustered up the most confident ministerial tone I could and hoped Owen couldn't read the terror beneath it. "It's not that bad yet, Owen. Let us all go. I'll tell the cops that you—"

"Shut the fuck up," he hissed. "Get the fuck over there by the old lady."

Pretty limited vocabulary, I thought as I moved toward Lydia and Rochelle. I knelt down by the two of them. *Your amateur detective work has gotten you into deep doo-doo again,* I thought. I forced myself to focus, not to give in to the dread I felt in my stomach.

I glanced at Owen who stood motionless, gun pointed at us. I imagined his mind going a mile a minute as he tried to figure out what to do.

I turned back to Rochelle. "How are you doing?" I asked.

"I feel a little woozy and my head hurts like blazes." She shivered. She wore dirty blue jeans and a white sweater over a blouse. The sweater had collected a lot of dirt. Her hair was matted, in need of a wash and brushing.

I looked at Georgina lying several feet away near Manetta and Lois, her face cloaked in a deathly pallor.

I noticed Rochelle shiver. "You're cold." I said, taking my jacket off. I turned to Owen. "Georgina looks like she's hanging by a thread, Owen. You don't want any more of your captives in that shape. It will just make things more difficult for you. Let me untie Rochelle's hands so she can wear my jacket. I think she may be in shock from the blow to her head."

Owen moved to the right and leaned against the wall. "Just cover her with the fucking jacket."

"It will keep her warmer if she wears it," I protested.

Owen looked preoccupied, probably still tying to figure out how to deal with the new situation. "All right. Just don't try anything stupid. Any of you."

I untied Rochelle's wrists and Lydia helped her into the jacket.

"Tie her fucking hands again, Reverend."

"Call me Rob," I said, even as I realized how ridiculous I sounded.

I tied Rochelle's hands again, leaving the rope a little loose.

Lydia moved to Georgina, touched her forehead. "Georgina is dehydrated, Owen. Do you have any water?"

Owen gestured with the gun toward a large plastic jug standing with bags of groceries in the corner.

Lydia moved to the jug, turned to me. "Got a clean handkerchief?"

I handed mine to her.

Lydia wet it, wrung it out and returned to Georgina with a cup of water. Lydia tried to get Georgina to take a sip and then bathed her forehead. Georgina groaned. There were old bruises on her face. Her breathing was ragged and shallow.

"Can you tell me what this is all about, Rochelle?" I said quietly.

"As near as I can tell, Benny's behind it." Rochelle responded in a hushed voice, squeezing her eyes shut, then opening them again. "I think he wants the Getaway closed or at least the go-go dancing ended, and he wants me out of there."

"Did Benny kill Hector and make it look like suicide?"

Owen slid down the wall and sat, gun still pointed at us. "Okay, that's enough with the questions, Rob."

At least we were on a first name basis now.

"Move the fuck away from Rochelle. Get the fuck over by Lydia." With a motion of his gun, he indicated the corner where Manetta and Lois sat.

Lydia stood up and moved toward Owen who rose from the floor now with catlike ease.

"That's far enough, Lydia."

She stopped. "I was just wondering if you could see your way clear to unload my gun and give it back to me. I'm real attached to it. It belonged to my late husband."

Owen smiled a lazy smile. "I don't think so, Lydia."

"Okay. I figured it couldn't hurt to ask. My husband fought in the Second World War. I gather you and Pookie were in Vietnam."

Owen said nothing.

Lydia shook her head. "I have to tell you that Rob and I never heard you sneaking up on us out there. You're really good. I guess you've had some experience doing that sort of thing."

The lazy smile again. He gestured with the gun in my direction. "Enough chit-chat. Get over there with Rob."

Lydia scowled. "I can't help wondering what your mother—"

"Shut the fuck up." Owen hissed. Then, "Sorry. Please," he added with a hint or sarcasm He gestured with the gun again, and Lydia came over to sit down with me.

No one said anything for a long time. Rochelle, Manetta and Lois slept. Lydia complained that she didn't have her knitting. Owen watched us with an alertness that was scary.

I sat with my back to the wall. I was getting cold. The pain in my neck and shoulders from Benny roughing me up was getting worse, and I had no aspirin with me. "Owen," I whispered, "is it okay if I get up and pace to keep warm."

He shook his head.

I thought about Jackie. I knew I was ready to support her decision to get an abortion. If I got the chance.

I checked my watch: 12:05. Jackie would be worried about me after my calling to tell her Lydia and I were going to try to enter the mine. I wondered if she'd tried to call Lydia yet to see if we'd gotten back to her place. I wondered if she might have contacted Johnson. I sent up another desperate prayer. Somehow, despite everything, I dozed.

I opened my eyes at the sound of voices approaching. Where was I? I saw Owen and remembered. Only 12:45 by my watch. Owen came to his feet and took out his gun in one easy motion. He moved next to the door. A moment later Pookie and Benny appeared. Benny had a wild look in his eyes, like he could be losing his tenuous hold on reality. He looked from me to Lydia. Shook his head.

"Where the fuck is the rope?" asked Owen.

"Benny was on his way in," said Pookie. "Met him just outside the door to the old workings. He decided not to wait till morning to come back. He didn't have no rope with him."

"What the fuck do we do now, Benny?" asked Owen.

"First thing, we take care of the redheaded bitch," said Benny. "She's not going to make it anyway. God's will. Take care of it Owen."

The three men moved closer to us. Owen continued on to Georgina, but not before Lydia and I moved in front of her cot. Rochelle struggled to her feet with her hands still tied and moved to join us. Not much of a barrier. Nonetheless, Owen hesitated, stopped, shot a look back to Benny.

"Please, Benny," pleaded Rochelle. "I'll do what you want. Don't let Owen kill her." Rochelle's eyes and face looked as if the life had gone out of her.

I doubted reasoning would work with Benny, but I appreciated Rochelle's attempt.

Benny seemed to be considering Rochelle's plea as he slouched against the wall. He shifted from one foot to the other. After a moment he said, "You won't go back to the Getaway."

"Okay," said Rochelle.

"And you'll leave Grand Rapids with me and won't try to run away."

"Yes, Benny." Her shoulders slumped. Her eyes spoke of defeat.

"You'll stop fucking up your dad's life."

"Yes."

"No more dancing. Period. You know we weren't raised that way."

"Okay."

All eyes stayed on Benny, awaiting his verdict.

At last, he pulled himself away from the wall against which he'd been leaning, his eyes looking a little less frantic. "Owen, take the redhead outside the mine and dump her somewhere where she'll be found in the morning."

"Thanks, Benny." Rochelle's shoulders slumped even further.

Was she that good an actress, I wondered, *or had Benny finally broken her?*

Benny looked at us and gestured with his gun toward Manetta and Lois. Rochelle, Lydia and I joined them over by the wall. Owen moved to Georgina's side and knelt.

As if she knew something was afoot, Georgina opened her eyes and looked at Owen. "No. Please." A weak protest.

Rochelle moved to Georgina's side. "It's okay. Owen will see that you get help."

Georgina extended her hand toward Rochelle, a look of fear and doubt in her eyes.

"I know Owen hurt you before. But he'll help you now. Trust me."

Georgina eye's fluttered closed.

"Okay, Rochelle," said Benny. Back by the others."

Rochelle complied, struggling again to her feet. Owen picked up Georgina's limp body, tossed her over his shoulder and began to carry her away. When I carried Andy that way he'd giggle and say, "I'm a sack of potatoes, Daddy." I bit my lip. *Would I get to see my little guy again*, I wondered.

I pushed that thought as far away as I could. "How about letting Lydia go with them, Benny?" I said. "Lydia can make sure that Georgina gets help in time."

Lydia elbowed me and scowled but said nothing.

Benny ignored me, put a hand out to stop Owen and whispered something in his ear. Then Benny nodded to Pookie who put the helmet on Owen's head and strapped the battery around his waist.

"Take Lydia's gun, Pookie," said Owen.

Pookie slipped the gun out of Owen's pocket and put it in his own.

Owen left with his burden.

I had a bad feeling that Georgina wasn't going to get the help Benny had promised.

Rochelle must have thought the same thing. "Remember, you promised, Benny," she said in a small voice.

"Don't worry, sweetheart."

I saw no love in Benny's eyes. There was a flash of something. Triumph, maybe.

"Benny?" It was Pookie. He stood next to Benny with his own gun pointed toward the floor.

Benny gave Pookie a look that silenced him. "Keep your gun on them."

Pookie's gun came up.

Rochelle took a step toward Benny. "You have to let the rest of them go now, honey."

I heard her make a small sound and wondered if she'd choked on the endearment.

Benny seemed not to notice. His lips curved in a smile, but his eyes looked wild. "Sure, sweetheart. We'll all go in a few minutes."

Rochelle took another step toward him. Because her back was to me, I couldn't see her expression when she said, "Untie me so I can give you a hug."

"In a minute," he said.

Rochelle was working her hands free. Was she going to try something stupid? If she got hurt or killed, it would be my fault for re-tying her hands so loosely.

I glanced at Manetta and Lois. I thought I saw a mixture of fear and hope on their faces. I sensed the tension in Lydia's body.

A single shot erupted in the silence.

We all jumped, except for Benny. No one said a word. Benny merely grimaced. Rochelle staggered a couple of steps back until she stood next to me again.

The silence wore on, broken only by strangled sobs coming from Manetta and Lois.

At last, Rochelle spoke in small voice. "Benny, you said—"

"Shut up, bitch. You think I believed that little number about how you'll do everything I want? I thought my love for you could break down your shell. I figured that you just needed to get to know me. You never gave me that chance in high school and now I know you never will."

He raised his gun with a lazy motion. At the same time, Pookie's gun swung toward Benny. Everything seemed to slow down. It was like watching a slideshow instead of a movie, a few seconds on every frame.

I was hardly aware I'd moved. Another shot rang out. Or was it two? Deafening in the confines of the room.

CHAPTER 36

Somehow I'd fallen. It must have been raining because the ground was wet. My new dashiki was getting muddy and Jackie would kill me. Only last month I'd ruined a tie with food stains, and she'd been upset. Well, okay, it was the third tie that bit the dust in as many months. I didn't like ties anyway but I *loved* this dashiki. I was going to be on Jackie's shit list. Besides, I was on my way to a meeting. It was something important, but I couldn't remember what. Of course, if I didn't remember what the meeting was or where it was, the issue of getting there on time was moot. The puddle I lay in felt warm. How long had it been since I'd played in a puddle? Forget the meeting. Enjoy the puddle. Mother hated it when I played in puddles. But then she disapproved of almost everything that gave me pleasure. I'd bet anything that my real mom would have understood. Mommy wouldn't have cared if I got dirty. I could almost see her smiling at me now. Despite the photo I'd found of Mommy in dad's study, I couldn't quite bring her image to mind. I just knew how warm and loved I felt whenever I'd go into dad's study to sneak a look at the picture. I smiled, becoming one with the puddle.

* * *

Voices. Distant. Muffled. Irrelevant.

Sand dunes. Blue sky. Looking down at Lake Michigan. Water almost green. Waves lapping at the shore. Andy running down the dune. Me chasing him. Both of us falling. Rolling down the dune. Laughing.

A touch on my forehead. Someone holding my hand. Fingering the mole on the back of my wrist. Jackie's touch. Probably wanting me to wake up.

The dunes again and the lake.

Pain in my shoulder, chest. Dull, aching.

Voices. More insistent. Something in my mouth. A thermometer? Was I sick? Voices receding. Pain receding.

My hand. Jackie's touch. She was saying something. The words quiet.

Then louder: "If you don't wake up soon you will be on my shit list big time, Robert Vander Laan."

In resignation, my eyes fluttered open, closed again at the brightness. Opened again. Closed. Opened. Someone looking at me. Had to be Jackie. Gradually she came into focus.

"Hey, babe," I said with a voice I didn't recognize.

"It's about time," she said squeezing my hand and leaning over to kiss my forehead.

When she sat back, I studied her face, trying to figure out why she'd be crying. Then it occurred to me that I could ask her. That meant speaking in that funny voice again. What was the question?

"You're mad because I got my dashiki messed up. I'm really sorry about that."

Jackie laughed, tears streaming freely down her cheeks now. She shook her head.

"I see the patient is awake. How are we feeling, Reverend Vander Laan?" A woman in a nurse's uniform came into view.

A nurse? I looked around. "What in the world am I doing in a hospital?"

The nurse laughed. "Okay, we're definitely doing better."
She rearranged my pillow.

"I can do—urghhh!" Pain shot through by body.

"Just lay back and relax, Reverend Vander Laan."

"*We* would be doing better if you'd call me Rob," I gasped.

She laughed again. "Okay, Rob. Try to get some rest. I'm
going to let your doctor know you've decided to join the land
of the living."

Someone must have drawn a curtain, and I sank gratefully
into the darkness.

* * *

Voices again. Distant, coming closer. Jackie's voice.

I'd open my eyes in a minute.

Mother's voice.

Maybe I'd just keep them closed.

Dad's voice.

I blinked a few times against the light, then kept my eyes
open. "Hey, Dad. Hey, Mother." I squeezed Jackie's hand.

Someone stood in the doorway. My sister. All the way from
Iowa. "A family reunion," I said, my voice not sounding quite
as strange as I remembered it sounding before.

Then Dad was trying to shake my hand; my sister was
touching my arm. Jackie stood on the other side of the bed.
Mother stood at the foot of the bed, a hint of a smile on her face.
Everyone was talking at once. It was too much. I wanted to be
alone with Jackie.

After a few minutes, Jackie shooed people out of the room,
then returned to the chair by the bed and took my hand again.

"Jacks, what the heck am I doing here."

Before she could answer, a nurse walked into the room. It was Nora, the nurse I'd dated in college and who worked part time at Jackie's office and part time at the hospital.

"Hey, Nora?" I said. "Does this mean I'm in St. Mary's Hospital."

Nora smiled but seemed nervous. "Yes, you are." She checked the I.V. dripping into my arm, then listened to my heart, checked my pulse and took my temperature. She pulled a notebook from her pocket and made some notes. She didn't look at me as she said, "I'm sorry about, you know ..." She waved her hand vaguely.

I noticed for the first time that there was another bed in the room. It was empty. Then I realized there was a tube in my chest. "What's the tube for?" I asked.

"It's to expand your right lung," said Jackie.

I wondered if Nora had bathed me. With relief, I noticed a stirring in my groin. Things still appeared to be working down there.

All the same, I'd better not think about bathing. I probably needed a bath, though, after lying in the puddle. The puddle? The gypsum mine. I squeezed my eyes shut. Oh, shit.

When Nora left, I looked at Jackie. "Benny shot me."

Jackie nodded.

"How long have I been here?"

"You got shot Sunday night. Sometime after midnight, I guess. It's Tuesday night now. You've been conscious off and on since this morning."

"How bad?"

"Detective Johnson said you're lucky Benny was using a twenty-two pistol. If he'd been using a bigger gun or hollow point rounds, it would have made a much bigger wound. Plus, Pookie shot Benny a split second before Benny tried to shoot

Rochelle but got you. Pookie's shot only grazed Benny, but that threw Benny's shot off. The surgeon said it's a miracle that you're alive. If you hadn't been turning when the bullet struck you or if the cops hadn't come in at that moment and prevented Benny from putting another round into you ..." She took a moment to collect herself. "The bullet entered the upper right side of your chest and exited near your spine. Somehow it didn't hit a rib or any major blood vessels."

I couldn't take it all in. I'd probably have to ask her to repeat it to me later. "Georgina's dead?"

Jackie nodded. "They found her body with a bullet in her head."

"Lydia, Rochelle, the others?"

"Lydia was here earlier. You were conscious, sort of. You don't remember?"

I shook my head and winced.

"Lydia's fine. So are Rochelle, Manetta and Lois. The cops shot Benny when he started firing at them, and he didn't make it. Pookie's in jail. Owen got away. They don't know if he got out of the mine or got lost in it. It's over. Your only job now is to get better. Oh, those flowers"—she pointed to a vase of roses—"are from Rochelle. She's really grateful you saved her life."

"You could tell her that if she wants to stop in and show her gratitude—"

"I should bop you for that." Jackie brushed a tear away and squeezed my hand.

We were quiet for a few minutes, just looking at each other. Then I said, "About the abortion, I'm not comfortable with it, but I'm ready to support you. It's hard for me to think straight right now, but that's one thing I'm sure about."

Tears again in Jackie's eyes. "That means more than you'll know. But I miscarried while you were down in the mine."

"Aw, babe." I felt a mixture of sadness and relief.

We held hands in silence for a long time. I felt her love dripping into me like the medications and fluid coming through the I.V. I hoped she could feel my love for her as well. Finally I sent Jackie home and made her promise to give Andy hugs and kisses from me.

I slept for a while. When I woke, I felt pillows behind my back so that I was shifted slightly to my side. I opened my eyes and was surprised to see who was sitting in the chair by the bed.

"Hey, Super Rev," said Johnson.

"Hey, yourself, Sid. I hear you got the bad guys, except for Owen, and saved the fair maidens."

"Sorry we didn't get there sooner."

"It sounded like a riot in the lobby when I called the information desk," I said.

"That's exactly what it was. We broke up a concert that had no permit at John Ball Park earlier in the evening. Made some arrests and a bunch of the kids came to the Hall of Justice to bail out their friends and to protest, including some of your hippies. I'm afraid your message to the rookie at the desk got lost in all the confusion."

"So Jackie must have called to tell you Lydia and I had gone into the mine."

"Not exactly." Johnson squirmed.

"Not exactly? How else would you know?" Then I smiled. "The bug on my phone have anything to do with it?"

Johnson shook his head and grinned. "You know about that, huh? The Feds caught your call to Jackie about you and Lydia going into the mine and notified us. Jackie did call eventually, as well. I was off-duty and at my brother's. All off-duty cops were called in for the disturbance at the station. Anyways,

I contacted the Grandville cops. They checked with the only Titus they knew, and the rest is history."

"How did Benny and his sidekicks get access to the mines?" I asked.

"Pookie's been very cooperative, so we've got a pretty complete picture. Owen's father is a mine supervisor, and Owen worked there for a year before going into the army. He must have borrowed his old man's keys and had duplicates made. Owen helped Pookie get a job in the mines a couple of months ago, but Pookie quit a week ago. He couldn't hack it.

"Pookie kept tabs on Rochelle for Benny at the Getaway. Benny figured that enough trouble at the Getaway would convince Rochelle to quit her job there.

"So Benny and his boys robbed the Getaway and mugged you when you showed up. Apparently Benny got all freaked out because you were a minister. He'd seen you in the Getaway before he got bounced out of there and thought he should teach you to stay out of such a den on iniquity, so they took your wallet and your car."

"Did Benny kill Hector?"

"Pookie says Benny gradually began to feel called by God to get the go-go dancing at the Getaway stopped, so he nabbed Georgina as a warning to Ned. Then he killed Hector because he was coming on to Rochelle. Benny had Owen beat up Van because Benny wanted Van out of Rochelle's life."

"Why did Benny take Manetta and Lois? He already had Rochelle."

"Pookie says Benny was obsessed with the evil of dancing. Pookie and Owen tried to convince Benny to just leave with Rochelle. Benny wasn't ready. He said Ned hadn't gotten the message yet, so they kidnapped Manetta and Lois. Benny was ready to grab the other two dancers, too, if Ned didn't stop the go-go dancing."

"You feel up to telling us what happened down there?" Kincaid. I turned in surprise to see him standing on the other side of the bed, pen and notebook in hand. He'd been so quiet that I hadn't noticed him.

By the time I finished my story, I was exhausted.

Johnson got to his feet. "I can see you're tired. We'd better get out of here."

* * *

When I woke again, it was starting to get dark and I was alone. The other bed was still empty. The clock on the wall said 9:20. Visiting hours were over. Somehow, while I'd slept, a couple of other things had jelled for me. I'd have to contact Johnson in the morning.

I was wondering if I could reach the remote on the bedside table to turn on the TV when someone stopped outside the doorway and peered into the room.

"Elliot," I said. "Come in. I'm surprised you're here after visiting hours."

"I told them you'd requested a pastoral call from me."

I had a bad feeling about Elliot's visit. His possible role in the Getaway trouble was what had fallen into place for me earlier.

He stepped over to the side of the bed, asked how I was doing and thanked me for saving his daughter.

"How is she?" I asked.

He looked at the floor. "I guess she's okay. She doesn't want to see me. I don't understand why she's rejecting me." He raised his gaze to mine. "But I didn't come to talk about my troubles."

It was too much for me. "Is it really a surprise, Elliot, given the way you keep trying to control your daughter. In fact, the only contact you've had with her for the past six months, is when I insisted she contact you, isn't that right?"

He looked at me steadily for a long time. I held his gaze. He turned and closed the door quietly. "You know, don't you?"

I said nothing.

"I may have hinted at some little things Benny could do for me. For Rochelle, really. I guess I shouldn't have done that."

"Do you mean little things like kidnapping the dancers, killing Hector, beating up Van."

"Benny was kind of a loose cannon. Vietnam messed his head up pretty badly. I couldn't control him. Whatever I tried to do, it was really for Rochelle."

"Was it?" I said. "Or was it because Rochelle was screwing up your career path? How could a man whose daughter is a go-go dancer ever be appointed president of seminary or Stated Clerk of the denomination?"

Elliot's eyebrows shot up in surprise.

"You had to either get Rochelle to become a good Christian Reformed young lady or get her out of the picture. Not much chance of the former."

"The denomination needs me, Rob. I couldn't let anything jeopardize that."

"So you did it all for the denomination."

"I wouldn't expect you to understand."

"The denomination will have to get along without you, Elliot. You have to tell Detective Johnson what you've told me and deal with the consequences. I'll do my best to stand by you and see you through this once I get out of here."

Elliot smiled. I noticed perspiration on his upper lip and his brow. "I don't think so. I'm afraid you won't be getting out of here."

"But Pookie will testify against you, Elliot. Rochelle will too. You're not thinking clearly."

"They don't know. They thought Benny was acting on his own."

Shit!

At that moment, the door opened. Nora walked into the room with a hypodermic needle. She looked at Elliot who nodded at her. "Time to give you something to help you sleep," said Nora. And then, to Elliot, "Sorry to cut short your pastoral visit." Despite her attempt at a professional tone, there was a look of naked fear in her eyes and a tremble in her voice.

"Do not give me that shot," I said as a cold shiver passed through me. "When I go to sleep, Elliot's going to kill me."

For a moment, Nora's eyes met mine. Then she looked away. That's when I realized she already knew about Elliot's intentions. I remembered Jackie complaining that Nora caved in to male authorities.

I struggled to get up but was too weak. I collapsed back onto the bed.

Nora's hand holding the needle shook. She took hold of the I.V. tubing, stood with the needle poised, face reflecting indecision.

I struggled to roll over in the bed, reaching to pull out the IV.

Elliot stepped quickly to the bedside and placed shaky restraining hands on my arms as I resisted futilely.

"Why would you do this for Elliot, Nora?" I demanded.

"I can help you out there, Rob," said Elliot without looking at me. "I happen to know about some ongoing sins her father engages in with a few of his female clients." Nora's dad was a prominent psychologist in the city. "Actually her father has sinned with Nora too. I make it a point to learn things about people. You never know when these secrets will come in handy. Nora and I don't want this information to get out. Think of how devastating it would be for all concerned. Then there's the fact that you dropped her like a hot potato after dating her for three months in college. She never quite got over that."

"Go ahead, dear," he said to Nora, "I think we've kept the patient waiting long enough."

I struggled feebly. "At least look me in the eye, Elliot!" His gaze slowly met mine.

Over Elliot's shoulder, I noticed the door opening slowly.

Both Nora and Elliot turned. Nora collapsed into the chair, needle dropping to the floor. Elliot let go of me with look of defeat.

"I see you're still awake, Rob." A deep baritone voice from the doorway. The voice of God. Dark suit, white shirt and tie. Bible in his hand.

For the first time in my life, I was deliriously happy to see the Reverend John Vanden Berg.

The End

Made in the USA
Charleston, SC
13 February 2012